HELEN VIVIENNE FLETCHER

Broken Silence

First published by HVF Publishing in 2017

First Edition

ISBN: 978-0-473-39665-7

This book was professionally typeset on Reedsy.
Find out more at reedsy.com

Symbolic Death

Sad, poignant and darkly funny tales about Death. Want it for free? Find out how at the end of the book.

Dedication

For Mary. Without your support, this book never would have been written.

1

Chapter One

"Because she's your daughter!"

I don't open my eyes when I hear Pete say that. For the past twenty minutes I've been pretending to be asleep, listening to him yell down the phone at Dad. Of course I'm only getting Pete's side of the conversation, but it's not hard to fill in the blanks.

"And whose fault is that?" Pete shouts.

I'm guessing Dad just played the fact that he's barely seen me in the last ten years as a reason not to take me in. Parent of the Year, right there.

"Well what am I supposed to tell her?"

That's a good question. What *is* Pete going to tell me? He obviously hasn't realised how thin the walls are, and I don't even want to think about the other implications of that.

"Whatever. I have to get to work." Pete slams the phone down and storms down the hallway. I flinch as the bathroom door crashes shut.

Honestly, I'm not sure what Pete was expecting. Dad's not going to suddenly turn into someone who cares, just because I've got no place else to go.

The phone rings again, making me jump. I stare at it, the light on the base blinking at me, like it's sending Morse code. I'm annoyed at myself, but I feel a little squirm of hope that it might be Dad calling back to say he's changed his mind. I'll pick up if no one else has by the time it gets to three rings.

One ... Two ...

"Kelsey?" Pete calls from the bathroom. "Can you get the phone?"

I sigh, then roll on to my side and reach for the receiver. "Hello?" I wait for an answer. "Hello?"

Silence.

"Hello? ... Hello? ... Last chance ..."

Still silence. Not Dad, I guess.

"Okay then." I put the phone down and flop back against my pillow.

Directly above my bed there's a brown leak stain on the ceiling, the shape of Australia. At home, I'd be seeing the *My Little Pony* pictures I stuck all over the walls when I was seven. Okay, of course I'm not into *My Little Pony* any more, but still I miss them. Opening my eyes and seeing signs of decay is just depressing.

My stomach hurts when I remember that I'll never wake up in my own room again. Instead I'm here in Pete's dingy flat, where everything is dirty and the wallpaper's just itching to peel off in long sheets, like a lizard shedding its skin.

Pete appears in my doorway. "Who was it?"

"Dunno. Wrong number, I think."

Pete hovers beside the bed, a tangle of overly-tall gangliness. He's wearing his work shirt and tie, but still has his pyjama pants on. It makes his already long arms look stretched, like he's a balding orang-utan in half a suit.

"Did you get hold of Dad?" I ask.

Pete hesitates, and I see on his face, a second before he says anything, that he's going to lie.

"No, I just got the machine."

I get out of bed and start gathering my stuff for school. "Must be at work," I say.

"Must be." Pete avoids looking at me.

"So that was his answer phone you were yelling at for the last twenty minutes?"

"What?" Pete's eyes flick up to meet mine. He frowns and then a red flush shoots up his face. "If you knew I was talking to him, then why act like–"

"Because you obviously weren't going to tell me!"

"I didn't want to upset you."

"Yeah, well you did a great job of that." I turn away. Out of the corner of my eye, I watch the flush retreat back down his neck.

"I'm sorry," he says.

I shove my books into my backpack instead of answering.

He sighs. "Kel, if you want to talk about any of this stuff–"

"I don't."

"Yeah, but ..." Pete clears his throat. "If you ever do." He gives me his best sympathetic look.

I feel myself soften. "I don't need to talk," I say. "But thanks."

Pete nods, then he grins. "Are we supposed to hug now or something?"

I scoff. "No way. Go have a shower. You stink."

"Thanks. That's what I get for trying to be a caring brother."

I poke my tongue out at him.

He laughs. "Hey, Ben and Aiden are making breakfast."

I roll my eyes. "Protein shakes, I'm guessing?"

"Well, you could do with a bit of fattening up." Pete goes to squeeze my arm.

"Don't!" I jerk away from him.

He frowns, dropping his hand to his side.

"Sorry." I say. "I ... hurt my arm at soccer." I pick at my nails, as my cheeks grow hot. I don't think Pete notices.

He nods, then tilts his head towards the door. "Come have some breakfast. Ben said he can give you a lift to school."

I wait until Pete's gone, then close the door. My suitcase is wedged halfway under the bed. I pry it open to take some clothes out. It's stupid. I know I'm not going home, but still I can't bear to unpack. It makes it too permanent, too irreversible.

I slip my pyjama top up over my head, wincing as it brushes my arm. I see the bruises clearly as I look in the mirror – five small ones and one large one, like somebody grabbed me with purple paint on their hand.

I flick my hair across my shoulder so it covers the bruises and glare at my reflection. I look like an angry pixie. I'm so pale, my skin is practically see-through, and my eyes look deer-in-the-headlights big. I scowl at the mirror again, and get dressed.

"So, how long is she staying with us?"

I stop outside the kitchen door as I hear Aiden's voice. Pete keeps saying his flatmates don't mind me staying with them, but I'm not so sure.

Ben's like another brother to me – he and Pete have been friends practically since the womb – but since I've moved in he's been acting weird. He keeps giving me funny looks and gets all intense. Aiden … well, I don't really know him, but if first impressions are anything to go by I'd say he was weird to begin with.

I flatten myself against the wall so I can peer into the kitchen. I watch as Aiden slathers his toast with marmalade and bites into it.

"I don't know." Ben glances at the ceiling. "Their mum's pretty sick. Pete's tried calling their dad a couple times, but he said Kel couldn't stay with him."

So Pete was honest with Ben, even if he wasn't with me.

Ben cracks an egg into the blender and flicks the switch. I want to gag, watching the liquid slosh against the sides. Judging from the look on Aiden's face, he feels the same way.

"How can you drink that stuff?" he asks.

Ben smiles and sculls it straight from the blender.

Aiden grins. "Kelsey's kinda moody, isn't she?"

I close my eyes. I don't want to hear this.

"Have you met a seventeen-year-old who's not?"

"Have you met a *girl* who's not?"

I've heard enough. I walk into the kitchen. "Morning."

"Hey, Kel." Ben looks guilty, but Aiden just stares at me. I stare back until he looks away.

"Morning, people." Pete bounds into the kitchen behind me and starts piling cereal into a bowl. He's like a kid, trying to prove he can eat the most in one sitting. I never got why you'd want to do that. More than half a bowl and I feel like I'm going to burst.

Ben pushes the blender towards me. "Want some?"

I make a face. "Ben, that's disgusting."

"I drink it." He swishes the pinkish liquid around.

"*You're* disgusting." I grin.

"Cereal, then?" He grabs the box off Pete.

"Eugh!"

"Toast?"

I shake my head, my chest feeling tight. "I'm not hungry."

"Well, you have to eat something." Ben's voice has an edge to it.

I frown at him. "Since when do I *have* to do anything?"

"You're too thin." Ben stares at me.

I glare back, feeling sick. He's a boy. They're not supposed to notice stuff like that.

I pick up an apple. "Happy?"

"Come on, children." Pete puts his arm around me. "It's too early for fist fights."

I shake him off and go and stand in the doorway. When Ben's not looking I drop the apple in the bin.

"Pete, can I get a ride to work with you?" Aiden creeps forward. He'd been standing there like a startled guinea pig.

Pete stirs his cereal into mush. "I'm up at the Manners Street office today. That okay?"

Aiden nods. "Yeah, I've got a meeting there."

I'm only half listening to Pete and Aiden talk about work. I stare at my hands. They look like bundles of twigs sticking out from my sleeves. I curl my fingers up, and it looks like they're going to break.

"You ready to go, Kel?" Ben pushes his hair out of his eyes, but it flops straight back down over them.

"Sure." I stuff my hands into my pockets.

"I just have to get my briefcase. Meet you at the car?"

I can feel Ben watching me as I walk outside.

I step on an ashtray right outside the back door. The butts spill out over the doorstep, and I stumble as the ashtray flips under my weight. I scowl and kick it under a bush.

I get halfway to the car before I realise that was a stupid thing to do. It's not going to stop Pete smoking, and it will just mean he ends up chucking his butts in the garden.

Ben appears before I can turn back and retrieve it, so I get in the car instead.

I stare out the window while Ben fiddles with the radio.

"This okay?" he says, picking a station.

"Sure." I don't look at him.

He sighs. "Come on, Kel. Don't sulk."

"You don't want to check my lunch box? Make sure I haven't packed all junk food?"

Ben rolls his eyes and doesn't answer.

The car groans and shudders as we back out of the driveway. For a moment I think it's not going to make it. I watch Ben's hands gripping the steering wheel. I can tell he's annoyed, but it's mixed with something else.

He glances over at me. "Don't chew your hair, Kel." He pushes my hand away from my mouth. I spit out the end of my ponytail and my hair sticks together in little wet spikes. I'm pretty sure there's a string of saliva stuck to my chin too. I crack up as I see Ben's expression.

He shakes his head. "Very classy, Kel."

I laugh. "Shut up." I pluck strands of hair from my lip, and rub at my face. "I didn't even realise I was doing it this time."

Ben chuckles. He turns up the radio as a song he likes comes on. "Hey, do you want me to pick you up after school?"

I shake my head. "Thanks, but I'm going to Mike's."

Ben wrinkles his nose, and his lips part like he wants to say something. I get in before he can. "Aren't you supposed to be working, anyway?"

He grins. "You seem to be under the impression that I care about my job."

I raise my eyebrows. "Pete says you love it."

"Your brother says a lot of things."

I smile. "That he does."

"You going to see your mum this weekend?"

I shrug. I stare out of the window, but my eyes start to burn and I have to blink hard.

"You should go with Pete."

I swallow. The air in the car feels thick. I can almost see Ben oozing concern.

"You'll regret it if you don't."

"Don't you start. Pete tried to have the 'sensitive brother' conversation with me this morning."

Ben laughs. "I would have paid to see that."

"Yeah, he got all uncomfortable."

Ben glances over at me. "He does care about you, though."

I sigh. "I know. It's just ... hard."

"It's not that bad living with us, is it?"

"Why doesn't Dad want me?" I don't plan to say it, it just pops out.

"What?" Ben doesn't look at me. I can tell he's playing for time.

"Pete told me this morning."

Ben goes quiet. "I'm sorry."

"It's not your fault." I have to blink back tears again.

"Kel, it's not your fault either. Your dad's a jerk. He always has been. You know that."

"I know, but ..." There isn't really a way to finish that. Instead, I press my palms into my eye sockets and wipe away the tears before they fall, then make an effort at being cheerful. "So I'm moody, am I?"

"Hey, it was Aiden who said that, not me."

"Yeah, but you agreed with him!" I give Ben a weak smile then close my eyes and sing along to the radio under my breath. Well, perhaps that's an exaggeration. I don't know the words, so I hum an approximation of what I think they might be. Ben chuckles, clearly enjoying my version more than the real one.

"You can drop me here," I say as we reach the street around the corner from school.

"Oh, I see." Ben pulls into the kerb. "Happy to take a lift from me but don't want to be seen being dropped off."

I laugh. "Whatever."

I go straight to the form room. As usual, it smells sickeningly of spray deodorant. It wouldn't be so bad if it actually covered up the smell of BO, but instead they just merge together into a smorgasbord of odours. I hold my breath to punch in my locker combination. The door jams.

"Aw, come on!" I give the door a fierce shake. It rattles, but refuses to open. "Damn it!" I slam my hand against the locker.

"Easy!"

I spin around. Mike's behind me.

"It won't open," I say.

"Here." Mike fiddles with the lock and the door swings free.

"Thanks." I try not to sound irritated that he fixed it so easily, but my voice still sounds sulky.

Mike hands me a box. "I brought you something," he says.

My stomach tenses and I can't look at him. I stare at the box in my hand, wondering what he'd do if I just threw it away without opening it. He doesn't give me the chance to find out.

"Here." He flicks the lid back.

"A cupcake," I say. "Thank you." It comes out as a whisper. The cake is covered in green icing and blotched with multi-coloured sprinkles. It makes me nauseous just to look at it.

"You deserve it." He kisses the side of my head, his lip piercing grazing my temple. "Hey, sorry about the other night."

I swallow. "It doesn't matter." I put the cake in the back of my locker. I want to smash it with my fist. For a moment, I even want to hit Mike.

"Aren't you going to eat it?"

My stomach tenses again. "I will ... just not now. I'll be late for class otherwise."

"Cool, see you at lunch."

I check my timetable. Geography first period. I pause outside the classroom door. Usually I try to get there early so I can sit somewhere by myself. Today I'm late. I take a breath before heading in. The desks are grouped in pairs with aisles in between each set. There's not a single empty pair. Every one of them has at least one person sitting at it, or has a backpack marking territory. I never thought I'd miss assigned seating, but that would be so much easier right now.

Some guys are chucking a rugby ball around at the front of the room. I duck and let out a shriek as it flies towards my head. This is apparently hilarious.

Tash grabs the ball off them and refuses to give it back. She glances at me and raises her eyebrows. I roll my eyes in the direction of the guys.

"You can have it back, if you promise not to hit anyone else." Tash gives them her version of a flirty smile.

One of the guys makes a "cross-my-heart" gesture and takes the ball off her. A second later, he throws it straight at me, whacking me in the stomach.

"Dick!" Tash yells.

I shove the ball at the closest guy, and they fall about laughing as I scuttle away.

Tash follows me. "Are you all right, Kels?"

I nod. I don't trust my voice at the moment, especially as that really knocked the air out of me.

Tash smiles. "Hey, do you want to come to mine after school? Stupid twin's ditching me for rugby."

"Doesn't Jacob ditch you every day?" I grin. "Anyway, I can't. I'm going to Mike's."

Tash scrunches up her face. I turn away before she can start. She doesn't need to say it. I know she disapproves, and thinks I can "do so much better". God, even Mike knows she thinks that. It's no wonder he doesn't want me to hang out with her.

Tash calls after me. "Jacob and I are having a party this weekend, if you want to come."

I aim a vague nod in her direction then go over and stand beside an empty desk. Well, it's not quite empty. Amber has dumped her bag on the chair while she's sprawled across the one next to it. She's talking to Sophie, who's sitting across the aisle. They lean their heads in together and lower their voices. I don't know why people do that. The best way to make people want to eavesdrop is to act secretive. If they really want to keep it private they should just speak normally. It's not like anyone will hear them over everyone else talking.

Amber pulls at a chain around her neck as she laughs at something Sophie said.

"Can I sit here?" I feel like I'm eight years old. At age seventeen, I shouldn't have to ask if I can sit somewhere.

Amber stares at me. I could be speaking another language for all the reaction I get. Either that or she's trying to dissolve me with her eyes. I'm not sure whether to just move her bag and sit down, or to walk away and try to find another seat. She's still staring at me, and now Sophie has joined in. It's unnerving, like having two life-sized dolls judge you with their glass eyes.

You'd never think Sophie and I were best friends when we were little from the way she acts now. It's hard to take someone trying to intimidate you seriously when you've seen them wet their pants twice in one day.

I'm about to turn away when Mr Humphries walks in. There's a rustling as everyone organises themselves into seats, and I decide it doesn't matter whether Amber wants me to sit beside her or not. I dump her bag on the floor, sit down and take out my textbook.

The more I stare at the map of Norfolk Island, the more I feel like I'm taking an ink blot test. The topographical colours swarm into Freudian images.

"Kelsey?"

"Huh?" I look up at Mr Humphries.

"Answer to number nine?"

I glance down at the blank page in my exercise book where my homework should have been. "Ummm ..."

Beside me, Amber sniggers. I look back at Mr Humphries.

"See me after class, Kelsey."

As everyone else files out I go and stand by Mr Humphries' desk. He keeps reading his papers and doesn't look up. I stare at the floor, feeling my face settle into a sullen frown.

Mr Humphries has a full face with pouchy cheeks and wet lips. It makes him look like a cross between a bullfrog and a trout. I try not to laugh.

"How are you coping, Kelsey?" he says once everyone has left.

I look up.

He stares at me over the top of his glasses. "This is the third time you haven't completed the homework assignment. Normally I'd give you a detention, but given the circumstances–"

"I don't want special treatment." I'm sick of everyone treating me like I'm broken. It's bad enough when Ben and Pete do it, but this is too much.

"So, you'd prefer the detention?"

I smile, despite myself, and shake my head.

"Try your best to get your homework done. I can only be so lenient."

At lunch I go up to the common room. I settle down in the corner and try to disappear into the wall. It's a bit difficult since it's silvery-grey and my top is purple-and-black striped.

I look around for Mike and try not to catch anyone else's eye. Everyone's split off into little groups. I'm like the lone zebra in a field of gazelles. I contemplate going to the bathroom so I look like I'm doing something and not just sitting here by myself. Then I think of the sinks, blocked with all manner of things, including hair, and decide against it.

Instead I open my backpack and pull out my lunch. I stare at the food I packed last night, and feel sick.

"Hey." Mike sits down next to me.

I relax as he does. "Do you want my sandwiches?"

"What? Are you on some kind of diet?" Mikes smirks.

"Nah, I'm just not hungry," I mumble.

"Yeah, okay then. Thanks." He bites into the bread. "You staying at mine tonight?"

I shake my head. "Can't. It's a school night."

"So? Your brother's not going to care."

"He promised Mum he'd keep her rules." I shrug and look down at my hands.

Mike's thick, black eyebrows pucker into a frown. "He's only – what? Three, four years older than you? What's he going to do? Ground you?"

My throat feels dry and it starts to ache. I find it hard to form words. "I don't want to go against Mum," I say.

Mike's eyes narrow. "It's not like she'd care, Kel. She's practically a vegetable."

My chest feels like it's imploding. A sound like a hiccup comes out of my mouth. I get up and stumble towards the bathroom.

"Hey, Kel, I'm sorry ..."

I hear Mike calling after me, but I don't stop.

2

Chapter Two

Ben looks worried as he opens the door to the sick bay. It's strange on him. He usually has a kind of calm, Zen expression with bit of a Crouching-Tiger-I'll-attack-if-provoked undertone to it.

It's weird; even when he's upset he still looks like he's smiling. He has one of those mouths that are permanently turned up at the corners. Most of the time, it makes him look like he's stoned, though I know with him that's unlikely.

I've wrapped myself up in the duvet from the bed. There are bright yellow bumble-bees on the cover; it's obviously intended for kids. It's the kind of sickeningly cheerful thing the nurse, Miss Bently, thinks is cute.

"You okay, Kel?" Ben sits down next to me.

I nod. "I didn't want them to call you."

"Better me than Pete – seeing you with that much mascara over your face would have made him very uncomfortable."

I cringe and rub at my cheeks.

Ben laughs. "Here." He hands me a tissue. "You wanna tell me what happened?"

I shake my head. It's too hard to talk about.

"Okay." He looks around the room and sighs. "You know, I spent nearly every Monday morning in this room when I was at school."

"Let me guess, maths?"

He grins. "Not just maths, Mrs Henderson's weekly quizzes. Come on, I'll take you home."

The door opens and Miss Bently comes in. She looks ridiculously cheerful. I'm always surprised she doesn't skip everywhere. She has a bouncy vibe to her, only partly due to her mass of frizzy hair, which actually does bounce with a momentum all of its own.

"Good, I'm glad I caught you before you left." She tips her head to the side and gives me a sympathetic look to rival Pete's. I can't look at Ben for fear of laughing.

"How're you doing, sweetie?" she asks.

"I'm okay." She's got Broken Kelsey Syndrome, I can feel it.

She waves a manila folder at me. "I was wondering if you'd like to talk to someone. A professional, I mean."

"What? Like a shrink?"

Miss Bently smiles. "Not exactly. A counsellor."

"You think I'm crazy?" My voice comes out all croaky.

"No, of course not. But a girl your age having to look after her mother like that–"

"Her mother's in care now." Ben's voice is quiet. It only ever gets like that when he's angry. He gestures for me to stand up.

"I know, but still …" Miss Bently looks baffled. She came in trying to help, and I freak out and Ben gets angry.

I'm not exactly sure why I'm upset. It's just hard. I think I'd be okay if people left me alone. Actually, I'm not sure why

Ben's angry either.

"I don't want to talk to anyone," I say.

Ben takes my arm and pulls me towards the door.

"If you change your mind ..." Miss Bently calls after us.

I stumble after Ben. He's still pulling on my arm, and I don't think he realises he's walking much faster than I ever do. I'd detach myself from him, but we're walking against the flow of students going back to class and I'd get swept away without him.

"Stupid, interfering biddy," he mutters when we get to the car.

"Why are you angry?" I shake his hand off.

"What? I'm not."

"Yeah, you are."

Ben takes a breath then gives a forced smile. "I'm not, honestly, Kel."

I hesitate. I'm not sure what's going on in his head but it makes me nervous.

He gives another smile. "I just didn't want her to upset you, that's all."

We don't talk on the way home. Ben puts the radio up loud so we listen to that and ignore each other.

His car makes this weird ticking noise, like the engine's going to explode. I find myself shrinking back in the seat, as if I could avoid any flames by being a few centimetres further away.

One of those whiny girl-groups comes on over the speakers.

"How come there's only angsty-girl music and no angsty guys?" I say.

Ben shakes his head and grins. "Do you really want me to answer that?"

"No."

Ben laughs. A few minutes later we pull into the driveway at Pete's place. I'm always surprised when we get here. I have the direction sense of a carrot, so I never recognise when we're getting close. Actually that's probably unfair to carrots – they at least know which way to grow. The fact that I never visited Pete after he moved out of home doesn't help either.

Ben picks up my bag and carries it into the house. "Why have I got this?" he asks. "You're big enough and ugly enough to carry it yourself. And what have you got in here? It weighs a tonne."

I laugh. "Think of it as weight training."

He dumps the bag just inside the door. "Pete said he'd try get home early. Do you want me to stay until he gets here?"

"Nah, it could be ages. Pete lives in a different time zone to the rest of us."

"You sure?" Ben does the sympathetic head tilt and screws up his mouth.

I roll my eyes. "I'm sure. Now get lost. I don't want to be the reason you get fired."

Ben laughs. "See you later, Kel."

About ten minutes after Ben leaves, the phone rings. I stare at it and sigh. It's weird Pete even has a landline. He insists he needs it for work, but then he ends up using his cell phone for everything anyway, and I'm the one who has to answer the stupid thing.

I pick up the receiver. "Hello?"

Silence.

"This isn't funny."

There's a sound like wheezing, heavy breathing.

"Grow up!" I slam the phone down.

A second later it rings again. I stare at it, my skin prickling with anxiety. I count the rings. One … two … The call minder will pick up after eight. Seven … eight.

I let out a wobbly breath as it stops ringing. It's stupid that I'm getting so worked up, but I can't help it. I head into the kitchen and start making myself a sandwich.

My mouth is glued shut with peanut butter I just licked off the knife, when the phone rings again. I swallow hard then answer it. "Hello?"

The heavy breathing starts straight away.

"You're disgusting!" I hang up and close my eyes.

Just some stupid kid, I think. *Just some stupid kid.*

I take the phone off the hook and go back to my sandwich. The annoying thing is, I'm not even hungry anymore. If I hadn't skipped lunch I wouldn't worry, but my blood sugar must be getting pretty low by now.

Lunch makes me think of Mike, and tears squeeze themselves out of the corners of my eyes. Why does he have to be such a jerk?

I pick up the peanut butter, but it slips and I drop the jar on the floor. "Damn it!"

I'm crying properly now, like a total idiot. "Just forget it," I say aloud, to no one in particular. I run up the stairs to my room. Except it's not my room. It's my brother's spare room. It's nothing like home and it never will be. I curl up under the duvet and cry.

✑

It feels like only a minute later when I hear Pete calling me. I must have fallen asleep.

"Kel? … Kelsey? Kel, where are you?"

I groan and open my eyes.

"Kel?" Pete opens the door to my room. He shakes his head as he sees me. "Geez, you scared me. I've been phoning all afternoon." His mouth pulls into an ugly shape as he speaks.

I give a lazy stretch and yawn. "There was a prank caller. I took the phone off the hook."

"Then I get home and the kitchen's a mess and you don't answer when I call you."

"I was asleep."

Pete sighs. "Look, Kel, I know I said make yourself at home, but come on."

"What? What did I do?" I sit up. He looks angry and I immediately feel defensive.

"It's not just me living here. You can't expect us to clean up after you."

"I didn't. I was going to clean up." I hate it when Pete tries to tell me what to do. Even when we were kids he seemed to think that because he was older, he was somehow in charge.

"You're not at home anymore. You can't leave things like that."

"I know that." I have to grit my teeth to stop myself from saying something stupid.

"And Ben and I can't keep taking time off work."

"It's not my fault. Miss Bently insisted on calling. I could have walked home." I struggle with my sheet, trying to unwind it from around my feet so I can storm out.

"What happened, anyway? You were fine this morning."

"Nothing!" I scream. I push past Pete and thunder down-stairs.

He follows me. "That's not good enough, Kel. You can't take time off school for nothing."

I don't answer. I start cleaning up in the kitchen.

Pete stands by the door and watches me. "I don't mean to yell at you–"

"So don't." Out of the corner of my eye I see him shake his head and walk away.

I do feel kind of bad, though. The peanut butter didn't have a lid on and it's slurped all over the floor in a big oily puddle.

The doorbell rings, but I don't get up. It's Pete's place; he can damn well answer his own door. He stomps through the house, obviously making a thing of it.

"Is Kel here?"

I feel sick as I hear Mike's voice.

"Yeah, she's in the kitchen. But watch out, she's in a foul mood."

I feel shaky. I don't want to talk to him. I don't want to see him. I just want him to drop off the face of the earth.

I stare at the floor as he walks into the kitchen.

"Hey." He shifts his feet. That's all I can see of him. Right now, it's more than I want to.

"Hey," I mutter.

"I'm sorry."

I scrub at the floor. Mike sits down next to me then lies down when I ignore him. He swivels around so his head is pretty much in the peanut butter, and I have no choice but to look at him.

He makes a puppy dog face. "I'm sorry."

I laugh, despite myself.

"That's better."

"I'm still mad."

"I know." He strokes my hair. "Of course you are. I'm a jerk." He looks so sad.

I sigh. "You're not a jerk. You're just an idiot."

Mike nods. "You forgive me?"

I close my eyes. "Yeah." I feel an ache down near my belly button.

"Let me help you clean up."

Mike makes himself a sandwich and I finish making the one I abandoned earlier. We sit on the couch in the lounge to eat. It's always dark in this room. I'm pretty sure it's only because the windows are grimy and streaked with dirt. If they were washed it would brighten the place up a lot. That doesn't mean I'm going to volunteer to do it, though.

I tear my sandwich into little pieces and try to swallow without tasting. Even so, it sticks in my throat.

"Hey, Pete?" I say as he walks into the room.

"Yeah?" He still looks angry.

"I'm sorry. You were right. I'll tidy up after myself and you won't have to miss any more work, I promise."

His face softens. "I'm sorry I yelled at you."

I wave away the apology.

"I'm putting the phone back on the hook," Pete says. "Now Mike and I are here to protect you from prank callers."

I roll my eyes. "I feel so much safer."

Pete seems to be in a better mood now, so I decide to try my luck.

"So, Pete," I say with a grin. "When do I get to meet this 'Jenny'?"

He scoffs. "Um, never?"

Mike raises his eyebrows. "Jenny?"

"His girlfriend," I say to Mike, then turn back to Pete. "Come on." I laugh. "You've met Mike."

Mike raises his hand as if he thinks Pete might have forgotten who he is.

Pete shakes his head. "And my life is so much richer for it. You're still not meeting Jenny." He hangs up the phone then dials the call minder number. "I left you a message," he says. "I'm just going to ... What the ...?"

"What?" At first I think he's trying to distract me, then I see his frown.

"Seventeen messages." Pete pauses, listening. "Was the prank caller a heavy breather by any chance?"

"Oh my God! He left messages?"

"Yeah, and a lot of them." Pete puts the phone down. "It's probably just a kid. They'll get bored if we ignore them."

Mike flicks on the TV and puts his arm around me. His bare skin is hot against my neck. I want to shuffle away, but my hair is trapped between his arm and the back of the couch. I try to focus on the cartoon flashing across the screen.

"Did you talk to Tash today?" Mike says in the ad break. "She and Jacob are having a party this weekend. You wanna go?"

"I don't know. Maybe." I lean my head against his shoulder. Even if there wasn't the awkwardness between Mike and Tash, I hate parties. Everyone's always wasted and they all look at us like we've gate crashed. Mike, of course, doesn't notice because he's busy getting more wasted than anyone else.

Over the sound of the TV, I hear keys in the front door lock.

"Honey? I'm home," Ben calls in his best 1940s TV-husband voice. He comes into the living room. "Hi." I can't help noticing Ben's shoulders stiffen as he sees Mike.

"Hey. Pete's upstairs if you want him," I say. It's not a comment so much as a suggestion. As in: please go anywhere except here.

Ben looks from me to Mike. "I think I might go train for a while." He goes out to the garage. After a few minutes, we hear the thump and squeak of him hitting the punching bag.

Mike turns and stares at the door. "What's he doing in there? Killing a cat?"

"Kickboxing. He's got a fight in a couple of weeks."

Mike nods, then unwraps his arm from around me. "I'd better get home." He kisses my forehead. "See you tomorrow, yeah?"

I wait until Mike's gone then go out to the garage. Ben's sweating heavily already. He kicks the punching bag hard and I flinch at the noise.

Ben glances up then hits the bag again. "Mike gone already?" There's a bite to his words.

"Why don't you like him?"

"What?" Ben steadies the bag as it swings back towards him.

"You don't like Mike. Why?"

Ben shakes his head. "Don't, Kel."

"I want to know." My hands are shaking. Say it. Just say it.

"I just don't." Ben aims a gentle punch at the bag.

"Why?"

He shakes his head again. "Leave it, Kel."

I can tell he thinks I'm angry, that I'll try to prove Mike's a good guy. Instead I close my eyes. "Whatever."

Ben stares at me then goes back to training.

3

Chapter Three

My eyes shoot open as the phone rings. I look at the clock beside the bed: 2.57am. The phone doesn't ring in the middle of the night unless it's something bad.

I pick up the phone. "Hello?"

Heavy breathing.

"You're a jerk, you know that?" I slam the phone down.

I swing my legs out of bed and sit on the edge, shaking. "Mum's okay," I say to myself. "She's okay, it's just a stupid prank caller." I turn the light on.

I can't cope with this. For once I fall asleep at a decent hour and the blimming prank caller rings. I get up and pull a sweater on over my pyjamas, then creep down the stairs to the kitchen.

All I can see are grey outlines of things. I keep blinking, waiting for my eyes to adjust to the dark, but they don't. There's a yellow aura around the window where the street light's edging in around the blind, so I move towards that, then make my way over to where I think the light switch is.

I can never remember things like that. After living in the same house my whole life, finding my way around in the dark was more natural than blinking, even with my poor sense of direction. Here, I can barely remember where things are in the daylight.

I see the shape of something leaning against the wall. It looks like a person.

"Pete, is that you?"

No answer.

The figure doesn't move. I can't stop shaking as I reach out to feel the way around.

A hand grasps mine.

I draw breath to scream.

"Kelsey?"

"Yes," I whisper. The light flicks on. "Aiden," I breathe. "Why the hell didn't you say something? I nearly wet my pants." I blush. I wish I could go back three seconds and not say that.

Aiden gives me a twisted half-smile and lets go of my hand.

"What are you doing up?" I try to pretend I'm not embarrassed.

"Phone woke me. You?"

"Same."

He opens the fridge. "You want some hot milk?"

"Yeah, thanks." I press my lips together to suppress a smile. Aiden doesn't seem like the kind of guy to be fond of hot milk.

I watch as he pours milk into two mugs and stirs in some honey. "My mum used to make this for me and Pete when we couldn't sleep." I instantly regret saying it. I've been avoiding talking about Mum. Suddenly I can feel the words piling up behind my tongue, desperately wanting to tumble out.

Aiden smiles. "I can't imagine Pete as a little kid."

"I can show you photos," I say. "Ben's got some really funny ones."

Aiden puts the mugs in the microwave. "I'm sorry about your mum." He kind of mumbles it, and he's turned away from me, so at first I'm not sure he really said it.

"It's okay." It's a stupid answer. It's not okay, but I don't know what else to say.

Aiden rubs at his face. He has strangely long fingers, feminine in a way. Actually, he's kind of feminine all over; I don't think he even has to shave. If I knew him better, I'd suggest he became a drag queen. I have to hold back a laugh.

Aiden sighs. "My mum died too. Last year."

I blink, wondering if I've misheard him. "My mum's … she's not dead," I say eventually.

He looks up at me. "I didn't mean–"

"I know. Sorry." I curse myself for how blunt that must have sounded. "It's just hard to remember sometimes. She's not dead. Everyone acts like she is, but she's not."

Aiden's eyes trace my face, like he's searching for something. I drop my gaze and tug at the hem of my sweater. When I look up, he's still staring at me. He nods and hands me the mug of milk.

"I'm sorry your mum died," I say.

Aiden shrugs and shakes his head. "Yeah, well–"

"Early morning party, eh?" Ben comes into the kitchen, followed by Pete. Aiden looks at me like he wants to say something else, then he closes off and turns away. I want to reach out to him but I don't know what to say.

"Who do we have to thank for waking us up?" Pete breaks open a banana and takes a bite.

"Prank caller," I say. "Again."

"Bloody hell." Pete's mouth is full so it comes out more like "Uddy ell." He swallows then continues. "It's three in the morning."

"Yeah." I hate it when people point out the obvious. It's like they think they're more intelligent than you.

"Any idea who it could be?" Pete stares at me.

I shrug and pretend I haven't noticed he's singling me out.

He tips his head on the side. "It's not one of your friends, is it?"

"No." I frown, not sure whether to be insulted or to laugh.

"You sure?"

I roll my eyes.

"Well, who is it then?"

I raise my eyebrows. "I don't know. Maybe it's someone from your work."

"Don't be sarkie, Kel."

Ben clears his throat. "We should just leave the phone off the hook." He reaches over to pick up the receiver.

"Don't." I put my hand over his to stop him. "They might call about Mum."

Ben goes tense as I touch him. He doesn't look at me, but I feel a little twist of something like butterflies in my stomach. I stare at him, confused, and let my hand drop to my side.

Pete clears his throat. "It's okay, Kel. They've got our cell numbers."

Ben looks up. "Okay?"

I find I can't meet his eye. "Sure," I say. But it's not okay. I don't want them to call on my cell phone. Somehow it feels safer if I just have to worry about the landline ringing.

Ben doesn't look at me again, and I force myself not to stare at him.

I pick up my mug from the bench instead. "I'm going back to bed. Thanks for the milk, Aiden."

He gives me an awkward salute. I go back up to bed without looking back at Ben.

❦

When my alarm clock rings, I feel like I've been asleep for all of twenty seconds. All night I kept thinking the phone was ringing, and dragged myself out of sleep to answer it. Each time I did, I'd wake with a sick feeling in my stomach and sweat on my upper lip.

When I was asleep, I dreamt that I was lost in Mum's nursing home. I heard her screaming my name, but couldn't find her. I ran down every corridor but I couldn't remember the way back to her room.

I go straight into the kitchen without pausing outside the door. Eavesdropping on any more conversations doesn't seem like a good idea.

I needn't have worried. Ben and Aiden are caught up with full mouths, and Pete's absorbed in reading the back of the cereal packet.

"Morning," he mumbles, without looking up.

I sit down at the counter, next to Ben. I decide I must have imagined the moment between us last night. I was tired, and it was making me see things that weren't there.

Ben slides a plate of toast with jam in front of me. He's not looking at me, but I can tell he's using his hypersensitive ninja-skills to observe my reaction. I don't say anything. It takes all my resources to not start shaking as I pick up a piece and start chewing. Ben relaxes as I do.

"Hey, I've got a meeting on the other side of town first thing," he says. "I won't be able to give you a lift. That okay?"

I nod. The toast is still going around in my mouth and I'm scared I'll spit it out if I try to speak. This would be so much easier if I didn't feel like he was watching every bite. Finally I manage to swallow. "I can walk."

"Or I could take you."

I look up. Aiden's staring at me.

"Are you sure? It's not out of your way?"

"No worries."

Ben and Pete both have to rush off. Aiden heads upstairs to get something, and doesn't come back down for ages. I wander around the living room, waiting. Ben's left his laptop on the couch. It's still on, so I sit down to check Facebook.

I should probably get a job and save up to buy my own computer. Pete gets annoyed when I ask if I can borrow his. Ben doesn't mind, but I feel bad when he's already putting himself out so much for me. At the very least I should see if I can afford a better phone, but for the moment I'm stuck with the painfully slow one my mum gave me when I was ten. It's too frustrating to even try to connect to the wifi.

"What are you doing?"

I jump as I hear Aiden's voice. I hadn't even realised he'd come back downstairs.

"Sorry, I was just checking my messages."

He stares at me. He looks pissed off, but I can't tell why. He glances at the laptop.

I look down at it. The screen looks completely different from the last time I borrowed it. There are all these extra icons, including one for some type of movie maker. The others are all technical sounding.

"Is this yours?" I say. "I thought it was Ben's." I put it back on the couch. "Sorry, I wouldn't have–"

He shrugs. "Forget it." He hovers, then sits down next to me and picks the computer up. "You can finish ..." He goes to hand it back to me.

"No, no." I'd feel like an idiot sitting there scrolling through my newsfeed in front of Aiden. Chances are it'd just be hundreds of notifications from Mike, linking me to stupid YouTube clips, anyway.

Aiden wraps his arms around the laptop so he's hugging it to his chest. He sits really far forward on the couch, just perching on the edge. I struggle to think of something to say. He glances at me, then away again. I swear I can hear my own hair growing, it's so quiet.

"I was wondering why Ben had movie-making software," I say eventually. I wasn't really wondering that, because I'd only just noticed. Now I'm wondering why Aiden has it, though.

He wrinkles his nose. "It's from work. I'm supposed to be testing it for bugs."

I don't really know what he means by that. Aiden and Pete have these mysterious IT jobs. As far as I can tell, they spend most of their time on the internet.

"I'll show you sometime, if you like."

I want to groan when he says that. Any time Pete wants to show me something, it ends up being some weird motivational speaker encouraging me to sort my life out. I'm seventeen. I haven't got a life to sort out.

Aiden makes a popping sound with his lips. There should be a neon sign above our heads, flashing "Awkward Silence!

Awkward Silence!"

Aiden glances at his phone and makes a face. He tucks the laptop under his arm. "Come on. I'm supposed to be at work by nine."

I pick my backpack up from beside the door where Ben dropped it yesterday.

Aiden raises his eyebrows. "So I guess you didn't have much homework last night?"

I poke my tongue out at him.

We're halfway out the door when the phone rings.

"I'll get it," Aiden says when he sees my face. He picks up the receiver. "Hello?" He listens for a moment, then glances at me and rolls his eyes. He makes exaggerated heavy breathing sounds into the phone and hangs up.

"What?" he asks when I gape at him.

"I just never thought of doing that."

Aiden shrugs. "Probably won't make a difference."

I clutch my school bag on my lap in the car. Aiden's not the best driver. I find I'm closing my eyes as we approach each corner. He's taking them too fast, and the car shudders as he nearly loses control.

He glances over at me. I try not to look terrified.

"What?" he asks.

"Nothing."

"Are you this scared when Ben drives?"

"Not exactly. His car does seem like it's going to fall apart around us, though." I gasp as Aiden swerves to avoid a car pulling out.

He smirks. "Are you a nervous passenger or am I a bad driver?"

"A little of both?" I grin.

"Any reason for that?"

"What?

His eyes flick over to me. "Do cars naturally scare you, or is there a reason?"

I shrug. "My dad was a bad driver. He crashed the car with me in it when I was five."

Aiden frowns. "I thought you didn't live with your dad."

"He walked out on us straight after that."

Aiden doesn't answer. I decide to tell him about it anyway.

"I was hurt pretty bad." I stare down at my hands. "Mum and Dad had a huge fight at the hospital. Mum blamed Dad. Dad left. Pete blamed me." I look out the window. I can't seem to stop talking. "Pete was always closer to Dad than to Mum. He's never really understood her. He even went and lived with Dad for a while, but ... well, our dad's not a very nice person."

I watch Aiden out of the corner of my eye. He stares straight ahead, frowning. He's kind of funny looking. His skin's really pale, which makes the colour of his lips look too dark – like he's wearing lipstick all the time. Plus, his nose is crooked, like he's got a fault line running down his face.

"But Ben's driving doesn't scare you?" he asks eventually.

I smile. "Not as much, but that's partly because he talks and has the radio on and stuff. I'm better when I'm distracted."

"I'll remember that." Aiden pulls into the kerb around the corner from school. "Have a good day, Kelsey." There's a weird sincerity to the way he says that. It catches me off guard.

"Thanks," I mumble. "You too."

I keep my head down for most of the day. I've done absolutely no homework from yesterday, and I think the Mum excuse is wearing thin. The teachers are just itching to give me the "You have so much potential, Kelsey," speech.

Mike meets me outside my last class for the day. His face lights up when he sees me, which gives me a strange mix of warm fuzzies and anxious gurgles inside.

"Ready to go?" he says.

"Go?"

His smile droops and the anxious gurgles win out over the warm fuzzies.

"You said you couldn't stay at mine because it was a school night. Tonight's not a school night." There's a hint of smugness to the way he says it. Like he thinks he's outsmarted me or something.

I sigh. "I just have to get some stuff from my locker." I hate the way Mike's just assumed I'm staying at his place. All the same, I'm not willing to argue with him about it.

He talks about some band he likes as we walk to the form room. I "mmm" and "ahhh" in the right places, but I'm not really listening. He likes that hard-out death-metal, which just sounds like noise to me, and there's only so long I can fake interest.

Amber's leaning against my locker in the form room. Hers is right next to mine and she does this all the time. Normally, I just wait until she's finished her conversation, but Mike's not as patient as me. He pushes her sideways with his shoulder.

"Hey!" She catches hold her of locker door as she stumbles.

Mike turns to me, ignoring her. "So, do you want to go?" he says.

Amber glares at me over Mike's shoulder. She mouths "bitch". I'm not sure why she's blaming me. I was willing to wait.

I look back at Mike. I realise I have no idea what he's talking about. "Huh?"

Mike frowns. I can tell he knows I haven't listened to any of it.

"I said: do you want to go to the concert when they play here?"

"Sure." I try to hide my disgust at the idea. "I'd have to check with Pete, though."

I busy myself with opening my locker so I don't have to see Mike's reaction to that last part.

"Hey, Kel?" Mike's voice is gentle. He touches my shoulder.

My body tenses. I have to force myself to look at him. "Mmm?"

"Are you okay?"

"What d'you mean?"

Mike shifts awkwardly. "I mean, with your mum. I know you and Pete never got on ... and stuff..."

I swallow. The warm fuzzies are back. "I'm okay. Really." I give Mike the most sincere smile I can manage.

He takes my hand as we walk home.

4

Chapter Four

I leave a note for Pete on the kitchen bench. Luckily, neither he nor Ben is home. Pete would get really uncomfortable if I asked him if I could sleep over at my boyfriend's house, and I don't think I could cope with another one of Ben's disapproving looks.

Mike does the talking on the way back to his house. I tune out every time he starts a sentence with, "I was so wasted ..." He used to not drink, because I didn't. Now it's almost as if he drinks more because of it.

When we get to Mike's place, he reaches up to grab the key from the top of the doorframe.

"You shouldn't leave it in such an obvious place." I cringe as I hear my mother's voice coming out of my mouth.

Mike shrugs. "Have to, otherwise Dad'll never find it." He opens the door. "Hello?"

"In here."

My stomach flips at the sound of Mike's dad's voice.

Mike frowns. "I didn't think he'd be home yet."

His dad's sprawled on a bean bag in the living room, beer in one hand – obviously not his first – and his wife-beater shirt stained with something unrecognisable.

He leers at me. "Hello, Kel-sey."

I hate the way he says my name, kind of sing-song and mocking.

Mike puts his arm around me and pulls me close to his side. "Where's Mum?"

"Kitchen." He jerks his thumb towards the doorway.

"Come on, Kel."

Mike's dad's hand brushes my leg as I walk past. I bite my tongue and swallow hard.

I've always thought the kitchen is the nicest room in Mike's house. It's light and, above all, it's clean. The rest of the house makes Pete's place look as spotless as Martha Stewart's mansion.

Mike's mum greets us with a nervous smile. She's really pretty, but her eyes are always watery and anxious, and over the last few months the lines around them have deepened. I find myself staring at those and seeing the rest of her face less and less.

"Kelsey, so good to see you, my darling." She gives me a hug.

"What's Dad doing here?" Mike's voice is accusing.

His mum gives a false, fluttering laugh. "Why shouldn't he be here?"

Mike scowls and looks away. "Come on, Kel."

We go and hang out in Mike's room. His walls are completely covered with posters of bands with names like Vomit Leftovers. When I met him, I think he had maybe one poster up. I can't remember who was on it, but I'd put money on the fact that it wasn't a band with a name that involved regurgitation.

You could actually see the floor back then, too. Now there's a path carved into the crap on the floor – just enough to get in and out of the room. I'd like to say that the state of his room is just down to his mum giving up on trying to make him clean it, but it's more than that. Somewhere along the way he just stopped caring.

Mike sprawls across the bed with his head in my lap. He seems so different to the guy I started going out with. I feel like I'm spending all my time waiting for him to stop being such a dick, and start acting like himself again.

I run my fingers through his hair and wait for him to say something, but his skin is taut over his clenched jaw. I pick at the lumps of old gel and flakes of black dye in his hair.

I cringe at the sound of a crash from another room. Then I hear Mike's dad yelling. Mike's mum answers, her tone rising with anxiety.

Mike sits up, presses play on the CD player and flops back against me. For once I'm glad to listen to his roaring death-metal. It blocks out all but the loudest crashes.

Mike still hasn't said anything. I can't tell whether he's angry or upset. I risk a peek at his face, then lean forward and kiss his forehead, leaving my lips pressed against his skin.

"It's okay," I murmur.

"Shut up!" He pushes me away.

I flinch as he shoves his chest of drawers, sending CDs flying.

"You think this is okay?" He kicks the bed. "You think it's okay the way he treats her?"

I cover my face as he throws a book at the wall behind me.

"He's a fucking asshole." He slams his fist into the mattress next to me.

I get up and head for the door.

Mike blocks my way. "Where are you going?"

My voice doesn't seem to want to work. I hear my breath coming out in little gasps.

"You can't leave." His eyes cut into me.

I stumble backwards. Mike lunges towards me. I scream and try to dodge him, but he grabs my arm. "This is bullshit." He shakes me. "You're going to leave me, aren't you?"

I twist away from him. He jerks me, snapping my head back. "AREN'T YOU?"

"No." I have to force the word out.

He makes a disgusted sound in the back of his throat.

"I'm not, I swear." I squirm, unable to lift my eyes to his face.

Mike's breathing slows. He lets go of my arms and pushes me towards the bed, where I collapse. I curl up in ball against the wall.

A couple of hours later, Mike touches my shoulder. His parents are quiet but he still has the music on. He's switched it to one of my CDs. I think that's his idea of an apology.

"Kel?" He runs his hand along my arm.

"What?" I flinch as his hand touches the bruises.

He moves his hand to my hair and kisses my neck. My jaw's shaking and I don't trust my voice to say anything. He pulls me over to face him. I can't look him in the eye, but he doesn't seem to notice.

He kisses me, pulling me close against him. "I love you, Kel," he whispers.

I can't think clearly. Part of me feels sick, like I want to run away and never come back, but the other part doesn't have the energy for that.

Mike slides his hand up under my top. We jerk apart as the door bursts open. Mike goes red when he looks up, and I feel my cheeks colour, too, as I see Mike's thirteen-year-old sister, Jo, standing in the doorway.

Her eyes flick around the room looking at anything but us. "I can come back later."

"No, it's okay, Jo." Mike disentangles his hand from my hair.

"Really?" She looks at me.

"Yeah, come in." I tug at the hem of my top, trying to make myself look more respectable.

Jo sits down on the floor. "Mum's locked herself in her bedroom."

"Yeah." Mike tries to sound neutral, but I hear the hollowness in his voice.

"Do you think Dad'll be back tonight?" She looks up at us with anxious eyes. Her hair's scraped back into the bun she wears for ballet class and she still has her leotard and cross-over on, covered by her jeans.

"Nah, we won't see him for a couple of days."

"You think so?"

Mike glances at me then down at the mattress he keeps on the floor, in among the clothes, for Jo to sleep on when things get really bad. "You can stay in here if you want."

Relief breaks across Jo's face. "You don't mind?"

Mike shakes his head.

"Of course not," I say.

Jo talks to me while I try to make something edible out the few ingredients I find in the fridge. There's half an orange and a bowl of whipped cream in there, but not much else.

I find pasta in the cupboard, and I start to make a sauce out of what's left in the vegetable drawer. There are two tomatoes but they've obviously been there for a while. They have black spots around the centre, and they collapse into a pulpy mush when I cut them. I find a single carrot – it's so old I can bend it in half and it doesn't break – and an onion with a long green stalk sprouting from the top. I nearly put in half a pumpkin from the bottom shelf of the fridge, but when I see the gelatinous state of its centre I can't bring myself to do it. I drop it in the bin instead.

"Mum's been on night shifts for the last couple of weeks." Jo sounds apologetic. "She hasn't had time to shop."

Mike's straightening out the living room. I ask Jo about her day at school, and if she needs any help with her homework. Someone should talk to her about that stuff, and I know Mike won't. Also, it keeps me distracted from the smell of the food cooking.

"Kelsey?" she says.

"Hmmm?" I'm trying to squash dry spaghetti into a small saucepan, so I don't look up.

"Can I come and stay at your place? You know, just for a couple of days or something."

Out of the corner of my eye, I see Jo twisting her mouth up as she bites her lip. I close my eyes and take a breath before I turn to her. "Hun, I'm living at my brother's now. There's barely room for me."

"But couldn't you just ask him? It wouldn't be for long."

I shake my head. "If I was still with Mum maybe, but–"

"Please? I can't handle it here." Jo's eyes are watery and for a moment she looks like her mum.

I shake my head again. I feel like I'm being ripped down the middle, like a paper doll.

I put my arms around her and she presses her face into my shoulder.

"I'll talk to Mike," I say. "We'll sort something out."

"Dinner ready?" Mike walks into kitchen, and the spaghetti spits and hisses as if answering him. He frowns. "What's wrong?" He gives Jo an awkward pat on the back and she mumbles something into my shoulder. He looks at me.

"Later," I mouth over the top of Jo's head.

Jo falls asleep almost as soon as she gets into bed, but Mike and I lie awake, talking.

"She wanted to come stay at my place," I whisper.

Jo's breathing has slipped into the regular pattern of sleep, and I don't want to wake her.

"Why?"

I shrug. "She's stressed, and I don't think she's really coping."

Mike sighs. His face is just a few centimetres from mine on the pillow, but he seems far away. He doesn't say anything for ages, and after a bit, I think he's gone to sleep.

"Thanks for talking to her." He opens his eyes. "I would myself but ... you know."

I attempt a smile. "Any time."

I wake up in the middle of the night. Mike's asleep with his arm draped heavily over me, and I can hear Jo's breathing from the floor. At first I'm not sure what's woken me, then I hear it again. The phone. I can hear it ringing in the other room. My heart speeds up and I get a tingling feeling on the tips of my fingers. I run through the options of who it could be in my head. Mike's dad, calling from God knows where wanting God knows what. Pete calling about Mum …

The ringing seems to get louder and the sound makes my skin crawl. I edge out from under Mike's arm and get up to answer it, just to make the ringing stop.

I pick my way around Jo and out of the room.

In the hall I fumble around until I find the light switch, then stand beside the phone listening to it ring.

I hold my breath as I pick up the receiver. "Hello?"

My whole body goes cold at the sound of the exaggerated breathing. I'm not at home. How does he know I'm here? I stand frozen with the phone glued to my ear. The heavy breathing continues.

"Leave me alone!" I scream, then slam the phone down as hard as I can. I hope the noise damages his hearing.

I go back into the bedroom and shake Mike awake. He groans and rolls away from me.

"Mike, wake up!"

"What?"

"There was a prank caller." I lower my voice so as not to wake Jo.

"So?" Mike hasn't opened his eyes, and his voice is clogged with sleep.

"I think it's the same guy who's been calling my house."

"Yeah?" Mike's not really listening to me. He's drifting back asleep.

"Mike!"

"What?" His eyes finally open as my voice shoots up with anxiety. Jo turns in her sleep.

"It's the same guy. That means he knew I was going to be here tonight."

Mike groans. "For God's sake, Kelsey."

"What?"

"He's probably calling all the houses around here. Take the phone off the hook and go back to sleep."

"But–"

"I said go to sleep, Kel." Mike's eyes flash. "It's the middle of the night."

The other things I want to say dissolve on my tongue. Mike rolls over and goes back to sleep. I sit on the edge of the bed, feeling cold and shaky. Just a coincidence, I say to myself. Just a coincidence.

I wake late the next morning. Jo's mattress is empty, but Mike's still sprawled on the bed next to me.

I rub at my eyes. "What time is it?"

Mike looks at his cell phone. "Just after ten."

My stomach drops. I get up and put on my jeans.

"What's wrong?"

I struggle to pull on my top. It has a narrow waist and tight sleeves and my arms get stuck in it. "I'm supposed to go see my mum today. I'm going to be late." I twist and wrench, but the top won't come down over my head. I look at Mike. "Help?"

He gets out of bed and yanks my arm through one of the sleeves. "Can't you go tomorrow?"

I push my other arm into its sleeve. "No, Pete works on Sunday mornings."

Mike tugs the hem of the top down over my waist. He frowns as his hand brushes my ribs. "You've got really bony. It's nasty." He slaps my belly. "Plenty of flab here though."

Bile rises in my throat as he laughs.

"You want some breakfast?"

"No, I'll eat at home." I shove all my stuff into my backpack and rush out the door. Mike follows me.

"Tell Jo bye for me," I yell over my shoulder.

5

Chapter Five

I run most of the way home, my backpack jerking against me. It seems like it's taking ages to get there, then I realise I've taken a wrong turn. I really need a phone with maps on it.

I backtrack for a couple of streets then find myself near school. I nearly scream with frustration.

"Kelsey?"

I look up to see my geography teacher, Mr Humphries, walking towards me.

"Are you all right?"

I flap my arms in a gesture of defeat. "I'm lost."

He frowns and glances around. "Well, you're right outside school ..."

"I know that! I can't find my way back to my brother's. I have terrible direction sense."

Mr Humphries nods. "I'm starting to understand your geography results."

I roll my eyes. "Very helpful." I say it under my breath, but I think Mr Humphries hears.

He chuckles. "What's your brother's address?"

"34 Brian Cres–"

"You're not far away." Mr Humphries cuts me off. "You turn left at the next corner then right at the end–"

"Wait, slow down. Left, and then?"

Mr Humphries laughs and shakes his head. His cheeks wobble with the movement, like chicken fillets. He has a horrible sallow complexion, and his teeth are all yellow. He's like a walking anti-smoking campaign.

I blush. "Street names? I think I can figure those out." I feel like an idiot. I can go somewhere if I know the way, but giving and receiving directions is beyond me.

Mr Humphries smiles. "My car's just down the road. I can give you a lift."

I hesitate. My instinct tells me I shouldn't go with him. I know him as a teacher, but does that really mean anything?

My desire to get home wins out. "Thanks, that'd be great."

I follow him to his car. Much to Pete's and Ben's disgust, I know nothing about cars, but I know this one is old and pretty beaten up. It's white and looks like a fridge on wheels.

"Sorry, it's a bit of a mess." Mr Humphries shoves a pile of papers off the passenger seat so I can sit down, then starts up the engine. "I had to come in and pick up some marking. I know how eager you all are to get your results back." He chuckles as I groan. "You're a bright girl, Kelsey, you could do well if only you–"

"Applied myself. I know, I know. I have so much potential."

Mr Humphries laughs again. "Well, it's true. Just look at your marks from a year ago. You were doing much better then. It's obvious you haven't been putting the effort in."

I stare out the window. "I've had other things on my mind."

"Of course, I'm sorry. That was insensitive of me."

Mr Humphries lights up a cigarette. I wait for him to open a window but he doesn't. The smoke creeps over to me, making my throat itch. I rest my hand against my mouth as he exhales.

Mr Humphries is silent. He probably thinks he's upset me. I'm actually not bothered. He's been really nice and given me more slack than the other teachers, even when I haven't been all that grateful for it.

"I'm glad to see you've joined the soccer team again this year," Mr Humphries says. He coughs, sending smoke in all directions.

I make a face. "Mum wanted me to play a sport. I hate it."

"But you're so good."

I laugh, but it comes out wheezy. I cough and clear my throat. "Really, I'm not. I just run up and down the field trying to look busy."

"I remember you scoring a few goals last season."

He's right. I was never the best player on the team, but I did okay. After all, I got through the try-outs and not everyone did. It was probably just that Mum wanted me to, so I made the effort. I don't have the energy anymore.

I shrug. "Everyone's sick of me being distracted. They'll probably cut me if I don't get my act together soon."

Mr Humphries glances at me. "Well, I enjoy watching you anyway." He gives me a smile.

I look away quickly. Did he really just say that? Ew!

I feel like I'm holding my breath until we get to Pete's place. "Thank you for the ride." I pick up my backpack from the floor of the car.

"Not a problem. Perhaps you should draw yourself a map of the way from Mike's house to yours."

"How did you know I was at his place?"

Mr Humphries' cheeks colour. It's like watching a map of blood vessels appear across his skin. "I'm sorry, I just assumed. I saw you leaving school together yesterday, so I thought ..." He trails off.

"Thank you for the lift home," I say. My voice comes out tight and prim. Mr Humphries nods then starts up the car and drives off. I watch until he turns the corner and goes out of sight.

I turn back towards the house. Pete's car is still in the driveway, so at least he hasn't gone without me. With any luck, he slept in and hasn't even noticed I'm late.

"Pete?" I call as I open the door. "I'm home."

He comes out into the hallway. "Where the hell have you been?"

"At Mike's. Didn't you get my note?"

Pete's jaw clenches. He shakes his head, but I'm not sure whether he means no or if he's just angry. I feel my face going ugly and defiant.

"You should have asked me," he says.

My eyes narrow. "And what exactly would your answer have been?"

Pete looks at me. I can tell he didn't expect this. He takes a breath. "Given your age, I would have said no."

I laugh. "You had girlfriends over when you were my age. Younger, too, if I remember correctly."

"That was different."

"Why? Because I'm a girl?"

"No, because I had Mum's permission. We had a long talk and–"

"Don't be ridiculous. You never had a long talk with Mum

in your life, and anyway, Mum was fine with me sleeping over at Mike's." My chest hurts with the anger building up inside me.

Pete's lips pull back into a snarl. "You're going to play it like that? She probably didn't even know what she was agreeing to. You took advantage of her state."

"How the hell would you know? You weren't there. You didn't look after her; I did."

"That's not fair. You could have called me and you didn't."

"I shouldn't have had to call you," I scream. "You never visited once after you moved away. I saw Ben more than I saw you."

I push past him. My eyes blur, but I can feel him follow me.

"You should have called me, Kel."

"Why the hell would I call you? You obviously didn't care about us."

"Of course I care–"

"Well, you didn't show it." I spin around to face him. "Mum didn't want me to call you. She knew you'd just put her in a home."

Pete's face goes slack. I stare at him, watching his expression going from angry to hurt to guilty.

I turn away. Ben's watching us from the stairs. I run past him and up to my room.

I lie down on my bed and stare at the leak stain on the ceiling. My eyes are suddenly dry and my insides feel like they've been rubbed down with sandpaper.

Ben opens the door. I turn over and stare at the wall instead. The bed squeaks as Ben sits down on the edge.

"Do you ever worry that you're really a terrible person?"

"You're not a terrible person, Kel."

I shake my head. "How could I say that to him?"

He chuckles. "Pete held his own."

"Yeah, but nothing as bad."

"Maybe he needed to hear it." Ben's voice is soft. I turn to look at him but he doesn't elaborate. "Come on. You need to get ready."

"For what?"

"Going to see your mum, remember?"

I close my eyes. "I don't think Pete will want to take me."

"No. But I do."

For some reason that starts me crying.

"Hey, hey, hey." Ben pulls me up into a hug. "Shhh."

"I'm sorry," I say.

"For what?"

"I don't know. Crying?" I give a weak smile into his chest.

Ben laughs. "I'm pretty sure I can cope with that. Now come on. You really need to get ready."

I follow the signs through the home to the dementia ward, then get one of the nurses to unlock the door and let me into the visitors' room. Hearing the click of her locking me inside makes me nervous. I know it's necessary, but still it makes me feel trapped.

Mum's hair is pulled back into a ponytail, but most of it's escaping, giving her a halo of blonde fuzz. She's talking and laughing with Pete, which is good. It means she's more lucid today.

I wanted Ben to come in with me, but he insisted on waiting outside. I don't see why. He's just as much family as we are.

I feel out of place here without him. Everything is pastel pink and green, except for the long, black streak behind the door, where the rubber seal has bumped against the wall. I almost want to stand next to that, so my black top doesn't stand out so much.

Pete looks up as I come over. The corner of his lip twitches as he fights a frown.

"Hi, Mum," I say.

She looks at me blankly. "Yes?"

"Mum, it's me. Kelsey." I take a deep breath as I realise she doesn't recognise me.

She frowns, puzzling over my words, then shakes her head. "You'll have to come back later. I'm talking to my son."

I look at Pete for help.

He leans towards her. "Mum, it's Kelsey. Remember? Your daughter?"

"Well, tell her to go away. I don't have time right now."

Pete looks at me and shakes his head.

"Mum? Come on, Mum, you know me." My voice cracks.

"I said go away!"

"Please ..." I put my hand on her shoulder.

She bats it away. "Leave me alone!" When I don't move, she pushes me.

"I think you'd better go, Kel." Pete doesn't look at me. He takes Mum's hand, drawing her attention back to him. She blinks a couple of times then smiles.

"Mum." It comes out as a whisper. She doesn't even look up. Neither does Pete.

I back away. When I get to the door, I bang on it until the nurse comes over and unlocks it. She twitters something about disturbing the residents. I stumble down the corridor towards the outside door, focusing on the lino beneath my feet. It's patterned in a motley mix of the same pink and green pastel colours. It makes me dizzy, but I like the feeling.

I shove the door open and step out into the parking area. I take a deep breath, then squat down, covering my face with my hands. I hear Ben open the car door.

"Kel?" He touches the back of my neck. His palms are cold, and a chill creeps down my spine. I push him away.

"What happened?"

I can't breathe. I stand up and struggle with my jacket, trying to pull it off.

"Kel ..."

I scream in frustration as I can't get my arms from the sleeves.

Ben tries to help, but that frustrates me more. I push him away and tear at the fabric, busting one of the seams I'd been meaning to mend.

"Kelsey, stop it."

I hurl the jacket at the ground.

Ben grabs my shoulders. "Calm down." His voice is a command. My heart rate slows as if in response. I stare at him, feeling my face dissolve into shock and sadness.

He pulls me into a hug.

"She didn't know who I was," I say. "Not even when we told her."

"I'm sorry."

"She knew who Pete was, but ..." My voice falters. I don't have words to explain that it's worse that she remembers Pete and not me. At least, not words that don't make me sound jealous and petty.

"She loves you, Kel. It's not her, it's the disease."

"I know, but ..." Again I don't know how to finish the sentence. I know I should be understanding. Instead, I'm angry and hurt.

"Shhh." Ben strokes my hair. After a bit he draws back to look at me. "Do you want me to take you home?"

I nod. He gives me a gentle squeeze, which presses my bruised arms. I grit my teeth to stop from flinching.

I sit at the kitchen counter while Ben makes some lunch. I swear, he could turn sandwich making into an art form. He spends ages lining up the salad so it fits exactly between the slices of bread, then cuts it all into perfect triangles. Even so, I struggle not to pull a face when he puts the plate down in front of me.

His eyebrows draw together into a frown. "Just eat it, Kel." He bites into his own sandwich.

I look down at the counter. "Do you think I'm fat?"

"What?" Ben splutters. It's like watching a cartoon character. I half expect to see his eyes bulge out of his head.

"I'm serious. I mean, I know I've lost a lot of weight, but–"

"Is that what this is about?" He shakes his head. "You think you're fat?"

"No. I don't know."

"You're actually starving yourself." He runs his hand through his hair. His eyes take on a wild look. "I thought you were just stressed."

"I am. I mean, I don't think I'm fat, I just haven't been hungry." My words run together as I try to explain. "It's just, Mike said–"

"Of course. That guy, I swear–"

"It was nothing." I hear my voice rising. "It's my fault. I shouldn't have said anything. Look." I stuff the bread into my mouth. It hits the back of my throat and I start to cough.

Ben whacks me on the back and I spit the half-chewed food onto my plate. "All right?" he asks.

I nod. "Yeah, sorry." The kitchen disappears into a blur as my eyes stream.

Ben sighs. "Kel–"

"I know. I know." I fight the urge to roll my eyes. "I just can't eat when I'm worried, that's all."

"Yeah, but if you think you're fat … I mean look at these bird wings." Ben grabs my arm and flaps it.

"I'm not anorexic."

He lets out an exaggerated breath and crosses his arms. Then he just stands there, staring at me. I try to meet his eye, but it feels really uncomfortable. I resist looking down at the sandwich.

"Kelsey …" Ben's voice is measured. I close my eyes, waiting for his lecture. He stops as Aiden walks into the room.

"Hey." Aiden's eyes flick between us.

Ben doesn't look up. He just keeps staring at me. His jaw's clenched, making his face all jowly, and his hands are balled into fists across his chest. He's not just worried, I realise – he's angry. I can't tell whether it's with me or Mike, and that makes me want to squirm.

"I can come back later." Aiden hovers by the doorway.

"No, I've got stuff I need to do." Ben's words come out all clipped. Then he lowers his voice. "I'll talk to you later." He eyeballs me as he says it, which makes it feel more like a threat than anything else. He throws his own sandwich in the bin as he walks out.

"What was that about?" Aiden looks from me to the pile of mushed bread on my plate.

I shake my head. "I'm not even sure I know."

"Yeah, Ben can be like that." Aiden smirks.

"What do you mean?"

Aiden opens the fridge and gets out a Coke. "I don't know. He's just kind of serious. He makes a big deal out of little things."

"Yeah, I s'pose." It doesn't really sound like the Ben I know, but it has been a while.

"Oh yeah, and you know how he's ridiculously calm all the time? Well, sometimes he gets hard-out angry. It's like he bottles it up or something."

"Really? But–"

I feel like I should try and defend Ben but the phone rings, interrupting me. I look at Aiden, raising my eyebrows.

He sniggers then picks up the receiver. "Hello? Yeah sure, she's right here." He hands me the phone. "For you."

I shake my head to clear it. "Hello?"

My breath catches in my throat as I hear the wheezing. I slam the phone down and glare at Aiden. "That wasn't funny."

Aiden backs away a step. "What?"

I follow him. "Do you think the whole heavy-breathing thing is amusing? Did you think it was funny when he woke us up the other night?"

Aiden smiles nervously and holds up his hands. "I don't know what you're talking about."

"Just don't give the prank caller to me!" I turn to walk away, but Aiden catches my arm.

"That was the prank caller?"

I shake Aiden off. "What? You mistook him for an asthmatic telemarketer?"

Aiden's eyes are wide and his face pales. "No, Kel, he asked for you. He asked if he could speak to Kelsey."

6

Chapter Six

I sit on the couch and stare at the carpet. It used to be purple, but it's faded to a mottled mixture of browns and greys, like the kind they have at school. Designed to hide the dirt. I could probably throw up on it and no one would notice.

I can hear Ben and Aiden talking in the kitchen. They've lowered their voices, so it's almost definitely about me. Well, me and the prank caller. I can't quite wrap my head around it. Who would want to prank call me? I'm not popular or glamorous. In fact, hardly any of the kids at school even notice me.

My cell phone rings, making me jump. I struggle to pull it out of my jeans pocket.

Ben comes and stands behind me as I answer it. He rests his hand on my shoulder, which is kind of nice but mostly just irritating.

"Hello?" My chest tightens as I wait for an answer.

"Hey."

I relax as I hear Mike's voice. Ben looks at me, his eyebrow raised. "Mike," I mouth. Ben makes a disgusted face and I wave him away.

"How's your mum?"

I get another attack of warm fuzzies at that, like an army of Furbies. "You know. The usual." I don't want to jinx his sudden episode of thoughtfulness by telling him the truth.

"What time am I picking you up tonight?"

"Huh?" I run through our conversation this morning, but I can't remember anything about tonight.

"Jacob and Tash's party."

"Oh, right. I'm not sure if–"

"You said you wanted to go."

I said *maybe* and I didn't even mean that. "I know, but–"

"Come on, Kel, it'll be good."

"Yeah, I don't know."

There's silence on the end of the line.

"You could come over here," I say. Ben makes gagging noises which I ignore. "We could watch a movie."

Mike still doesn't say anything.

"Or you could go by yourself."

"I don't want to go by myself. Come on, it'll be a laugh."

"It's just ..." I hesitate, wondering how to word this. "We're not exactly friends with Jacob, and Tash and I hardly ever hang out anymore."

"So? It's an open invite, and Jacob and I hang out some-times."

I sigh. Mike thinks everyone's his friend when he's drunk. He doesn't realise they're all making fun of him.

"Mike–"

"Are you coming or not, Kel?" Mike's voice rises. My heart rate speeds up as I imagine his face. He has this look when he's just about to blow – stony, and kind of like his eyes are going to jump out of his head and slap you.

"Yeah, all right. Pick me up at eight."

We say goodbye, then I hang up. I look at Ben, who's staring at me.

"Did you have to stand there and listen?"

He gives a twisted smile.

I hear the back door open, and Pete walks in. He still looks mad at me. I take a breath, as pins and needles prick my fingertips.

I glance at Ben. He gives me a little nod which I think is meant to be encouraging.

"Mike and I are going to a party tonight. Sorry about before." I run the two sentences together.

Pete stares at me and sighs. He rubs his forehead. "Whose party is it?"

"You remember my friend Tash?" I'm half hoping that Pete will say no so I'll have an excuse not to go.

"Yeah, okay. Just be home by one." His voice sounds flat, like he's really tired. "Write down Tash's address for me."

Pete doesn't look at me. I swear right now the sound of my swallowing would be loud enough to cause an avalanche.

"I really am sorry," I say. I feel a big lump forming in my chest.

Pete nods and lets out a long breath. I think I'd feel better if he yelled or laughed at me. Anything really.

"The prank caller rang again," I say. "Aiden answered it, but he asked for me."

Pete looks up. "What?"

"Aiden said he asked to speak to Kelsey," I say. "And he rang last night at Mike's. He didn't say anything; it was just the heavy breathing again."

"You didn't tell me that." Ben leans over the back of the

couch to look at me.

"Yeah, I forgot. It didn't seem important until now."

Pete looks from me to Ben. I hadn't noticed before, but there are heavy bags under Pete's eyes.

"Maybe we should call the police," he says.

"No, don't do that." I roll my eyes at his overreaction.

Pete squints at me, screwing up his face. "Do you think it's someone from school?"

I shrug and look away. Pete wouldn't understand. He was Mr Popular at school.

He sighs. "You probably shouldn't answer the phone from now on."

"Yeah, all right. Just ask who it is before you give it to me."

I go up to my room and start sifting through my clothes. I have to really focus on the textures of the fabric to stop myself from thinking about the caller. They feel surprisingly rough when I take the time to notice.

I've got to find something for tonight that covers my arms and still looks presentable. Who am I kidding? Mike's going to be so drunk I could wear a potato sack and he probably wouldn't notice, and it's not like anyone else will be paying me attention.

I pick out a dress and a wrap-around shirt to go over it. Then I realise I'm getting ready way too early. I decide to make good on my promise to finish my homework, so I spread out my exercise books and try to do some calculus. The numbers seem to get up and rearrange themselves when I'm not looking. I swear a minute ago that three was a seven.

I give up and read for a while, but even my old copy of *Catcher in the Rye* doesn't hold my attention. I've read that book so many times most of the silver has flaked off the cover, but today I can't focus on anything. My brain feels like it's been replaced by candy floss.

Even though I don't want to go to the party, I'm almost relieved when it's time for me to get dressed.

I'm putting my mascara on when Mike arrives. The doorbell rings and I rush downstairs, hoping to get there before anyone else. I'm too late. Ben and Mike are having some kind of Mexican stand-off in the hallway.

"Come on, let's go." I try to bustle Mike backwards out the doorway before Ben can stop us, but he's too quick for me.

"I've made some dinner. Do you want something to eat before you go?"

I resist the urge to turn and glare at Ben. "Nah, we're fine."

Mike doesn't take the hint. "I could eat."

I fix him with a stare. "We'll get something on the way there."

He frowns. "What's wrong with your face?"

I feel like bashing my head against the wall. He seriously knows how to make me feel like crap. He rubs at my cheek with his thumb and a smear of black comes off on his hand.

"Bloody mascara." I rush upstairs to re-do my make-up.

I hear laughing from the kitchen as I come back down. Right now I think I'd rather become a rodeo clown than go in there, but you probably have to pass a fitness test for that, so I head inside.

It's not just Ben and Mike; Pete and Aiden are there too. They all stop laughing as soon as I walk in, which makes me feel sure one of them was saying something about me.

Ben's serving up big bowls of pasta. He probably thinks I haven't noticed his eyes flicking between me and the pot.

"You should cook every night, Ben." Pete talks with his

mouth full which puts me off even more.

Ben pulls out a chair for me and places a bowl in front of it. My face goes really hot and my throat feels like it's constricting. Suddenly the Mexican stand-off isn't between Mike and Ben anymore. It's me, Ben and the pasta.

"I'm not hungry," I say.

"More for us, then." Pete reaches out for the food, but Ben pulls it away from him.

"Come on, you've got to eat something before you go." Ben's all smiles but his tone is clipped.

I start playing out arguments in my head. In all of them, I start screaming at him and Mike and Pete. Even Aiden's not faring well. On the plus side, if I did that, Pete probably wouldn't let me go to the party. On the downside, I'd have to deal with Mike afterwards.

I choke down the food. It doesn't really taste of anything, but it sits inside me like I ate the bowl as well as the contents.

I stare at the dish. It's one of the old ones Mum gave Pete when he moved out of home. I remember eating ice-cream out of one like this when I was little. It's mud-brown with a darker stripe around the top, and there's a crack running down the side where it's been glued back together. I trace my finger over it.

"Remember to be home by one," Pete says as we get up to go. He gives me a forced smile and pats me on the shoulder. I return the smile with the most sincere one I can manage.

The food rolls around inside me as we walk over to Tash's house.

"I always thought Ben was a bit of a dick, but he makes really good pasta," Mike says.

I don't have the energy to answer that, so I just nod. Mike

keeps talking. I probably should try to pay attention, but I'm distracted by the noise my stomach is making.

"What were you guys laughing about?" I ask when he pauses for breath.

Mike chuckles. "They were telling me about when you were little."

"Like what?" I run through all the embarrassing things Pete could have told him. There are too many to even list.

"Oh, nothing."

"No, tell me."

Mike just laughs.

"Miiiike." I use my most ingratiating, whiny voice.

He sighs. "Pete was telling me about how you spilt juice on your dad's shirt and hid under your bed for five hours to avoid being told off."

I blush. I was so scared of being yelled at, I wouldn't come out. Eventually Dad had to drag me out from under there.

The windows of Tash's house are all open, and there's techno music blaring at ear-bursting volumes. The neighbours must be thrilled. People are shouting and laughing inside, and I swear I can smell the alcohol already.

Mike grins at me and takes my hand as he opens the door. I stare down at the doormat. It used to say "Welcome", but the W and the ME have worn off so now it says "elco".

Just inside the door there's a table absolutely covered with beers, which of course Mike heads straight for. He offers me one, but I shake my head. There's a coffee table set up with some chips and dip so I wander over and try to look busy.

I scan the room while simultaneously trying to avoid making eye contact with anyone. Usually there's at least one person looking as awkward and out of place as me. Either that or there'll be someone who's had a little too much to drink and is in the emotional, talkative stage. I always try to attach myself to that person. It gives me some semblance of feeling like I fit in.

I pick up a chip and put it in my mouth, then gag and spit it out into my hand. It comes out as dry brown flakes. I look down at the dish I got it from. Great. I just ate a piece of potpourri. I move the 'bowl of chips' away so no one else makes the same mistake.

The house is all white with a red feature wall, and has a matching red-and-white-striped couch that probably cost more than all the furniture in Pete's place combined. I don't fancy the place's chances of surviving the night unscathed. The house is packed with people and most of them are dancing, rave style.

I thought Mike would come over with me but I've lost him. I scan the crowd again but I can't see him. Amber knocks my back as she goes past, making me stumble. She glances back over her shoulder and smirks. I feel my cheeks colour as she turns to Sophie and laughs.

There's a group of guys from the school rugby team huddled in the corner, with Jacob at the centre. From the level of their laughter, I can tell they're pretty drunk. Jacob catches my eye as I look over at them. He says something to the others and they all laugh. He breaks away from them and heads towards me.

"Here's the star of the show," he says.

"What?" My voice comes out kind of shaky, so it sounds more like "wait?"

Jacob grins. He leans down and whispers in my ear. "When are you going to break up with Mike and go out with me?"

I stare at him. "Jake ..."

He laughs, and I blush as I realise he's joking.

"Just say the word, Kels. Just say the word!"

I laugh despite myself. "Sure, I'll keep that in mind."

Jacob glances back at the other rugby guys. I frown as I see they're coming over to us.

"Uh-oh." Jacob grins and shakes his head.

"What's going on?" I back away.

He doesn't answer. He picks me up and throws me over his shoulder. I scream as he spins around on the spot. The red and white turns into a candy-cane swirl. I close my eyes, but I can hear everyone laughing. All I can think about is how embarrassing it would be if I chucked up spaghetti all over Jacob.

"Jake! Put her down!"

I hear Tash's voice, but I don't want to risk opening my eyes to look for her.

Jacob swings me down and puts me back on my feet. I can't balance and have to cling to him to stop from falling over. He laughs and holds me around my waist.

"What are you doing? Leave her alone." Tash takes my arm.

Mike comes out of the kitchen. I register the surprise on his face just before it turns into a glare.

I stumble towards him but Jacob pulls me back. "Where're you going? The party's just started."

"Leave me alone." I push him away, but the rugby guys surround me.

"Jacob!" Tash is blocked from my view.

"What do you want?" I try to back away. One of the other guys grips my shoulders. I can't see who it is but I elbow him in the stomach and he makes an "oophf" sound.

"Aw, come on, Kels, we're just having some fun." Jacob pulls me towards him and wraps his arms around my waist. The other guys laugh.

"Where's your boyfriend, Kel?"

"Don't tell me Dicky-Micky let you out on your own?"

I can't even tell who's saying what. My head starts to pound. I stare at a scar on Jacob's arm. It's long, and still shows the marks where stitches held the flaps of skin together, beige against the dark of his skin.

"Please let go of me," I say.

Jacob frowns. "Relax, Kel. It's just a joke." He loosens his arms though, letting me pull away.

"Come on, Kel."

I spin around. Billy Atkins stares at me with an inane smile.

"We're just having a good time." He makes air quotes around the words "good time". He juts his chin out like he's the most attractive guy in the room. In reality he looks like a pumpkin head jack-o-lantern.

Someone thrusts a piece of paper at me. I stare at it, feeling a fizzing in my mouth.

FOR A GOOD TIME CALL
KELSEY MORGEN
021 354 376.

At first I can't even form words. I want to scream, but that seems stuck in my throat as well. "Those calls ... they were because of you? Do you have *any* idea ...?" I don't know how to finish the sentence. "My mother is ... the middle of the night ..." I'm not even making sense now, but I don't care.

Billy scoffs. "Lighten up, Kel, it was just a joke."

I contemplate punching him in the face, but it would probably be like trying to chop wood with a butter knife. Instead I slam the paper into Jacob's chest as hard as I can. A chorus of "Oooo," goes up from the guys and they laugh.

"Jake! What the hell are you doing?" Tash forces her way through to me. Behind her I see Amber and Sophie snickering.

I push Tash away. "All of you, just leave me alone." I run out, grabbing a beer from the table as I go.

7

Chapter Seven

I stagger down the road as fast as my high heels will let me. I feel like such an idiot. All I want is to get as far away from the house as I can, before I lose it.

Once I get down the road a bit, out of sight of the house, I stop. I struggle with my shoes, kicking them off, then I scull most of the beer. It goes straight to my head. One beer and I'm drunk. Even I think that's pathetic.

"Kelsey." Mike's following me.

I move towards him and reach out, expecting a hug.

He pushes my arms away. "I bet you enjoyed that." He moves so his face is lit by a streetlight. He's glaring at me and the light casts shadows under his eyes, giving him big hollows where his cheeks should be.

"What? You're mad at me?" I laugh. It comes out all high-pitched and weird.

Mike pushes my shoulders, hard. I stumble backwards.

"You think that was funny?" he says.

"No." I'm still laughing, but it's coming out in little puffs. I can't remember why I started. The bottle slips from my hand and I laugh harder as it smashes against the pavement.

"Shut up!" He pushes me again.

I nearly trip this time. "Stop it."

"Slut." He spits the word at me.

I stare at him, feeling the corners of my mouth pull down. "What?"

He sneers. "You heard me."

"Fuck off, Mike," I say with as much venom as I can manage, then turn and start to walk away. He hits me hard in the middle of my back. I fall forward, only just managing to put my arms out in time to save my face. My wrists jar, pain shoots up my forearms, and my hands prickle like I'm holding ice. I try to get up. Mike kicks my side and I land splat on the pavement again.

"Don't!" I scream.

He kicks my side, again and again. Somehow I turn over onto my back and cover my face with my arms. A kaleidoscope pattern of flashing gold and black plays on the insides of my eyelids.

"Enjoyed the attention, did you?" He lands a kick on the word "did".

"No," I try to say, but it doesn't come out properly.

Mike breathes heavily. He backs off a bit and stares at me. I don't move. It's like I'm playing dead. He swears under his breath then squats down, covering his face with his hands. I still don't move, though I can't stop the sounds coming out of my mouth – a cross between whimpers and gasps.

"Kelsey," he says. He's crying.

"Go away," I say. My voice is cracked and hoarse.

"Kel ..." He reaches out to touch my shoulder.

"Get away from me!" I scream. It hurts to speak. I want to groan but I hold it back.

Mike gets up. He's crying as he walks away.

I don't move, even after he's gone. It starts to rain, and the drops feel heavy and oily against my skin. I wait for the pavement to swallow me whole like a whale opening its mouth.

It doesn't happen.

I ease myself up. The heels of my palms are skinned and there are pieces of grit lodged in the raw skin. I shudder as I flick them out with my nail. The thought of touching the inside flesh of my hand makes me feel sick.

There's a piece of beer bottle sticking out of my leg. Somehow this doesn't bother me as much as the grit. It's like I'm watching myself pull it out. It hurts, but not nearly as much as I would have expected. A trickle of red creeps down my leg and lands as a snowflake on the ground. In another setting, I'd think it was beautiful.

I freeze as I hear someone clear their throat. The streetlight casts a circle around me like a spotlight. I couldn't be more obvious if I tried.

I peer into the shadows around me. Down the road, back towards Jacob's house, I see the light of a cigarette butt being flicked into the gutter. Then, as my night vision kicks in, a figure among the shadows. I watch, but he doesn't seem to have noticed me. Either that, or he's pretending I'm invisible so he doesn't have to deal with this. He coughs then starts to hum as he walks around the corner, out of sight. The tune floats back to me. It's a lullaby, I know that much, but I can't think which one. I squint, trying to remember, then I let out a breath. My ribs give a stabbing shock of pain as I do. I clutch at my chest, then my stomach heaves and I throw up in the gutter. So much for Ben's attempt at feeding me. I start to laugh, but it hurts so I stop and wipe my face instead.

My toes curl up against the cold of the pavement. I look for my shoes but they've disappeared into the bushes. The streetlight's glow doesn't reach far enough for me to see, so I give up and hobble home in my bare feet.

I go in through the kitchen door. There's a note on the bench from Pete.

STAYING AT JENNY'S. SEE YOU IN THE MORNING.

I stare at it for far too long, reading it by the light from the window. It seems to take my brain an extra five minutes to understand each word.

I look up as the kitchen light flicks on. Aiden's standing by the door, staring at me. He rests his hand on the wall as if grounding himself. His other arm hangs limp by his side. I glance down at the dirt on my dress, my shoeless feet, and the blood dripping down my leg. I can just imagine what my face looks like.

"Shit," he whispers.

"Don't tell Pete." I swallow and it hurts.

Aiden hesitates, then nods.

"Or Ben," I add.

He nods again. His face has gone blank and distant. It creeps me out not knowing what he's thinking. I walk past him and go upstairs.

I lock myself in the bathroom. My hands shake as I go through the first aid kit. I find the disinfectant, then sit on the edge of the bath and dab at myself with it. The scrapes on my hands and the cut on my leg sting as I do. I almost enjoy the pain.

I'm surprised at myself. I should be falling apart, but I'm not. At the very least I should be mad, but I'm not really that either. My strongest feeling at the moment is a desire to throw up again. I think I've put everything in the too-hard-to-deal-with-right-now basket.

I wrap my leg with cotton wool and gauze bandages, then shuffle down the hall to my room. By the time I get there, blood's oozed through the bandage, leaving a red patch like the Japanese flag.

Downstairs, Aiden's moving around in a restless, pacing sort of way. I probably should feel bad, but instead I'm irritated by the noise.

It hurts changing into my pyjamas. I have to coax my body to bend enough to get my head through the neck hole and my arms into the sleeves. My head's pounding and I'm too wound up to sleep, so I flick on the radio. After a couple of minutes I turn it off again. It feels like the ads are drilling themselves into my brain. I bet I'll wake up in the morning wanting to buy a personalised number plate and a vacuum cleaner.

Just as I'm falling asleep, the phone rings, sending a jolt through my whole body. I grab the receiver, feeling a fizzing in my mouth and throat.

"What? What do you want?" My chest spasms as I force the words out. I have to hold back a cough.

There's silence on the line.

"Who is that?" I say. "Jacob? Billy?"

I wait for the heavy breathing to start but instead he starts humming. The lullaby.

"Oh my God!" I drop the phone on the floor, then fumble to pick it up so I can hang up. I slam it down as hard as I can then squeeze my hands against my mouth. My insides feel like they're swelling up and they'll come pouring out my mouth if I don't hold them in.

The phone rings again.

I pick it up and scream into the receiver. "Just leave me alone you sick freak!" I have a horrible moment as I realise it could be Pete or Ben. I'm almost relieved when he starts to laugh.

"What do you want?" I can't even make my voice sound assertive. It comes out wobbly and quiet.

"To talk to you," he says.

It's the first time I've heard his voice and it doesn't sound like I imagined. He's younger and his voice is grainy, like he's smoked a pack a day since he was seven.

"I saw what he did." His words go up at the end of the sentence, making it a question rather than a statement.

The air in my lungs feels like it's gone solid. "What?"

He doesn't answer. I can hear him breathing but it's soft – just what you'd expect from a normal call.

"Just ..." My voice breaks and I can't finish the sentence. Instead I scream and hurl the phone against the wall. The plastic cracks and something inside me breaks.

It's late when I wake up. I want to stay in bed forever but of course I need to pee, so I ease myself out of bed and creep down the hall.

I feel a lurch inside me as I open the bathroom door. There's blood from my leg on the side of the bath and on the floor, and the first aid kit's open, spread out around the sink where

I left it. I lean forward to start cleaning up, then gasp as my ribs burn.

"Kelsey?"

Pete stands in the doorway, in his work clothes. My eyes flick around the walls as I wonder how I can cause a diversion big enough for him not to notice the state of the room.

His brow creases as he reads my mind. "I saw it when I came in."

"I'm so sorry. I'll clean it up." I reach for the first aid kit. This time I clasp at my chest and bite down on my lip, to stop from making a noise.

"Leave it." Pete touches my back.

I look up at him.

His eyebrows draw together into a concerned mono-brow. "What happened?"

I have a moment of delayed reaction, then attempt a laugh and self-deprecating roll of my eyes. "Nothing. I'm just clumsy."

"Yeah?" Pete doesn't sound convinced.

I look away. "I fell over on the way home. I shouldn't be allowed to wear heels." I force another laugh. My cheeks burn as Pete watches me.

He crosses his arms. "Were you drunk?"

I look at him, feeling my eyebrows shoot up. It takes a moment for me to process, then I hang my head in what I hope looks like shame. "Yeah."

Pete sighs. "So, I suppose Mum let you drink as well?"

I frown at the sarcasm in his voice. "No."

"I didn't think so."

I roll my tongue around the inside of my mouth. "So what? Are you going to ground me?" I have to stop myself from sneering at him.

Pete shakes his head. "Someday soon you're going to have to start acting like a grown up, Kel. And yeah, maybe I should ground you. Maybe then you'd take some responsibility for yourself." He starts to walk away. "Clean that mess up," he calls over his shoulder.

I alternate between fuming at Pete and bouts of tears as I clean up the bathroom. I can't even cry quietly now. It comes out as a weird, hiccupy sound. At least if Pete hears me, he'll think I'm just mad at him.

I finish my half-hearted cleaning effort. The mess isn't much better; I end up smearing the blood around with hot water, leaving a streaky red pattern. I should have used bleach or something, but I couldn't be bothered. I go back to bed.

My whole body seems to have dissolved into a dull, throbbing ache. I hear Pete leave for work, then start to doze again. It's weird. I'm still aware of lying in bed but I'm having dreams as well. It feels like there's someone pressing hard on my chest with their palm and another, smaller person sitting on my forehead.

I wake properly as Ben opens my door. I wish he'd knock, but I don't have the energy for that argument right now.

"Hey." He grins at me.

I blink in reply.

He comes and sits on the edge of my bed. "Are you sulking?"

"No." It comes out sounding petulant, and exactly as if I am sulking.

He laughs. "It's not that bad. I bet Pete will have forgotten about it by the time he gets home from work."

"Go away." I close my eyes and turn my face to the wall.

"Come on, Kel, time to get up. Best thing for a hangover is a big breakfast." He pulls the duvet off the bed.

I scream at him and scramble to grab it back. He dodges me and I tumble out of bed. I land heavily on my bruised side.

Ben laughs, then stops as I groan. I start to cry in a pathetic, whimpery sort of way.

"Shit." He picks me up and puts me back on the bed, then sits stroking my hair. "What's wrong?"

I push him away. "Don't."

He moves his hand, resting it on my shoulder.

"Don't touch me," I say, but I don't think he hears me. My words just come out as sobs. I try again. "Please, go away." I hiccup in the middle of saying it, which takes some of the force away.

Ben passes me the glass of water from beside my bed. It's about three days old and has a dead spider in it. I drink it anyway.

"Did something happen last night?"

I blink a couple of times then decide to go with half-truths. "I had a fight with Mike," I say.

Ben shakes his head. "Him again."

My chest seems to swell up and burst into angry words. "That's your idea of sympathy? 'I told you so'?"

"No, I didn't mean–"

"Well, you can stuff off then." I shove the empty glass at him and turn over to face the wall.

"Kel …"

I cover my ears with my hands. Probably my most immature moment to date, but it works. When I turn to look a couple of minutes later, he's gone.

Half an hour later, the phone rings in the other room. I stare at my smashed phone on the floor and wait until someone else picks it up. A second later it rings again. Then again. After three phone calls my cell starts. I groan and cover my head with my pillow. I'm not sure why people do that. It doesn't block out any noise. Well, I suppose it might, but only if I held it down firmly enough to smother myself.

I miss four calls before I get up and pull my cell out of my jacket pocket. I'd like to think that the missed calls are all from the prank caller, or the entire rugby team, as I now think of it, but I bet some of those calls were from Mike. My phone buzzes as it rings again, and I nearly throw it, it gives me such a fright. The caller ID says "Private Number Calling". I'm so relieved it's not Mike, I answer it before thinking.

"Hello?"

Silence.

I groan. "For God's sake, if you're going to call me you could at least talk."

"What do you want me to say?" He says it softly. It catches me off guard.

"I–" I stumble over my words.

There's a pause. I hold my own breath as I listen to his.

"Why are you with him?" he asks.

The air in my lungs comes out in a rush. "What?"

"You don't know, do you?"

"I ... Everything is just so screwed up and I don't know how to fix it." The words come out in a rush, and I'm not sure where they came from. I press the *end call* button, but my phone rings again straight away.

"What?" I try to sound assertive.

"Don't hang up on me." His voice is icy.

I go cold. "What do you want?" It comes out as a whisper.

He doesn't answer. I'm annoyed at myself, but I'm actually scared to hang up.

"You know what?" I say. "You saw what happened last night, right? Why the hell didn't you do anything? Did you think it was cool to just stand there and watch me get ...?" I stop myself and rub my hand under my eyes.

He doesn't answer straight away. I wait, listening to my own pulse echoing in my ears.

"Would you have wanted me to do anything?" He says it so quietly, I almost miss it.

I frown. "What?"

There's a click as he hangs up. I stare at the phone then turn it off. My hands are shaking, and I have to remind myself it's just Jacob or one of his mates. I toss the phone onto a pile of clothes in the corner of my room and go downstairs.

My legs hurt so much, I have to edge down stair by stair. Much as I'd rather stay curled up in bed, I'm actually hungry for the first time in a couple of weeks.

Aiden's at the stove stirring something in a big pot, and it looks like Ben's out.

Aiden looks up as I come into the kitchen. "You want some soup? It's good hangover food."

"I'm not hungover." I watch him carefully as I say that.

He nods. "I know, but let's just call it that."

"Huh?"

He smirks and hands me a bowl. "Just eat your soup, Kel."

I sit down at the kitchen counter. The moment I do, I have a flashback to the pasta last night. My breath feels like it's convulsing, trying to force itself into a sob.

Aiden hands me a spoon, but doesn't say anything.

I feel better as soon as I swallow my first mouthful. The

soup is warm and salty, with big chunks of vegetables in it. The potatoes hit my stomach and it's like they're anchoring me, keeping me safe.

"Where's Ben?" I ask.

"Out. Don't know where. What did you say to him?"

I frown. "What do you mean?"

"He was pretty pissed off." Aiden ladles more soup into his bowl. He offers me some, but I shake my head.

I shrug. "I did tell him to stuff off."

Aiden grins. "Why?"

"He–" I stop. I actually can't remember why. I remember telling him to "go away" and that he made me fall out of bed, but I can't remember why I was angry with him in the first place. "I don't know," I say. "I don't think I was mad at him."

Aiden nods. I hold my breath but he doesn't ask.

I stare down at my hands. "I just … I didn't think it would ever get this bad."

"No. No one ever does."

I look up at Aiden when he says that. He says it with a weird sincerity, like he really knows what he's talking about. I watch him staring down at his bowl, stirring his soup. His crooked nose is more obvious at this angle. I wonder if it was always like that, or whether it was broken and didn't heal properly.

My chest hurts as I put things together.

I take a breath. "Aiden …"

He meets my eye, and his look is bordering on a glare. It's like he's daring me to ask, but I can't make the words come out.

The back door opens and Pete comes in. He smacks the mail onto the table next to me, making me jump. When I look back at Aiden, he's closed off again and I know it's too late to say anything.

"Finally got out of bed, then?" Pete raises his eyebrows at me.

I stare down at the table and don't answer.

Pete and Aiden talk about work over my head. I try to catch Aiden's eye, but he doesn't look at me. Eventually I get up and put my bowl in the sink. As I'm heading up to my room, I hear Pete say something that sounds like "stroppy madam". I almost want to go back in there and yell at him, but he and Aiden are laughing and I'm too embarrassed. Instead I go back up to my room and stare at the wall.

8

Chapter Eight

"Get up!" Pete's face is purple. Me staying with him must be giving him high blood pressure.

"No!" I pull the duvet over my head. I remember having this same argument with Mum when I was five. It was easier for her, though, because I was small enough then for her to pick me up and put me in the car in my pyjamas. I'd like to see Pete try that. He's probably strong enough to pick me up, but there's no way I'd let him carry me downstairs quietly.

"You're going to be late for school."

"I don't care. I'm not going." Now I sound like I'm five.

Pete groans. He doesn't say anything for a bit. I almost want to peek out from under the blankets to see what he's doing.

"Fine, Kel, do what you want."

He closes the door. I lie still, feeling a strange mix of satisfaction and guilt. On the one hand, I like the fact that I can now stay in bed and Pete won't hassle me. I don't think I could handle going to school and pretending everything's okay between me and Mike. On the other hand, Pete doesn't know why I've been so grumpy lately. He probably thinks I'm just a real bitch. The kind of sister he'd rather not live with. I bet he's downstairs ringing up all our relatives, trying to find someone who'll take me.

I sigh and get out of bed. My ribs hurt more today than they did yesterday. I struggle to get my pyjama top off, then gasp as I see the state of my side. It looks like I've got six aubergines growing under my skin.

I ease myself into my bra, but it takes a couple of goes to get it done up. My arm doesn't seem to want to bend that way anymore.

My door bursts open. I jerk, bashing my elbow into my side.

"Hey, Kel, Pete sent me to ..." Ben trails off and just stands there, staring at me.

It takes me a minute to find my voice. "Get out of my room!"

"Oh my God."

"I said get out!" I grab my pyjama top and hold it across my chest.

"What happened?" Ben moves forward and tries to touch the bruises on my side.

"Nothing." I back away from him, but he follows. "Don't touch me!"

"Who did this? Mike? I swear I'll kill him." Ben's hands curl up into fists.

"No. I fell over. I was drunk." My breath comes out in short gasps, like I'm crying, but there are no tears.

"It looks like you've got broken ribs. You didn't do that falling over."

"I got hit by a car."

"What?"

"I got hit by a car. I didn't want to tell you because it was my friend driving." I know that doesn't make any sense, but I'm hoping Ben won't notice.

"Kel-"

"No, Mike didn't ..." I cry properly now. Ben touches my shoulder.

I flinch away from him. "It's not his fault," I say. "His dad's horrible. He's always drunk, and Mike and Jo-"

"Kel ..." Ben tries to look me in the eye. I stare at the floor so he can't.

He gestures to the bruises. "Nothing excuses that."

"You don't understand. It was my fault. I told him-"

"It is *not* your fault." He reaches out to touch my face.

I push him away. "Get out of my room. I have to get ready for school."

"You have to go to the hospital."

"No, I don't. I-" I scream as my chest spasms.

Ben grabs my arm and sits me down on the bed. I cover my face with my hands. Ben strokes my back. His palms are warm against my bare skin.

"Please, go away," I say into my hands.

"I want to help you."

"I don't want your help. I want you to leave me alone." My voice comes out in a monotone.

"Please, Kel."

I turn to look at him. "I love Mike. How're you going to help me with that?"

Ben's lip curls up, like he's smelt something bad, then his face droops.

"Go away," I say again.

Ben closes his eyes. "I'm going to go downstairs so that you can get dressed, then I want you to come talk to me, okay?"

I nod, but I don't look at him. Instead, I stare at his hands. They're pressing into his thighs so hard that his knuckles are white, and I bet he's left marks on his legs. He moves his hand as if to touch me again, then seems to think better of it and walks away instead.

As soon as he's gone, I pick up my phone from the corner and turn it back on. I ignore the missed calls and go straight to the text messages. From Mike: I'M SORI. From Mike: PLZ CAL ME. From Mike: I LUV U. His text language annoys me even more than usual. The least he could so is spell "sorry" properly. I turn the phone off again. My head hurts. I rub it with my fingertips, but it doesn't help.

I need to get out of here. I need air. Only thing is, if I leave, I won't want to come back.

I dump the contents of my school bag out onto the bed. Clumps of lint and pencil shavings scatter out from under my books. I try to wipe them off the duvet, but they leave grey smudges across it. I fill up the bag with clothes instead. After a moment's hesitation, I chuck my cell in there, too.

I get dressed as quickly as I can, then creep down the stairs. From the hallway I can hear Pete and Aiden talking in the kitchen, and the thump and squeak of Ben hitting the punching bag in the garage. It's louder than usual. He must be picturing Mike's face on the bag.

I make a dash for the front door. As soon as I'm outside, I have to stop as my breath is reduced to an aching wheeze. I set off down the road at the pace of an injured power-walker.

I don't really know where I'm going. I find myself outside the park Mum used to take us to when we were little, and that seems as good a place as any so I go and sit on one of the swings.

The park's nearly empty. Probably because everyone – me included – is supposed to be at school. There are a couple of mums with really little kids. They're all cute and squidgy – still in that stage where they look like jellybeans. I look away as I realise I'm getting clucky. There's no way I could look after a baby. I can't even pretend to look after myself.

I fish my phone out of my bag to check the time. It beeps as I turn it on. Missed call from ... I check the call list. Ben. Didn't take him long to notice I was gone. I switch the phone off again and stuff it down the bottom of my bag.

I scuff my feet against the plastic meshing under the swings. It's this spongy stuff with big holes in hexagonal and circle shapes. It makes me dizzy just looking at it. I think it might actually make me ill if I was swinging above it. When I came here as a kid, there was just concrete. I guess kids these days are less durable. Or maybe my generation's parents just didn't care on the safety front.

I hang out in the park all day. Several mothers come and go. They all look at me like I'm a drug addict. I suppose the fact that my eyes are pink from crying, and that I'm hanging out in a park when clearly I should be at school, doesn't help my case.

Every so often I check my phone. The missed calls and messages have built up to the point where it says "no space for new messages" when I turn it on. I don't clear out the inbox. It's easier to just ignore it all.

At five o'clock it starts to get dark. I know I have to make a decision, but that's as far as I get. It's not until five-thirty that I take out my phone again. I turn it on and it rings straight away. *Private Number Calling.*

I shake my head and answer it. "Now's not such a good

time. I can't talk at the moment." It sounds so stupid and formal, like I'm in the middle of a tea party or something.

There's a pause, then he says: "Where are you?"

"I'm at the park," I say. I feel like my brain is trapped in toffee. If I could think clearly, I wouldn't have told him that. "I'm sorry, I have to go now. I have to call Mike."

"Don't–" he says, just before I cut off the call and dial Mike's number.

Mike answers on the second ring. "Kel? I'm so sorry. I never, ever meant to hurt you. It'll never happen again–"

"Meet me at the park in fifteen minutes," I interrupt him, then hang up. I start crying as soon as I do.

I go out on to the pavement outside the park to meet him. I see Mike coming from down the street. He walks with his head down – like there's a weight dangling from his neck – and his hands are shoved into his pockets, making him look shrunken, smaller than me even.

He sits down on the wall beside me. We don't say anything. It's quiet except for my breathing. I think I'm getting dehydrated. I'm like a robot leaking oil.

Mike touches my hand. "I love you."

I nod. His palms are dry and rough; they scratch my skin as I pull my hand away.

"I don't know what to do," I say. I'm lying. I know exactly what I'm going to do, I just don't know how.

His arms are bare. I watch as goosebumps rise on his skin, making the hairs stand up. He fiddles with the zip on the pocket of his jeans. The fabric pulls at the seams as he does. The thread is loose, inching its way out, undoing the stitching. I bite my tongue to stop myself automatically offering to mend it.

"I'm sorry." He looks up at me.

I look away. There's moss growing on the wall. I edge it off with my thumbnail, leaving a round, wet patch on the concrete. It leaves green smears on my fingers. I pull the clump apart, forcing the dirt under my nails.

"I don't want you to call me anymore," I say.

Mike goes really still. I have to force myself to keep staring in the other direction.

"Don't come around, either." I measure each word, making my voice come out steady. My insides have turned to porridge, but my vocal cords are holding strong. I give myself a second to let my legs solidify, then stand up.

Mike grabs my arm. "Don't." His voice is soft. "Please."

I jerk away from him. He claws at me, gripping tighter every time I pull away. I stop as his fingers bite into my arm. His breathing is jagged, like he's about to hyperventilate. "Don't!"

I take a breath, keeping my eyes on the ground. "I'm leaving now." I try to pry his hand off my arm. Something ugly flashes across his face. I shriek as he bends my fingers back. The crack on the pavement between my feet looms closer. I watch a trail of ants walk along it.

"No." He twists my arm.

I scream again.

He claps a hand over my mouth. His head is right by my ear, his voice low. "You're not going to leave."

"Ben knows," I say into his hand. "He saw the bruises."

"What?" Mike jerks my head around to face him.

"Ben saw the bruises. He knows what happened."

Suddenly Mike's hands are around my throat. I want to scream but there's no air.

"Did you screw him?"

I try to shake my head. I think I'm going to be sick.

"Did you?" Mike shakes me.

I can't answer. Black spots prickle against my eyes. I reach out, trying to push Mike away. He lets go and punches me in the face. I fall backwards. I hear a crack as my head hits the wall. There's a moment where everything swims, then pain. Mike stomps on my hand, but I don't feel it. I catch a glimpse of someone standing next to Mike then everything goes grey, like snow on the TV. I think I hear voices but I'm not sure. I blink. I feel myself sinking.

I close my eyes and let everything go black.

I have this feeling of being at the bottom of a bowl of jelly. I reach for the surface but it's too thick to swim through.

I manage to open my eyes a couple of times, but only long enough to see a hint of things. At one point there's a man I don't know touching my head. I can't focus on him properly. All I see is a Santa Claus beard. He says something to me, but I sink under before I hear him.

I hear my name being called over and over again, until it sounds like nothing. Then I hear it once more and I recognise the voice. I open my eyes and see Ben. He seems to be moving, then I realise I am too. Everything's fuzzy around the edges, but this time I stay on the surface instead of sinking.

I'm lying flat, rolling down a corridor. The ceiling whips past above me. I hear people talking, but it's all echoey and the volume fades in and out.

Ben touches my face.

I open my mouth to speak, but instead my stomach heaves and I throw up on his hand. The jelly overwhelms me again and I close my eyes.

When I wake again, things are sharper at the edges. My face hurts and my right eye's all squinty. I'm in a room – a hospital room I guess, judging by the fact that the walls are made of curtains. There's a doctor, or at least a woman in scrubs, sticking a needle in my arm, attaching a drip. It takes her a minute to notice I'm awake.

"Kelsey? Can you hear me?" She has an English accent.

I nod, but it makes my head swim. "Yes," I say.

She takes out a torch and flashes it in my eyes. I flinch away from the light.

"Do you know where you are?"

"Hospital?" My voice is scratchy, and my throat burns.

"Can you tell me what happened?"

"I threw up on Ben," I say.

The doctor smiles. "Before that?"

I try to think, but all I remember is pain.

The doctor picks up the chart from the end of my bed and writes something down. "That's okay. Can you tell me what day it is?"

I close my eyes to think. "Monday?"

"That's right. Now, can you touch my finger?" She holds out her hand in front of my face.

I go to lift my right hand and feel a stabbing pain. I gasp as I look down. My fingers are swollen and purple. There's a split across my knuckle, like a burst sausage.

"Try with your left hand." Her voice is matter of fact. I touch her hand with my left index finger. The latex gloves she's wearing are too big for her. They have these spongy, wrinkled bunches at the ends where they're just filled with air.

"Now touch your nose," she says.

I tap my nose with my finger.

"And touch my finger again."

When I do, she nods and writes the result down in her notes. "I'll be back to do some more tests in a minute. Would you like to see your family?"

"Yes."

It takes until Pete, Ben and Aiden come into the room for me to work out what she means by my family. For a moment, I thought she might have meant Mum was here.

Aiden hangs back by the curtain. He looks nervous, like he thinks he might catch something from me. Pete's a little better. He makes it to the end of the bed. Ben comes right up to me and takes my hand.

"I'm sorry I threw up on you," I say.

"That's okay." Ben smiles as he says that, but then his face slouches back into concern.

I start to sniffle again. "What happened?"

Ben glances back at Pete. "You don't remember?"

I shake my head and feel the room spin.

There seems to be some kind of non-verbal conversation going on among my "family". Finally Aiden breaks the silence. "You were beaten up." He shifts his weight. His eyes flick around, looking at anything but me. "You hit your head."

The fogginess in my brain starts to clear. "I was at the park," I say, "then I called Mike ..." I groan and close my eyes. "Mike." Suddenly, I feel really cold. I start to shiver. A second later I'm shaking, and my breath is making shushing noises as it comes in and out.

"Kelsey." Ben squeezes my hand, making me look at him. He swallows then continues. "Mike's in hospital too."

9

Chapter Nine

The doctor comes into the room. Ben moves towards the door to make room for her. I try to get up and follow him, but the doctor gently pushes me back into the bed.

"You have to stay lying down," she says.

"I have to see Mike," I say. I grab the IV line and pull it. A red berry of blood grows as the needle comes out.

The doctor grips my hand. "Don't do that."

"Let me go." I struggle with her. The room spins and I can't breathe properly.

"Can I have some help in here?" she calls, then she turns to Ben and lowers her voice. "I asked you not to say anything. She's not well enough."

"I have to see Mike," I say again.

The doctor turns to me. "Listen to me, Kelsey. You won't be able to see him for a while yet. We need to look after you first." She presses the call bell.

"What's wrong with him?"

She doesn't answer. My breathing gets faster until it comes out in big, whooping wheezes. I can't get any air. The doctor checks my chest with a stethoscope. A guy comes in and helps her put the bed flat. His hands look too big for him. They splay out, like he's got more than five fingers on each hand, and they're covered in little tufts of hair. I focus on the star-shaped nurse's badge hanging from his scrubs.

"Breathe slowly now, Kelsey," the doctor says.

I try but it doesn't work. Ben's crying. His tears reflect the blue of the curtain, like oil. He stares into the air above my feet and turns to stone. It's like his eyes are leaking of their own accord. The tears fall straight down, barely touching his face.

I try to wrestle away from the doctor and the guy holding me but I'm light-headed. The room swirls like I'm falling.

"Come on, Kelsey." The doctor places her hand on my shoulder and looks me in the eye. "Breathe with me. In, two, three ... Out, two, three ..."

I take a couple of short gasps, but my hands won't stop shaking.

"What happened?" I say. It comes out as a crackle.

"Anxiety attack," the doctor says. She fixes up the IV line I pulled out.

I swallow. My mouth feels thick. "I mean, what happened to Mike?"

She sighs and glances at the nurse. "Don't worry about that right now. You need to concentrate on getting better."

"What ...?" I stop and I shake my head. "Is he going to be okay?"

She makes a face that's somewhere between a sympathy-smile and a grimace. Ben looks down at his feet.

I feel like the bed is folding up in the middle. My stomach drops through my spine, towards the floor. I make a sound, but it's just a little sound – one that's far too small. The doctor touches my shoulder then leaves. I close my eyes and cover my face. Something inside my chest is getting bigger. It swells, making everything ache. I wait for it to burst, but it doesn't. When it does, I'm sure I'll explode. I block out everything except that feeling.

It could be hours or minutes later when I hear Aiden's voice.

"Kelsey?"

I try not to move, so he won't know I can hear him.

"Kel?"

I feel him move closer to the bed.

"Kelsey?" He whispers this time, like he's leaning right over me.

I drop my hand and open my eyes a crack. Aiden gives me a half smile. I stare at the beads of liquid dropping from the IV bag into my arm. They swell and shudder before falling, like the flesh of a peach blooming then plunging from the tree. Everything on my face droops. It will all slide off if I'm not careful.

Aiden sits on the end of the bed. It takes me a moment to notice Ben and Pete aren't behind him.

"Where's Pete?" I ask. My voice comes out raspy. I'm surprised Aiden can even understand me.

"He and Ben couldn't handle ..." He waves his hand in my direction. "They went to get some coffee. I said I'd stay in case you snapped out of it." Aiden's still smiling but he's frowning as well. It makes his face look smooshed up and shorter than it should be.

"Thanks," I say, though I'm not sure whether I'm being sarcastic or not.

"Kelsey?"

"Yeah?"

Aiden doesn't answer straight away, so I open my eyes again and look at him.

"What do you remember?"

"I was at the park all day, then I called Mike." I stop. My memory gets a bit fuzzy after that. I get a wave of nausea as I think about it. "I was trying to break up with him." I look up at Aiden, but he doesn't react. "He punched me. I hit my head."

Aiden nods. "After that?"

"Don't know. I blacked out?" I shift, trying to make myself more comfortable. "How did you know I was here?"

"Huh?"

"At the hospital. How did you know I was here?"

Aiden shrugs. "Ben was the one who called the ambulance."

Aiden's words roll around inside my head instead of going straight to the part of my brain that makes sense of them. I mouth them to myself, as if that will help.

"He told us what happened. When you didn't come back he had us out looking for you." Aiden pauses. It makes me think he's leaving something out. "Ben found you," he adds.

I feel a rush through my chest, like it's been flushed with cold water. I want to turn away, but I force myself to keep looking at Aiden.

"What about Mike?" My voice cracks when I say his name. "Ben didn't ..."

Aiden's eyes slide away from mine. "I saw Mike when I

came in. His head was all smashed in–"

"Oh my God!" The air around me feels thick. I have to force myself to keep breathing it.

"I wasn't supposed to tell you that," Aiden says, but it's more to himself than to me. "Ben said he was lying on the pavement next to you. No sign of whoever did it."

The doctor comes back in. She smiles when she sees I'm not having hysterics anymore.

"We're going to take you up to X-ray now." She turns to Aiden. "Would you like to come up with us?"

Aiden looks thoroughly uncomfortable with this idea, but nods anyway.

"I'll just get one of the dis–orderlies." She laughs at her own joke. Aiden glances at me and shrugs.

I close my eyes as we roll down the corridor. It makes me dizzy otherwise. When we get to the X-ray lab, Aiden peels off to the waiting room. He looks relieved he doesn't have to come in with me.

The X-ray guy looks like human contact scares him. He keeps muttering things – I have no idea what he's saying – then occasionally he'll look up and give a smile to no one in particular. It's endearing in a weird way.

He moves my hand around until he gets it just right, then shoves wedges of red foam in between my fingers to hold my hand in place. They look like slices of watermelon, which doesn't help with my queasy stomach, and my hand is in the most unnatural position possible. I close my eyes as my fingers start to burn. He mutters something that sounds like "high pain threshold" and goes off to start the X-ray. He comes back in between flashes to rearrange my hand. By the end, it hurts so much it almost feels numb.

The chest X-rays aren't so bad. I suppose that's because they can't exactly ask me to move my ribs around.

After that, I'm back being rolled down the corridor again. We pick up Aiden from the waiting room and head back to the lifts.

He grins at me. "Painful?"

"Yeah." I look away, irritated by how cheerful he is about that.

Ben and Pete are waiting in the A&E room. Ben's eyes are red-rimmed. It makes me uncomfortable to know he was crying over me. His gaze flicks back and forth across me, as if he thinks I'll disappear if he doesn't watch me every second.

I try to smile but it doesn't really work.

Ben gives me an equally pathetic smile. "How're you feeling?"

Before I can answer, the doctor comes back in, followed by a different nurse.

"Angela here," she gestures to the nurse, "will put a cast on that hand of yours, then we'll get you up to the ward."

"I have to stay here?"

"Her hand's broken?" Ben and I talk over each other.

The doctor smiles and turns to Ben first. I'm annoyed by that. It's like there are a whole lot of conversations going on about me, but not with me.

"Yes. Fortunately it's a reasonably clean break."

I think the doctor and I have different definitions of the word "fortunately".

"And her ribs?" Ben asks.

"Bruised but not broken." She turns to me. "You'll be here for the night at least. You've got a concussion. We need to observe you."

Angela asks me if I want to choose the colour of my cast, like I'm five years old or something. I stare at the wall above her head and don't answer.

"Purple," Ben says. "She likes purple."

"Purple's my favourite colour," I say. Mike doesn't know that, I nearly add.

Ben takes my good hand in both of his and squeezes it. His knuckles are bruised. I run my thumb over them then look away, feeling sick.

He seems to read my thoughts. "I was punching without gloves this morning. I was … angry."

I want to throw up again. "I'm sorry," I say.

Ben's eyebrows draw together into a frown. His bottom lip drops, making it a sad frown rather than an angry one. "Why are you sorry?"

"Because …" I'm not sure how to articulate what I'm feeling. "It's all my fault. I shouldn't have … And now Mike … and you …" My head pounds. I feel dizzy and sick again. I close my eyes and feel relief as they shut against the light. Ben touches my face. I think of the bruises on his hand, and want to pull away.

"It's okay," he says. "It's not your fault."

Angela finishes the cast, and I'm moved to the ward. Ben seems to be attached to me. He stays right by my side as we roll along the corridor.

I catch sight of Jo and her mum as we're being loaded into the lift. No sign of Mike's dad. Jo sees me and gives a little wave. Her skin looks green, she's so pale. She's not crying, but her eyes have a dead look to them. I want to call out to her, but the lift doors close before I can.

Ben sits next to my bed on the ward. Aiden goes home. He

says he's got to sort out some work stuff, but I think he just feels uncomfortable. I'm glad when he leaves; his hovering was making me nervous. Pete doesn't say anything. He barely even looks at me. He stares out of the window, though I'm pretty sure he can't see more than I can – the rust stains on the side of another building. It occurs to me that he hasn't said a word since he got here. At least, not to me.

"Is there anything you need from home?" Ben asks.

I surprise myself by gripping his hand. "You're not going, are you?"

"No, no. Not for a while yet." He smiles and strokes my arm in a way that's meant to be soothing. I stop myself from flinching away. My skin feels sore as he touches it.

"Kelsey Morgen?"

I look up as a woman comes into the room. She's followed by a surly-looking policeman. He's young – fresh out of police college, I'd say. One side of his face is raised into an angry rash where he's shaved too close. I look away as I realise I'm staring, and focus on the woman instead. She has a warm, sun-splotched face and reminds me of Mum, despite the fact that she's probably about twenty years younger.

"I was wondering if we could have a word."

I nod before I even think about it. I'm pretty sure she didn't mean it as a question anyway.

There's an awkward moment, where they just stand there, before the policeman clears his throat. "Alone?" He looks at Ben and Pete.

Pete mumbles, "Of course," and practically bolts for the door. Ben hesitates and looks at me.

"I'll be fine." I'm reassuring myself as much as him.

The woman watches him go then asks if she can sit down.

The guy stays standing by the door. He fidgets in an agitated way that makes me want to squirm too. I look at her instead.

"I'm Detective Jenkins," she says, "and this is Officer Brian."

Officer Brian nods as she mentions his name.

"We were wondering if we could talk to you about what happened today."

Again, I don't think she's really giving me the option to say no, so I don't say anything.

"Can you tell me what you remember?" She gives me what she must think is an encouraging smile, but in reality it just looks like she's baring her teeth.

I swallow. "I walked out this morning-"

"What happened before that? Why did you walk out?"

Officer Brian takes out a notebook and starts to write.

I force myself not to look at him. "I had a fight with Ben."

"Was Ben the man who was in here before?"

I have a stupid urge to laugh at that. I never really think of Ben as a "man". He's still Ben who I grew up with. I bite my lip and nod.

"And what relation is he to you?"

"He's ..." I pause, trying to think how to explain it. "He's my brother's flatmate. I guess my flatmate too."

"So you live with your brother?"

"Yes."

"What was the fight about?"

I look away. My chest seems to expand again as I think about it. "It doesn't matter." I swallow hard, not wanting to cry in front of her.

Officer Brian clears his throat in an irritated way. Detective Jenkins leans away from me and says something to him.

I catch the last part of it: "bruises on his hands".

"Ben's a kickboxer," I say. "He got the bruises from that."

Detective Jenkins looks annoyed that I heard her.

I keep talking, hoping she'll forget about it. "I walked out," I say, "and I went to the park." I look at Detective Jenkins. "Mike met me there and ..." My voice catches, and I can't get the words out.

Officer Brian clicks his tongue and shifts. I cover my face so I don't have to look at him.

"What happened then?" Detective Jenkins' voice is soft.

I force myself to look her in the eye. "Mike punched me. In the face. I fell and hit my head."

Detective Jenkins goes very still. She shoots a glance at Officer Brian. I can tell this wasn't what they were expecting.

"It wasn't the first time." My voice comes out really flat. I tell them about the party.

Neither of them says anything. I don't know what I was expecting. Some measure of comfort or reassurance maybe? Instead it's like talking to a couple of mannequins.

"And Ben found out about this, this morning?"

"Yeah." I rub my eyes. "I didn't tell him exactly what happened, but he saw the bruises."

"Did anyone else know?"

"Aiden ... Pete's other flatmate," I add when she looks blank. "He saw me when I came home."

"Anyone else?"

I remember the phone call. "Someone from the party. I don't know who."

"Okay." She looks over at Officer Brian, to make sure he's written that down, then continues. "Do you remember anything else?"

"No. I don't think so."

"Did you see anyone else at the park today? Maybe someone who might have got angry if they saw what Mike had done?"

I start to shake my head, then stop. "I think ... I think there might have been someone."

"Yes?"

"Just before I passed out, I think I saw someone."

"Was it someone you recognised?" She sounds eager, and I realise where she's going with this.

"No," I say as firmly as I can. "There was a man with a beard," I add. "But that was later on. He might have been an ambulance officer?"

Officer Brian writes that down.

"Okay then," Detective Jenkins says. "We'll let you get some rest." She stands up.

"Is Mike ...?" I can't finish the sentence. I'm not even sure why I'm asking.

Detective Jenkins bares her teeth again. "We'll keep you informed of any developments in the case."

I frown. I don't like the way she didn't actually answer the question. She pats me on the arm as she leaves.

Ben comes back into the room by himself. He sits on the chair by the bed and stares at me for a second, then covers his face with his hands. There's a horrible moment when I realise he's crying, and I have no idea what to say. There's this cringing feeling in my stomach, and I have to fight the urge to shrink away from him.

"It's okay," I mumble. I try to pat him on the back but the IV line gets tangled and pulls at my skin.

"Are you okay? What's wrong?" Ben sits up.

I shake my head. "Just got this tangled." I hold up the line.

Ben lets out a breath and sits back in the chair. He picks at imaginary lint on his jersey. "I'm sorry."

I swallow and look away. He seems to take this as me being mad at him and continues. "I shouldn't have pressured you this morning."

"Don't," I whisper, but he doesn't hear me.

"I should have – I don't know – listened? I didn't ..." He shakes his head. "I'm sorry."

"Stop it!" I yell. I surprise myself with the volume. "It was my fault. I knew what would happen, and I called him anyway."

"It's not your fault–"

"Stop saying that! It's *all* my fault. *Everything* that happened today is my fault."

Ben clasps my face in his hands and makes me look him in the eye. "Listen to me." His voice is fierce. "It is not your fault. You did not deserve this. This is no one's fault except Mike's."

We glare at each other. I let out something that sounds like a sigh, and Ben lets go of my face.

I lick my lips. They're dry and scaly under my tongue.

He doesn't look at me. "Okay?"

I nod. "Thank you," I say, though I'm not exactly sure what I'm thanking him for.

He picks up his coat from the chair. "The nurse says we have to let you get some rest. I'll come see you tomorrow."

Suddenly, I'm really glad he's going. I feel like I could sleep through a drumming workshop right now. Ben kisses my forehead as he goes.

I've only just dropped off to sleep, when I'm woken by the sound of a phone ringing. By the time I figure out it's my cell phone, stowed in a basket under the bed, it's stopped.

I get out of bed and hunt through my bag for the phone. It rings again straight away. *Private Number Calling.* I feel a funny squirm inside me as I realise I was expecting it to be Mike.

I sigh and answer it. "Yeah?"

Silence.

I screw up my face. "Look, I'm in hospital and my boyfriend–"

"You asked me to do something." His voice is soft.

"What?" I go cold. *"What?"* I shiver as I think of the last call. *"Would you have wanted me to do anything?"*

"What did you do?"

He doesn't answer.

"Oh my God!" I say.

"Don't tell anyone." There's a beep as he hangs up.

I drop the phone on the floor. It makes a satisfying clunking sound. I'm shaking so much, I can't pick it up. It's like there's a rubber band around my chest, stopping me from getting any air. I stare at my hands. There's blood under my fingernails. Each one has a red crescent-shaped curve at the tip, like I've had some perverse type of French manicure. I rub them against my shirt, but the blood doesn't shift.

"Oh my God." I squeeze my hands into fists and press them against my mouth. The heat of my breath swirls against my palms. I focus on that feeling.

The phone rings again. The side of it is scratched, like someone took a nail file to it.

"Hello?" I'm not sure whether I press the answer call button before or after I speak. At this point I don't think it matters.

"I thought it was what you wanted." He doesn't ask it like a question, but he seems to want a response.

"No, I–"

"He would have killed you."

"What?"

"If I hadn't, he would have killed you." There's a little catch in his voice.

"I don't …" I'm not sure how to end that. There don't seem to be any words that fit.

"Should I have let him?" His voice is gentle.

It makes my stomach hurt. "Leave me alone!" I hang up the phone. I want to throw it out of the window, as if by doing that I could make it not true. My chest feels like it's cracked in half. I cover my face and press my elbows into my sides to hold myself together.

Ben was wrong. It *is* all my fault.

I wake the next morning when a woman brings in a breakfast tray. She sits me up in the bed and puts the spoon in my hand, as if she thinks I don't know how to do it myself.

My phone stares at me from the top of the bedside cabinet. I cover my face so I don't have to look at it.

I hear someone walk into the room, but I don't look up. There's silence, then they clear their throat. I pull my hands away from my face and stare at the man at the end of my bed. He looks like a ten-pin bowling pin. His head is far too small for the shoulders that swell out from his neck. Then, his body tapers down to thin legs and tiny feet. I assume from his suit and tie, and from the fact that he has a follower – a short, dumpy woman with a smile too big for her face – that he's a doctor. My eyes are leaking and I can't stop hiccuping.

He clears his throat. "Hello, Kelsey." He seems uncomfortable, but I can't work out why.

My face screws up as another wave of tears breaks inside me.

The woman bustles forward. "It's so good to meet you, darling. I'm Cathy, but you've probably already figured that out."

I look back at the man, and finally focus on his face. The clouds in my brain slowly roll back. "Dad?"

He nods, looking as upset as I feel.

"Yes, well," Cathy says, obviously trying to fill the silence. "I suppose it has been a while since you've seen each other."

I shake my head to clear it. "Nice to meet you …" I trail off, not sure what to call her. I have an urge to say "step mum", but that doesn't seem right.

She comes to my rescue. "Cathy. Call me Cathy, dear. It's good to finally meet you, though I wish it was in better circumstances."

I feel snot creeping down my face under my nose. Normally I'd be disgusted with myself, but right now I don't care. Dad stays hovering by the end of the bed.

Cathy decides to make herself useful by rearranging my blankets. "I was so upset when Pete called me last night," she says. "I told your dad we must drive down here straight away."

I look at Dad, figuring things out. He wouldn't have come

if Cathy hadn't made him. In fact, I bet if Pete had got hold of him instead of her, Dad would have pretended he'd never got the call.

"It was too late to come see you by the time we arrived, so we just checked into a hotel, but I wanted to make sure we came as soon as possible."

I'm not sure whether I'm supposed to answer that. Instead, I just stare at her and wish they'd both disappear.

"You poor darling." Cathy moves to touch my face then seems to think better of it. "Is it painful?"

"It's okay," I say, that being the simplest answer.

I'm saved from having to say more by Pete arriving. He greets Dad with a handshake, but I suppose in my dad's world that's as close as you get to a hug.

"I just popped in before work." Pete looks at Dad as he says that. I think it might be an attempt to get Dad to ask him about his job. If it is, Dad doesn't pick up on it. I feel sorry for Pete. It must be hard caring what a man with the emotional range of an alarm clock thinks of you.

Dad and Pete talk, but I don't really listen to what they're saying. Cathy keeps staring at me, which freaks me out.

"When can I go home?" I interrupt Pete.

He and Dad look at me.

Pete gives me a weird half-smile. "They said tomorrow."

I look away. "I want to go home now," I say, more to myself than anyone else.

Cathy rubs my arm. "Soon, darling. They've just got to make sure you're well enough."

My mouth twists up as I try not to cry again. "I don't want to stay–"

"Don't be stroppy, Kel." Pete sighs.

I look at him and fail in my attempt not to cry. Cathy tuts and puts her arm around me.

Pete rubs his face. "I'm sorry. I didn't mean that."

For some reason, that makes me cry more. "It's my fault," I say. It comes out all slurry and incoherent.

Cathy shushes me and tries to be soothing. "Look, maybe should let you get some rest. You'll feel better if you have a sleep." She smiles.

Pete glances at me, then back at Dad. "Why don't you two head off? I need to have a word with Kel."

Dad steps towards me. I'm not sure what he's doing at first, then he gives me a hug. His chin ends up pressed against the top of my head, and I think he's squeezing more of the pillow than he is me. I keep my arms by my sides. This is awkward enough without me adding to it.

Pete walks them to the door then comes back into the room by himself. Actually, it's not as simple as that. He edges forward, not looking at me, then eventually comes and sits on the end of my bed. He stares at his hands, then out the window, before turning to me. I'm not sure whether to be amused or frightened. I watch him playing with the end of his tie. He seems to want to say something, but so far no words have come out.

"Kelsey." He stops as I look up at him. I wait as patiently as I can for him to continue.

"I wanted to say I'm sorry." He's back playing with his tie.

"What for?" I have to admit this isn't the direction I thought he was going to go in. I was pretty sure he was going to suggest I move out.

"For ... you know. I had no idea until Ben told me."

I shrug. I'm irritated, but I'm not really sure why.

"I mean, I didn't realise why you were acting … how you were acting."

I roll my tongue around the inside of my mouth. I love how he comes in to apologise and all he does is comment on "how I was behaving". No mention of his bullshit. He seems to want me to say something.

I take a breath before opening my mouth. "It doesn't matter now."

He doesn't notice the strained note to my voice. He smiles and pats my leg. "I'll come pick you up tomorrow," he says.

I nod. I guess that's as close as we're going to get to a proper brother-sister moment. I feel myself drifting off to sleep as he goes.

10

Chapter Ten

When I open my eyes again, the room's empty except for a nurse. My face feels hot from crying and my head aches when I move it. Someone's turned the main light out which is nice. It feels much calmer with less light.

"How are you feeling?" the nurse asks. She detaches the IV bag, leaving just the line in my arm.

"I'm ..." I'm not sure what the right answer is to that question. I'm messed up, would be my first choice. "Okay," I say eventually. I want to crawl into a hole and disappear, I nearly add.

She nods. I like this nurse. She's very matter of fact. She even looks matter of fact, if that makes sense – serious without being morose. She has lined skin that has an almost powdery quality to it.

"What's that for?" I point to the empty IV bag in her hand.

The nurse clicks her tongue. "You were a bit dehydrated last night, so we had to get some fluids into you. We gave you some painkillers as well."

I hate to think what it would have been like if they hadn't given me pain relief. It was bad enough with it.

The nurse pulls the blanket off me. "I need to get you up to weigh you."

I don't move. "Why?" The last thing I need is another lecture about how thin I am.

"For the medication doses. We had to guess last night."

The nurse gets a scale then helps me up and onto it. I refuse to look down at the numbers, but watch her face instead.

She frowns as she writes on my chart. "Have you been eating properly lately?"

I shrug. She looks at me in that serious, matter-of-fact, way and I find myself shaking my head.

"I'm not anorexic," I mumble. My voice comes out sulky, which irritates me.

"I didn't think you were." She helps me back into bed, but doesn't pull the covers up. "I need to look at your leg," she says. We both wince as she pulls off the bandage and cotton wool I stuck on at home.

She tuts and starts to clean up the cut. "Never use cotton wool on an open wound, Kelsey. You'll need antibiotics for this." She re-dresses my leg, doing a much better job than my patch-up attempt.

"Is there anything I can get you?" she says when she's finished.

I start to shake my head, then stop. "Some water?" I ask.

The nurse nods and hands me a paper cup from beside the bed. I feel stupid for not noticing it there, but she doesn't seem to mind. Most of the water ends up down my neck, because I don't sit up properly before trying to drink. She takes the empty cup from my hand.

"This arrived for you." She points to a helium balloon bobbing up and down in the corner of the room.

I squint at it. My head's still fuzzy, so it just looks like a big red blob.

"There's a card too." She hands me an envelope.

The words inside the card are printed in block capitals. They slant backwards like they're about to topple over.

FEEL BETTER SOON.

The tops of the Ts curve down like little umbrellas, and the L curves up like a backwards J. He's drawn a smiley face next to that, but his pen's slipped, making one half of the mouth droop down, like the smiley's had a stroke. At the bottom of the card, in smaller writing, are the words:

REMEMBER: YOU ASKED ME TO DO IT. TELL ANYONE AND I'LL KILL YOUR BROTHER.

As I read the last line, I gasp and start shivering.

The nurse glances at me. "Is everything all right?" She moves as if to take the card from me. I tear it up before she can.

"Yes," I say. "Please, just leave me alone."

She frowns. The corners of my mouth pull down, and I have to sit very still or I'll start screaming. The nurse leaves. I think she says something to me as she goes, but I don't hear it.

Would he really hurt Pete? I don't know, but I can't risk it. This isn't Jacob. I don't believe that any of the guys from school would do this. But if it's not one of them, who is it? I cover my face with my hands and stay like that.

Eventually, I get up to go to the bathroom. I stare at myself in the mirror. My right eye is so swollen it won't open properly, and it's all blue and purple. I have to touch my reflection, then my own face before I believe it's me.

Why did I ask him to do something?

I lean my head down against the taps. The sink bowl is cleaned to hospital standard, but down the plughole I can see white growths of sludge. I groan as I hear my cell phone ringing in the other room.

"Go away!" I scream into my hands, then I start to shake.

I can't face going back to my room, so I creep out into the corridor. There aren't any nurses around to stop me. My feet seem to know where I'm going before I do. I walk down the corridor, checking the names on each door.

I'm probably assuming a lot by thinking Mike will be on this ward. He could be anywhere in the hospital, or ... I can't even let myself think about the alternative.

I almost don't recognise it when I read the name: Michael Furlong. It takes me a moment to connect it with Mike.

The door's open, which is good. It feels like less of an invasion to go through an already open door.

The curtain is drawn around the bed. My hand shakes as I reach out to pull it back. I focus on the fabric. It's blue, faded in patches by the sun, so it looks like it's been painted with watercolour paints. I edge the curtain back just enough so I can slip through.

It's like I'm falling when I see Mike. I don't even recognise him. His head's bandaged up and there's a thick tube down his throat. He's attached to a whole lot of machines, which I can't even take in. There's a steady beeping noise in the room, but it seems to be coming from inside my head.

Mike's face is a colour I've never seen on skin before –

burgundy – and it's all puffy. His eyes don't look like eyes anymore; they're more like crescent wounds carved into his face.

I feel a pain in the middle of my chest which shoots up into my throat, and I make a strangled sort of sound. I grip the end of the bed to steady myself.

"I'm so sorry," I say to him. "I didn't know he'd–"

"Kelsey?"

I turn. Jo's standing behind me. I didn't hear her come in.

"I ..." I don't know what I'm trying to say. "I'm sorry" seems so pathetic. "How is he?"

Jo's mouth pulls down at the corners and it wobbles. She just stares at me, her eyes slowly filling up.

"I'm so sorry." I let go of the bed and reach out to her.

She backs away from me. "How could you?" She spits the words at me.

I stand frozen with my arms held out to her. A tingling chill creeps down from my hairline.

"How could you?" she says again. "How could you say that about him?"

I shake my head. My arms drop to my sides by themselves. "What?"

"The police told us you said he *hit* you." She says the word "hit" like it tastes bad in her mouth.

I shrug, not sure what else to do. "I'm sorry."

"Why would you lie?" Her lip pulls back in disgust. "How could you do this?"

I shrug again. I don't want to tell her it's true, but I'm not sure what else to say.

"How dare you come in here?" Her eyes spill over and she jerks a hand across her face. "Get out. I don't want you here.

I hate you."

"Jo ..." My voice cracks. I stumble, my legs giving way beneath me. I grip the bed and sink to the floor.

"I said get out! I hate you!"

Something inside me breaks and I yell at her. "It's not my fault! He hit me." I go cold as soon as I've said it.

"Get out!" Jo screams at me. She covers her face and starts to sob.

I shiver. It was my fault.

"He's not Dad," Jo mumbles.

"I know," I say.

"Go away," she says, but it doesn't have much force. I want to tell her I would if only I could make my legs work. Instead, I lean my head against the bed.

"Dad didn't come. Mum called him but he didn't turn up. He doesn't even care."

I'm not sure if Jo's talking to me. She seems to be trying to convince herself. I try to pull myself up. It doesn't work. I just end up flopping back down.

Jo goes really still. She stops sobbing but doesn't move her hands from her face. "Who do you think ...?"

I don't answer. She peels her hands back and looks at me. "Who did this?" Her eyes flick over to the bed. They squint as they brush over Mike.

I swallow, thinking of the phone call, then shake my head.

Her face screws up and she starts to cry again.

The curtain around the bed shoots back. Aiden looks down at me and his face seems to flit through a million emotions at once.

"Get out!" Jo's voice screeches, but Aiden ignores her.

He comes forward in a jerk. His hands hover above my

shoulders, but he doesn't actually touch me. His eyes flick up to Mike in the bed, and he makes a little noise in his throat. "I'll get Ben," he mumbles, then calls: "She's in here."

Ben seems to arrive instantly.

"Go away! All of you just go away!" Jo sounds hysterical now.

Ben ignores Jo and doesn't even glance at Mike. He pushes Aiden out of the way and pulls me to my feet. "Come on, Kel."

My legs give way again.

"Shit." Ben runs his hand over his face then stares at me. "It's okay," he says and picks me up. "You're okay."

"I'm sorry, Jo," I say over his shoulder, but I can't tell if she heard me. Ben carries me from the room.

In the morning, Cathy helps me get showered and dressed. She won't just let the nurse help me – she insists on doing it herself. She must think that because she's my step-mum, it'll be less awkward for me, but let's be honest, I've known the nurses for about the same length of time as I've known her.

Pete's assembled a weird assortment of garments. I can only assume it was really dark in my room when he grabbed them. There's a pair of cut-off shorts which I would normally never wear without tights underneath. Of course there are no tights. To go with the shorts he's given me a grey sweatshirt, which I think is actually Ben's, and a pair of gloves.

I'm not sure what I'm supposed to do with the gloves. It's not like they'll fit over my cast.

There's no underwear in the bag. On one hand, I'm not

terribly pleased that I'll have to keep wearing the same pair I've had on for two days, but on the other, I'm quite thankful that Pete wasn't rummaging through my underclothes.

Cathy has a real giggle when she sees what's in the bag. "Well, that's boys for you," she says.

It's only when they bring me my old clothes that I realise why Cathy insisted Pete bring me clean ones. There are bloodstains splattered like a pattern of flowers on my top. They go all the way through to my bra. I guess my nose must have been bleeding when I came in. There's vomit on the shoulder too. The top is blue-and-black striped, so the blood and sick only show up on the blue bits. Still, it looks pretty bad. My jeans are covered with dirt and more blood. Possibly Mike's blood.

The sweatshirt is like a dress on me. It comes down further than the shorts.

Cathy's giggles turn into hysterics when she sees that. "Well, at least it covers your lebby tubbon."

I frown, wondering if the concussion has damaged my ability to process speech.

Cathy smiles at my confusion. "Belly button. That's what the kids call it."

"Oh, right." I blush. It's weird hearing her talk about my half brother and sister. I've never met them, and to me they're not real. I'm not even sure how old they are. Pete's shown me pictures from when he went to visit Dad, but I can't remember how long ago that was. For all I know they could be anywhere between one and eighty-three.

"You should come up and visit us when you're feeling better." Cathy says this like it's a genuine invitation. I'm pretty sure Dad wouldn't be too pleased about that, so I make a non-committal noise in my throat.

"Perhaps we could stay for a while to help look after you? I'd really like to get to know you and your brother better." Cathy bites her lip. It's like she's seeking my approval, and I'm not sure what I'm supposed to say.

"You'll probably need some help. It's not like those boys will have a clue," she adds.

"Um–"

I'm interrupted by Pete calling from the other side of the curtain. "Can we come back in now?"

"Yeah, come in."

Pete draws back the curtain and he and Dad come into the cubicle. It's hard to judge which of them looks the most uncomfortable. I'd probably go with Dad. Something about his expression makes me feel anxious, although maybe I'm projecting. Dad in general makes me anxious. Pete looks me up and down and his expression goes from uncomfortable, to something between confusion and amusement. I'm now more convinced than ever that he chose these clothes in the dark.

"I was just saying, maybe we should stay a while, to help look after Kelsey," Cathy says before I have a chance to stop her. "You'll be wanting to get back to work, Pete, and Kelsey will need someone around for at least the next few days. What do you think, Martin?" She turns to Dad.

Dad shifts. "What about the kids?"

"I'm sure Marie won't mind looking after them for a couple more days. Marie's my sister," Cathy adds, looking at me.

Dad clears his throat. "Do you even have enough room for us?" He glances at me and forces a smile.

"Kel's in the spare room, so I guess …" Pete's face falls.

I take a breath, hating myself for giving in to Pete's sad look. "I don't think I'll be able to manage the stairs. I'll probably have to sleep on the couch." I leave it at that. I don't want to be responsible for actually inviting Dad to stay.

Pete's face lights up again. "Then you can stay in Kel's room."

I try not to notice how uncomfortable Dad seems.

We have to wait another hour for me to be officially discharged. Then there's the performance of removing the IV line. The nurse has to hitch up the sweatshirt sleeve to pull it out. It starts to bleed, and I have to leave while pressing a cotton wool ball to the inside of my elbow. The nurse gives Pete a couple of prescriptions to fill for me, and he pushes my wheelchair down the corridor. I ask Pete if I can go see Mike before we go, but he pretends not to hear me.

Cathy puts her arm around me to help me out of the car when we get home, but my legs don't want to co-operate. They give way and Pete half catches, half lowers me back onto the car seat. I end up walking between Pete and Cathy, with them both supporting my weight. I'm not sure what Dad's doing. Staying out of the way would be my guess.

There's a purple helium balloon tied to the front door handle. I groan when I see it.

"Do you need to sit down?" Pete asks.

I shake my head. "I'm fine."

Pete sets me up on the couch when we get inside, then goes out to get the balloon. "No card," he says. "Know who it's from?"

I shake my head. Pete tries to hand it to me, but I close my eyes and turn my face away. After a second, I hear him walk off.

Cathy sits in the chair next to me and talks non-stop. I stare at the wall and ignore her. I don't mean to be rude, but I just want to zone out at the moment. After a bit I realise she's stopped talking and is sitting looking at me. I think she asked me a question and is waiting for an answer, but I can't for the life of me work out what it was.

I stare at her. She says something else, but it sounds like gibberish to me. Her eyebrows slowly creep down in the middle until they almost join together over her nose. She goes out into the kitchen and comes back with Pete. I watch his mouth moving as he talks to me, but forget to listen. He touches my shoulder, and I go back to staring at the wall.

The phone rings at about four o'clock. I shiver as I think about the call in the hospital, and have to cover my face with my hands to stop from screaming. Pete answers it. I listen to his side of the conversation.

"Hello? Hey, Jen ... Sorry, I can't ... No, of course I want to, it's my sister ... Yeah ..."

His voice trails off as he goes upstairs. I wonder what it is he's not doing because of me.

The phone rings a few more times. Each time, Pete answers it, then a second later he slams it down. After three calls he takes it off the hook.

Aiden arrives home not long after that. He goes into the kitchen then comes back out eating a banana. He stands back from the couch and tips his head on one side to look at me.

"Hey, space cadet." He smirks.

I blink at him.

"Cathy says you're off in La-La land." He takes a bite of his banana and continues with his mouth full. "Can-you-hear-me?" He grins at me.

I give a weak smile.

"I told her you were just faking." Aiden smiles, a proper smile for once, and sits down. "What's your dad still doing here?"

"Cathy offered to stay." I stretch, testing out whether it hurts to move. It does.

Aiden frowns. "And you wanted them to?"

I shake my head. "No, but Pete did."

Aiden nods and finishes his banana. "Okay if I put the TV on?"

I shrug and yawn. Aiden takes that as a yes. He stares at the screen and I watch it with half-closed eyes. He turns the volume up, which makes my ears hurt. I shift as my head pounds. Aiden looks over at me and turns it back down.

"Sorry," I mumble. Aiden frowns as I do.

When the ads come on he presses the mute button. He keeps his eyes on the screen.

"So, Cathy's got kids?"

"Yeah. She tell you about them?" I push the duvet away from my face to look at Aiden.

He nods. "Showed me pictures too." He gives a little shake of his head. "Lots of pictures."

I smile. "Sorry."

Aiden sniggers. "What's with the apologies? Is this some new compulsion?"

"Huh?"

He looks at me. "How is it your fault Cathy forced photos on me?"

"She's here because of me. If she wasn't …" I shrug.

Aiden shakes his head. "Did you tell her to show me pictures of her kids?"

"No, but–"

"Then how is it your fault?" He tips his head on one side and watches me.

I hesitate, feeling my forehead crease into a frown. This feels like a test and I think I'm failing.

"Well?" Aiden raises his eyebrows.

I swallow. "It's not, I guess."

Aiden looks back at the TV, smirking. "Then don't apologise." He turns the volume back up.

A preview for a film comes on. A guy slaps a girl across her face. She flinches away, but he keeps hitting her.

I cover my mouth. In my head the guy has Mike's face.

Aiden glances at me and frowns. He aims a finger gun at the screen. "Line them up and shoot 'em." He makes a gunshot noise and mimes the kickback.

I stare at Aiden. His face goes cold. He runs his teeth over his bottom lip, biting at the dead skin.

The girl cowers on the floor, the guy kicking her side.

"That's what he deserves," Aiden says under his breath.

"Aiden …" My voice cracks and I can't finish that. The hardness in his face scares me. He looks so distant, just like he did when … I stop, feeling sick. *He saw me when I came home from the party. He knew Mike had …*

Aiden starts to laugh. "I hate that guy. He can't act for kittens."

I look back at the screen as a gunshot sounds. A guy in a trench coat fills the screen. "Line them up and shoot 'em," the guy says as he drops the gun.

I let out a breath.

Aiden shakes his head. "This film looks so stupid."

I laugh at my overreaction. "Kittens?" I ask.

Aiden shrugs. "PG version."

I hear his phone beep. He pulls it out of his pocket and frowns at it. I start to laugh again.

Aiden glances up at me. "What?"

I shake my head. "Nothing."

Of course Aiden's not the caller. He answered the phone in the kitchen. He spoke to the caller before he handed it to me. I'll be suspecting Mum next, if I think someone as weedy as Aiden could have beaten up Mike.

I'm still laughing at myself when Ben walks in. He smiles at me, which makes me smile back. Then he hands me a banana, which makes me feel less like smiling.

"You don't have to eat it," he says.

The tendons in his neck pop out. He's trying so hard to be relaxed, it's making him tense. I take the banana. Ben laughs as I make a rather pathetic attempt at opening it. I hand it back to him, and he opens it for me.

He lifts up my feet and slides himself onto the couch underneath them. I'd complain, except it's surprisingly comfortable.

"How're you feeling?" He rests his hand on my leg. I'm glad of the duvet. This would be way too weird if there wasn't a layer of synthetic padding between us.

I shrug and chew the banana, slowly.

"So, your dad's staying here?" Ben taps his hand against my leg.

"Yeah." I can feel him watching me.

"You okay with that?"

I shrug again. "As long as he doesn't try to drive me anywhere."

Aiden sniggers but Ben just looks blank. I look at him, waiting for him to click, but he doesn't so I shake my head. "Never mind."

Ben frowns and tilts his head to the side. "What's that you're wearing?" he asks.

I giggle. "Pete's idea of clothes. Is this yours?" I pull at the sweatshirt sleeve.

"Nah, it's mine." Aiden glances over at me.

I blush. "I'm sorr–" I catch myself just before I say it. "I'll wash it and give it back."

"Whenever." Aiden flicks the mute button on again as the TV goes into another ad break. I watch him pulling stuffing out of a hole in the fabric of the armchair he's sitting in. He pitches the pieces across the floor into a little pile on the other side of the room. He knocks his banana skin from the chair arm into his lap, so he chucks that across the floor too.

"You want anything else to eat?" The tendon in Ben's neck pops out again.

I shrug. It seems easier to just go along with his re-feeding programme. "I don't know. Maybe some milk?"

Ben smiles. "Chocolate?"

I nod and he goes off to the kitchen.

Aiden turns to me as soon as Ben's gone. "What's up with him trying to feed you all the time?"

I scowl. "He thinks I'm anorexic."

Aiden starts to laugh, then he stops. He looks me up and down, which makes me squirm.

"Are you?" he asks.

I shake my head. "I don't think so."

"Wouldn't you know if you were?"

I look at him, wondering about that.

He shrugs. "I guess if you were you wouldn't want chocolate."

I roll my eyes at his logic.

Ben comes back into the room and I sit up, partly so I can drink from the glass he hands me and partly to free up enough seats. Pete, Dad and Cathy come back in with him. I end up smooshed between Cathy and Ben on the couch. It's only a two seater, just long enough for me to lie on with my legs curled up, but not quite long enough for three people to sit. Dad takes the other armchair – frowning as he passes Aiden's banana skin but not picking it up. Pete grabs a wooden chair from the kitchen.

Cathy asks me how I am, but I manage to take a sip before I have to answer. I'm getting a bit sick of that question. She arranges the duvet over my knees, but it's so big she ends up tucking me and Ben in together.

"What're you drinking?" Dad asks me. At first I'm puzzled by the question, then I realise this is probably as close as it gets to him starting meaningful conversation with me.

"Chocolate milk."

Dad makes a little noise in his throat. "Lot of calories in that," he says.

Ben goes stiff beside me. I run my tongue over my teeth. My mouth feels all clogged up, like I just ate a lump of butter.

"Martin ..." Cathy's voice has a warning tone. I find myself warming to her.

I force myself to take another sip, for no other reason than to spite Dad. Ben half relaxes as I do. He reaches forward and squeezes my shoulder.

After that it doesn't seem so hard to drink the whole glass.

The volume on the TV's still off when the hourly ad for the news starts. A picture of Mike flashes up on the screen. Except it's not really Mike. It's a picture of him in the hospital, his skin purple and his eyes swollen shut.

I put a hand to my mouth.

Ben grips my arms, steadying me. He turns to Aiden. "Turn it off, will you?"

Cathy touches my face. "Are you okay, honey?"

I look down at Ben's hands. The bruises look worse today than they did yesterday. I push him away. "I think I'm going to be sick." I get up and hobble to the bathroom.

11

Chapter Eleven

I make it to the bathroom, but not quite to the toilet, before throwing up. Fortunately, the sink is close enough. I splash some water on my face and sit down on the lid of the loo.

The whole household seems to have gathered outside the bathroom door to discuss me.

"Do you think we should call the hospital? Isn't vomiting one of the things they said to look out for?" Cathy lowers her voice, but I can still hear the concern.

"I think it's more a sign of the fact that she hasn't eaten for weeks and decided to celebrate with milk."

I'm surprised Pete even noticed I wasn't eating. Ben probably thought he should tell him.

"Why wasn't she eating?" Dad asks. That's such a dad question. Couldn't he figure it out? He does sound worried, though. I suppose he feels guilty over the chocolate milk comment now.

"I don't know, maybe because her boyfriend hit her, her mother lost the plot and you turned her away so she had to come live with us. Do you think it might be that?" Ben's practically spitting his words out.

"Martin ...?" Cathy leaves it at that, but I can tell she didn't even know Pete had asked if I could stay.

"Is she still throwing up?"

I smile as I hear Aiden's voice. He sounds bemused by the whole thing.

There's a knock on the door. "Sweetheart? Can I come in?" Cathy opens the door without waiting for an answer.

I keep staring at the floor. There are patches of mould growing around the edge of the bath and in the cracks in the lino.

I've got the post-vomit shakes. Cathy picks up a clean flannel off the towel rack and wets it under the tap. She presses it to my forehead then wraps her arm around me. I lean against her shoulder.

"You poor darling."

I close my eyes. Until she speaks it's easy to pretend she's Mum.

"How about we get you out of those clothes and into some pyjamas, and I make you something to settle your stomach?"

I nod and Cathy moves to face me. She has flecks of mascara and eyeliner creeping down her face under her eyes. It looks like her eyelashes have fallen out and scattered themselves down her face.

"Now, where will I find pyjamas?"

I grimace. "The suitcase under my bed or the pile of clothes in the corner of my room."

Cathy chuckles. "You're just like your father."

"No, I'm not," I say, but I don't think Cathy hears me.

We reassemble in the living room. It's awkward without the TV on. Not that I'm about to suggest we turn it back on, but now it's really obvious we don't have an awful lot to talk about. Aiden resumes pitching armchair stuffing across the room. Cathy offers to make some dinner, so Pete goes to show her around the kitchen. Dad follows them.

I pull at the stuffing from the seat of the couch and pitch a piece onto Aiden's pile. He squints and throws a piece of his own. A second later Ben pulls a piece from the back of the couch and throws it over too. I grin at him. By the time Cathy comes back in with dinner I'm surprised the couch is still standing, we've removed so much stuffing.

"I made you some soup, Kelsey. Just eat as much as you like." Cathy hands me a bowl.

I'm glad she's not trying to make me eat any more than that. She's made what looks like a beef stew, and I think I'm having a vegetarian moment at the sight of it. Everyone else seems to think it's great though, so maybe it's just me. I put the bowl down on the coffee table.

Ben puts it back in my lap. "You need to eat something with your pills." He rattles the prescription bottle.

I don't remember Pete going out to the pharmacy, but I suppose it must have been while I was zoned out.

Ben doles out some pills and gets me a glass of water. "Antibiotics and painkillers." He gives me a little smile as I eat some of the soup.

"It's about time for the news, isn't it?" Dad pats his chair, looking for the TV remote. Aiden, who has the remote, ignores him.

Ben glances at me. "I don't think that's a good idea."

Dad looks at me too. He shifts as he meets my eye and mumbles something that I swear sounds like "pickled onions". The silence this time is only broken by en masse swallowing.

When I've finished eating, I start to yawn. I do the whole grit-my-teeth and suck-in-air-through-my-nose thing, but still Cathy notices.

"Come on," she says. "We'd better get out of here and let poor Kelsey go to sleep."

"You don't have to go," I say. "It's still early."

"Don't be silly, dear. You need your rest." She kisses me on the forehead. Dad, Pete and Aiden head off after her.

Ben hangs back. "You okay?"

I shrug and don't look at him.

"You need anything?"

I shrug again. The corners of my mouth pull down as I think about being left alone in the dark.

Ben frowns. He sits back down next to me. "What's wrong?"

"I'm not tired," I say, except it's punctuated by a yawn so it's probably not that believable.

Ben presses his lips together. I think he's trying not to laugh at me but it's not really working.

"How about I stay until you go to sleep?" he says.

I look up at him. "You'll be here a while."

"That's okay."

Ben settles himself in the armchair next to me, and I tuck down on the couch. He turns out the lounge light but leaves the one in the kitchen on. Even if he hadn't, it's still reasonably light outside and the glow from the streetlights creeps in through the dirty windows.

"Dad didn't look happy about being sent to bed early," I say.

Ben chuckles.

"I suppose he couldn't really argue, though," I say, "since

it was Cathy's idea."

"Mmm."

I look up at Ben. "She invited me to go stay with them."

"Yeah?" His eyebrows bob in a miniature frown.

"I'm not going to go."

Ben nods. He rests his head on his hand and looks at me, a faint smile on his lips.

"Did she show you pictures of her kids?" Part of me feels bad calling them "her kids". I could just as easily have said my brother and sister. Or Annie and ... crap, I can't even remember my own brother's name.

"Yeah, she showed me a few," Ben says.

"What'd she say about them?"

Ben chuckles and rubs his hand across his eyes.

"What?" I sit up a bit to look at him.

"You're supposed to be going to sleep."

I screw up my face and he laughs again.

"Just try."

I rest my head back down on the pillow. "I'm not tired." Even as I say it, I can feel myself dropping off. I watch Ben through half-closed eyes. He smiles at me as though I amuse him.

I don't remember falling asleep, but I remember waking up. I open my eyes and Mike's standing over me. He snarls and draws back his arm to hit me. I close my eyes and scream.

"Kel, wake up!"

I open my eyes as I hear Ben's voice. He crouches on the floor beside the couch. I'm so cold, and clammy. I sit up and manage to bash myself in the head with my cast as I try to wipe my face.

Ben presses his hand against my forehead. His palm is cool and soothing, though it hurts where it presses against the top of my bruised eye.

I rest back against the couch.

Ben's hand drops away. "You had a nightmare." He sits down beside me, wrapping his arm around my shoulder.

"What are you still doing here?"

"Huh?"

"You said you'd stay until I fell asleep." I push the hair out of my face. It sticks to my skin in little clammy threads.

"You only just dropped off."

I don't think that can be true. It looks a whole lot darker outside than it was when we were talking before. I squirm at the thought that he might have been sitting there, watching me sleep.

I pull away from him. "I had a dream about Mike."

"Yeah?" Ben goes stiff beside me. His hand falls from my shoulder to his side.

"He was about to ... He was going to hit me." I feel shaky as I think about it.

"Bastard." Ben spits the word out.

I stare at him, feeling my skin tingle. Don't speak ill of the dead, I want to say, but that doesn't seem quite right. For a start, Mike's not dead. I shudder as the image of his distorted face comes into my head.

"Do you want to go back to sleep?" Ben asks.

I shake my head.

Ben settles beside me. "How about we watch a movie?"

I don't remember much of the film. I'm pretty sure I fell asleep right near the beginning and dreamt the rest of the plot. Either that or Johnny Depp's character really did turn out to be an alien who was part horse.

When I wake again, it's early morning. I'm flopped across Ben, my head against his chest and his arms wrapped around me. From his breathing I can tell he's still asleep. One of his hands rests on my thigh and the other on my stomach, in the gap between my pyjama top and bottoms. His fingers twitch in his sleep, tapping against the bare skin of my belly. I cringe as I realise he can probably feel every ounce of fat on my stomach. Just being this close to him is making me blush. He's so warm, though, and weirdly enough, this is pretty comfortable.

The bottom button's missing from my pyjama top, making the gap bigger than it should be. There are little bits of thread that used to hold the button in place sticking out, which must be tickling Ben's hand. I'm surprised it hasn't woken him up.

I wonder if I should edge out from under his arms without waking him, or if I should just sit still until he wakes naturally. Of course, as I'm trying to decide, I realise I need to pee and that makes the decision for me.

I slide my hand underneath his until my own hand is on my leg. Then, I try to ease it sideways. Ben wakes with a jerk. The hand on my stomach shoots up under my top. I grab it before it goes higher than my bottom ribs. He stares at me, his eyes wide like a bush baby's, and makes a sound like "woophf". I can't help but laugh. He blinks a couple of times then starts to laugh too, though I'm not sure he knows why. He smooths out his hair and rubs his eyes.

"Sorry, I didn't mean to wake you." I try to stop laughing.

"'S'okay, babe."

I freeze as Ben says that. No one's ever called me "babe" except Mike, and even he hardly ever said it. I swallow and look away. Ben doesn't seem to notice. He pats the couch, looking for something which he doesn't find, then leans back and closes his eyes. He opens them again as I get up.

"Where're you going?" He looks puzzled, almost hurt that I'm leaving.

"Bathroom," I say.

When I come back, he's more alert. He smiles at me and moves back the duvet for me to sit down. I pretend I don't notice and sit in the armchair instead.

"What time is it?" Ben asks.

I shrug. "Don't know. I don't have a watch."

He nods towards the window. "Must still be early."

"Don't know how you can tell." I nod to the window myself. "They're so dirty it could be any time and the light would look the same."

"You offering to clean them?" Ben grins at me.

"Hey, I'm injured, remember?"

He smiles. "Can't use that excuse forever."

I tuck my legs up underneath me and prop my head up on my hand. My feet are cold, making my toenails mauve and my skin a sickly greyish colour. Ben watches me in a sleepy way that makes him look even more like he's stoned than usual. I hate to think what his boss will say.

"What time do you have to be at work?" I ask.

He groans and closes his eyes. "Maybe I'll pull a sickie."

I frown. "You can't. You've already taken so much time off because of me."

"Who says it's because of you?" Ben smiles, keeping his eyes closed. When I don't answer, he opens his eyes a crack and peers at me.

"You know what I mean," I say. My voice comes out all huffy and cold. Ben's forehead creases up as he watches me. He's not smiling anymore. I look away and stare at the wall instead.

Pete comes clattering down the stairs. He stops as he comes into the lounge. He does a startled fawn impression as he sees us sitting up, awake.

"Hey, it's early. What're you doing up?" he asks.

I feel Ben glance at me.

"Kel couldn't sleep, so I stayed down here," he says.

Pete doesn't answer. In my peripheral vision I see him fidget.

"Why are you up so early?" Ben asks.

Pete clears his throat. "I thought I'd go visit Mum on my way to work."

I look up at him. "Can I come? It'll only take me a minute to get ready." That's a lie. At the rate I'm moving it could only take me a minute to get ready if I was going in my pyjamas.

Pete's mouth pulls down at the corners. "I don't think that's a good idea."

"Why not? I'll be okay."

Pete looks down at his feet. "It's not that." He takes a breath. "It's just, she didn't recognise you last time."

"So? That doesn't mean anything."

"Yeah, but with your black eye ..." Pete trails off. I stare at him until he continues. "I think you might scare her."

Pete looks at me, like he's waiting for me to yell at him. Instead I shrug and look away. Pete lets out a long breath, though I can't tell whether he's relieved or frustrated.

"I'm going to see if I can get someone from the phone company to come round this afternoon," he says.

"Why?" I ask without looking up at him.

"I want to get a caller ID installed. Then maybe we can sort out this prank caller."

A feeling, like a wave, ripples down from my forehead to my toes. I haven't turned my phone back on since I got home from the hospital. The term "prank caller" doesn't seem appropriate anymore.

Pete squints at me. "Unless you know something?"

My fingertips tingle. "I–"

"What? You know who it is?"

I try to answer, but I can't make the words come out. My head starts to hurt. I rub my temples with the heel of my palm.

Pete's face goes red. "If this has all been some pathetic joke–"

"Pete," Ben says softly.

Pete doesn't hear him. "Bloody hell, Kelsey. I thought you were more mature than that."

My throat clogs up with words that all want to come out at once. "I didn't–"

"What? Think? Yeah, that sounds about right."

I screw up my face. "You have no idea what–"

"What a brat I have for a sister? Yeah, you'd be surprised."

"Pete, stop it," Ben says. He looks at me. "She's made a mistake, that's all."

"How dare you?" I make a noise in my throat. "You have

no idea … You have …" I shake my head. "I'm trying to tell you …" I look at Pete.

He stares at me like I disgust him.

I feel my expression mirror his. "Forget it. Just forget it." I try to walk away.

Ben catches my arm. "Kel–"

I jerk away from him. "Stuff you." I look at Pete. "Stuff both of you."

∽

"What are you doing?" Aiden plonks himself down on the couch next to me.

I glare at him. "What does it look like?"

"Like you're bashing yourself in the head with a hairbrush." Aiden smirks.

I give a little shriek of frustration and hurl the brush at the floor.

This afternoon, Cathy brought me a whole lot of stuff down from my room, including my hairbrush and cell phone. It took me ages to work up the courage to turn the phone on. I felt sick every time I tried.

I spent the past half hour trying to delete the built-up messages – not so easy using only my left hand – and every time I got rid of some, new ones came in. There were a whole lot of texts from the caller: I WAS TRYING TO HELP, and PLEASE TALK TO ME. Then finally the same threat as at the hospital: TELL ANYONE AND I'LL KILL YOUR BROTHER. He probably left voice messages, too, but I didn't check those. I couldn't bring myself to delete the messages from Mike and that got me more annoyed than anything. I wish I could just feel one way and stick to it.

Pete called my cell phone to say he was going to Jenny's after work. Even though it came up saying it was Pete, it still took me ages to answer it. By the time I did, Pete was pissed off. He didn't say it, but I could hear it in his voice.

On top of all that, I tried to brush my hair and, as Aiden said, just ended up bashing myself in the head. I tried gripping the brush in my right hand, but I couldn't get my fingers close enough together because of the cast.

Aiden picks up the brush from the floor. "Here." He gestures for me to turn around.

I stare at him, feeling my eyes narrow.

He sniggers. "You prefer bashing yourself in the head?"

I roll my eyes and, against my better judgement, turn my back to him. "Ow!" The brush catches in a tangle, and I pull away from Aiden.

He grabs my shoulder and pulls me back. "Sit still. You're worse than Becky."

"Who's Becky?"

He doesn't answer. I turn my head to look at him. He appears to be concentrating very hard on removing a knot from my hair.

"Your girlfriend?" I make my voice innocent. Secretly, I've been dying to ask Aiden if he has a girlfriend … or a boyfriend, for ages. He's always been such a question mark in that department. In fact, I wouldn't be surprised if he turned out to be completely asexual.

Aiden rolls his eyes. "She's my sister." He glances up at me. "I brushed her hair for her when she broke her arm."

I try not to sound disappointed. "You've never talked about your family before," I say.

"No."

I glance back over my shoulder. Aiden's still concentrating on the knot in my hair. I wait for him to continue but he doesn't.

"Is she older or younger?" I ask.

"Becky? Younger."

Again I wait for him to continue, but he doesn't. I try to think of another question to get him talking.

"What the hell did you do to your hair?" Aiden sniggers. "It's in dreads."

I run my hand over my head. I hope I don't have to cut it all off.

My cell phone buzzes in my lap, making me jump. My head swims as I look at the caller ID: *Mikehome Calling*. I have a stupid moment of relief when I see it's not *Private Number Calling*. Then I think about it and want to throw up. I must have made some kind of noise, as Aiden stops brushing.

"What?" he asks. "Prank caller?"

I shake my head and show him the phone. He tries to take it out of my hand, but I cling to it.

"It'll be Jo," I say.

He grunts. "So?"

"I should answer it." It's a bit of a stupid thing to say, as by now the phone's stopped ringing.

Aiden doesn't say anything. He probably doesn't get it. I go into my contacts list and look up Mike's home number. It takes me a second before I can press dial. Jo answers almost straight away. "Hello?" She sounds like she's been crying.

I wonder if I'm having an allergic reaction. My throat feels like it's closed up.

"Hello?" Jo says again.

"Jo," I say when I find my words. I want to add "honey" or some other form of endearment, but I can't make it come out.

Jo sighs in response.

"Is something wrong? Do you need something?" I regret saying it as soon as it's out of my mouth. It makes it sound like she has to have a reason to call me.

"No, I don't need anything."

I can almost hear her adding "from you" in her head. Her voice is so cold. It makes her sound much older. It seems to be my turn to speak, but I don't know what to say. I'm very aware of Aiden sitting next to me. He's staring at the floor, but I can tell he's listening. I get up and hobble out of the lounge.

"Jo, I–"

She cuts me off. "Do you hate him?"

"What?" My head seems to have detached itself from the rest of my body.

"Do you hate him? Mike?"

I don't know what to say. I'm not even sure if I know the answer to that. "I don't know," I say eventually, then I swallow and try to be honest. "I do hate him, but I love him too." Or I loved the person he used to be.

Jo takes one of those shaky breaths that come just before you start crying.

"Jo–" I say, but she hangs up before I can say anything else.

Aiden looks up as I come back into the lounge and sit down next to him. He's pulling the hair out of my brush, leaving it in a pile beside him on the couch. It looks like a group of giant daddy longlegs.

"Okay?" he asks.

I shake my head. "I don't know." I pinch at the skin on my left hand, making a pattern of pink fingernail imprints. Aiden sees me doing it and pushes my hand away. He starts brushing my hair again.

It takes him an hour to get all the knots out. He makes an attempt at braiding my hair to stop it re-knotting itself. I don't tell him, but it's killing one side of my head because it's pulled so tight. The other side's got clumps of hair creeping down my neck as they escape from the braid. I wait until he goes into his room, then get Cathy to re-do it for me.

She undoes the bobble and shakes my hair out. "You've got lovely hair," she says. She runs her hand down the length of it. It tickles as she touches the back of my neck.

I flinch away.

Cathy laughs. "Sorry. Didn't realise you're ticklish. Annie's like that. Hair like yours too."

I twist my mouth up. I'm not sure what I'm supposed to say when she talks about them.

"You know, Annie's always wanted a big sister. She'd love to get to know you." Cathy gathers my hair into bunches and starts plaiting.

I take a breath. "Cathy, I–" I'm interrupted by my phone ringing. I look at the caller ID. *Mikecell Calling.* I let out a breath. I'm glad Jo's calling back, but I still don't have a clue what to say to her.

I glance back over my shoulder at Cathy. "I have to take this." I gesture to the phone.

"Sure." Cathy slips a bobble over the end of my half-finished plait.

I ease out of the chair and go out into the hall, then press the answer call button. "Jo, I–"

"It's not Jo."

My chest contracts at the sound of the caller's voice. "What? How did you–"

"I took his phone." He says it like it's nothing, almost like he thinks it's funny.

"You took his …?" I cover my mouth with my hand.

There's a silence. The blood pounds in my ears. I move my hand to hang up. He speaks before I can.

"Did you know you talk in your sleep?"

"What?" My skin goes cold. "How do you know that?"

"I know a lot more than you think." He laughs.

"You are really sick!"

"Ignore my calls and you'll see just how sick I can be." He hangs up before I can.

My hands shake and I drop the phone. He was in the hospital. He was watching me in the hospital. I cover my face, but I don't cry. I've exhausted the supply of tears. Instead I just sit there and wait for things to stop hurting.

I'm back on the couch, half asleep when Ben gets home. I sit up to make room for him.

He comes in and sits down next to me. "Are you still mad at me?"

I shake my head. "Not really. No."

"Good." He leans his head against my shoulder and closes his eyes. My heart rate speeds up. If I'm honest with myself, this is kind of nice. His hair's soft against my face. Not like Mike's, which was always prickly and sticky with gel. I go cold and pull away.

He blinks and sits up. "Sorry. It's been a long day." He looks at me.

I do my best to smile, but I can't help screwing up my mouth as I try not to let it shake.

Ben's eyebrows draw together. "Kel ..." He rests his hand down on the couch. A second later he makes a sound like a backwards scream. The air wheezes in instead of going out. He lifts up his hand – in it is the ball of dead hair from my brush. "What the?!"

I laugh. It feels weird, like I'm doing something wrong.

"Eugh!" Ben screws up his face in disgust and drops the ball into my lap. "That's worse than when you chew your hair."

"I'm sorry." It doesn't sound like a particularly genuine apology, as I laugh my way through it. "I thought Aiden threw it out."

"Aiden?" Ben's eyebrows bob as he smiles.

"Yeah. He brushed my hair for me." I run my hand along my braid as I speak.

Ben chuckles. "I'm surprised Aiden knows what a hair-brush looks like."

I frown. "He said he used to brush his sister's hair when she broke her arm."

Ben raises his eyebrows. "Well, can't say I would have expected that."

"Why were you so late?" I ask after a bit.

Ben shakes his head. "Day from hell, I swear. I really wish I had pulled a sickie." He settles back against the couch. "Where is everyone?"

"Aiden's in his room, Pete's at Jenny's. The rest are in the kitchen."

"The rest?" Ben's mouth pinches up as he tries not to laugh at me.

"You know – Dad, Cathy. The rest." I smile as I say it. No love lost in my family, that's for sure.

"You had dinner yet?"

I groan and look away from Ben.

"What?" He sits up to look at me.

"Don't start." I feel my teeth clenching.

"I wasn't–"

I flap my arms in what's supposed to be a gesture of irritation, but probably looks more like a demented version of the chicken dance. "Can you just let it go? I'll eat when I'm hungry, okay?"

I hear Ben swallow, then he lets out a breath. "Okay," he says eventually.

I'm not sure I believe him. He'll probably just try to be more subtle about the way he checks up on me, but let's face it – he's a boy. They struggle with subtlety at the best of times. I stare at the blank TV. Well, it's not really blank. I can see a wobbly reflection of me and Ben sitting on the couch together. We look a funny shape, like children with arms and legs too long for their bodies.

Ben nudges my arm and lowers his voice. "You sick of your Dad being here yet?" He grins at me.

"I was sick of him before he got here." I laugh then shrug. "He hid from me most of today. Cathy's doing her best to recast herself as my fairy godmother."

"Annoying?"

I shrug again. "Not too bad. She kind of reminds me of Mum." Tears prick the back of my eyes as I say that. I press my fingers against my mouth.

Ben touches my shoulder.

"It's okay." I laugh in that depressed way people do when they're really about to cry. "I just miss Mum."

Ben puts his arm around me. "I'll take you to see her next week, yeah?"

I nod then think of something. I think Ben notices me go still. He tenses up, too, as he braces himself, waiting.

"Ben …" I wince as I hear the ingratiating tone come out of my mouth.

"Yeah?" His voice is cautious. He can tell he's not going to like what I'm going to say.

"Will you take me to see Mike as well?"

Ben doesn't even seem to breathe, then he unwraps his arm from around me and pulls away. "No. I won't."

I expected reluctance, but not a flat out "no". I feel my blood pressure rise. "Why not?"

Ben gets up and moves away from the couch. He doesn't look at me. "Because he was a bastard and you should forget about him."

I get up and follow Ben. "I love him. He loves me." I swallow down my doubts as I say that, pushing away my conversation with Jo.

"Yeah?" Ben turns suddenly to face me. I almost bash into him, I'm following so close.

"He didn't love you, he controlled you. He hit you, for God's sake." Ben glares at me.

I feel myself shrink. "He did love me." It comes out as a whisper.

"I thought you were smarter than that, Kel"

I can see on his face that he regrets it straight away, but I don't want to give him a chance to apologise. I start to hobble away as fast as I can. Unfortunately, that's not very fast.

"Kel, I'm-"

"I don't care," I scream.

He tries to stop me by grabbing my wrist, but I shake him off. I go and sit in the bathroom. It's the only private place I have left now.

A little while later, there's a knock on the door. I expect it to be Ben, or maybe Cathy, but when I don't answer, Dad calls out. "Kelsey? Can I come in?"

I figure he must actually need to use the bathroom, since I can't imagine him wanting to talk to me. I get up to open the door.

He stands in the doorway, fidgeting. "Can we talk?" he asks.

I frown, then stand back to let him in.

Dad leans against the wall. I sit back down on the side of the bath. Dad doesn't say anything. I wonder if I'm supposed to start this conversation, but since I don't know the topic it's a little difficult. Instead I just stare at my feet. They're bare, and I'm a little disturbed by the amount of mould they must be touching.

Dad clears his throat. "I honestly thought I was doing the best thing."

"Huh?" I look up at him.

Dad looks uncomfortable. "By saying no to you coming to live with us."

I think he wants me to absolve him of guilt, but he's got seventeen years' worth of that stashed up.

"You would have had to change schools - leave all your friends. You wouldn't have been able to visit your mother easily-"

Dad must have been preparing a list of why he was justified in rejecting me. He's performing it like a speech now.

"You've never even met Annie and Greg—"

Greg. Of course.

"It would have been too much of an upheaval for you." Dad pauses. I think he's waiting for a response from me, so I nod.

He sighs. When he continues his tone is more honest, less like he's trying to get me to vote for him. "You're closer to your brother than to me. I thought it would be better."

I swallow. "It's fine," I say.

"If I'd known …"

I close my eyes and shake my head. Dad trails off. He was recycling that bit from Pete, anyway.

"It doesn't matter now," I say.

Dad lets out a breath. "What I wanted to say was …"

I look up at him, and he stops. I have to fight back the urge to prompt him.

"Cathy and I have talked. If you want to come live with us, you'd be most welcome. It might be good to have a … a fresh start."

I laugh and shake my head. "Are you kidding?"

Dad shifts his feet. "Well, it sounds like you're struggling a bit here. Pete said—"

"Does Pete want me to leave?"

"No, but—"

"Is Cathy making you offer?"

Dad looks at me like I've slapped him. "What?"

I laugh again. "Come on. Do you honestly want me to stay with you, or do you just feel bad?"

Dad starts to go red. "I didn't—"

"You don't have to pretend. I know you blame me for

breaking up you and Mum. It's okay. Pete does too." I get up to walk out.

Dad catches my arm. "Did your mum tell you that?"

I shrug. "No. I figured it out for myself. That's why you never wanted me to come visit."

"Kelsey" Dad pulls me towards him, almost knocking my feet from under me. "That's not true."

"It's not a big deal," I say, then wonder why I said that. Of course it's a big deal.

Dad sighs. "Look, you really are most welcome to come stay, or live with us. For as long as you like."

I look away. I'd have left by now, but Dad's still holding my arm. It's starting to hurt where he's pressing against one of the many sets of bruises.

Dad rubs his hand across his mouth. "Cathy and I have to get back. The kids, you know." He stops and looks at me. "We're leaving the day after tomorrow, but if you change your mind ..." he trails off. "I really am sorry, Kel. I wish ... I wish things could have been different."

I take a breath, one of those long shaky ones that squash down emotion, and nod.

Dad gives my arm a little squeeze. "Your brother ..."

I look up at Dad, wondering what he could possibly have to say about Pete.

"Your brother loves you. Be kind to him, okay?"

I nod, unable to think of another way to answer that. Dad seems satisfied. He gives me a little smile as he leaves.

12

Chapter Twelve

"I don't want to go," I say. I don't look at Ben as I say it. I'm sitting on the couch, in my pyjamas, with my legs folded up underneath me. Dad and Cathy left last night, but I slept down here again anyway. I don't know how Pete can possibly think I'm ready to go back to school, when I can barely manage the stairs in the house.

Ben leans forward to try and catch my eye, but I keep my head turned in the other direction. Aiden's sitting in the chair next to me. He seems amused by this conversation. The corner of his lip keeps twitching up into a smile.

"It'll be okay," Ben says. "I promise."

Aiden snorts. "How can you possibly promise that?"

I smile despite myself.

Ben rolls his eyes. "I can't," he says to Aiden, then to me: "but I bet it won't be as bad as you think."

My lip starts to shake. "Everyone will stare at me."

Ben touches my hand. He was training early this morning and he's still sweaty. His hand is slimy against mine. "No one's going to stare at you."

Aiden shakes his head. "Of course they're going to stare at

her. She's got a black eye for God's sake."

"Aiden!" Ben's voice rises. He looks about ready to hit Aiden.

I can't help but laugh.

Aiden smirks. "See, at least I made her laugh."

Ben lets out a breath and chuckles. For a moment, I think I've got the better of him, then he starts again. "Look, Kel, Pete doesn't want you to miss any more school."

I shake my head and close my eyes. "Please don't make me." I keep thinking about the picture of Mike from the news. Everyone's going to know what happened.

Ben doesn't say anything. Somehow the silence is worse. I open my eyes to see what he's doing. He stares at me in a serious, concerned way. I'm annoyed at myself as I cave.

I groan. "Fine, I'll go." I stand up.

"How did you do that?" Aiden says to Ben. Ben laughs in answer.

I storm out of the room in the stroppiest way I can manage.

All my trousers press against the bruises on my side. My skin's turned a yellowy-green colour, rather than the aubergine it was originally, but it still hurts a lot. Too much for me to be able to cope with something pressing against it all day.

I rummage through my clothes until I find a loose T-shirt dress. With a pair of tights underneath it would be okay, and the tights wouldn't dig too bad.

When I put the dress on I realise, with all the weight I've lost recently, it's more like wearing an empty bean bag. On the bright side, if people are staring at that, maybe they won't notice my punching-bag face. Or maybe they'll just think I had an accident with my eye shadow, since they'll have to assume I got dressed in the dark.

Pete insists on driving me to school himself. It's either a nice, caring gesture or he's trying to make sure I actually go. To be fair, wagging had crossed my mind. He has talkback radio on in the car, which makes me feel ill. The self-important voices remind me of Dad, and I can't make sense of what they're saying. I lean my head against the car window, which is nice and cold but it sends vibrations down the left side of my body every time we stop.

It's weird being in Mum's car again. Pete figured it was easier to keep her car for himself and sell his old one to Aiden. Mum probably wouldn't have minded him taking it, but I'm pretty sure she'd be pissed off if she saw the amount of mess he's created in the backseat.

I sit up and open the glove box.

Pete glances over as I do. "What are you doing?"

I rummage through the junk he has in there. Actually, "junk" is probably the wrong word. Knowing Pete, I bet it's all extremely useful stuff like the car owner's manual and map books and enough cash to solve any possible emergency. I'm surprised when I find a half-eaten pie and some movie ticket stubs in there.

Right at the back I find what I'm looking for: a bag of peppermints. I pull them out and hold them up for Pete to see. "Looking for these," I say. I pop one in my mouth and lean back against the seat.

Pete frowns. "Are you car sick?"

I nod.

Pete looks at his watch. "We've hardly been driving for five minutes."

I shrug and close my eyes. Pete turns off the radio which

makes me feel better straight away.

"You were like that when you were little," he says. "Especially after the accident."

"I don't really remember," I say.

"Yeah, I'm not surprised. You were lucky you weren't brain damaged."

I look over at Pete. He stares straight ahead, the model image of a good driver. I have this weird feeling that I can't remember him as a kid. It's like he's always been my adult, prematurely-balding, older brother.

"I read to you while you were in the hospital," Pete says.

"Huh?"

He glances over at me. "After the accident. I read to you. Ben and I took turns."

"I don't remember that," I say. I can't even remember Ben coming to the hospital. He would have been just a kid then. Same as Pete, I guess.

Pete shrugs. "You wouldn't. You were unconscious most of the time."

I stare at Pete, wondering why he's telling me this.

"Dad took off and Mum was out of it she was so upset." Pete wipes his hand across his mouth. "I stayed at Ben's place and he came to the hospital with me. We didn't know what to say to you so we read you books."

I'm not sure what to say. I'd always thought that when Dad walked out, Pete followed him. Or tried to, anyway. I forget that he was only nine and probably scared out of his head. I never thought of Mum not being able to look after him, never even considered that he might have had to go stay somewhere else.

"Ben said he was coming to support me, but I knew he

wanted to be there for you as well." Pete pulls over to the kerb outside the school and stops the car.

I just sit there, staring at him, making no move to get out.

Pete sighs and pinches the bridge of his nose. "Look, Kel, you and Ben–"

"I know. I'm sorry. I shouldn't argue with him so much. I–"

"It's not that." Pete stops and looks at me. "You're my little sister, Kel, and Ben's a lot older than you."

It takes me a moment to click as to what he's saying, then I shrink in embarrassment and cover my face with my hands. "Aw, Pete, no!"

"If you're staying with us we have to talk about this stuff." Pete sounds just as embarrassed as me.

I shake my head and pull my hands down my face. "No, we don't. Ben and I are just friends. He's like another brother to me."

"Are you sure about that?"

"Yeah," I say, but my voice kind of wobbles. "And anyway, Mike ..." I find I can't finish that sentence.

Pete sighs and then nods. "Come on. You'd better go or you'll be late." He helps me out of the car and puts my backpack on for me. I feel like every single person walking through the school gates is staring at me. I keep my head down and get inside as fast as I can.

The form room is packed. I take out my cell and pretend to text as I walk in. This would have been a great move to avoid drawing attention to myself, except I trip and drop the phone. The battery detaches itself and goes shooting off along the floor. By the time I've picked it up, my black eye is probably less obvious, as I'm sure my face has turned beetroot.

I swear I never used to be this clumsy. The concussion must be throwing my balance off.

When I open my locker, a sickly, greasy smell greets me. It takes me a moment to realise where it's coming from. The cupcake Mike gave me is still sitting where I left it, behind my books. I stare at it. The green icing has melted, leaving oily patches on the top which seem to be doing their best to dissolve the sprinkles. By the smell of it, the whole thing has gone rancid. I fish it out, unsure what to do with it. I almost want to make myself eat it as some kind of penance. In the end, I can't make up my mind so I dump it back in my locker.

My feet feel heavy as I walk down the corridor to class. They don't seem to want to be pulled off the floor and into steps. If I didn't know better, I'd swear the lino has been replaced by Velcro. I'm vaguely aware of people staring at me as I pass them, but I can't remember why I cared about that before. They could be replaced with smiley-face helium balloons and I probably wouldn't notice the difference.

I sit down at the front of the room in English class and take out my lined refill. It probably looks like I'm being extremely studious, but instead I draw a picture of a hand holding a marble. Well, that's what it was supposed to be, but it looks more like a grape balanced on top of a bunch of bananas. My art skills aren't helped much by my broken hand.

Halfway through the class, my English teacher appears beside my desk and picks up my refill. She looks at it and a little frown line pops up between her eyebrows, just above her glasses. I can't even be bothered to make up an excuse. I just stare at her shoes. They're black platform things with silver studs in them. Very un-teacher-like.

She sighs. Her hand hovers over mine for a second, then

she changes her mind and gives me back my refill.

Even after that I don't start working. I add shading to the hand/bananas. I couldn't tell you the topic of the class if I tried.

There seems to be a consensus among the teachers not to tell me off today. I do no work, which must be very obvious, but none of them says anything or calls on me to answer questions. They do all give me their own versions of awkward sympathy smiles. My maths teacher even goes so far as to pat me on the shoulder. I flinch away from her and she doesn't try again.

At lunch, I can't face going up to the common room, so I head outside instead. I can feel people looking at me as I cross the sports field, but I keep my head down and they lose interest.

I sit down, cross-legged, on the ground behind the gym. It's cold here, as the building blocks out the sunlight, and there's a composty smell coming from under the trees. At least there's no one to stare at me, though.

I take out my lunch and lay it on my knees but make no move to start eating. My eyes have gone on protest and refuse to stay open. I lean my head on my hands. If I just fall asleep for a couple of minutes I'll feel better, I'm sure of it. My cell phone buzzes in my pocket. I fish it out. *Mikecell Calling.*

I have to choke down a bad taste in my mouth. My hand hovers over the reject-call button, then I remember his threat and answer it. I hold the phone to my ear but don't say anything. I can hear him breathing, but it's soft, not exaggerated.

"I saved your life," he says. His voice is really quiet. I have to strain to understand him. "He would have killed you."

I shake my head, rattling the phone. "I'm not going to thank you." I swallow. My throat aches as I do.

"What?" He sounds breathy, like I've startled him.

I realise he may not have meant for me to hear him. I force myself to continue anyway. "For saving my life. I'm not going to thank you."

He doesn't answer.

"I would have rather ..." I trail off and rub my forehead.

He sighs. "I thought I was helping."

I close my eyes. There were other ways, I want to say.

I count his breaths. They're faster than mine, like he's been running.

He coughs then clears his throat. "If I call when you get home, will you answer?"

I shake my head. I'm about to say no, then I hear his voice in my head: *"Ignore me and you'll see how sick I can be"*.

"Yes," I say, before I can think about it. I go cold as I do.

"Okay." He hangs up.

I listen to the beeping on the line for a moment, before I turn off my phone. My chest and throat do a little spasm, making a sob come out of my mouth. I dump the phone on the grass next to me, then squeeze my eyes shut and cover my face.

I take some slow deep breaths. It makes me dizzy. I have this weird feeling that I'm being watched. My skin prickles, like someone's trying to pull all the hairs off my arms using only static electricity. I resist the urge to open my eyes and look around.

Someone clears their throat. I jump and look up. Jacob's standing next to me, or over me would be more accurate.

"Hey." He shifts his feet.

I hold his gaze for a second then look away.

"You okay?" He sounds uncomfortable. His voice comes out with a laugh in it.

I stare in the other direction. "I'm fine."

He scoffs. "Why do girls do that?" He pauses. I'm pretty sure he wants me to ask "what", but I don't bite. When I don't say anything, he sits down next to me.

"I'm fine, *I'm fine*, really I'm *fine*." He mimics a high-pitched voice, then laughs at his own joke.

I keep my head turned away. I'm annoyed at myself, but I think I'm going to cry. Jacob rummages in his pocket. He pulls out a pack of cigarettes then holds them out, offering me one. When I ignore him, he lights one up himself.

"Come on, Kelsey." He sighs.

I keep ignoring him.

"Kels," he nudges my side, "Kels Bells," another nudge, "Kelly Belly."

I turn and glare at him. He laughs and blows smoke over me. His teeth flash white against his skin as he does. He has beautiful teeth. I run my tongue over my own. Mine aren't awful, they just don't make a nice crisp line like Jacob's. His sit in his mouth like a row of corn kernels on the cob.

I cough as the smoke hits the back of my throat. "You shouldn't smoke."

He shrugs and coughs himself. I don't know how he manages to play rugby after smoking. I'm barely fit enough to play soccer and my lungs are healthy. I take the cigarette out of his hand and stub it out. He stares at me, his face like a startled possum, then he laughs. He pulls out another cigarette and lights it.

I blush and look down. I unwrap my lunch to give myself

something to do.

When Tash and I were little, we made a pact that when we grew up, I'd marry Jacob and she'd marry Pete, so we could be sisters. Even though Jacob's a bit of a dick, I still probably got the better end of that deal.

Jacob pulls at the grass beside him. "Why're you hanging out back here? You like the smell of rotting leaves?"

"Where else am I supposed to go? It's not like anyone will want to hang out with me now." I squint my eyes up, irritated at myself for having said that. "What do you want?"

He shrugs and throws a handful of grass at me.

I flinch away as the pieces scatter over me. "Shouldn't you be playing rugby or something?"

He leans back against the wall of the gym, closing his eyes. "I skipped practice."

I stare at him, then shake my head. "Well, could you maybe 'skip practice' somewhere else?"

Jacob laughs in a way that tells me he's not going anywhere. I make a noise in the back of my throat, and get up to leave myself.

Jacob jumps up and follows me. "Where're you going?"

I shrug without looking back.

"Kel-sey," he calls my name in a sing-song way that reminds me of Mike's dad.

I spin around to face him. "Can you please just piss off?"

He grins. "You forgot your phone." He holds it out to me.

"Thanks." I reach out for my phone, but Jacob pulls it back. He grins and spins it in his hand.

My whole body seems to swell up and burst into angry words. "What is your problem?" I scream. "Why can't you just leave me alone?" If I could run away, I would. Instead I turn, and make a rather pathetic attempt at limping off.

"Kelsey, wait."

I don't look back. Of course it takes Jacob only a few seconds to circle around me, and block my way.

He holds out the phone. "Here." His face has gone all serious and apologetic. It makes him look five years old. I look at the phone and something wells up inside me. I grab it and throw it into the bushes. Then I stand there, feeling childish and stupid.

Jacob looks from the bushes to me. "Sorry," he says. I can tell he's not entirely sure what he's done wrong.

"Whatever."

"About the party too. I'm sorry."

I shake my head and look away. Jacob's still standing in my way, otherwise I'd have walked off by now. I think he knows that.

He shrugs. "It wasn't even about you. We were trying to piss off Mike."

"Yeah? Well, it worked." I stare Jacob straight in the eye. "He was so pissed off he beat me up."

His eyes flicker away from mine.

I swallow. My mouth feels really dry. "Is it you?" My voice comes out as a whisper.

"What?" Jacob frowns.

"The phone calls. Is it you?"

Jacob shakes his head. "I don't know what ..."

I can tell from his face he has no idea what I'm talking about. I push past him. He could easily stop me, but he lets me go. I can feel him watching me as I walk away.

I sit down, taking my place at the front desk of geography class. I spent the rest of the lunch hour hanging out in the girls' toilets. Two of the sinks were blocked, this time with what looked like a combination of hair and toilet paper, and one of them was filled with a mysterious grey liquid. Not really an enjoyable place to be, but at least it was quiet.

I look up as Tash sits down next to me.

She smiles and hands me my phone. "Jacob said to give you this."

"Thanks." I take the phone and slide it into my pocket.

Tash doesn't look anything like Jacob. Most people wouldn't pick them as brother and sister, let alone twins. Tash is petite and dark. She has this tightly wound curly hair that she holds back with a scarf, and her nose is little and turns up at the end. Kind of like a pug. Except, a really beautiful, glamorous pug. Okay, so not really like a pug at all.

Tash starts to unpack her books. Her eyes flick from my face to the cast on my wrist. Then she catches my eye and smiles. "Got any plans for this weekend, Kels?"

I stare down at the desk in front of me and shake my head. "No." Then I remember. "Oh my God, Ben's fight is this weekend."

She frowns. "Ben?"

"Pete's friend – our flatmate. He's got a kickboxing match on Saturday. I can't believe I forgot."

"That sounds like ..." Tash wrinkles her nose, "fun."

I laugh. "I know." I glance around the classroom. "How come you're not sitting with what's-his-face?" I nod my head in the direction of the guy Tash has been pining after for the last few weeks.

Tash looks over at him. "Danny? He turned out to be a twat." She smiles. "I'm happily single, thank you very-"

Tash is interrupted by Mr Humphries walking in. He gives me his version of a sympathetic gesture - a little nod and no-eye-contact smile - then starts the lesson.

Tash sits with me in history class too. "So, I suppose you won't be coming back to the soccer team this year?" She gestures to my cast, then blushes and looks away.

I shrug. "No big loss." I laugh. "To me or the team."

Tash glances up at me. "You're not that bad."

I love the qualified compliment. I'm not good, but I'm not that bad.

I shake my head. "I never wanted to play in the first place. It was Mum's idea." My voice cracks on that last bit. I swallow, and look down at my hands.

Tash touches my arm. "I'm sorry about your mum, Kels."

I nod, but don't look up.

Our history teacher arrives and launches into a lecture about Medieval England before she's even properly in the door. I stare at the clock and watch the minutes tick by.

As soon as class is finished, I rush off to my locker. Tash follows after me.

"So ..." Her forehead creases up as she struggles to find something to say. "Can anyone come to the fight this weekend?"

"What?" I shift my books under my arm, trying to get a hand free to open my locker.

"Your flatmate's fight. Can I come?"

I turn and stare at her. "Why?"

She shrugs. "I don't know-"

"Are you a kickboxing fan?"

She shrugs again. "Not really. But–"

"Then why on earth would you want to come? *I* don't even want to go." I turn back to my locker and try to open it. The door jams, and I make a rather pathetic attempt at shaking it.

Tash looks down at her feet. "I don't. I was just trying to be nice."

I sigh and lean my forehead against the locker. Broken-Kelsey-Syndrome again. I turn back to Tash. "That's sweet of you, but you don't have to." I gesture to my face. "You don't have to hang out with me just because you feel sorry for me."

Tash frowns. "Is that what you think of me?"

"I–"

"We've been friends for years. You act like that was nothing." She shakes her head and blinks. I realise she's about to cry, and my stomach drops. I reach out to touch her arm, but she pulls away.

"I'm sorry," I say. "I didn't mean ..."

She rubs her head. "Kels, you've got to stop acting like everyone hates you."

I shake my head and stare down at the floor. Tash shifts beside me. I open my mouth to say something, then just shrug instead.

She sighs and her voice goes quiet. "It really hurt when you chose Mike over me."

I look up at her. "Tash, I–" I start to shake my head, but she cuts me off.

"I mean, I get it now, but ..." Her eyes flick over the bruises on my face.

"I didn't ..." The words disappear in my throat. I had no

idea she felt like that. It always seemed like she was the one who pulled away from me.

"You just let him push me away." She shakes her head. "And it sucked!" She stares at me for a moment, then starts to laugh.

I laugh too. "It did suck," I say.

She hesitates, then wraps her arms around me. "Don't you ever do that again!"

I hug her back. "I'm sorry," I say into her shoulder.

She nods, then giggles. "Jake said we should set you up with Billy, then you'd forget all about Mike."

"Billy? Ew!" I shake my head. "God. That's such boy-logic. It's like Ben. He thinks he can solve my 'anorexia' by feeding me." I try to make air quotes around "anorexia", but with my books in one hand, and the cast on the other, it doesn't really work.

"You're anorexic?" Tash pulls back to look at me. Her eyes shoot to a whole new level of wideness.

I laugh. "No, of course not." I give my locker door a fierce yank, and it finally opens. A piece of paper falls out on to the ground. Tash picks it up.

Her eyes flicker from me to the page. "Did you write this?"

"What is it?"

She hands me the paper. In the middle of it there's one, typed line:

DO YOU THINK MIKE SCREAMED?

I fold in on myself, my spine bending like a paper clip. I squeeze the sides of my head with my hands. The pressure hurts but I squeeze harder.

Tash takes the paper back from me. "Who would write this?"

I shake my head. On the back of the page there's a splattering of red marks, like someone dropped it in tomato sauce.

Tash looks at me, then glances around at the other people in the form room. I stare at her shoes. They're green, but the toes are cracked with a web of white lines where the vinyl's split. They blur in and out of focus.

"Kelsey? Come on. Get up." Tash pulls on my arm, until I stand.

"How did he get in my locker?" I ask. I'm not sure if I'm asking Tash, or just the universe in general.

It's Tash that answers. "I don't know." She shakes her head. "Come on. Let's get out of here."

"I thought ..." I don't finish that. Someone brushes against me as they walk past, and I jump like they've hit me.

Tash puts her arm around me and negotiates the crowd. "Come on." She half leads me, half pulls me towards the sick bay.

Miss Bently calls Pete. I can hear her talking to him in the other room. Tash sits with me on one of the bumble bee beds. I've got cold sweats suddenly. I keep trying to wipe my face, but just end up bumping it with the heel of my cast.

Tash passes me some tissues. I run them over my face, but it feels more like I'm smearing the sweat around rather than wiping it off.

Tash looks back down at the page from my locker, and

shakes her head. "I can't believe anyone would pretend they beat up Mike."

I stare down at my lap and make a line across the back of my hand with my fingernail.

"Kels?" Tash leans forward to look at me. I keep staring at my hands. "Kels? You don't think they really-"

I look up at her. "I don't know. I really don't know."

Tash fiddles with her hair. "If you do know something," she speaks slowly, measuring each word, "you should go to the police. I'd come with you if you wanted."

I just shake my head. Tash's eyes narrow. She stares at me as though she thinks she'll be able to read my thoughts just by looking at me. I can't meet her eye. I don't know why I don't just tell her the truth anyway. It would probably be a relief to tell someone.

"Tash-" I'm interrupted by Miss Bently coming in. She sits down on the bed next to me. I'm surprised the bed doesn't collapse with the weight of all three of us.

"Pete said he'd get his flatmate to come get you." She rubs my shoulder. "How are you feeling?"

I shake my head again.

"Look at this." Tash shoves the paper at Miss Bently.

I try to grab it back, but Miss Bently's already read it - I can tell from the way her mouth is pulling down and her forehead has turned into a valley of frowns.

"It's nothing," I say. "Just a stupid joke."

Miss Bently looks up at me. "Kelsey ..." She seems unsure how to finish. She tries to put her arm around me, but I flinch away.

I take the piece of paper out of Miss Bently's hands and screw it up. "It's nothing," I say again. I stare at the ball of paper in my hands. If I had a cigarette lighter I'd burn it. Then maybe the whole thing would go away.

Miss Bently touches my shoulder. "Do you want to talk about it?" When I don't say anything she sighs. "I know how close you and Mike were–"

"I hate him." It pops out before I can stop it. I look up at Miss Bently and register the shock on her face, before she melts her expression back into the listening one.

"I mean …" I falter, not really sure what I mean. "I loved him but when he hit me, I hated him." I close my eyes. Tash shifts beside me.

"Listen to me." Miss Bently's voice is firm. "What you're feeling is normal–"

"No, it isn't," I say. "None of this is normal." My heart starts to pound again. "Just … just leave me alone." I lean forward and rest my head against my knees. If I sit like this for long enough, maybe a cocoon will form around me and turn me into something else. I don't know that I'm keen on the idea of a butterfly, but maybe a bee. If nothing else, I could sting people.

Miss Bently rubs my back. I hunch up my shoulders to try and communicate with her that I want her to go away, without actually having to say anything. My ribs are hurting and I can't breathe properly, but I don't want to sit up until I know that I'm alone. Eventually I have to, though. It's either that or suffocate.

"Here." Miss Bently holds out her hand.

I stare at it, wondering what she wants. When I don't move, she pries the used tissues and ball of paper out of my hands. She drops the tissues in the bin as she goes back into her office. She keeps hold of the ball of paper.

I don't look at Tash. She's staring at me, though; I can feel it.

"It's not Jacob," she says.

"Huh?"

She looks up at me. "The note. It's not Jacob, if that's what you're thinking. He wouldn't do that. I know him better than anyone, and I know he wouldn't."

I roll my tongue around the inside of my mouth and nod. She doesn't need to tell me. I could tell from Jacob's face when I asked him that he didn't know anything about it.

We both glance up as the door opens. Aiden comes in.

"Hey." He shifts his weight.

My stomach drops when I see Pete's sent him and not Ben. I can't help myself, but I burst into tears. Aiden's eyes go wide and they flick around the room, looking for something else to focus on. I stand up and try to stop crying. Aiden reaches out to me. I lean against him, then realise he was probably going for a pat on the shoulder not a hug, but it's too late. His shirt smells of lemon soap powder and coffee. I can feel the bones of his back under my hands. He falters. He moves as if to pull away from me, then changes his mind and gives me a gentle pat on the back. It's the way I would hold a child whose nappy needed changing.

I pull away from Aiden and stare at the floor. "I'm sorry," I mumble. "I don't know why I did that."

"Yeah, well ..." He touches the front of his shirt where I've left a wet blotch. He rubs his fingers together, and his face screws up in disgust before he catches himself. "Pete told me to come get you." He shifts again and stares at the ceiling, then he glances at Tash and seems surprised.

"This is Tash," I say. I don't look at her, but gesture towards her. Aiden raises his hand in greeting. Tash mumbles a hello.

I'm glad that Aiden doesn't talk much. He doesn't ask me what happened. Instead, he nods then just stands there. After a second I realise this is probably his way of asking me if I'm ready to go.

I pick up my bag and follow him out.

"Good luck with your fight," Tash calls after us.

Aiden glances at me and frowns.

"She thinks you're Ben," I say.

Aiden's mouth twists up into a smirk. I smile too, at the image of Aiden kickboxing. I suppose it wouldn't be so bad if he was fighting someone just as scrawny as him. Or if he was fighting me. We might even be well matched.

He drops me outside home. The phone rings before I can even get the door open. I have this stupid moment where I think the caller must be watching me, and has phoned because he knows I'm home. Then I realise he's probably been calling from the moment school finished, and I just haven't been here to hear it. It's stopped ringing by the time I get properly inside. I dial the call minder number and brace myself for the messages. The computerised voice tells me I have four new ones. I hold my finger above the delete button, ready to punch it if it gets too much for me.

I let my hand drop to my side as I hear the start of the first message. "This is a message for Pete Morgan. My name's Jackie, I'm calling from the Thompson Rest Home."

My chest goes tight as she says that. I press my thumb nail into my thigh to distract myself from the worst-case-scenario parade playing in my head. She dithers, explaining they've "lost track" of Pete's work number. I just want her to get to the point of why she's calling. Finally she does.

"Unfortunately, your mother had a fall this morning."

I press my hand against my mouth.

"She's been assessed by the doctor, and she's fine, but she's been asking to see you. I'll keep trying to reach you on this number, but please give me a call when you get this message. Thanks."

I run through the other messages. They're all from the home. I start to search for Pete's work number. I can't find it, until I remember he stuck it on the fridge for me. I'm about to call him, when the phone rings again.

I pick it up. "Jackie?"

There's a pause, then he speaks. "No, it's me."

I bite down on my lip, and close my eyes.

"I ... You said I could call?" His voice rises up. He sounds anxious.

"Why?" The word comes out clipped, as I let the anger slide out.

"Huh?"

"Why did you ..." I stop as my voice fails me. "You said you were trying to help, so why the hell would you put that fucking note in my locker? I hate you, you know that? I hate you, you sick bastard!" I scream the last part, retching the words from my throat. It burns as I do, like my voice is toxic.

"But–"

I slam the phone down, cutting him off.

13

Chapter Thirteen

Mum's not in the visitors' room when Pete and I get to the home. The nurse takes us through to her bedroom. I hate the rooms here. They're really tiny and dark, and make me feel like I've stepped into a rest home from the seventies. Actually, I probably have. I think this home has been around at least that long, and while the main areas have been redone, the individual rooms have only been touched up. It's like putting a band aid on an operation wound.

Mum's room has dark green wallpaper with little white diamonds on it. There's a wooden desk attached to the wall, which folds out, so you can sit and write letters. I'm not sure I get the point of that. If the other residents are as out of it as Mum, then letter writing is going to be a bit beyond them. The whole thing makes Mum's hospital-type bed look like something out of the space age.

"Hi, Mum." Pete sits on the side of Mum's bed.

I sit down in the chair. Mum's got a bandage on her arm and another one on her forehead. She quite pale, but I think that's more from shock than sickness.

She peers at us. She looks like she thinks she should know

who we are, but I don't think she does.

"It's me, Pete. And Kelsey." Pete gestures towards me.

Mum frowns as she puzzles over that. "I have a son named Pete," she says eventually, then she loses interest in us. She picks at a freckle on her arm.

Pete sighs and rubs his face. I sink back into the chair. There isn't much else we can say.

After a while, Pete raises his eyebrows at me, and we stand up to go.

I lean over to kiss Mum goodbye. I don't know if it's a good idea, since she doesn't even know who I am, but it's instinctual.

"I love you, Mum," I say.

She catches my face in her hands and stares at me. "Kelsey?" She frowns and runs her fingers over my black eye. "What happened? Did someone hit you?"

My chest tightens and starts to hurt. I swallow and Pete shakes his head.

"No, Mum," I say, and force myself to smile. "I just had an accident."

Mum responds with a smile of her own, but her eyes are filling up. She pats the side of my face. "Love you, darling," she says.

I take a breath and gently peel her hands back from my face.

I wait while Pete goes to talk to the nurse. He lowers his voice, so I can't hear what he's saying. Instead I watch as he rubs his hand over his temple again and again, until it seems like he'll wear a hole through his skin. The nurse pats him on the shoulder, which reminds me of the sympathy gestures the teachers gave me at school. There's something about them that communicates not sympathy, but a desire to look caring without actually getting involved.

Pete stops when we get to the car. He doesn't unlock the doors but just stares at me. I think he might be about to cry, and I have no idea how to deal with that. But he doesn't end up crying. He just looks up at the sky then tries to get in the car before he realises he hasn't unlocked it.

"Shit." He fumbles with his keys then finally manages to open the door.

I walk around to the passenger's side and climb in beside him. He doesn't say anything, just starts up the car and takes off.

I blow my breath out onto the window beside me and draw a pattern with my finger tip. It's supposed to be abstract but it starts to look like a flower with pointy petals, so I try to make it that. Of course, when I do, it stops looking like a flower and goes back to being abstract.

Pete glances over at me. "Don't do that." He clicks his tongue. "I'll have to wash that off now." He glares out the windscreen and shakes his head.

I drop my hand to my side and lean my head against the window. My hair sticks to the moisture from my breath. "Ben's fight is this weekend," I say.

"Yeah?" Pete glances at me. "I'd forgotten about that."

"Yeah, me too." I fiddle with my earring. "I think we should throw him a party or something."

Pete doesn't say anything. I look over at him to make sure he's listening. He taps his fingers against the steering wheel, and his eyes narrow.

"After his fight, I mean."

Pete sighs and rubs his head. "Why?"

"Because if he loses, he'll need cheering up, and if he wins, he'll want to celebrate."

Pete frowns. He touches the back of his head, then drops his hand to the wheel. He's been doing that a lot lately. I think it's because he's just noticed his hair's thinning. He got it cut really short last time he went to the hairdressers, and he's started growing one of those designer-stubble beards to compensate.

He closes his eyes for a second and swallows. "Yeah, all right. We'll do that."

Ben's already home when we get there. He's sitting on the couch, with his feet up, watching a *Friends* re-run.

"Pete and I are throwing you a party," I say.

"What?" Ben looks from me to Pete.

"All her idea," Pete says. He gets a can of Coke from the fridge and goes upstairs.

Ben moves so I can sit next to him. He scratches at a spot on the couch cushion with his fingernail. I grab a glass of water from the kitchen and slip my shoes off first, then sit down with my feet curled up underneath me.

Ben pokes my foot with his finger. "So?"

"After your fight. You'll need cheering up if you lose." I bite my lip to stop from smiling. Ben looks hurt, then realises I'm laughing at him and pushes my shoulder.

"Who says I'm going to lose?" He grins at me.

I shrug. "You'll want to celebrate if you win, so either way."

Ben chuckles. "Little madam," he mutters.

"What was that?" I try to look stern, but I can't stop myself from laughing.

"You heard me." He grins.

I kick Ben's thigh. His eyes shoot open as he laughs. I kick at him again, but he grabs my feet before I touch him.

"Don't!" I squeal as he tickles me. I bat him away with my non-cast arm.

"This is what you get for kicking me."

I scream and laugh at the same time.

Ben shushes me. "Quiet! You'll get 'Dad' down here."

It takes me a second to realise he's talking about Pete. I giggle at the thought of Pete coming to tell us off, then scream again as Ben tickles me.

"Shhh!" Ben tries to put his hand over my mouth. I grab a handful of his hair and give it a tug.

"Ow!" He laughs and winds my hair around his hand.

"You wouldn't!" I try to grab his wrist. He ducks out of my way. "No, Ben, don't!"

He grins and reaches out to tickle me again.

I dodge him, but my side twists, making my ribs burn. I gasp and clutch at my chest.

"Shit, are you okay?" Ben's face flips into panic. He pats my arm as if checking for injuries.

"I'm fine." I smile. "Just a twinge."

"I'm sorry. This was stupid. I shouldn't have ..." He shakes his hand, trying to unwind my hair from it. The ends catch on his watch.

"No, it's all good." I giggle.

Ben struggles, trying to free my hair from his watch. "No, it's not. You're hurt and ... What the hell is wrong with your hair?"

I laugh and reach up to help him. "I know. It does this." I

have to lean right in close to him to be able to try and detach my hair without pulling it.

He swallows. "Are you sure you're okay?"

"I'm fine. Honestly." I look up. I blush as realise how close I am to Ben.

His face goes serious. He leans towards me.

We both jump at the sound of someone clearing their throat. I look up. Aiden's standing in the doorway. I feel my cheeks colour and I pull away from Ben, even though it yanks my hair. Ben frees the last of it from his watch. I feel like I've done something wrong, but I'm not sure what.

Ben glances at me then rubs his hand over his lip. "I better go train," he says, then stands up and goes out to the garage.

"Feeling better, then?" Aiden smirks at me.

I glare at him while trying not to laugh. "Shut up."

After a minute I hear Ben start hitting the punching bag. I chew on my fingernail and try not to think about him. I suddenly feel really sore. Play-fighting maybe wasn't my best idea, considering how covered in bruises I am.

The phone rings, and Aiden goes to pick it up. "Hello?"

I wait for him to slam the phone down, but instead he looks over at me. "Yeah, just a second." He puts his hand over the receiver. "It's for you. The police."

I go cold. I feel like the blood in my veins is turning me to stone. "What do they want?"

Aiden holds the phone out to me instead of answering.

I get up and take it from him, though it takes me a second before I can hold it to my ear. "Hello?"

"Kelsey Morgan?"

"Yes?" I have to clear my throat and say that again to make it understandable.

"This is Detective Jenkins, I interviewed you in the hospital?"

I think she wants some confirmation that I remember her, but I don't say anything.

After a pause she continues. "We'd like you to come down to the station. There are a few more questions we'd like to ask you."

"About what?"

"We'll explain all that when you get here. If you could be here in fifteen minutes?"

Just like in the hospital she's asking me questions that aren't really questions.

"Yeah, sure," I say, only because I know I don't really have a choice.

I hang up the phone and yell for Pete. Aiden goes into the living room and turns the TV on. He doesn't ever seem to just watch TV. He always glares at it. At the moment he looks like his forehead's about to crack, he's frowning so hard. I look up as Pete comes down the stairs. His eyes are bloodshot, so he's either been crying or I've woken him up. I pretend I don't notice and tell him about the police calling.

He rubs at his temple again as he listens. "Yeah, okay, come on, let's go." Pete grabs his coat, but I dawdle until he looks at me. "What are you doing? Come on."

I pull at the hem of my dress. "Can't you say you won't let them talk to me? I mean, you're my guardian, kind of ..."

Pete pinches the bridge of his nose. "It doesn't work like that, Kel. Anyway, you're seventeen and it's not like you're in trouble ..." He trails off. "Are you? God, Kel, what have you done now?"

"Nothing!" I shriek at Pete, which is unfair of me. But

then again, it's unfair of him to assume I've done something wrong.

"For God's sake! I cannot deal with another one of your tantrums right now."

I take a breath and try to think of something reasonable to say, but it's too late for that. Pete's already pissed at me.

He shakes his head. "Look, you don't have a choice. Just go get in the car or I'll make you walk there."

I rub my tongue against my teeth and press my lips together to stop from saying anything. I'm not sure how Pete thinks that's going to work. If he tried to make me walk, I'd just sit on the doorstep and refuse to move.

I fold my arms across my chest. "Car it is," I say. Pete follows me outside.

Detective Jenkins shows me into a little room at the back of the police station. I'm starting to wonder if Pete's right. Maybe I have done something wrong. This really feels like I'm in trouble, but I can't for the life of me think what for. Maybe the packet of raisins I stole from the supermarket when I was three has finally caught up with me.

"Have a seat, Kelsey." Detective Jenkins smiles – a no-teeth smile which is less alarming than the teeth-baring one.

I try to smile back, but my mouth makes a sideways S shape instead.

She looks down at her papers. "We just wanted to check in with you to see if you remembered anything else about what happened."

"I don't."

I say it a little too quickly. Detective Jenkins glances up at me, her look sharp.

I swallow. "At least, I don't think I do."

Detective Jenkins nods and looks back down. "You may not realise you've remembered anything, but if we go through what happened again-"

"No." I surprise myself by interrupting her. A trickle of sweat creeps down the side of my face. They must make it extra hot in this room to make people feel guilty even if they're not.

Detective Jenkins' mouth pinches up into a tight little line. "I understand it's difficult for you to talk about, but-"

"Mike hit me then I blacked out, that's all I remember."

Detective Jenkins shuffles through her papers. "When we talked to you in the hospital, you said you remembered seeing someone."

I shake my head. "The guy with the beard? I'm not even sure that was real."

She produces a photo. "Was this him?"

I stare at the picture. I have no idea whether it's him or not. All I could see was his beard, and that could be just about anybody. Well, anybody with a beard, that is.

I shrug. "Maybe. I don't know. Who is he?"

"The ambulance officer who brought you in. You said in hospital that you saw someone else. Just before you passed out?"

I look down at my hands. "I don't remember."

Detective Jenkins sighs. "You said someone from the party knew Mike had hit you. Can you tell me a bit more about that?"

I shrink back into the chair and focus on sitting very still.

"I don't remember saying that." I can't look at her.

She reads over her notes. "You told us both your brother's flatmates were aware of the assault, and you thought someone from the party–"

"Your notes are wrong. I never said that." My shoulders hunch up as I try to disappear.

Detective Jenkins puts down her papers. She leans forward on her elbows and stares at me. "Kelsey, if you know something, you really need to tell me."

I lick my lips. "I don't know anything."

Detective Jenkins draws a pattern on the table top with her fingertip. "You know, I'd understand if you felt some sympathy towards the person who attacked Mike. It must have been a relief to know that Mike would never hurt you again."

"What?"

She ignores my interruption. "If, perhaps, you had discovered that it was in fact someone you knew who had–"

"It's not," I say, but again she ignores me. The back of my head starts to ache.

"If, let's say, it was someone you were very close to, maybe even someone you lived in the same house as, I could understand if you were reluctant to turn them in."

"Stop it!" I clench my hands to stop them shaking. "I don't know anything. I don't know who beat up Mike, and you know what? I'm not even sure I care."

Detective Jenkins rubs her tongue over her teeth. She studies my face. "I see."

We sit in silence.

"Can I go now?" I ask. "Unless you're going to charge me or something?"

Detective Jenkins sighs. "Of course. You're free to go."

I stand up, but she puts out her hand to stop me. "This is my direct dial number." She writes a number on the back of a business card. "I want you to call me if you change your mind." She holds out the card. I stare at it, then take it and put it in my pocket. It's easier than arguing.

She calls out to me as I reach the door.

"Kelsey?"

I look back.

"We'll be in touch." She gives me a tight smile.

I'm turning away from my locker when Tash calls out to me. She comes across the form room, pushing a boy in front of her. He's gangly-looking, almost like his elbows bend the wrong way.

He looks embarrassed. It crosses my mind that Tash might be about to try and set us up, and that makes me want to run.

"Hi," I say. The word comes out elongated and weird.

Tash stops in front of me. "Adam has something he wants to say to you."

I turn to the guy. "I'm guessing you're Adam?"

He nods and scowls at his feet.

"Go on." Tash jabs him in the ribs.

Adam rolls his eyes. "I put that note in your locker. I got the combination from the office."

Tash jabs him in the ribs again.

"I'm sorry," he mumbles, then turns to Tash. "Can I go now?"

She sighs. "Off you go."

"Wait."

Adam starts to leave, but I call after him. He turns back to me, looking for all his worth like a sulky three-year-old.

I look him the eye. "The phone calls." I lower my voice. "Is that you too?"

He frowns and shakes his head. "Look, I just put the note in your locker because Billy dared me to. That's all."

He's not as easy to read as Jacob. I can't tell if he's telling the truth. Even if he is, that poses another problem. If Billy dared him to do it, is Billy making the calls?

Adam shifts his feet. "Now can I go?"

Tash nods then turns back to me as he goes. "Jacob heard Billy talking about it yesterday."

"Did Jacob make him come and apologise?" I ask.

Tash smiles. "No. I did."

I shake my head. I can't imagine having enough power to make anyone do anything, let alone make them apologise when they don't want to.

"Thanks," I say.

We have assembly first period. I lean my head down on my hands during announcements and wonder if anyone would mind if I fell asleep. As long as I stayed upright, instead of toppling over onto the person next to me, probably no one would notice. Actually, the girl next to me seems to have her own problems. She keeps fiddling with her earring. Her earlobe looks infected. The silver stud has a red, scabby halo surrounding it. It makes me want to rip out my own earrings and disinfect everything in sight.

I realise I'm staring and force myself to look back at the stage. The light keeps catching on the thick lenses of the principal, Miss Borowitz's, glasses. It sends rainbows of colour darting across the side of her face. I wonder if she can see when that happens, or if everything dissolves into a multi-spectrum glare.

I glance over to the clock near the door. My breath catches as I notice someone standing by it. Someone in police uniform. I try not to stare at her, but I can't help it. She scans the crowd. Her eyes brush over me, but I think she knows exactly where I am.

I tune in to what Miss Borowitz is saying. "Now, Detective Jenkins would like to speak to you about the recent assault on two of our pupils."

Detective Jenkins comes forward. I can feel students' eyes flick towards me, then slide away again. Before I think about it, I stand up. The girls on either side of me shift and stare. I falter, then edge my way along to the end of the row, out into the aisle. The carpet's come unstuck on the stairs and my foot catches in the cave-like pocket it's created. I stumble, nearly falling, and little fibres of brown carpet wool come loose as I move my foot. They float up into the air before sinking again. Detective Jenkins hasn't spoken yet. I think she's standing there watching me leave.

I pass Mr Humphries on my way out of the hall. He follows me. I shake my head, trying to communicate that I don't want to talk, but that doesn't deter him. He moves in close to me, as if he might pat me on the shoulder, but then he doesn't; he just stands there. I step back, trying to reassert my personal space.

He steps forward, missing my hint that I need room. I have to crane my neck up to look at him.

"This must be very difficult for you," he says.

"Yeah." I back away and break eye contact.

He still doesn't get it. He steps forward again. "You know, I always thought you and Mike were an odd couple."

"What?" I look back at Mr Humphries.

"You could have done a lot better. I always thought that." He smiles, and I feel an icky squirm inside me. I step backwards again, but my back grazes the wall. I glance behind me. Mr Humphries steps forward and I find myself trapped.

"Mr Humphries ..." I'm not sure what to say next. My shoulders hunch up and I stare at the ground. I press my palm against the wall. It's pitted and dented, like pock-marked skin. I feel it leaving an imprint on my palm.

"I don't think you value yourself enough, Kelsey." Mr Humphries falters. He looks up as the bell for the end of the period goes. "I hope you'll think about that." He smiles again, then just hovers. I wonder if he's waiting for me to say something. The only thing I can think of is telling him he creeps me out.

He turns away as students pour into the corridor. He glances back at me, but doesn't add anything else. He gives another smile, but this one is crossed with a frown. He pats me on the shoulder and walks away.

I see Tash waiting for me. She comes over.

"I saw you leave." She gestures towards the hall.

"Yeah. What did they say?"

She wrinkles her nose. "Nothing. Just warnings about safety and all that." She stares after Mr Humphries. "What did he want?"

"Nothing ... I don't know." I shake my head.

Tash narrows her eyes. Her voice comes out measured. "I'd avoid being alone with him if I was you."

"Why? Because he's weird?"

Tash makes a noise in the back of her throat. "Let's just say, if he hadn't left his last school he would have been fired."

I roll my eyes. "You shouldn't listen to rumours, Tash."

"I'm serious." She touches my arm. "You should be careful."

"People just say that because he's got no idea about personal space. He gave me a lift home and it was fine." I swallow as I say that. My skin starts to crawl.

"He gave you a lift home?" Tash frowns.

"Yeah," I say. "It was all normal, except ..."

Tash stares at me. "Except?"

I shake my head. "It's nothing. He just said something creepy, that's all."

"Like?"

"We should get to class." I turn away. I sigh as I realise it's geography. Tash follows after me, but she doesn't say anything.

I take my usual seat at the front of class and Tash sits down across the aisle.

Mr Humphries comes in, starting the lesson. I flick through my book, looking at notes I don't remember taking. There's absolutely no way I'm going to be able to pass the exam at the end of this year. I've probably already failed anyway. I don't think I've got enough credits, even if I pass every assessment from now on.

Mr Humphries has stopped talking and the class is quiet. At least, as quiet as our class ever gets. A couple of people are still talking. Someone at the back gives a hyena-type laugh and is shushed by a look from Mr Humphries.

I look around to see what everyone else is doing, but I can't tell. Tash is writing something in purple pen on yellow lined paper. I'd try to read over her shoulder, but the colours make me feel ill. My focus drifts, and I read the fire evacuation notice by the door.

"Kelsey?"

I look up. Mr Humphries is standing by my desk. I hadn't even noticed he was there.

He frowns as he looks down at my desk. "Do you need some help?"

I nod, and he sits down in the empty seat next to me.

He flicks my textbook open to a page with some flow-chart type diagrams and questions. "Question one." He lays a thick finger on the page next to the first question. The words on the page seem to blur in and out of focus.

Mr Humphries stares at me, waiting.

I swallow and try to concentrate. It gives me a headache.

Mr Humphries sighs. "This is revision, Kelsey. You've already learnt this."

I shrug. "I don't remember."

"Okay." Mr Humphries gets up and leans right over me. I shrink away from him, but he's a human barrier and I'm trapped. I try to concentrate on what he's saying. All I can focus on is the fact that he smells like a combination of sweat, cigarettes, and overripe bananas. I look down at the page where he's writing the answers in block capitals. His letters slope backwards, like they're about to fall over. I run my finger over them and get a feeling that's not quite déjà-vu.

The card.

"Oh my God," I say. It doesn't sound loud enough, so I say it again. "Oh my God!"

"What?" Mr Humphries sounds alarmed, but he doesn't move.

"Oh my God!" I don't seem to be capable of saying anything else. I push my chair backwards, bashing into Mr Humphries.

"What's wrong?" He holds up his hands as if in surrender, then changes his mind and reaches out to touch my shoulder.

I jerk away from him. "Don't!" I cover my face with my hands. I'm shaking so much, my whole body seems to vibrate.

He shakes his head. "Kelsey–" He reaches out again.

"Don't touch her." Tash stands up, putting herself between me and Mr Humphries. She turns to me and lowers her voice. "Did he do something to you?"

"I can't ..." I don't even know what I'm trying to say.

"What did he do?" Tash raises her voice this time, making sure everyone can hear.

I just shake my head.

Mr Humphries looks from Tash to me, his face somewhere between anger and confusion. Then the anger wins and he goes red. "Girls, sit down now."

I don't move. A nervous laugh goes up from the class. I'm surprised they're not rioting by now.

"Sit down now!" Mr Humphries goes from red to purple. A little vein in his forehead pops out.

"I have to ..." I look at Mr Humphries, and can't finish that sentence. I head for the door instead.

"Come back here!"

I ignore him and slam the door behind me. My legs go wobbly as soon as I'm out in the corridor. I lean against the wall and sink down to the floor, then cover my face with my hands. The door swings open.

"Pervert!" Tash slams the door behind her.

I stare up at her. "He knew I was at Mike's that night and–" I'm interrupted by the rest of the class dissolving into chaos. Some of the guys are chanting "Pervert" over and over. Everyone's laughing and yelling. Mr Humphries is screaming, but it barely makes a dent in the noise. He comes out into the corridor. "You two," he points his thick finger at me and Tash. "Principal's office. Now!"

Tash and I sit on the chairs in the corridor outside Miss Borowitz's office. Tash asks me what happened, a couple of times, but I ignore her. I press my lips into a thin line and stare at the wall. There's a crack running down through all the bricks. It's been filled up with grout, but that's chipping away and the crack is reappearing. Probably it will all come down in an earthquake and anyone sitting here will be crushed. Personally, I'm hoping the big one will hit in the next five minutes, or at least before Miss Borowitz gets off the phone.

I jump at the sound of Miss Borowitz's door creaking open. Paint flakes off the hinges as they move, and the whole thing is in desperate need of oil. Miss Borowitz sighs as she sees us. "Come in, girls."

I follow Tash into the office. The whole room seems thick with dust, but I think it's just that it's catching in the blinding sunlight streaming between the gap in the curtains.

I sit down in one of the chairs in front of Miss Borowitz's desk and stare at the carpet. Someone's dropped a big lump of gum on it, which has turned grey with age and dirt. I kick at it, but it's stuck fast.

"So, what's this about?" Miss Borowitz leans forward on her desk and tilts her head to the side. Her eyes flick from me to Tash. She looks like an owl when she does that, especially with the thick glasses. I half expect her to spin her head too far around to the left, but I'm glad she doesn't, as that would be more Exorcist than bird.

"Mr Humphries is sexually harassing Kelsey." Tash goes red as soon as she says that. I swallow an urge to laugh.

Miss Borowitz gives a little shake of her head. "I'm sorry?"

"I mean, he …" Tash looks at me for help.

I rub my hand across my face. I suddenly feel very cold.

"He was being inappropriate. He gave Kelsey a lift home, and he said …" Tash falters.

Miss Borowitz sighs. "Perhaps I should talk to Kelsey alone."

I love how they're talking about me as if I'm not here. Or as if they think I'm too stupid to understand. I stare at the clock as Tash leaves. It's stopped at eleven past four. The seconds hand jerks back and forth as if it's having a seizure. Watching it makes me want to twitch too. I find myself fidgeting in time with the clock's movements.

Miss Borowitz looks back at me, as Tash closes the door. "I understand you've been having a hard time lately, Kelsey?" Her voice is soft.

I nod, then have to rub my face as my eyes spill over.

"And sometimes, when we're having a hard time, we see threats when there aren't any. Do you understand what I'm saying?"

I chew on my lip. "I don't think Mr Humphries is sexually harassing me."

Miss Borowitz lets out a breath and leans back in her chair. "Okay. Then can you tell me what this is about?" She gives me a little smile. She seems so relieved, I almost don't want to say anything.

"I've been getting phone calls ... and a card ... from a guy. Scary phone calls."

"Have you told the police about this?"

I shake my head. "No. I don't know, I probably should have, but I didn't." I swallow as I think of the threats. "Anyway, I was staying at Mike's one night and the guy called there. He didn't say anything, just like heavy breathing and stuff–"

"So he was calling you before Mike ..." She stops, unable to find a tactful way of saying "got the crap beaten out of him."

I look down at my hands. "Yeah, he's been calling for a while. He didn't talk at first, but then ..." I shake my head. "Anyway, Mr Humphries gave me a lift home the next day, and–"

"Mr Humphries did actually give you a lift home?" Miss Borowitz goes very still. A frown line pops up between her eyes.

"Yeah, but it wasn't like Tash said. I mean, he said some creepy things, but–"

Miss Borowitz sighs and rubs her head. "Thank you, Kelsey." She stands up and opens her door.

I don't move. "But, Miss Borowitz–"

"I'll look into this, I promise." She smiles in a tired way.

I shake my head. "But what about the phone calls? What am I supposed to do?"

She looks down at her hands. Eventually she looks up. "You need to talk to the police about that. I'm not sure there's anything I can–"

I cut her off by looking away.

"I'm sorry, Kelsey."

I shake my head and get up. My shoulder brushes against her as I walk out into the corridor. She turns her head and draws away from me, as if she thinks I'll wrinkle her clothes.

Tash is sitting on one of the chairs, waiting for me. "What'd she say?"

I suddenly feel really angry. It makes me feel like my teeth are too big for my mouth. I want to scream, or bite something, to get the feeling out. Instead I clench my jaw and walk.

Tash catches up with me. "What happened? Is she going to do anything?"

I shake my head and keep walking. When we get outside I let it out. I scream and scream until my teeth don't hurt anymore. Tash covers her mouth with her hand and backs away. She must think I've lost it, that I'll attack her next.

"She didn't even listen. I tried to tell her, and she didn't even listen." I sit down on the ground and lay my head in my hands. "I don't … I don't know what to do." I look up as the bell goes for the end of class. In a moment the whole place will be streaming with students. I look over at Tash.

She pulls her cardigan closer around herself, then crouches down next to me. "It's going to be okay, Kelsey." She reaches out to hug me.

I pull away from her. "No," I shake my head. "No, it's not." I get up and hobble away.

14

Chapter Fourteen

The rest of the day passes in a blur. Everyone stares at me, but I suppose that's to be expected. That's what happens when you lose the plot in the middle of class. It's weird. I always thought any attention would be better than being completely ignored. Now I'd do anything to go back to that. I wish I could just go home and never come back.

I'm by my locker, packing up my stuff, when Amber and Sophie come up to me. They stand way too close to me and stare at me with their unnerving, glass-like eyes.

I look from one to the other. "Yeah?" I try my best to sound assertive, but it comes out more surly than anything else.

Amber hands me a pile of books. "You left these behind."

I take the geography books from her. "Thanks, I'd forgotten about that."

They keep staring at me. If I could, I'd turn back to my locker, or walk away, but they're standing so close it's difficult for me to do anything other than just stand there. Sophie puts her head on one side as she stares. Amber rolls her labret piercing around with her tongue. I swear both of them have perfected the art of not blinking. If they'd done this a couple of months ago, I would have burst into tears. As it is, I'm beyond caring.

"For God's sake, what do you want?" I step forward, forcing them to back away.

"Is it true you got Mr Humphries fired?" Sophie asks.

I shake my head. "Who told you that?"

"Everyone's talking about it." Amber gives a little smile. One like a cat would give a half-dead bird.

"No, that's ridiculous. Miss Borowitz wouldn't even listen to me."

Amber and Sophie glance at each other.

"So you tried to get him fired?" Sophie asks.

"No!" I rub my eyes. "I didn't try to get him fired. I didn't do anything."

Amber pushes her piercing so far forward it looks like it's going to rip through her skin. "We heard he got you in the back of his car and tried to molest you." Her eyes light up as she says this.

I can't help but laugh. "That's the stupidest thing I've ever heard."

She and Sophie visibly sag. It's sick that they're so disappointed that it's not true.

"So why'd you flip out in geography?" Amber pouts in a sulky way as she speaks.

I shiver. "It doesn't matter." I start to walk away. Amber and Sophie keep pace with me, flanking my sides.

"So, none of it's true?" Sophie asks.

I shake my head. "Look, he gave me lift home, that's all. This is all so stupid."

"Wait," Amber catches my arm. "He actually did give you a lift home?"

"Yeah. So what?" I shake her hand off.

She ignores me and turns to Sophie. "Maybe he really has been suspended then."

I frown. "What? Why would he be suspended for that?"

Amber sighs, like she's being forced to explain things to a small child. "It's against school policy for teachers to give students lifts. Especially male teachers." She emphasises the last part like I'm supposed to read more into that.

I shake my head. "They wouldn't suspend him just for that, would they?" I'm not sure why I'm so worried. If he is the one making the phone calls, I don't really care what happens to him.

"Let's just say, this isn't the first time he's given someone a 'lift'." Amber makes air quotes around the word "lift".

I'm pretty sure this is like every other rumour in this school – completely blown out of proportion. But something inside me feels icky. Every rumour I've heard has also had some basis in truth.

"I have to go," I say, and I push my way through the crowd away from Amber and Sophie. They laugh as I do.

I'm halfway home before I think of looking at my geography book again. I flick it open to the page with Mr Humhpries' writing on it. Something drops in my stomach then bounces up again, like I've got a trampoline sitting at the level of my pelvis. I wish I'd kept the card so I could compare the two sets of handwriting. They looked the same to me before, but now I'm not sure. I trace the letters with my finger. Yeah, they both slope backwards, but other than that I don't know. Mr Humphries' letters are pretty straight. The Ts and Ls on the card were curvy.

I knock the book against my forehead. "Idiot, idiot, IDIOT!" I swallow as I think about it. I got him suspended and all he was trying to do was help me out.

I can't make my keys work when I get home. The phone's ringing inside, but I don't care. It doesn't matter who it is, I'm sick of phone calls. I fumble with the keys, then completely drop them. It's hurts too much to lean over to get them, so I sit down on the doorstep and pick them up from there. They've landed in a damp patch of moss. It looks like a miniature rolling hillside. I'm pretty sure I'm sitting in another patch of moss. The moisture is creeping through my dress to my skin. Either that or I've suddenly become incontinent. I'm really hoping it's the moss.

I squint as I notice something. Down the street, near the corner, is a girl. My eyesight's never been that great – things get a bit blurry in the distance – but I'm pretty sure it's Jo. I think I can even make out what she's wearing – her jeans and ballet cross-over, like that night at Mike's. She doesn't move or wave or anything, she just stands there and stares at me. I raise my hand in a half greeting, but she doesn't react.

A white car pulls up across the street. It looks more like a fridge than anything else, and I wonder where I've seen it before. Then it hits me like I just swallowed a peach pit. Mr Humphries' car. I stand up, unsure whether to run or stay and try to explain. He must be pretty pissed at me, so I'm not sure I want to stick around for that.

He doesn't get out of the car. He takes out his cell phone and dials a number. A second later, the phone inside starts ringing. It feels like my skin is trying to shrink and grow at the same time. I squeeze my hand around the keys until they cut into my palm. I swear I can see the cell phone microwaves going from his car to inside the house.

I turn and shove the keys into the lock. My hands move like I'm wearing seven pairs of gloves, and I can't make the key turn.

"Kelsey?"

I look back over my shoulder.

Mr Humphries slams his car door. "I just want to talk to you."

"Leave me alone!" I finally manage to turn the key and jerk the door open.

"Kelsey, wait!" Mr Humphries jogs across the road.

I slam the door behind me and lean against it.

Mr Humphries bangs on the door. "Open the door ... open the door now."

"Go away!" I scream.

"Kelsey, please! My wife said she'd leave me if anything like this happened again. She'll take the kids. I'll never see them again–"

"I don't care!" I scream the words, but even to me they don't sound true.

"Please! Just open the door."

I press my hand against my mouth and shake my head, even though I know he can't see me.

Mr Humphries goes quiet and I hold my breath. I think I hear him walking away, but it could just be the blood pounding in my ears.

I ease myself back and stretch up on my toes to look through the peephole. The doorknob rattles. I dive for the lock. I'm pushed backwards away from the door as it swings inwards.

"Kelsey-"

I throw my weight against the door.

Mr Humphries screams as his arm gets trapped. "Let me in, you stupid bitch."

"Just leave me alone!" I push harder against the door.

Mr Humphries makes a noise that's somewhere between a grunt and a scream. He throws himself against the door. It bursts open and I'm thrown backwards. I scramble to get up. My feet slip against the carpet.

Mr Humphries grabs my arm, pulling me up by my wrist.

"Let go of me." I try to kick Mr Humphries.

He dodges out of the way. "Listen to me, you little slut." He pulls me close to him, bending my arm so I can't move. "You're going to call Miss Borowitz and tell her you made a mistake. You're going to say I never gave you a lift home, that you made the whole thing up and then you're never going to come back to my class. Do you understand?"

I try to speak, but all that comes out is a whimper. Stupid thing is, that's what I was going to do anyway.

Mr Humphries shakes me. "Do you understand?"

"Yes." My voice comes out wobbly.

He shakes his head and leans in close to my face. "You're a stupid little bitch, you know that?"

"Yeah? Well you're a fucking psycho!" I bring my knee up and smash it into his stomach. He makes an "oophf" sound and folds in on himself. I bring my cast down over his head, then run for the door. He grabs my arm.

I let out a shriek. "Help! Help me!"

Mr Humphries claps his hand over my mouth. "Shut up! Just shut up!" His eyes dart around, like he's losing it.

The door swings open again. Jo appears. The light behind her gives her an aura, and I wonder if I'm having a religious epiphany. Her eyes and mouth go wide as she sees us.

She looks from me to Mr Humphries and her face goes hard. She backs away, pulling out her cell phone. "Let go of her or I'll call the police."

For a second Mr Humphries' fingers tighten against my face. The tips press into the flesh under my eye. His nails are stained with greasy nicotine rings. I want to scrub at my face to get the feeling off.

He lets go and backs away, holding up his hands. "This wasn't supposed to ..." He shakes his head. "It wasn't ..." He looks at me. "I just wanted to talk to you." He takes a step towards Jo. She backs away and presses buttons on the phone. He mutters to himself and edges his way out the door past Jo. He keeps his hands held up. "This wasn't supposed to happen," he says. "I didn't do anything wrong." It seems directed more towards himself than anyone else. Jo turns to watch him walk away. I hear his car start up.

I rub my hands against the sides of my face. They're cold, really cold, or my face is really hot; I can't tell. I dig in my pocket for a tissue. There's only a used one, and it tears and rolls into little worm-like fragments as I touch it. I rub it across my face and feel the fibres stick to me. The tissue comes away, limp and damp with sweat as drops bead on my lip.

Jo hovers, but she doesn't say anything. I don't look at her. Eventually she disappears into the kitchen. I lean against the wall and slide down to the floor.

Jo comes back with a cup of tea. She sits down next to me and hands me the mug. "Drink it. All of it."

I sip at the tea. My breath makes the steam puff out over my hands. A layer of moisture settles and cools on my skin. It tickles, and I have to set the mug down to rub it off. The tea tastes like she's made it with half a cup of sugar. I drink it anyway.

Jo pulls at the carpet, as if she's picking grass. Bits come off in her hand and she rubs them on her jeans, leaving streaks of fluff, like a nearly-bald cat has rubbed up against her.

She doesn't look at me. "Are you going to tell me what happened?"

I stare down at the tea. "No," I say. "I'm not."

Jo nods. "Okay."

I finish drinking and put the mug down on the floor next to me. It tips over and a trickle of liquid dribbles out onto the carpet. I rub it in with my foot.

"Look, Jo ..." I look up at her properly for the first time since she got here. There's a purply-blue bruise running down the side of her face and jawline, and there's dried blood in her hair. "Oh my God! Are you-?"

"I don't want to talk about it." She looks me in the eye. "You didn't tell me what happened and I'm not going to tell you. Okay?"

I bite my lip and nod. Jo picks at the blood. It comes off in a powder that scatters down the side of her ear.

She swallows. "Can I stay here? I know you said no before, but-"

"Yeah, of course. I'll square it with Pete." I reach out to take her hand, but she pulls away from me.

"This doesn't mean I forgive you." Her eyes are hard and cold.

I find myself nodding. "I can deal with that."

Jo and I make dinner. I figure Pete will be more willing to accept Jo if he's got a full stomach. It's easier than cooking at Mike's. There's actually food for a start. Except all the meat's frozen. I contemplate carving some frozen mince into little slices so I can fry it, but it seems like too much effort. Instead, we put some potatoes in the oven to bake and stir-fry some vegetables, bacon and cheese to go in them.

"How's school been?" I ask Jo. I hope that doesn't give her the idea to ask me the same question.

"I haven't been going."

I look over at her as she says that.

She pulls a piece of dead skin off her lip with her teeth, then wipes it away with her finger. She looks at me and shrugs. "Mum's at work all the time and Dad doesn't care. You and Mike were the only ones who did."

I swallow. I hate how I'm in the past tense for her.

"What about you?" Jo doesn't really look at me when she says that. "How've you been?"

I shake my head and that seems to be answer enough.

The food's cooked by the time Ben gets home. I'm glad he's here first. I figure he's the most likely of the three to be on my side over Jo.

I grab him before he comes into the kitchen. "Can I talk to you?"

"I was just going to–"

"Now?" I try to pull him upstairs, but stumble as I try to climb them sideways.

He grabs my waist to steady me, and we stop halfway up the stairs. "What's wrong?" He frowns. His hands don't move from my sides.

"It's okay," I say. "I mean it's not. But it is." I place

my hands on top of his, but he doesn't move them. This is probably the first time in my life I've ever been taller than him. I have to fight an urge to run my hands through his hair just to see it spring up again.

"What's wrong," he repeats. His fingers tap against my hips.

I squeeze his hands with mine. "It's Jo," I say.

"Who?"

"Mike's sister? I don't know, maybe you never met her." I shrug. "Anyway, she's here."

"What? Why?" Ben glances around, as if he thinks Jo might have snuck up behind him.

"She needs a place to stay. She's only a kid and she hasn't been going to school. She turned up here all bruised and–"

"Someone hit her?" Ben shifts his hands, making me sway towards him. I rest my arm against the wall to steady myself.

"Her dad, I think. I don't know; she didn't want to talk about it." I rub my temple as my head starts to hurt. "Anyway, can you persuade Pete to let her stay?"

Ben sighs and leans against the wall next to me. I rest my cheek against the top of his head and feel his curls brush my neck. He smells of coconuts – of my shampoo. I like that our hair smells the same. He goes very still, except his shoulders rise and fall with his breath. I reach out to take his hand, then I remember myself and pull away. He closes his eyes. I sit down on the step and lean my chin on my hand.

His Adam's apple bobs as he swallows. "We really should call the police."

I flap my arms against my sides. "Please don't. She just needs a place to stay. If we call the police now, she'll disappear. She needs to be ready."

Ben rests his head back against the wall. He mutters something to himself, but I think I catch it. "Disappear like you did."

He opens his eyes. "Okay. She can stay. I'll talk to Pete. But you need to call her mum. Make sure it's all right."

I don't know what Ben says to Pete, but he doesn't object to Jo staying. He even sets up a mattress for her on the floor of my room.

I call Jo's mum after dinner.

"Hello?" She sounds worried, even in just that word.

"Mrs Furlong? It's Kelsey."

She doesn't say anything. I'm not sure whether to wait for her to speak, or keep talking.

In the end I decide to just carry on. "Jo's here. She's going to stay with us for a while."

She still doesn't say anything.

I take a breath. "I don't think she wants to see you at the moment, so don't come over."

She makes a sound, like a sob, then takes a couple of breaths. "Look after her, won't you?" Then she hangs up.

When I get off the phone, Aiden's standing there, staring.

He gives his weird half-smile. "Eventful day?" He smirks as if this is the most hilarious thing he's ever said.

I shake my head. "You have no idea. I got a teacher suspended too."

Aiden snickers. "Yeah, that sounds about right."

He looks like he's going to say something else, but then Ben and Jo come downstairs. Ben offered to show her where the bathrooms and everything are.

Aiden glances at them and wrinkles up his nose. He goes off to his bedroom and closes the door.

It's weird sleeping in the same room as Jo again. I half expect to roll over and find Mike next to me. Jo doesn't really say much, but then again she never really did when I slept over at Mike's. Usually she'd fall asleep way before Mike or I did. Tonight I can see she's lying there awake, though.

She jerks up into sitting position as my cell phone rings. I grope across my bedside table, not wanting to put the light on, until I find the phone.

"Hello?" I whisper. I don't know why I make that a question. I know who it's going to be.

"Hi." His voice is all soft and breathy.

I glance at Jo. She stares through the dark at me, her face lit by the light from the window.

"Hold on a second?" I get up and go into the bathroom. "Who is this?"

There's a silence, then he says: "You know who this is."

I sigh. "No, I don't. Not really. I got one of my teacher's suspended today because I thought he was you. Then he assaulted me, so if you are him, I don't really want to talk to you."

"Your teacher assaulted you?"

I shake my head. "Yeah. Well, kind of. He forced his way into my house, then he grabbed me and threatened me and ..." I don't even want to think about what might have happened if Jo hadn't turned up. I swallow. "I don't know why I'm telling you, I should go to the police."

"No, you don't need to." He sounds really distant, almost like he's reading from a script. "I'll take care of it."

I stand up, jerking forward. "No, don't do that."

My hands start to sweat, making it hard to hold the phone steady. "Please, don't–"

"It's okay. It'll be okay."

"No, wait–"

He hangs up, cutting me off.

15

Chapter Fifteen

Jo sits up as I come back into the room. I turn on the light and search for my jacket.

She rubs her eyes. "What are you doing?"

"Nothing." I glance over at her. "Go back to sleep."

"But–"

"Just leave it, Jo! I don't want to talk about it."

She lies back down on the mattress. I feel bad for yelling at her, but I don't have time to explain.

Pete moved all my stuff around when he set up the mattress, so I can't find anything. Finally I spot my jacket under the bed. I search through the pockets for Detective Jenkins' number.

"Who are you calling?" Jo asks, when I start to dial.

"No one. It doesn't matter." I go back out into the bathroom.

The line rings, but no one picks up. Finally it clicks through to an answer phone.

"Fuck!" I hang up and cover my face. What the hell am I supposed to do? It's not like I can just call emergency services and tell them I think someone's going to beat up my teacher.

I dial the number again and wait for the answer phone.

"Detective Jenkins?" I say when it picks up. Then I stop, wondering what to say. It's not like I can explain the whole story in an answer phone message. "This is–"

My phone beeps telling me there's a message.

I press the end call button. My hands are shaking. I press them to my mouth as I remember the threat from the card. *Tell anyone and I'll kill your brother.*

I shove the phone into the cupboard under the sink and wedge the door closed.

The landline doesn't ring in the morning. I keep staring at the phone, but it stays silent. At this point, I'm not sure whether I'm more scared of the caller or Detective Jenkins ringing.

I don't take my cell phone out of the bathroom.

Pete drops me off in the morning then takes Jo on to her school. She looks pretty surly at the idea, but I suppose I can't exactly expect her to be happy about it. She didn't talk to me this morning. It's weird. I'm used to her being so friendly. She seems like a different person.

Things at school seem to have gone back to normal. Every-one's returned to completely ignoring me, rather than staring at me like I'm contagious. We have a sub for geography class. I don't think she really knows what she's doing. They might as well have let me teach the class – we're probably evenly matched on knowledge of the subject.

No one mentions Mr Humphries.

At lunch I head out to my spot behind the gym. It smells like someone's turned the rotting leaves under the trees, making them more composty than ever. Even if I'd actually felt like eating, it would have put me off my food.

"Hi."

I look up. Tash is standing next to me.

I give her a little smile. "Hey."

"Jacob said I'd probably find you here." She sits down next to me and leans back against the gym. "It'd be nice back here if it didn't smell so terrible." She glances at me and grins.

"Yeah." I run my hands through my hair, fluffing it out. Tash plays with the end of her scarf, then takes the whole thing off and reties it. It's weird how that happens. One girl starts fixing her hair, or make-up, or something, so all the other girls around do too.

"I'm sorry I flipped out yesterday," I say, not looking at her.

Tash shrugs. "It's okay. Did you hear he resigned?"

"Huh?" I almost give myself whiplash, jerking my head around to look at Tash.

She doesn't look at me but keeps staring into the bushes. "Mr Humphries. He came in this morning, packed up his desk and handed in his resignation."

I let out a breath. "Wow." My brain dissolves into a whole load of little sparks as I think that through. I'm relieved – one, because I'll probably never have to see him again, and two, because he's still alive. Or at least he was this morning.

"I thought you'd want to know." Tash shifts her gaze down to her feet. She runs her fingers through the grass, like she's stroking a cat. "You know, if Mr Humphries did do something, you should really–"

"He didn't," I interrupt her. I turn and look her in the eye. "At least, nothing I want to talk about."

Tash narrows her eyes then nods once, a sharp jerk of her head.

We both go back to staring into the bushes. There's a little bit of a breeze. It blows from Tash to me, bringing with it the smell of watermelons. I used to have a watermelon lip balm, but it smelt more like gone-off kiwi fruit. This must be her shampoo or something.

A blackbird in the bushes is attacking a worm. The bird's feathers are all oily and separated out from each other. It looks like the kind of animal that would spread bubonic plague, or rabies, if we had those here. I look away as my skin starts to crawl.

"We're having a party for Ben after his fight," I say to Tash. "You could come if you wanted." I blush. It's stupid how I feel I'm imposing on her just by asking her to a party.

She nods. "Yeah, that'd be cool."

I write down Pete's address for her.

She twists the paper around in her hand, then looks up at me. "If you ever do want to talk about it ..." She seems to be holding her breath as she waits for me to answer.

I'm not sure what to say so I just nod.

"Kelsey, you don't ..." She stops as a shadow falls over us.

We both look up. Jacob grins at us. He rocks back and forth around the side of the gym.

"Thought I'd find you here." He nods to me. "Hey, Kels."

"Hey." I glance at Tash. She rolls her eyes in Jacob's direction.

"Ta-ash." Jacob stretches her name into a sing-song, wheedling sound.

"Wha-at?"

He grins. "Can I check my biology homework against yours?"

"In other words you haven't done it and want to copy my answers?"

Jacob chuckles and taps her leg with his foot. "I'll love you forever."

She sighs. "Yeah, all right. Come on."

Jacob helps her to her feet.

She turns back to me. "See you later, yeah?"

"Yeah, sure."

"Hey," she lowers her voice, "I really mean that. If you want to talk–"

I shake my head and glance at Jacob.

Tash nods. "Later."

❦

Jo meets me outside the school gates at the end of the day. I wasn't expecting to see her but it's nice to have someone to walk home with.

"How was your day?" I ask.

She gives me a look – like a cat just peed on her foot – but then she smiles.

"Yeah, pretty much the same here." That's not strictly true, my day wasn't all that bad, but it's like when you complain about the weather just to have something to say.

We walk in silence for a bit. I amuse myself by kicking a piece of gravel along in front of me.

"Do you have a new boyfriend?"

I look up at Jo as she says that. She stares at the ground in front of her and keeps walking. I can tell she's watching me in her peripheral vision, though. She fiddles with the chain around her neck. It's this thick silver thing with a pink glass bauble hanging on it. I picked it out for Mike to give to her.

"No, honey, I don't."

Jo stops and turns on me. "Don't call me 'honey'. Not if you're lying to me." Her face contorts as she tries not to cry.

I take a breath. "I'm not lying," I say. "I don't have a new boyfriend."

Jo's face relaxes, but she chews on the inside of her cheek. "Then who was that call from?"

I make a noise in my throat. "That. It was no one."

Jo's eyes narrow.

I shrug. "Well, of course it was someone, but no one important. Just this weird guy who's been calling me. I don't know who he is. Not really." I swallow. Technically I haven't lied, but it feels like I have.

Jo pulls on a strand of hair that's escaped her bun. She winds it around her finger then tucks it behind her ear. "What about Ben?"

"What about Ben?" I repeat, changing the emphasis. I try to keep my voice light.

"Do you like him?" Jo looks up at me.

I shrug. "Ben's ... Ben."

Jo sighs. "That's not really an answer, is it?"

I feel myself blush. "God. What's with everyone trying to pair me and him up? He's like a brother to me." I cross my arms and speed up my pace.

Jo keeps up with me. "Thing is, Kel, you're not like a sister to him."

I feel her watching me, but I can't look at her. I rub my hand against my cheek to cool my face. "You don't know what you're talking about." It comes out much harsher than I mean it to. "You're thirteen," I say, as if that makes a difference.

She shrugs and looks away.

I stop at the dairy on the way home and buy a ton of butter, along with some sugar, chocolate chips and flour. Ben comes home from work early so he can have extra time to train. By the time he does, I've made three trays of cookies and a batch of rather unsuccessful muffins that wouldn't come out of the pan. I'm working on some new muffins when he comes into the kitchen.

I'm not sure where Jo is. Last I saw she was upstairs doing her homework.

Ben stops in the middle of the room. His eyes get wider as he takes in the baking and mess I've created. For a moment I think he's going to yell, then he starts laughing.

"What are you doing?" He picks up a cookie, but I grab it out of his hand.

"They're for your party. It's all the things you can't eat before your fight." I realise this might not have been the great idea it seemed like on the way home.

Ben runs his hands through his hair and laughs.

I shrug. "I'm sorry. Maybe this was a stupid idea."

Ben shakes his head, and chuckles. "No, it's a great idea." He puts his arm around my shoulder and kisses the side of my head. I feel myself flush and busy myself with trying to pour the mixture into the muffin pan. It's not that easy to do with my hand in a cast.

"Here." Ben takes the bowl from me and holds it while I fill the pans. He licks some mixture off his finger. "Mm, this is good."

I tap his wrist with the spoon. "You're not supposed to eat it yet!"

He laughs. I put the muffins in the oven then turn back to him.

"Kel, you've got …" He reaches out to touch my face.

I dodge away from him.

He drops his hand to his side. "Flour. In your hair."

"Thanks." I run my fingers through it, then wash my hands. Ben goes quiet. He scratches at some burnt mixture on one of the tins. I swear we're both swallowing and breathing in sync.

I struggle to find something to say. "You didn't have any recipe books, so I had to make them up. I don't know. Might be terrible. The first lot of muffins didn't rise. Everything else seems okay though." I'm babbling now. I look up at Ben. He stares at me then starts to smile. I'm blushing, I can tell. He presses his lips together in what I think is an attempt not to laugh.

"What?" I shift. My arms and legs seem to stick out at odd angles, like I'm a doll that's been put together wrong.

Ben shakes his head. "Nothing. I'm going to go." He gestures towards the garage. "See you later, Kel." He smiles again. I feel like he knows something I don't.

"Ben …" I start to say, but I falter and the word peters out. Ben glances back at me and grins. He keeps walking towards the door.

Pete yells at me when he gets home. Of course. I was expecting him to, so I'm immune to it.

"Look at this mess … So irresponsible … Bloody disrespectful …"

He doesn't even really need to say it. I could have quoted

his rant, word for word, before he even started. He thinks I'm so stupid that I wouldn't realise I'm supposed to clean up after myself. It's not like I wasn't going to. His face gets red and blotchy, like he's going to have a heart attack. I make him a cup of decaf and he calms down. I don't tell him it's decaf.

"But you'd better bloody well clean it up."

I nod and don't make eye contact. He seems appeased by the fact that I'm not arguing, but that's really because I'm not listening.

Jo comes downstairs while I'm cleaning up. She hovers in the living room doorway. I can see her from the kitchen, but she doesn't look at me.

When Ben comes out of the garage on his way to the bathroom, she accidentally-on-purpose gets in his way.

"What's up?" he asks. He's all slimy with sweat. He rubs his face on a towel, which I hope he's going to put straight in the washing machine.

Jo fiddles with the hem of her top. "I need a ride to the hospital. I want to go see Mike."

Even from where I'm standing, I can hear Jo swallow. She looks up at Ben. Her mouth pulls into a funny shape.

Ben sighs. He tilts his head back and stares at the ceiling. "Yeah, sure. Just let me have a shower and get changed first."

Jo catches my eye as Ben goes into the bathroom. I look back down at the counter and act like it's taking all my energy to wipe up the spilt flour.

I don't look up as she comes into the kitchen.

"Are you going to come?"

I keep staring at the bench. It feels like her eyes have turned into lasers. I'll probably have a couple of holes in my temple after this conversation.

"Are you?" Jo tilts her head forwards, so I'm forced to look at her. "I know you haven't been since you left the hospital."

"It's not that simple," I say, even though I know it's a cop out.

"Yeah, it is." She stares at me then walks away.

Ben comes downstairs. Jo's standing by the front door, like she thinks Ben might forget unless she reminds him with her presence. He fluffs around, picking up his keys and jacket, then goes out into the hallway. I get up and stand next to Jo.

Ben's face crinkles up in confusion, then he closes his eyes and shakes his head. "Kel ..."

"I asked Kel to come with me." Jo shifts, stretching her neck and shoulders higher. She stares at Ben without blinking. I cross my arms over my chest and stare at the floor.

Ben rubs his hand over his eyes. He lowers his voice. "Are you sure you want to do this, Kel?"

I force myself to nod. My cheeks burn as I do.

Ben sits in the waiting room while Jo and I go in to see Mike.

Jo sits down and takes Mike's hand. I'm not sure if I'm supposed to do the same. Even if I am, I can't bring myself to do it. I can't even bring myself to look at him.

"Sit down." Jo doesn't look at me, but I can't imagine she's saying that to Mike so I sit down in the chair on the other side of the bed. I stare at the wall above Mike's head.

"I'm staying at Kelsey's."

I'm confused at first, then I realise that Jo's talking to Mike.

"That's why I wasn't here yesterday." Jo looks up at me.

"He can hear us, you know," she says.

I'm not sure what I'm supposed to say to that, so I just nod.

Jo rolls her tongue around her mouth and her eyes narrow. My stomach clenches when she looks at me like that.

She turns back to Mike, and her expression melts into a sad one. She reaches out to stroke his cheek. "I'm going away for a while, so I won't be able to come see you every day."

I blink at Jo. "Where are you going?"

Jo looks back at me, her expression hard. "To Auckland. I've booked the bus ticket for tomorrow."

"You can't just go off by yourself."

"I'm not going by myself. My aunty's picking me up at the bus station." She looks down at her hands. "I can't go home. Not without Mike there."

I sigh. "Jo, I didn't–"

"You didn't what?" Jo's eyes shoot up to meet mine. "Think about it? You know what it's like there. What were you going to do? Send me home as soon as your brother kicked me out?"

"No, I–"

"You hadn't even thought about it, had you? You're too wrapped up in your own stuff."

"That's not true!" I swallow and lower my voice. "Jo–"

"You don't even care!" Jo shakes her head. "You haven't even looked at him."

"What?" My chest starts to hurt. I take a breath, which makes it hurt more.

"Mike. You haven't even looked at him."

I stare at Jo. My eyes sting. I have to blink and drop my gaze.

"Look at him!" Jo stands up and points, her finger in Mike's face.

I look up at the ceiling. In my head I see the picture from the news. *That's not Mike,* I want to say, but the words won't come out.

"Look at him." Jo's voice is softer this time. Somehow that's worse.

My forehead creases up as I look at Mike. The swelling in his face has gone down. He almost looks like he used to, just asleep. Something inside me breaks. I get up and run from the room.

16

Chapter Sixteen

Ben chases after me. "Kel, stop!"

My breath rasps out of me, like I've been running for hours. I grab the wall as my legs give way beneath me. Ben's arm goes around my waist, catching me.

"Kel–"

"No!" I push him away, but he holds me fast. "Let me … go." I can't get enough air to say that. I push at Ben and try to stand. My legs crumple. "Let me go!" I shriek it this time.

Ben holds my arms so I can't move. "Shhh, Kel. Just stop, okay? Stop."

"No!" I struggle against him. "Let go!" I scream. The middle of my chest hurts. I feel someone else's hands on me, on my face and on my wrist. Ben holds me. I try to scream again. It doesn't come out. I cry instead, in big quaking sobs. I hear Ben's voice.

"Kel …? Kel? Come on, Kel." He shakes me.

I raise my head, but it's wobbly, like my neck's not strong enough.

"Has she had panic attacks before?"

I hear the woman's voice, but I can't see more than her

217

hands. I think she's a nurse. She'd better be a nurse, otherwise she's just some stranger touching me.

"One. Yeah." Ben's arms shift, going from restraining to holding. "In the A&E. Things have been … bad." He moves me, so I'm resting back against him. I flop like over-cooked pasta.

"Ben?" My voice cracks even in just that word.

"It's okay," Ben touches my face. "You're okay."

Jo sits in an angry huddle in the back of the car on the way home. I'm too tired to hold my own weight, let alone care about what she's doing.

Mr Humphries' car is parked across the road from the house when we get home. I groan when I see it. Ben keeps asking me "What? What's wrong?" But I don't answer. What can I say? It's my fault Mike's in a coma? It's my fault my teacher might be dead?

Ben wraps his arm around me as we walk up the path. It's like I've forgotten how to walk in a straight line.

The zip of his jacket presses against my face. It's cold and it digs in. I try to push it away from my cheek, but I can't. It starts to hurt, then to go numb.

Ben moves Jo's mattress out of my room, into the living room. I don't even bother to get changed before climbing into bed. Ben sits with me for a bit, but I don't look at him. I don't answer his questions. I just shut my eyes and cover my face with my hands until he gives up and leaves me alone.

I wake early in the morning. It's still dark out and the air feels cold against my cheeks. I turn my face to the pillow and try to go back to sleep.

I open my eyes as I hear Jo clear her throat. I roll over to face her. "Jo–"

She cuts me off. "I'm leaving now. Aiden's going to take me to the station."

I sit up. "Jo, I wish …" I rub my face. "I wish things were different …" My voice peters out. It sounded better in my head.

Jo nods and looks away. "Yeah. Me too."

I reach out to her. After a second she hugs me, but her arms are stiff and her head sits awkwardly against my shoulder. I squeeze my face against her hair.

She draws back. "I'd better …" She gestures to the door and turns away.

"I love you, Jo."

Jo stops, but she doesn't look at me. She shifts her head, as if she's thinking of turning back, but then she takes a breath and walks away.

When I wake again, later in the morning, there's a hole inside me. It's not like an empty hole; it's like a black hole slowly sucking my insides into it, until one day I'll implode.

No one woke me up, so I assume Pete doesn't care whether I go to school or not. Either that, or they're all so freaked I'll flip out, they'd rather just let me sleep. I get up and go downstairs. My head hurts when I move it. Everything feels thick, like I'm covered in mucus.

Ben's in the kitchen. He's making another one of his horrible egg-smoothie things. I remember him saying something about taking today off to prepare for the fight. Out the window I can see Mr Humphries' car, parked where it was last night. The sun glints off the side mirror at me, in greeting. The rays shoot out like the quills of a porcupine.

Ben looks up as I come in. "Hey." He gives me a half smile. "You okay?"

I shake my head. "No. I'm really not."

He stares at me for a long time, then nods and sighs.

I watch TV while Ben trains. I don't change my clothes from yesterday. A couple of times I jump when a phone rings on the TV, but our phone doesn't ring. By the time Pete and Aiden get home from work, I'm ready for bed again.

As I come out of the bathroom, I hear Ben talking to Pete. I move to the living room doorway and watch the backs of their heads bobbing as they speak. They're both focused on the TV, but it's on mute.

Ben rubs his face. "It's serious. She's completely out of it."

Pete shakes his head and scoffs. "She's a bloody drama queen."

"Pete–"

"Trust me. She'll be fine."

"She's not …"

I must have moved, or something, because Ben stops and glances over his shoulder at me. His mouth droops, then he tries to smile. "Hey."

"I'm going to bed, okay?"

Ben seems puzzled, and I realise it must have sounded like I was asking permission.

"Goodnight," I add.

He gives me a little nod.

❧

Aiden drives us to the venue for Ben's fight the next evening. He drops us off and goes to park the car.

Inside's not what I expected. I'd imagined a really dark room with a chalk circle drawn on the floor and people standing around it, screaming at the fighters and making bets. But I was probably picturing an illegal dogfight, not a professional kickboxing one. This is more like a gym, with big raised blue rings set up. I don't know why they call them rings. They're squares not circles. I suppose boxing squares sounds stupid.

Ben looks really nervous. I don't think I've ever seen him nervous about anything before. He goes quiet then laughs too loudly and too quickly at things we say. Mostly when they're not funny. He goes off to warm up and we sit down.

Aiden hasn't reappeared so Pete leaves a space for him. I make sure we take seats at the back so Ben won't see us and be put off.

Ben's fight is first up. I'm glad about that. Hopefully we can leave straight after. I want to support Ben, but watching people smash each other in the face just isn't my thing.

Ben comes out and the crowd stand up and cheer. I clap, or do my best to with my hand in the cast. If I could wolf-whistle I would, but that's not in my list of talents. The other guy comes out and the crowd cheer again. I feel like I should boo or something, but that's probably from watching too much TV.

The overhead lights glint off the sweat on Ben's forehead. I clench my hands in my own version of crossing fingers.

They touch gloves and the ref blows a whistle. The crowd cheer as they start to circle. I twist my hands in the fabric of my dress to stop from screaming. Ben jabs at the other guy. It doesn't connect. I shrink back as the other guy hits Ben. The punch lands square on Ben's jaw. I cover my mouth with my hand, pressing my fingertips into my face. In my head I see Mike's arm drawing back. I feel the force as it hits my face.

"Oh God!" I cover my face.

Pete jerks my hand away from my face. "Do not do this now!"

I stare at him and try to breathe.

He shakes my wrist. "Kel ... Kel!"

I squeeze my eyes shut. The crowd is so loud.

Pete pulls me to my feet. "Just go outside then." He pushes me towards the door.

The air outside is so cold after the heat in the gym. I shiver and collapse onto a bench outside the door. My skin rises up into goosebumps. I wrap my arms around myself and bury my head in my knees.

"Kel?"

I look up. Aiden walks over to me.

I shake my head to clear it. "You didn't come in."

He gives me something that almost passes for a smile. "Too violent for me." He sits down next to me. "What happened?"

"They'd just started. Ben took a hit. Don't know after that."

Aiden looks down. He smiles at his feet. "I mean to you. Why are you out here?"

"I'm just being pathetic."

Aiden coughs. He takes a packet of cigarettes out of his pocket and offers one to me. I shake my head. He lights one himself and takes a drag.

"I didn't know you smoke," I say. I don't think it would go down well if I stubbed his cigarette out, so I just turn my face away as he blows the smoke out.

"Yeah, I don't advertise it." He coughs and looks up at me. "You know your brother does too?"

I nod. "I found his ashtray."

Aiden twists up his mouth. I blush as I realise it was probably Aiden's ashtray, not Pete's. He must have thought I was so weird for hiding it.

"Pete told me he quit," I say, to cover my embarrassment.

"Yeah. He did." Aiden shrugs. "Then he didn't anymore."

"You know Ben used to smoke, too?" I say. "Can't imagine it now, with how fit he is."

Aiden shrugs. "What happened?"

"With Ben? I think he just got sick of it."

Aiden smiles. "I meant with you. In there." He gestures with his cigarette then takes another drag.

I shake my head. "Nothing."

He scoffs, making me look at him. His face is blank, but he keeps staring.

I hunch up my shoulders. "What do you care?"

His eyes flick away from mine. "It was a flashback, wasn't it? To Mike hitting you?"

I swallow, then shrug when he looks at me.

He stares up at the sky. "I used to get them all the time.

My step-dad. Anything violent, TV or whatever. That's why I didn't go in."

"He hit you?" I try to make my voice gentle.

Aiden nods. "Me, my mum, Becky, he even took a swing at the neighbours. That's how Becky broke her arm. I got out of there as soon as I was old enough."

I let out a breath. "I'm sorry."

"Why? You didn't hit me." He takes a drag and blows the smoke out above our heads.

I watch it break up into the air. "Does it get better?"

"Huh?" Aiden stops, with the cigarette halfway to his mouth.

"Does it ... Am I ever going to feel normal again?" It sounds so melodramatic once it's out of my head. I wrinkle up my face and shake my head. Aiden doesn't answer so I look at him.

"Becky ..." His eyes go wide and he blinks a couple of times.

The doors open and Pete comes out, interrupting Aiden. I can hear the sound of cheering. Aiden drops his cigarette and crushes it underfoot.

"Ben lost." Pete looks at me as if he thinks it's my fault.

The door swings closed, blocking out most of the noise and light from inside. I go very still as I wonder whether it *is* my fault, then Aiden clears his throat.

"Come on." He touches my shoulder. "We'd better go show our support." It sounds sarcastic, but I don't think he meant it that way.

"Wait." I lower my voice and turn my face away from Pete. "What were you saying about Becky?"

Aiden shakes his head. "Another time."

Ben's hunched over in his chair. They've moved him to a back room, away from the crowd. I hear the next fight starting. Even away from it, the noise still makes me jump. Aiden hangs back by the door. He crosses his arms and studies the ceiling. Pete stands next to me, letting his arms swing. I'm not sure what to do, so I just wait.

Ben's pressing a cloth to his temple. He hasn't realised we're here. There's a medic guy checking him out. His face pinches up as the medic removes the cloth. There's so much blood, all down his face and neck. It doesn't look real. It's like cornstarch blood in a bad horror movie. Then Ben moves and I see his black eye.

"Oh my God!"

Ben looks up. I didn't mean him to hear me. His face screws up as he sees me, then he winces as the medic starts to clean up the wound. I move forward. Pete makes a little noise in his throat but doesn't try to stop me. I move around the medic and kneel down on the other side of Ben. I take his hand in mine. He doesn't react. His hand stays limp.

"Is it bad?" I ask. Ben stares at the ground and scowls.

The medic smiles at me. "Lot of blood, but nothing's really wrong."

I let out a breath. "Good."

"I'll just get this cut sorted out, then you can deal with the rest at home." The medic smiles at me again.

"Thanks."

Ben glances at me and sighs. I do my best to smile. He closes his eyes and links his fingers through mine.

We wait while Ben goes and has a shower then head back

to the car. Ben doesn't say anything on the way home. He stares out of the window. Pete and Aiden don't talk either. I feel like starting a monologue. Then Aiden puts on the radio, and the silence isn't quite so deafening.

I drag Ben up to the upstairs bathroom when we get home, even though he keeps saying he's fine. He sits on the vanity, beside the sink, and I dissect the first aid kit.

"Here." I give him a couple of arnica pills. "Take them," I say when he just stares at me.

He drops the pills onto his tongue.

I rummage through the kit looking for the arnica cream. Ben kicks the bathroom cabinet with his heel, then looks down at his hands and goes very still. I stop and stare at him. Eventually he looks up at me.

"If you're going to sulk, I'm leaving. You can sort yourself out." I hope Ben doesn't notice my hands are shaking. I want to be all tough-love, but I'm not very good at it.

He sighs and rubs his hand over his face, then winces as he brushes the black eye.

I shake my head. "So, you didn't win. That wasn't the point, was it?"

Ben shrugs.

"Ben, win or lose, it doesn't matter. You did well."

Ben scoffs and shakes his head.

"What?"

He doesn't answer.

I take his chin in my hand and force him to look at me. "What?"

His eyes flick away from mine. "You wouldn't know if I did well. You left right at the start."

I drop my hand. He looks back at me.

I cover my face with my hands. "I'm so sorry. I'm so ... I didn't mean you to see. I just ..." I peel my hands away and look at him. "I couldn't handle it, watching you get hurt and it made me think of ..." I shake my head. "It doesn't matter. I should have been there for you."

He stares at his hands and winds his fingers around each other.

I rub my cheek against my shoulder. "Look, things have been so screwed up, and, I don't know. I've been so wrapped up in my own stuff, and I didn't realise how it would affect you." I take his hand in mine. "I'm really sorry if I put you off."

Ben sighs and shakes his head. "It's not your fault, Kel. He was just better than me. It doesn't matter."

"It does matter. If you want we don't have to go through with the party tonight. If you just want to-"

"No, I'm being a dick. Ignore me." Ben attempts a smile, then winces again.

"Here." I dab the arnica on to his face. I blush as I feel Ben's eyes on me and have to concentrate very hard on what I'm doing. "Where else?"

"My shoulder." Ben slips his shirt off.

"Here." I try to hand him the tube of cream.

He doesn't take it. "I can't reach. Could you-" He bobs his head up and down.

"Sure." I don't look at Ben. His hand brushes against my side as I rub the cream into his shoulder. "There. Good as new. Kind of." I smile. Ben doesn't move his hand. I'm not sure whether to wait or just step backwards, making him drop it.

"Kel-"

I look down at my feet. "Ben, I–"

Ben stops me by lifting my chin with his hand. My face feels really hot while the rest of me goes cold. The blood on Ben's face has dried and is flaking off in a powder.

"I ..." My mouth goes dry. It hurts as I swallow.

I look away from Ben as Pete calls from downstairs.

"Ben? Where are you? People are here." Pete's footsteps thump up the stairs. I step backwards, and Ben's hands drop to his sides.

Pete opens the bathroom door. He stops as he sees us. I inspect the bath in great detail. I can't see what Ben's doing. Pete doesn't say anything for a bit. When he does, his voice comes out funny – very controlled, and like he's putting on an English accent without realising it.

"People are here. You should come downstairs."

Ben lowers himself off the vanity. "We'll be down in a minute." He looks at me.

So does Pete.

I shake my head to clear it. "Yeah, I'm coming." I walk past Pete without looking at him or Ben.

I'm a bit overwhelmed when I see how many of Ben's and Pete's friends have come. I duck out into the kitchen and busy myself with arranging food and drinks. Pete's bought half the bottle store. He's even got a couple of those frozen daiquiri mixes, which are sitting melting into a pink slush among the beers. I wonder if they were free. I can't imagine Pete choosing them.

The boys don't have any baskets or serving dishes, so I

dump the baking into some soup bowls and spread out the chips and dips on dinner plates. I'm only intending to put them on the coffee table, but people think I'm handing them out, so I end up mingling while shoving food at people.

Ben and Pete haven't come downstairs. I almost go up to hurry them along, then I realise they might be arguing and don't want to get in the middle of it. Aiden seems to have disappeared as well, but that doesn't surprise me. He's probably off hibernating, to avoid too many people.

I'm wondering if I should text Ben, to get him down here, when this girl comes up to me.

"So, did he win?"

I stare at her for a second, before I realise what she's talking about. "Ben? No, he lost."

She wrinkles up her nose. "Poos. What about you?"

"Huh?" I shift the bowls I'm carrying, trying to balance them against my body.

She gestures to my black eye and cast. "You look like you came off worse. You win your fight?" She smiles, revealing a gap between her front teeth. Somehow it's endearing.

I give an awkward laugh. "I'm not–"

"Yeah, Kel won her fight. Won the whole division."

I feel Ben's hands on my shoulders. He gives them a little squeeze. I lean back my head to look at him and mouth "Thank you."

He smiles at me then nods to the girl. "This is Michelle, from my work." He pats my shoulder. "This is Kel, my flatmate and fellow kickboxer." He rests his chin on top of my head.

Michelle takes a sip of her drink, then squeals and nearly spits it out. Ben and I both draw back.

"You're the girlfriend!"

Ben and I talk over each other. "Michelle, she's–"

"No, I'm–"

Michelle flaps her hand at us. "You're the girl from the photo! The one Ben has on his desktop. He's been so secretive about the whole thing, but–"

"I'm not his girlfriend." I pull away from Ben. "I'm not a kickboxer, either. My boyfriend beat me up, and now he's in a coma." I blush and take a breath.

Michelle snorts, as if that's the funniest thing she's ever heard, then looks from me to Ben. She covers her mouth and tries to stop laughing. "Don't mind me. I'm drunk." She snorts again and backs away, Pink Panther style.

Ben doesn't say anything. I shove one of the bowls at him. "Have a muffin."

"Kel–"

I walk away so he can't say anything else.

He follows after me. "Kel, I never said you were my girlfriend. She's just drunk."

I stop and look at him. "Why do you have a photo of me on your desktop?"

Ben shakes his head. "It's nothing. It's an old one of us. From that Christmas when Pete and I came round to your mum's house. You know, when my parents first moved away."

"Yeah, I remember." I'm not sure what to do next so I stuff one of the cookies into my mouth.

Ben watches me. "It's not a big deal," he says.

I nod. "I know. Eat the muffin."

Ben stares at me then shakes his head and smiles. "Okay, I'll eat the muffin."

Pete comes downstairs a little later. He goes straight up to a girl and kisses her on the lips. She'd been standing there looking lost, picking up her drink then setting it down again without taking a sip. I'd been contemplating going up to her and offering her some baked goods. Now I realise she's the mysterious Jenny, I wish I had.

She's a tiny thing. She looks even tinier next to Pete. I look away as he runs his hand down the side of her face. It feels like an intrusion to watch them. Also, it grosses me out.

When I look back, Pete appears to be telling a story. He waves his arms around and she laughs, like it's the funniest thing she's ever heard. She pushes the curtain of dark brown hair back from her face. I can't stop myself from staring as I realise she's actually into my brother. It's a weird thought.

Pete catches my eye and he points me out to her, leaning down to whisper to her. She laughs then smiles and waves at me. I force a smile back and raise my hand in greeting.

I do a double take when Tash arrives. I'd forgotten I'd invited her. I do another double take when I see who she's brought with her.

"Hey, Kels." Tash smiles nervously, then she pulls me aside. "I'm sorry. I told Jacob I was coming, and he wanted to come too. I didn't think it would matter, then he invited Billy and Billy invited–"

I interrupt her. "It's okay. I don't mind." I force a smile. "Just stay out of the way of my brother. I forgot to tell him I'd invited you, let alone ..." I gesture to the group of kids from school.

"I'm really sorry. I can tell them to go if–"

I laugh. "I don't think even you have that much power." I watch as Billy and Jacob find the beer. Amber and Sophie aren't far behind. I grab another cookie and break it into pieces.

Tash takes one too. "Why ...?" She gestures to the bowls of baking.

I shake my head. "I don't know. I thought it was a good idea at the time."

Tash looks puzzled, but she nods anyway.

Jacob comes over to us. His eyes are red-rimmed and I don't think the beer in his hand is his first tonight.

"Hey." He gives me a sleepy grin. He leans against Tash and nearly topples her over. She stumbles and he pulls her back up.

"Oops." He pats her shoulders but it's more like he's dusting her than comforting. "You okay?"

Tash pulls away from him and laughs. "Yes. Are you?"

"I'm all good." He grins again. He fixes me with a stare and takes a swig from his beer. I squirm under his gaze.

Tash shakes her head and glances at me. "Jacob, you need to eat something." She takes the bowl out of my hand. "Here."

"Awesome, cookies!" Jacob shoves three in his mouth at once. I look away as crumbs scatter down his chest.

Tash holds his face and looks him in the eye. "Jacob?"

He smiles at her, mouth full.

She sighs. "Are you drunk or stoned?"

I feel ill when she says that. Pete will kill me if they've brought drugs here.

Jacob raises his hand to his forehead. "Scout's honour, I am only drunk." He slurs his words, adding an S to only.

Tash looks at me and rolls her eyes. "He was never a scout," she says.

I look around as someone changes the music.

Jacob grabs my hand. "I love this song. Dance with me, Kelsey." He shoves his beer can at Tash.

"God, he must be drunk." Tash clicks her tongue, then she rests her hand on his arm. "Leave her alone, Jacob."

Jacob ignores her and looks at me. "Come on, Kels. You're not going to make me dance with my sister, are you?"

I laugh. "I don't think–"

He doesn't let me finish that. He swings me around and I lose my balance. I grab his arms, and he pulls me into an exaggerated version of a slow dance. We swing from side to side, in a way that makes me feel seasick.

"Jacob ..." I try to look at him, but he pushes my head against his chest.

"Shhh ... Just be in the moment."

I can't help but laugh. Jacob starts to hum along to the music. At least, I think he's trying to hum along. It's rather tuneless, so it could be a completely different song.

Jacob spins me out then pulls me back close to him. I lean back my head and laugh. Tash watches us. She tries to look stern, but it just looks like she's holding back a laugh.

"Kel?"

I turn as I hear Ben's voice. Jacob turns with me then dips me, so I'm staring up at Ben. Ben takes a sip of his beer and frowns.

I laugh as the blood rushes to my head. Jacob swings me up, and I stumble, lightheaded. Ben catches my shoulders.

"This is Jacob, from school," I say.

Jacob tries to spin me again, but Ben's still holding my shoulders. He ends up yanking my arm instead.

"Ow!" I pull my arm back against my body.

"Shit, sorry." Jacob hovers but seems unsure what to do.

Tash comes over and smacks his arm. "That was stupid."

"Let me see." Ben moves my arm then looks at Jacob. "You could have dislocated her arm."

I shake my head. "Just gave me a fright, that's all." I rub my arm.

Ben sways on the spot. His eyes look unfocused. Most of all, he looks far more angry than he should be.

I touch his face and make him look at me. "Are you drunk?"

He shakes his head, but it's more like he's trying to clear it than he's disagreeing with me. "Nah, I've only had a couple of beers."

I study his face. "You're dehydrated. Go drink some water. Or eat something." I grab the nearest bowl of baking and hand it to him. He shoves the food in his mouth with far more volume and speed than can be healthy.

I go out to the kitchen and try to look like I'm doing something, not just hiding. There are beer cans scattered all over the floor. I bend down to pick them up. When I stand up, I feel a hand on my side. I jump and look around. Billy's standing next to me. "Wanna dance?"

I shrug away from him. "No, not really."

"Why not? You danced with Jacob." He leers at me.

I shake my head, as I realise he's drunk too. It makes me wonder if I should start drinking. Being the only sober person in a room is just disturbing.

"That's not the same." I head towards the kitchen door.

Billy blocks my way. "Come on, Kel-sey."

I swallow, a bitter taste in my mouth. "Why'd you put that note in my locker?"

"Huh?"

"The note. In my locker. Did you think it was funny?"

A look creeps over Billy's face and he smiles, Cheshire-cat style. "I didn't put it in your locker." He thinks he's going to get out of it on a technicality.

I cross my arms. "No, but you dared Adam to do it."

Billy's face goes ugly as he realises I've caught him out. "It was just a joke."

"Yeah, real funny."

Billy sneers at me. "Whatever. You used to be hot, but now you're just bony."

I roll my eyes, and walk around him out into the living room. I hear him call after me: "Bitch!"

I go sit down on the couch. My head hurts with the noise of the people and music. I rub my temple and lean my head against my hand. Jacob is busy hitting on Michelle, from Ben's work. She's so drunk, it looks like he might have a shot. Billy's going after Tash. Unfortunately for him, she hasn't been drinking. I laugh as Jacob catches sight of him and gets all cave-man "leave my sister alone" angry. Tash has to get in the middle of them to stop them fighting.

Amber and Sophie come and sit down next to me. They both stare at me, until I turn and look at them.

"What do you want?" I know. I'm the least gracious host around. Well, maybe there're a few people worse than me. Like the ones who kill their guests.

"He doesn't like you, you know." Amber chews on her piercing as she speaks. Her face is fixed into a heavy scowl, and her eyes look like they're about to spill over.

I shake my head. "Who?"

"Jacob." Sophie juts her chin out at me. "He doesn't like you. He just feels sorry for you."

"You're not even his type," Amber adds.

Sophie looks at her and nods.

"I'm sorry?" I laugh as I realise they're serious.

"You should be sorry." Amber glares at me. "You shouldn't dance with other people's boyfriends."

"Jacob's your boyfriend?" I can't keep the surprise out of my voice. From the way Amber tucks her chin into her chest and Sophie rubs her tongue over her teeth, it doesn't go down well.

Amber shifts. "He's as good as. So keep away from him unless you want your eyes scratched out."

I roll my eyes at the threat. "Sure, whatever."

Amber stares at me. Her bottom lip drops, and her eyes spill over. "He is my boyfriend," she mumbles.

Sophie puts her arm around Amber. "Of course he is." She glares at me over Amber's shoulder.

"What would he want with a stick-insect like her?" Amber rubs her face and stares at me.

"Look, I'm sorry. I didn't-"

"Haven't you done enough?" Sophie hisses the words at me. "And don't you even think about going after Billy. I saw you talking to him."

I sigh. They've already decided I'm the bad guy and anything I say will just confirm that. I get up and walk away. I wonder if they even know they're in my house.

I catch sight of Ben. He's sitting in a chair by the stereo, a beer in his hand, his head drooping almost to his knees.

I go over to him. "What are you doing?"

He looks up and smiles at me. "Hey, Kel." He raises his beer in a solitary toast.

I take it off him. "I told you to eat something."

He nods. "I did. Lots of muffins. Lots of cookies. Cuffins

and mookies." He laughs in a sloppy, drunken way.

I shake my head. "How did you get drunk so quickly?"

"I'm not." He tries to stand. "Do you want to dance?"

I push him back into the chair. "I think you'd better stay sitting."

"Sit with me." He pulls me so I'm sitting on his lap.

I shake my head and try not to laugh. "Ben ..."

He reaches for his beer.

"No." I pull it out of his reach. "You need some water."

He smiles at me. "I need a hug. Give me a hug." He wraps his arms around me.

I squirm and try to free myself. "Stop it. You're drunk."

"No. I'm stone ... stone ..." He stops and puzzles over that. "I'm stonily sober." He smiles, pleased with himself.

I can't help but smile back at him. I free myself from his grip. "I'm going to get you some water."

"I've only had three beers."

I nod and talk to him like I'm explaining things to an unintelligent two-year-old. "Yes, but you're dehydrated from the fight. You need some water or you're going to be sick."

He rocks his head back and forth, in what might be a nod, then leans it back against the wall and closes his eyes.

I take his beer with me as I go out to the kitchen. I'm halfway there when a guy stops me. He must be one of Ben's kickboxer friends. I'm dwarfed by him and have to crane my neck up to look him in the eye.

"You Kelsey?"

I nod, too intimidated to say anything.

He hands me the cordless phone. "Phone for you."

I frown, wondering why he was answering the phone in our house, then decide I don't care. I take it and escape to the relative quiet of the kitchen. Even with the door shut I still have to block my other ear before I speak into the phone. "Hello?"

"Hi."

I freeze. Not at his voice – I'm used to that by now – but at the background noise. Down the phone line, I can hear the sound of the party.

17

Chapter Seventeen

I go back into the living room, taking the phone with me. "Where are you?"

He doesn't answer at first. "Where do you think?"

I scan the room. Jacob's on a cell phone. He's over the far side of the room, too far away for me to hear if it's him. He's turned away, so I can't see if he's speaking. I move towards him. Then I see another guy on a cell phone. One of Ben's workmates, I think. And another guy's texting. I look around again. Billy's in the garden, his phone to his ear. Along with about three others. I watch them through the window.

"Why haven't you been answering your cell phone?"

"I ..." I shake my head. "I lost it. It doesn't matter."

I think of ringing the police, but what would I say? Some guy at our party just called me? They'd hardly send someone out for that.

I spin on the spot, trying to lip read from the guys with phones. "Where are you?" I say again.

"That doesn't matter. You need to leave."

"Who-?"

"Leave the party now!" He screams the words at me, then

the line disconnects.

Jacob doesn't hang up. Neither do the guys outside. I grab the phone out of the nearest guy's hand and hold it to my ear.

"What the hell are you doing?" He takes the phone back, but not before I hear a woman's voice. Not him.

I move towards the next guy. The phone in my hand rings again. I answer it.

"Don't try to find me. Just leave."

"Why?" I spin, watching the guys with phones.

"Leave the party or I'll kill you!"

"I don't …" I'm not sure what I'm trying to say.

I feel sick at the thought he's in my house. There's a click as the line disconnects. I drop the phone and rub my face.

Where the hell does he think I'm going to go? It's dark outside. I can't just go wandering off, and how do I know I can trust him not to follow me? Maybe he only wants me to leave so he can attack me outside.

I look down at the phone, but it doesn't ring again. There's a creamy-coloured powder on the floor where a cookie's been ground under foot. I scuff at it, rubbing it in more. Someone appears beside me, but I don't look up.

"Hey, Kels, how's your arm?"

I raise my head at the question. Tash's lipstick is smeared at the corner of her mouth. It makes it look wider than it should be, stretched into a wound-like gash.

"I …" I shake my head to clear it. "I have to go to the bathroom," I say.

Tash squints at me. "Is something–?"

I nod and move away from her.

"Kels?" I hear her call after me, but I don't look back.

The bathroom door's locked. I don't really need to go, but

I'm not sure what else to do.

I lean against the wall and wait, but the door doesn't open. The wallpaper's come off in a bubble, leaving a pocket just big enough for my hand. I touch the wall underneath. It's rough with the remnants of wallpaper paste. I try to stick the paper back down, but it doesn't work.

The bathroom door still hasn't opened.

"Hello?" I knock on the door. "Is anyone in there?" No one answers, but I think I hear someone throwing up.

I head back down the hallway towards the stairs. There's a girl passed out on the bottom step, her head resting on her friend's lap. The two of them block the staircase pretty thoroughly. The unconscious girl doesn't look like she could move, even if I asked her to, and I don't fancy my chances of climbing over them without injuring one or all of us.

Someone touches my back as they brush past me. I jump, throwing my arms across my face.

The guy laughs. "Sorry. Didn't mean to scare you." He pats my arm.

"Don't touch me." I push him away, and add a little hysterically, "And stop calling me!"

I back down the corridor, towards Aiden's bedroom.

He shakes his head. "I think you've had too much to drink, sister."

I bang on Aiden's door. "Aiden? Aiden, are you in there?"

He doesn't answer. I yank the door open and turn the light on.

Once I'm alone, I feel better. And a little stupid. I'm not even sure who that guy was, but I doubt he's the caller. Even if he was, he's hardly going to kill me in the middle of my house, in front of two drunk girls.

Aiden's room is mostly tidy, except it looks like he got up this morning and threw everything on his bed onto the floor. The mattress is completely bare, and I have to wade my way over a pile of bedclothes to get even halfway into the room.

I don't know what to do now. There's no chair in here, and I'd feel weird about sitting on Aiden's bed. I'm hoping the caller will leave now I'm out of sight, but I can't stay in here all night.

I hover for a bit then give in to my temptation to snoop. There's a bookshelf with a few books on it. Nothing I recognise. Most of them look like old textbooks. Beside the bed there's a glass of water, with scummy lip marks around the rim, and another book. I open it to the bookmarked page. Well, it's not really a bookmark. It's a scrap of cardboard torn from a cereal box. I read a couple of sentences off the page then put the book down.

There's not much else in the room. I spot a photo in a frame on the windowsill and tramp my way over the bedclothes to reach it. It's half covered by the curtain. I flick the fabric out of the way and pick the photo up.

It's of Aiden, he's probably about fifteen, but it's still obviously him, and a redheaded girl. Her head's tilted back to look at Aiden, and she's grinning. Aiden stares straight at the camera. He's not smiling, and he has this look about him that makes me think he can't have blinked for the last hour before the photo was taken. I run my thumb over the girl's face. She looks like she might have Down's syndrome, but I'm not sure. I wonder if she's his sister, Becky.

I turn it over to see if there's anything written on the back of the frame. It slips from my hand and hits the window frame. I curse under my breath, then stoop down to pick it up. The glass has smashed. I sit down on the floor to gather up the pieces. One of them cuts my hand. I put my finger in my mouth and try not to get blood everywhere. Aiden stares up at me from the photo, and I can tell he disapproves.

I jump as the door behind me creaks. I shove the photo back into the frame.

"Aiden, I'm–"

"Not Aiden."

I turn around at the sound of Jacob's voice. He grins at me from the doorway. "I saw you come in here."

I shake my head to clear it. "Hey, sorry." I head back over the pile of bedding towards the door. Jacob moves forward, meeting me halfway.

I stop, confused. "You shouldn't be in here." I shrug. "Actually, I shouldn't be in here. This isn't my room."

Jacob glances around. "Pity." He looks back at me and fixes me with a stare. He takes a swig from his beer. He's so drunk, he's swaying slightly, as if blowing in the wind. It makes me want to sway too, to stop from getting dizzy.

I narrow my eyes as I stare at him. Then I shake my head and laugh. "Anyway ..." I gesture towards the door.

"What happened to your hand?" He catches my wrist.

I look down at my finger. It's started oozing blood again. "Nothing. I'm just accident-prone."

I go to pull away, but Jacob lifts my hand to his lips. He stares at me as he sticks my finger in his mouth, licking away the blood.

"Oh my God!" I don't know if he meant that to be sexy, but all it did is make me want to throw up. "Don't. That's disgusting!" I draw back my hand and wipe it on my dress. I feel like I need a shower.

Jacob laughs. "Come on, Kels. I see the way you look at me."

"Excuse me?"

He pulls me towards him and locks his lips over mine. He tastes of beer and rust. I gag as I realise that's the taste of my own blood.

"Don't!" I try to pull away, but his arm's tight around my waist. "Jacob, stop!"

"Shh. It's okay." He kisses me again. His hand slides down my back.

I shove hard against his chest. "Stop it."

His face screws up. "What's your problem? I thought you wanted this."

"Well, I don't." I wrap my arms over my chest. "Anyway, what about Amber?"

"Amber? She's a psycho." He grunts and rubs his face. "I like you, okay? You don't need to be so uptight."

I blink a couple of times, not sure what to say to that. I guess it's always nice to hear someone likes you, but this is beer talking, not Jacob. At the moment he'd probably tell his own cousin he liked her if he thought there was a chance of some action.

Jacob seems to take my not saying anything as being lost for words. He comes over and kisses me again. I go stiff, hoping he'll realise I'm not into it, but he doesn't notice. He gets more insistent, pulling at my clothes.

He was on a phone. He could be the caller.

"No!" I step backwards, pulling away from him. My foot catches in the bedding, making me stumble. I grab Jacob's arm, but he stumbles too. He falls forward, knocking me over and landing on top of me. His hand smacks my face and his weight knocks the air out of my lungs. The floor shakes as we hit it. Jacob groans but doesn't move.

White spots prickle the backs of my eyelids. My ribs feel like they're broken. I gasp as I start to black out.

The door creaks as it opens. "Kelsey?" Pete looks down at me from the doorway. His face goes red. "What the hell are you doing?"

Jacob moves his hand from my face.

I try to say something, but I'm still too winded.

Pete's eyes swell in his face. He grabs Jacob by the back of his neck. "What did you do to my sister?" Pete shoves him up against the wall. I groan as I try to sit up.

"What did you do to her?" Pete's shakes Jacob, his knuckles white as they grip his shirt.

Jacob wriggles, as if he thinks he'll be able to squirm his way out of his shirt without Pete noticing. His mouth gapes like a dying fish. "Nothing. I kissed her and she fell over."

Aiden and Ben appear in the doorway. Ben looks like he can barely stand. Aiden's trying to support his weight, but he's dwarfed by Ben and the two of them sway from side to side.

"What the hell?" Aiden's face moves from confused to something nearing amusement.

I take a breath, finally managing to force air back into my lungs. "He wouldn't ..."

Ben comes forward and nearly falls on top of me. He tries to crouch down, but he can't balance properly. He ends up leaning against the wall beside me. He touches my shoulder in what's meant to be a gentle pat, but with his co-ordination out the window, it turns into a push.

"I'll fucking kill you!"

I look up at Pete's shout. His hand goes around Jacob's throat.

"Pete, stop it!"

Pete doesn't even seem to hear me. Jacob gags.

Billy appears in the doorway. His grin morphs into surprise. "Shit." He goes to pull Pete back, but Pete elbows him in the stomach. Billy backs away and doubles over. Pete drops his hand back to Jacob's shoulder.

Ben gets up and stumbles forward. "Did you hurt her?" He looks angry but his eyes are unfocused. He lurches from side to side as he moves towards Jacob.

Aiden steps in Ben's way, but even a drunk Ben is stronger than a sober Aiden. Ben keeps coming forward.

"Ben, don't." Aiden pushes him back.

I stand up and step in front of Ben. "Pete, stop! Nothing happened. Not really."

Ben turns to look at me. He stares at me, like he doesn't recognise me, then his body seems to give and he crumples, leaning on my shoulder. I think my collarbone's going to crack under his weight. I edge out from under his arm. He stumbles then sits down on Aiden's bed.

Pete looks from me to Jacob. "What happened?" He jerks Jacob against the wall. Jacob looks like he's about to cry. Pete's face is purple. His jaw shakes as he clenches it.

"Let him go." I step forward, but trip on the bedding.

Aiden catches my shoulders. He doesn't look at me and moves his hands away as quickly as he can.

"Pete." Aiden doesn't say anything else, but it seems to be enough.

Pete lets go of Jacob and backs away. He points his finger at Jacob's face. "You need to leave," he says. "Now." His voice goes all quiet and controlled.

Jacob rubs his shoulder where Pete was holding him. "I didn't do anything."

Pete steps forward again. The corner of his mouth is crusted with dried spit. He rubs his hand across his face, and it flakes off. Aiden steps back, as if he's scared. His arm brushes my shoulder.

Billy steps between Pete and Jacob. "Come on." He takes Jacob's shoulder and pushes him towards the door. "Don't be stupid."

Jacob shakes his head. "Yeah, all right, I'm going."

Billy turns back once he's out the door. "Bitch!"

Jacob shoves him away before Pete can react.

I press my hands against my ribs. It hurts to breathe. Sweat drips down my temple with the effort of it.

Pete's mouth makes an ugly shape and he shakes his head. He looks at me. "Are you all right?"

Aiden looks at me too. He's still retreating. In a second he'll hit the wall and be stuck.

I shake my head. "It was nothing. I just thought–" My voice comes out in a little puff, making that less convincing than I'd like.

Ben groans and leans his head down on his hands. His face has gone a sickly waxen colour. His index finger wobbles back and forth as he moves his hand away from his face.

Pete looks at him, as if he'd forgotten he was there. "I'd better ..." He gestures towards Ben. "Get up, Ben." He puts his arm around Ben and heaves him up to standing. "You need to go to bed."

"No, I ..." Ben stumbles and Pete pulls him upright.

"Come on." Pete pauses at the doorway. He looks back at

me. Ben droops against his shoulder. "Are you sure you're all right, Kel?" He gives me a mouth shrug which I choose to interpret as a smile.

I nod and attempt a return smile. "Thanks, Pete," I say and try to ignore the fact that I'm thanking him for violence.

When they're gone I turn to Aiden. He looks around his room, like he's inspecting a bird cage after a cat has got in.

"Aiden, I'm–"

"What happened to your hand?"

"My hand ..." I look down at the blood on my finger. "Your photo."

"Huh?" Aiden peers at me from under his eyebrows.

"Your photo. I broke the frame." I wade my way over to the window.

Aiden follows me.

"Careful of the glass," I say, then shake my head. "I'm so sorry. I dropped it. I'll pay for a new frame."

Aiden takes the photo from me and sits down on the bed. He half laughs then rubs his hand over his eyes. For a moment, I think he's crying, then I realise he's still laughing.

"I'm really sorry," I say again.

Aiden looks up at me. He's not smiling anymore. "This is the only photo I have of Becky," he says.

I chew on my lip, unsure of what to say.

Aiden turns the frame over and shakes out the last of the glass. "What were you doing in here, anyway?" His tone is harsh. I realise I deserve it.

I feel my shoulders rise up. "I got this phone call." I go cold at the memory. "I wanted to leave, but ..." I shake my head. "It doesn't matter. I shouldn't have been in here."

"I should have locked the door." Aiden shrugs and looks

away. "You have blood on your face."

I touch my cheek where I rubbed my finger against it. The blood comes off in a red smear.

Aiden takes something out of his pocket. "I forgot to give you this." He holds out my phone. "I found it in the bathroom."

I stare at it. When I don't take it, he drops it onto the bed and shrugs.

"It kept ringing when I was in the shower." He smirks. "Any reason you keep your phone under the sink?"

"Thanks." I ignore the questions and put the phone in my pocket. "Why do you only have one photo of your sister?" I say, in an attempt to change the subject.

Aiden scowls at the photo in his hands. "How many photos do you think Pete has of you?"

I scoff. "None, but you guys sound like you're closer than us."

Aiden stares up at me and sighs. He takes the photo out of the frame and turns it over. "Becky happy as always. Aiden in a sulk," he reads, then hands the photo to me. "That's what my mum wrote on the back." He shakes his head and stares at his hands. He presses his fingertips together, one at a time, until he's made a pyramid, then he curls his hands down into fists. "Becky and I weren't close at all." He links his fingers together and twists them around. "I resented her. I ignored her and now ..." There's a little catch in his voice, like he's about to cry, but he doesn't. Something about what he just said niggles at me.

"Weren't close?" I say. The skin on my forehead prickles. I force my breathing into a steady pattern.

Aiden looks up at me. "Huh?"

"You said 'weren't.' Like you meant ..."

Aiden and I stare at each other, then he nods. "Yeah. Weren't." He looks away.

I sit down next to him. "What happened?"

"She died. Last year."

"I'm so sorry. I didn't–" I touch his arm.

He pulls away and shakes his head. "Don't."

I drop my hand to my side. "Don't what?"

He closes his eyes and leans his head back. He runs his hands through his hair. "You should go now."

"What?"

"Just go away." He opens his eyes and looks at me. "You're always here. You're not my sister. I shouldn't have to look after you all the time." He rubs his hand over his mouth.

I can't help but flinch at his words. I stare at him. He stares back, his eyes cold. Then he turns his face away. He goes very still and closes off. I think he's trying not to cry.

"Just go, Kelsey." He wipes his temple with the heel of his palm.

I swallow. I want to say something to make it better, but there just isn't anything. I place the photo on the bed next to Aiden and walk away.

18

Chapter Eighteen

I run into Amber and Sophie in the living room. Amber's eye make-up is smeared. It's all down her face in big black streaks. It looks like ash, and I have to shake my head to clear it. She sees me and shoves my shoulders. I stumble backwards.

"Slut!" Amber spits at me.

Sophie pulls her back. "Don't. She's not worth it."

"I didn't do anything," I say, but it doesn't come out loud enough.

Amber glares at me. "You're just after everyone else's boyfriends, aren't you?"

I shake my head. "It was him, not me."

"Skank!" Amber lunges at me.

Sophie pulls her away. She mouths, "You're dead!" over her shoulder as she leads Amber away.

"I didn't do anything," I say again. This time it really is to myself.

The party's dissolved into chaos. It looks like I'm the only sober one here. There's a guy passed out on the couch with his head dangling off the end onto the coffee table. That would be fine, except he's using a bowl of muffins as a pillow. Some of the people from Ben's work are playing cookie frisbee. Michelle's at the centre, trying to catch the cookies in her mouth. So far she's been hit in the head at least three times. The rest of the baking is in the process of being ground into the carpet.

I see the phone lying on the floor where I dropped it. One of these people is the caller. The thought makes me sick. I try to convince myself he left after he called, but I don't really believe it. I shiver and go up to my room.

I lie face down on my bed and put the pillow over my head.

There's a knock on my door. "Yeah?" I sit up.

No answer. They probably can't hear me over the noise from the party. I get up and open the door.

Tash smiles at me from the hallway. "Hey, I was hoping this was your room."

"Are you heading off now?" I force a smile.

Tash rolls her eyes. "Well, I would be if my useless excuse for a brother hadn't gotten himself kicked out and left without me." Tash peers past me, into my room. "You haven't seen Billy, have you?"

I give an awkward laugh. "He's not in here, that's for sure."

Tash blushes. "I didn't mean ..." She shrugs. "I've been texting him, but he's not answering, and I haven't got any minutes left. I was hoping he'd walk me home, but he's disappeared. Can you help me look for him?"

I hesitate. Rationally, I'm probably no safer in my room than anywhere else in the house. Somehow it feels better, though. I look at Tash. I guess safety in numbers might be good, too.

"Sure." I pull a sweater on over my dress and go out into

the hall with Tash. "I think he left with Jacob, though."

"What actually happened tonight with Jacob?" Tash doesn't look at me as she says that.

"So you heard about that?"

Tash smiles. "Twin ESP. Can't keep anything a secret." Then she shrugs. "Actually, Amber and Sophie told me about it, but I'm guessing their version isn't all that close to the truth."

I swallow and look down. "I don't really want to talk about it, if that's okay."

"It's just he tends to get a bit over-friendly when he's drunk, so ..."

I cringe as she says that.

She shrugs and shakes her head. "Never mind. I shouldn't be prying."

"I guess Amber and Sophie are out for blood now." I rub my tongue against my teeth.

"I wouldn't worry about them."

I look up at Tash. "Yeah?"

"Yeah. They're all talk." Tash wrinkles up her nose.

"Amber said Jacob was her boyfriend."

Tash snorts. "Yeah, she decided that a couple of months ago. Jacob can't stand her, but it's hard to break up with someone you were never going out with in the first place." Tash shakes her head and laughs. "Anyway, speaking of my brother ..." She tilts her head to the side. "He's not that good with ... well, anything except rugby, and I know you're all screwed up over Mike, so if he came on a bit strong–"

"We should look for Billy." I look up as I cut Tash off.

She stares at me then smiles. "Yeah, we should."

Tash knocks on the closest door, which happens to be Ben's.

She opens the door before I have a chance to stop her.

Ben's not in there. At the moment, his room resembles Aiden's. It looks like he tumbled out of bed, taking half the bedding with him.

I go inside, as if I'm going to find him hiding in there. "Where is he?"

"Who?"

I look back at Tash. "Ben. He was out of it drunk. Pete was supposed to put him to bed." I go back into the hallway and knock on Pete's door. When he doesn't answer, I open it. His room's empty too.

"Bloody hell. Where are they?"

"What's with all the guys disappearing just when we need them?" Tash grins at me.

I shake my head. "I know." I knock on the bathroom door. "Ben? Are you in there?" It's not locked and not even shut properly. Still, for obvious reasons, I don't like the idea of walking in on someone in the bathroom. "Ben?" I call again, then look at Tash.

She shrugs. "Worth a try, I guess."

I open the door. Ben's sprawled on the floor. He's got sick all down his front and is only semi-conscious.

"Ben?" I kneel down beside him.

He groans and tries to wipe his face. He's so drunk, he misses and ends up wiping my knee instead.

"Come on, Ben." I haul him up to sitting position. I have to prop him up against my legs to stop him falling over again. "Ben? Ben?" I tap the side of his face. He mumbles something but doesn't open his eyes.

"You need to wake up."

He doesn't answer. His head flops against my shoulder.

I shake him. "Ben, wake up!"

He groans and shifts against me. I nearly tumble over with the weight of him.

I look up at Tash. She sniffs. Her lips purse with disgust.

I sigh. "Can you go find my brother? I can't move him by myself."

Tash nods and goes off. My shoulder starts to hurt. I shift my hand to the back of Ben's neck to move his head. His skin is warm and smooth. The muscles move under my hand as I touch them. His eyes flicker.

I tap him with my fingertips. "Ben? Can you hear me?"

He makes a hissing noise and bubbles of spit appear on his lips. I yank some toilet paper off the roll and wipe it over his face.

He jerks away from me. "Kel?" His voice is croaky. He coughs and spits on the floor. It's gross, but I'm just glad he didn't spit on me.

"It's all right." I stroke his face.

He squints up at me then blinks and shakes his head, like a baby woken early from a nap. "What …?"

I shift him, pushing him further upright. "Can you get up?"

He stretches forward onto his hands and knees. He moves in slow-motion, lumbering like a giant panda.

I stand to help him up and he reaches for my hands. He makes it onto one knee before tumbling back down, taking me with him. My right shin hits the floor hard and I smack my elbow on the bathroom cabinet. It sends a jolt through my funny bone and my lower arm goes numb. I let go of Ben's hand to clutch my elbow.

He lies back down on the floor. "I have to tell you something, Kel." He looks up at me. "Can I tell you something?"

He coughs again, but this time it doesn't stop. He hacks away until it turns into a groan. He rolls onto his side.

I rest my hand against his head.

"I need to tell you–"

Tash comes back into the room. "Couldn't find your brother, but I found this guy."

Aiden follows her into the room. "Aiden. My name's Aiden." He stares at Tash and shoves his hands deeper into his pockets, then he looks at me. Our eyes meet for a second, then he swallows and looks down. I shift my weight and keep my focus on Ben.

Tash shrugs, like she couldn't care less what Aiden's name is. She hands me a glass of water. "Thought this might help."

I hold the glass to Ben's lips.

He squirms away from me and whines, like a temper-tantrumy child.

I hold his chin and force the water on him. "Drink it."

He closes his eyes and swallows the water. I stroke the hair back from his face. "Do you think you can help me get him up?"

Aiden doesn't answer straight away, so I look up at him. His eyes flick away as soon as they meet mine. "He's covered in sick." He shifts, as if he thinks the vomit is going to get up and crawl over to him.

"I know. I'll have to clean him up."

Tash and Aiden both look relieved when I say *I'll* have to clean him up, not *we'll*.

Ben pats my arm. "I have to tell you something."

I sigh. "You can tell us whatever you want once we get you up."

Ben pulls my hair, making me look up. "I love you, Kel."

I freeze as he says that. I feel, rather than see, that Tash and Aiden go still, too. My throat goes really dry.

"Ben …" My airway feels like it's closed off.

Ben shifts and looks up at Aiden. "And I love you too, Aiden, and you … you." He points at Tash and smiles.

I look at Tash. She covers her mouth and giggles. Aiden presses his lips together, trying not to laugh.

I can't help but smile. "All right, Ben." I rub his arm. "We love you, too."

Between the three of us we manage to heave Ben up to sitting on the toilet. Tash goes out while I try to clean him up. It's not so easy when he keeps trying to pull my hair.

Aiden goes to find him a clean top. Fortunately, the sick's only on his top half. I don't think I could ever face him again if I had to remove his pants.

I wash his face with a clean flannel and chuck his shirt in a bucket to soak.

Aiden comes back in with a clean top. He clears his throat. "Kel, about what I said before–"

I pull the T-shirt out of his hands. "You're right. You're not my brother, I shouldn't treat you like you are." I don't look at him. I busy myself with redoing my ponytail.

Aiden sighs. He stares at the floor.

We both jump backwards as Ben throws up.

Aiden's face goes pale and a sheen of sweat appears on his forehead. He swallows and wipes his fingers across his throat. His breathing goes all huffy.

"Are you all right?" I'm not sure whether I'm asking Ben or Aiden.

Aiden answers. "I just feel a bit …" He rubs his stomach.

"Go." I point out into the hallway. "I don't want to be

cleaning up after two of you."

Aiden nods and backs away. "All right if I kick out anyone who's still here?"

"Absolutely fine with me." I relax as I realise that means the caller will have to leave, too.

I get Ben another bucket and make him hold it in front of him, while I mop the floor. He drinks a couple of glasses of water and seems to perk up a bit. I hold his hair back as he throws up again – this time into the bucket, fortunately. I stroke the back of his neck as he leans over the bucket. It's weird. The sick is gross, but somehow this isn't so awful. Ben looks up at me, and I wash his face again.

"I really do love you, Kel." His eyes are watery, but I can't tell whether he's crying or if it's just post-vomitness.

I sigh and stroke his head. "I know you do, honey."

Tash helps me get Ben to bed. Aiden's gone back to his room and I don't want to disturb him, especially if he's going to throw up too.

"I don't know how I'm going to get home," Tash says to me, once we've got Ben settled. "Jacob was supposed to drive me, but I suppose he was too drunk for that anyway. I don't have money for a taxi, and it's too dark to walk by myself." Tash rolls her eyes. "Stupid twin."

"I'd get Pete to drive you, but he hasn't turned up either." I shrug. I'm about to ask her if she wants to stay the night, when her phone beeps.

She looks at it and laughs. "Jacob," she says. "He's on his way back here. He's suddenly remembered he has a sister." She rolls her eyes. "Typical boy."

"You can swap anytime." I wrinkle my nose. "Pete's going to have a spaz when he sees how messy downstairs is."

Tash smiles. "Come on. I'll help you tidy up before Jake gets here."

After mopping up Ben's spew, the living room's nothing. Tash cleans up the tables, while I run the vacuum. Tash puts some music on, but it's drowned out by the sound of the vacuum. She turns the volume up.

I collect up the empties and dump them in the kitchen bin. I jump as I realise Tash has followed me.

"Thanks for inviting me, Kels." She smiles.

"Anytime." I smile back. I hope she doesn't take me saying "anytime" to actually mean any time. That would be sure to make Pete's head explode.

Tash fiddles with the charm bracelet around her wrist. The charms bounce away from each other as they collide.

"Jacob should be here soon, I guess," I say.

Tash looks at her phone. "Yeah, he said he was just down the road." She frowns. "I don't know. Maybe he got lost?"

"He can't be far away. Do you want to watch TV while we wait?"

Tash nods.

"I'd better just check on Ben first. Go through to the living room."

I knock on Ben's door. He doesn't answer, so I open it. Downstairs, I hear Tash switch the music off. There's a moment of silence then the sound of the TV.

It takes a second for my eyes to adjust to the dimness of Ben's room. Even when they do, I can't be sure whether he's okay or not. The bed's such a mess it's impossible to tell where exactly he is on it. I go in to check.

"Ben? Ben, are you all right?"

He doesn't answer. I go right up to the bed and pull the

covers back.

He's not there.

I stare at the mattress, as if I think he's going to materialise, then I sigh and go check the bathroom. I left a bucket for him so he wouldn't have to get up if he was going to be sick, but you can't trust a drunken person to remember that. He's not in the bathroom either. I look in Pete's room, then mine, then go back downstairs.

"He didn't come back down here, did he?" I ask Tash.

She shakes her head. "Not that I've seen."

I check all the rooms then go knock on Aiden's door.

"Yeah?" he calls.

"Ben's not in there, is he?" I feel stupid talking to the door. If Aiden wasn't already pissed at me, I'd just open it.

"No. Why would he be?" There's rustling as Aiden moves around.

I sigh. "It doesn't matter."

I turn back towards the living room. The front door's wide open. I peer out into the dark then shut it. If Ben's gone wandering out there, I don't know what to do. It's like looking for a missing dog.

Tash looks up. "Any luck?"

I shake my head. The TV shows an infomercial for a bread maker that also cooks bacon.

I look back at Tash. "I'm going to call Pete," I say.

She runs her tongue over her lip. "Do you mind if I call Jake after that? He should be here by now."

I dial Pete's number. A second later I hear a cell phone ringing. I follow the sound. It stops before I find it, so I ring Pete's number again. I stop by the window. The sound's coming from outside. I pull back the curtain and stare out.

"Is that …" I try to focus on the dark shape on the front lawn. "Oh my God!"

I rush outside. My bare feet curl up against the cold of the driveway.

"Kelsey? What's wrong?" Tash follows me out. She hovers on the doorstep.

As I move closer, the dark shape morphs into a person – a guy, lying face down in the grass.

I giggle and squat down beside him. "Pete, I don't care how drunk you are, that's a stupid place to sleep."

He doesn't move. I shake his shoulder. "Come on. Get up." I reach for his face, but soft hair brushes my hand, and I jerk away. "Wait, I don't think that's Pete." He still doesn't move. I look back at Tash.

She holds up her hand to block out the glare from the streetlight. "Who is it then?"

I shake my head. "I'm not sure." I shove him, forcing him onto his back.

His mouth hangs open, his tongue slack against his lips. His eyes are blank, staring at me but not. There's a blade of grass stuck to his cheek.

"Tash …" My voice breaks up in the air. I hear her walking towards me.

I look down at his chest. There's a knife sticking out from it and a pool of brown creeping out over his shirt. I rub my fingertips against my thumb. They stick together. They're covered in the same brown from his shirt.

"Who is it?"

I turn and stare at her. "It's Jacob," I say.

Tash stops beside me and looks down. Then she starts to scream.

19

Chapter Nineteen

"Did you touch the knife, Kelsey?"

The policewoman has to repeat the question several times before I understand it.

"I don't think so … I don't know." I swallow down the bad taste in my mouth. "I touched his shoulder," I say. "There's blood on my hand." I hold my fingertips up for her to see. My hands are shaking. I want to wash the sticky feeling off. There's blood on my other hand, too, but I think that's my own.

"Is he …?" I don't know what I'm trying to ask. I know he's dead. Your eyes don't look like that unless you're dead. I want to ask if he's going to be okay, though. I want her to say he is.

A policeman has taken Tash down the hall to the kitchen, but I can still hear her screaming. They found Pete's phone in the grass by the garage. No sign of Pete, though.

My head hurts with all the lights. Every light in the house is on, and the ambulance and police cars flash red and blue against the living room windows. It makes my head hurt, but I don't want them to turn them off. I don't want it to ever be dark again.

"Why did you go outside?" The policewoman moves her head back and forth in an attempt to look me in the eye.

I blink, trying to make my eyes focus. "Pete's phone," I say eventually. "I rang it. I could hear it ringing outside. Then I saw Jacob …" I lean my head down on my hand. "Where is Pete?" I ask.

She doesn't answer. I don't think she even knows who Pete is.

I keep getting a hissing in my ears. My skin goes cold and everything goes grey. It's better now I'm sitting down, but I'm so clammy. I can feel sweat dripping down my neck. I press my hands into the fabric of the couch to ground myself. My hands start to hurt, and I realise I've got blood on the cushions.

"Is he really dead?" I look up at the policewoman. I want her to lie. If she says he's alive, I'll believe her. It doesn't matter what I saw outside. I'll put that all down to a nightmare.

The policewoman looks down at her feet. She's young, not much older than me. She rubs her fingers over the seam in her trousers. "I have to go write this up." Her throat bobs as she swallows.

"Wait." I pull my phone out of my pocket. "I got a call-"

"From Pete?" She takes her notebook out again.

I shake my head. "No. I … I don't know who from, but he was at the party. He said that I had to leave-"

"So, it was someone that you know?"

"No. Well, maybe. I don't know."

The policewoman frowns. She flips her notebook closed. Her face is closing off too. She's not really listening, and I don't know how to make her.

"Detective Jenkins?" I ask. "Can I talk to her?"

"She should be here soon. I'll let her know that you'd like to speak to her." The policewoman pulls at her ponytail as she walks away.

I try dialling Ben's number. He's left his phone behind; I can hear it ringing upstairs. Aiden comes and sits next to me. I don't look at his face but stare at his hands instead. They're pressed together so hard, his fingertips are red and his knuckles white.

"Where are they?" I ask him.

He shakes his head. I hear his throat click. "There was so much blood," he says. His voice shakes.

I cover my face with my hands. I hear myself groaning, but I'm not in control of it. "Why didn't I leave?" I say into my hands. "He told me to leave. Why didn't I leave?"

Aiden doesn't answer. I'm not even sure he heard me. The couch shakes as his leg jiggles up and down. He presses his heel into the floor and it stops. A second later, it pops up again and resumes shaking.

"Where are they?" I say again.

There was so much blood, too much for one person ... I shake my head to stop that thought. "Why didn't we hear anything?"

Aiden rubs his face. "The music ... and the TV."

"And the vacuum," I add. "We should have heard something, though."

Aiden nods.

"Where are they?" I stand up, but I get dizzy and have to sit down again.

I hear Pete's voice outside: "What's going on?"

I'm up and running before I even think about it. Aiden follows me. I grab Pete, wrapping my arms around him.

He squirms, as if he's going to push me away, then pats my back instead. "What's wrong? Why ...?" He gestures towards the police and ambulance.

"I thought you were dead," I say into his shoulder.

Pete laughs. "You thought I was ..." He stops and looks around. "What happened?"

"A guy was stabbed." Aiden shifts beside me. His shirt sleeve brushes my arm.

"Oh my God! Is he ..." Pete trails off as Aiden shakes his head. "Who was it?"

Aiden clears his throat. "The guy you ... kicked out."

Pete rubs his hands over his hair. "That's ... God, that's awful."

I pull back to look at Pete. "Where were you? I couldn't find you and ... Where did you go?"

Pete looks at me as if he doesn't understand the question. He pinches the bridge of his nose. "I had to give Jenny a lift home. She wasn't feeling well. God, this is horrible." He rubs his temples. "Do they know who ...?"

I shake my head. "Do you know where Ben is?"

"No, he's not with me." Pete keeps rubbing his face. It's lit by the flashing police lights. The blue makes him look sick, all dark circles and hollows; the red makes him look surreal, like a goblin or a devil. I start to shiver.

The policewoman from before comes up to us. "You need to go back inside. This is a crime scene." She turns to Pete. "Who are you?"

"Pete Morgan. I live here."

The policewoman makes a noise in her throat. "We'll need to interview you. Go inside, please."

Pete makes me some coffee. I ignore the bitter taste and

force myself to drink it. I get the shakes afterwards. Tash is still crying. She sits on the floor in the kitchen, rocking back and forth. I sit down next to her, but I don't know what to say. I touch her arm and she clings to me.

My cell phone beeps in my pocket. I pull it out, hoping it's a text from Ben.

Two new messages.

I unlock the keypad then open the first message.

I DID IT FOR YOU.

My chest and stomach hurt like they've been ripped open. I look at the second message.

TELL ANYONE AND I'LL KILL YOU TOO.

"Oh God!" I press my hand to my mouth.

Tash's sobs turn into wails.

I wrap my arms around her. "Shhh, it's ..." I stop myself. I was going to say, it's okay. But it's not. I rub her back instead.

"Kelsey?"

I look up as Detective Jenkins calls my name.

She squats down beside me. "You wanted to talk to me?"

I look down at my phone. "No. No, I didn't."

She frowns and glances at Tash. "Perhaps we could go somewhere and talk?"

"No." I shake my head. "I need to stay with Tash."

Tash doesn't move. She doesn't even seem to be aware of me holding her anymore.

"Kelsey, if you–"

"I don't." My eyes leak as I look at Detective Jenkins. "I

don't know who did this." I brush my hand across my face.

Detective Jenkins questions me for a while longer, but when I keep repeating the same thing, she gives up. She gives me another business card, but I throw it away as soon as she's gone. She thinks she can protect me, but she can't. He was in our house tonight. No one can protect any of us.

An hour later, the policewoman comes over to tell us they've found Ben. He'd fallen asleep at a bus stop. She tells us they've taken him to the police station to question him. She won't tell us why.

Pete tries to convince me to go to bed. I'm tired, but I don't want to. We all end up sitting in the living room, staring at the floor, or the ceiling, or the walls – anywhere but at each other. Tash's parents pick her up. I can't look at them. They go to the hospital or wherever it is that Jacob's gone. Jacob's body, I should say. I don't know where the rest of him has gone.

I don't want to fall asleep, but I can feel myself drifting off. I jerk myself awake every time my head droops, but eventually I have to give in to it.

I wake the next morning at the sound of the front door closing. There's this lovely moment before I remember. Then Ben walks into the room, and I can see from his face that it's bad.

He crouches down beside me as I start to cry. He puts his arms around me and holds me while I sob into his shoulder.

"It's okay, Kel. It's going to be okay."

I pull away from him. "He's dead. It's never going to be okay."

"I know, it's just ..." He doesn't finish that, but I'm pretty sure I get the gist of it. I don't know what else to say, is what he really means.

He shuffles around until he's leaning against the front of the couch. His hair brushes my arm.

"Why did they want to talk to you?"

Ben doesn't answer at first, so I twist around to look at him.

He presses his lips together into a thin line. "There was blood on my shirt." He looks up at me. "They decided it was mine in the end. My head started bleeding again."

"Who do they think …?"

Ben rests his head back against me. "They think it was random. Probably had nothing to do with him, or us, but …" He twists around to look at me. "Don't go off by yourself, okay? Especially after Mike."

I wonder if I should set him straight. It might not have had anything to do with Jacob, but it certainly had something to do with me.

"Where's Pete?" I ask after a bit.

"Outside."

"Where did you go last night?"

Ben shakes his head. I shift my arm as his hair tickles me.

"Apparently I was trying to buy a newspaper. I don't remember." He closes his eyes and draws his chin into his chest. His skin is hangover green. He groans. "I think I told some girl I loved her last night."

I swallow. "That was me."

Ben goes really still, then he turns to face me. He doesn't quite meet my eye.

I shrug and attempt a smile. "Me and Tash … Aiden too, actually."

Ben pushes air out of his lungs in something that might be a laugh. He rubs his hand across his eyes. "I'm never drinking again." He shakes his head. "Who's Tash?"

"A friend from school. She's Jacob's ..." It hits me like I've belly flopped into cold water. I look at Ben and my face crumples. His face matches mine. He puts his arms around me as I cry.

He sits with me until I fall asleep. I wake up as he moves away.

"Where're you going?" I cling to his arm.

"I'm just going upstairs to change." He squeezes my hand and tries to let go.

I claw at him, pulling him back. "Don't go! Don't leave me alone. He'll kill me if you leave me alone." I can't breathe and my chest hurts.

Ben crouches back down. "Shhh ..." He pushes the hair back from my face. "You're okay. No one's going to hurt you."

I grab his hands, then when that doesn't calm me, wrap my arms around his waist. "Don't go. Please don't go." My breath comes out in big, choking sobs. I swear if I let go the caller will slip into the house. My stomach contracts at the thought.

Ben unwraps my arms from around him. I struggle against him until he sits down and pulls me into his lap.

"You're okay, Kel." He presses my head against his shoulder and strokes my hair. "You're safe. I won't let anything happen to you."

"You can't stop him," I say. "He was watching me sleep!"

Ben doesn't say anything for a second. His Adam's apple bobs. "It was just a dream. You're safe, I promise."

I close my eyes and bury my face in his shoulder.

I wake later in the day. I'm lying flat on the couch, and Aiden's sitting in the armchair next to me. He's pulling the stuffing from the arm, but he doesn't pitch it across the room, he just drops it into his lap. I watch him for a while before he realises I'm awake. My breathing comes out slow and laboured as I try not to hurt my chest too much. Aiden tips his head to the side and peers at me, as if he's deciding something.

"Where's Ben?" I ask. My voice comes out all croaky.

"In the garage. Pete's at Jenny's."

My head throbs. I close my eyes against the light, then think of how dark it was last night and open them again. I sit up and run my hand over my hair. It's back in dreads. Aiden crosses his arms and tucks his chin into his chest. He shivers and closes his eyes.

"Do you keep seeing it?" My question comes out as a whisper. I shiver, too, and shake my head to clear it.

Aiden doesn't answer. He rubs his mouth, as if he's going to be sick. "It was …" His voice is thick. He shakes his head.

"I know." I close my eyes. I hear Aiden shift.

He clears his throat. "I think I'm going to go to out. I can't … I can't be here at the moment."

I sigh. "Yeah." I look at Aiden then stand up. "I'm going to go talk to Ben," I say. I hesitate as I pass Aiden. His eyes are still closed, but I think he feels me hovering. I touch his shoulder before walking away. He doesn't acknowledge it, but he doesn't flinch away either.

Ben is hitting the punching bag when I go into the garage. I sit myself up on the bench by the wall. Ben steadies the bag as it swings back towards him. He chews on his lip, watching me. I pull on the straggly bits of hair around my face.

I look up at him. "Can you teach me how to punch?"

"Huh?"

"Can you teach me how to … you know, defend myself." I look down at my pipe-cleaner arms and wonder if there's any point. Even if I knew how, I'm probably not strong enough to hit anyone.

He frowns. "Of course. Come here." He holds out his hand to me. I lower myself off the bench and go over to him. His hands brush my shoulders, setting me up in front of the bag, then he moves to stand next to me. "Arms up like this. Left foot forward."

I move to copy him.

He narrows his eyes as he watches me, then pushes my shoulders, making me stumble. "If you're centred that won't happen. Sink your weight over your legs so you're balanced."

I don't really understand what he means, but I move until I feel "centred" and he nods. I raise my arms again and jab at the bag, testing it out.

Ben grabs my wrist before it connects. He uncurls my hand. "Thumbs out. If you punch like that, you'll break your hand." He looks at my cast and frowns, but doesn't say anything. He pushes my fingers back down and lays my thumb over the top. "Okay?"

I nod and rearrange my other hand as best I can. My fingers don't really reach over the cast into a fist, but I hold my hand as if they did.

"When you punch, you start with your big toe."

I frown. Ben smiles at my confusion. "Watch." He turns his foot as he punches. His whole body twists around, bringing his hand forward. I drop my arms as I watch. They're starting to hurt already. Actually, my whole body is hurting. It aches just with the effort of staying upright. I shift my feet.

Ben turns to face me. "You try."

I attempt to square up my shoulders, and move my arms and feet back to where they were. I try to remember Ben's instructions. They were pretty simple, but my head's fuzzy. I twist my foot around and bring my arm forward. Something doesn't feel right.

"You need to move your hip too, Kel."

I shake my head. "Maybe this was a stupid idea." I turn away.

Ben catches my wrist and pulls me back. "Come on. You're doing okay."

I sigh. My hands dangle awkwardly at the ends of my arms. Ben presses his lips together and tries not to look amused.

"I'm really tired," I say. My voice cracks and I have to swallow a lump in my throat.

Ben's face goes serious. "I know." He scuffs his foot against the floor. "We can do this another time."

I take a breath then shake my head. "No, it's okay. I'm being stupid."

I shift back into position. This time Ben stands behind me. When I twist my foot around, he pushes my hip around too.

"Better?"

"Yeah, sort of." I move back and try it again.

Ben moves his hand to my side, guiding me. "Now keep your elbow soft ... Good." He brushes the hair back from my face. "You want to try it for real?"

I shrug. "I guess." My eyes flick up to Ben's, then away again.

He steps back. "Same thing, just harder and faster."

I settle my feet into the floor and stare at the bag. You're probably supposed to picture something on it, like someone's face, but that doesn't feel right. It makes me go cold to think like that. The bag shifts, like a giant blue chrysalis swaying in the wind. The stitching has come undone at the side of it. A flap pokes out at the top, marked with regular, machine-punched thread holes.

Maybe closing my eyes is the best choice. I practise the movement a couple more times, slowly, going through the motions, then I go for it. My hand connects with the bag. It feels numb, stinging, like an overenthusiastic high-five, but good too. I open my eyes just in time to see the bag swinging back towards me.

"Shit." Ben catches me as it knocks me backwards. "Are you all right? I'm sorry, I should have held it."

It takes me a moment to get my breath back. I suddenly realise Ben's hand is on my boob. He seems to realise at the same time, as he shifts it to my waist. I don't trust myself to move. My legs are shaky and everything's fuzzy around the edges. Ben turns me around. He looks down at me, his eyes wide with concern. I force a smile to show him I'm all right. He smiles too, then something else crosses his face.

"Kel ..." His eyes flick down to the ground, then back up to mine. "Kel, I ..."

He leans down and kisses me. He does it quickly, like he's afraid he won't get the chance again.

Before I can think about it, I'm kissing him back. He winds his hand in my dreadlocky hair. His other hand presses the small of my back. I twist my hands in the back of his shirt. Then he's kissing my face and my neck. I run my hand through his hair. It springs back up as I touch it.

Ben whispers into my neck. "I love you."

The words hit me like bits of hail. I stumble backwards, pulling away from him. He follows me, steadying me as I back into the punching bag.

"No," I say. I can't look at him. My hand hurts, and my arms are going numb.

Ben's face falls. "What's wrong? I thought ..."

I look back at him. His face blurs as my eyes spill over.

"You can't love me." I swallow, but the lump in my throat sticks. "I'm a horrible person."

"You're a ..." Ben half laughs then stops himself. He reaches out to me, but I pull back, afraid to let him touch me.

"What do you mean?" He frowns.

I press my hands to the sides of my face. "If you get too close, I'll hurt you. I won't mean to but ... It's my fault. It's my fault they're dead. I killed them."

"Who? What do you mean?" Ben comes forward.

I push him away, but he grabs my wrists and holds me.

"What do you mean?" he says again.

"Mike and Jacob." My voice cracks on their names. "I killed them. I didn't mean to, but–"

"Kel–"

"He did it. I didn't want him to, but ... I don't want him to hurt you."

"Who?" When I don't answer, Ben shakes me. "Who?"

"I don't know. I don't know. It's my fault." I cover my face with my hands. They shake so much my whole head vibrates.

"You don't know?"

"No, but–"

Ben pulls my arms away from my face. "Kel." He looks down at the ground and sighs. "I get that you feel guilty, but–"

"No, you don't! It's my fault!"

"It's not. It's not your fault." He kisses my eyes and cheeks as I cry.

I push him away. "No–"

I'm interrupted by the sound of the phone ringing in the house. My skin freezes. I stare at Ben, feeling sick.

He reaches out to touch my face. "Kel–"

"No." I back away from him. "No!" I run into the house, towards the sound of the phone.

20

Chapter Twenty

"Kel? Kel, stop!"

I ignore Ben and keep going.

He catches up easily. "Please, can we just talk about this? I thought–"

"No." I push him away and grab the phone.

"Kel, please!"

I close my eyes. "Hello?" I say into the phone.

Silence.

"Hello? Hello?" My voice shakes as I cry.

Still silence.

"Don't do this! Talk to me!" I scream into the phone. There's a click as he hangs up. I drop the phone down on the bench and cover my face. My throat closes up with sobs.

Ben wraps his arms around me and presses his cheek against the top of my head. "Please, Kelsey, just talk to me, okay? Just talk to me."

I cringe as I realise he's crying too. "I can't." I pull away from him, but he's too strong. "Let me go, Ben."

"Please." He kisses the side of my face. "Please, don't ..." He moves, pressing his face into my neck.

I scrunch up my forehead. His arms squeeze my stomach. I grip his wrists. "Ben ... Ben!"

"Please ..."

I shake his arms, forcing him to loosen his hold. "I don't love you, Ben," I say. The lie makes my throat ache. His arms go stiff around me. "I'm sorry," I say. I close my eyes and turn my face away from his.

He leans his forehead against my shoulder. I tense up, not letting myself react. I feel his breath against my skin. He drops his arms and backs away. I turn to face him. He doesn't look at me. I swear I can see him deflating.

I stare at the floor between us. "I really am sorry." I wish I could say something to make it better. There just isn't anything, though.

He raises his head but doesn't meet my eye. "I'm going to go ..." he gestures toward the garage.

I watch him close the door behind him, then I go up to my room. My head pounds and I feel like I'm suffocating. I lie face down on my bed. I want to disappear; I want to turn to stone. Instead, I cry until my insides hurt.

My head feels heavy, puffy, like it's swollen to four times its usual size. I roll over and lie on my back. The room spins as I do. My nose starts to bleed. I wipe it on my hand, then on a tissue when it doesn't stop. The blood makes me feel sick. I close my eyes so I don't have to look at it.

The phone doesn't ring again. I keep trying to make myself go downstairs, but I can't do it. Ben will never forgive me for this. I cringe every time I think about it. My hands move to the sides of my face by themselves, and I have to squeeze my head or I'll just dissolve into nothing.

After a while, I hear Ben moving around downstairs. It's getting dark outside. Condensation builds up on the inside of my window and dribbles down onto the sill. The wood's split and mouldy at the corner from all the moisture. There's a crash as Ben drops something, then muffled swearing. I swallow, enjoying the pain in my throat, then get up and go wash my face in the bathroom.

I go downstairs, into the kitchen. Ben's making a sandwich, but it appears to be more of an excuse to throw things around than anything else. He slams a loaf of bread onto the bench as I come in. He doesn't look up.

"I really am sorry, Ben." I hold my head up as I say it, but my voice comes out with a huge crack down the middle.

He pauses in buttering his bread but doesn't look at me.

"I ..." I close my eyes. There's something I should be saying, something that will make it all better. I'm just too stupid to know what it is. "I didn't mean to hurt you," I say eventually. It sounds pathetic even to me. I let my arms dangle, waiting for Ben to react, but he doesn't. I turn away.

Ben scoffs as I do. I look back at him. He meets my eye for a second then looks away.

I lick my lips. It's like rubbing my tongue over drywall. "Whatever you want to say, you can."

Ben's eyes flick up to mine again.

"Yell at me, whatever. I deserve it."

Ben shakes his head. "Forget it." He mashes a lump of butter into his bread. The bread tears and the butter smears across the bench. He throws the knife down on the bench top, making me jump. It bounces and falls to the floor. I watch

Ben's throat as he swallows.

"You could have told me," he says at last. He looks up at me.

I force myself to meet his eye.

"All this time, I thought ... You could have told me you didn't feel the same, and don't tell me you didn't know, because you did. You must have known."

"I'm sorry."

"Stop saying that!" He runs his hands through his hair. "You're not sorry or you wouldn't have let me ..." He shakes his head and stares at the ceiling. His mouth moves without sound. He sighs and drops his voice. "You wouldn't have let me think you felt the same."

I look down at my feet. I feel the symmetry of it, him looking up, me looking down. Then I realise it's not symmetry at all. We're just pulling in different directions.

He rubs his eyes and looks at me again. "I'm going out."

"Where?"

"Don't know. Don't care."

I follow him into the living room. "Don't go."

He picks up his coat from the couch. "Why? What's going to change if I stay?"

I peer into the growing darkness outside. A fizzing bubbles up inside me. "He'll kill you if you go outside!" The words wrench themselves from inside me. I grab Ben's arm and cling to it.

His face softens and his hand brushes mine. "Who, Kel? You keep saying ..." He raises his hands in a gesture of frustration. "Who?"

I shake my head. The rest of me shakes, too, in a tremor. "I don't know."

Ben sighs. He peels my hands back from his arm. "No one is trying to kill you, Kel."

"He killed Jacob." I clutch Ben's hands. "And Mike."

Ben looks down. I count his breaths as I wait for him to answer. Finally he looks up.

"What happened to Jacob," Ben swallows and bobs his head, "and to Mike was awful, but it's not the same thing. It doesn't mean ..." He squeezes my hands. "Maybe you need to talk to someone, Kel. What you're saying, it ... it doesn't make sense." He gives me something that's close to a smile and lets go of my hands. They tingle as he drops them. He turns away.

"Ben ..."

He hesitates but doesn't look back. My voice peters out. I shiver as I realise he's leaving me alone in the house, then again as I think of him alone outside. After the phone call last night, I half expect the caller to jump out at me from one of the cupboards. I'm picturing it happening. He's wearing a ski mask, then pulls it off. Underneath, his face is a mixture of Jacob's and Mike's.

I groan and stumble upstairs. Somehow it feels safer on the second floor. I wonder if the police would even believe me, if I tried to tell them. Ben obviously doesn't. He looked at me like I'm crazy. Maybe I am; I don't know anymore.

Ben screams.

I lose my footing, falling flat on my face. My chin hits the carpet, and I hear my teeth crack together.

Everything happens very slowly. I pick myself up. He screams again. I think I'm running, but it's all so slow. My feet thud against the stairs. The sound echoes my pulse.

"Ben? Ben?" My feet hurt as they hit the gravel on the path.

I see Ben, on his knees beside his car. I run towards him. He topples over into the grass.

"Ben!" I catch his head in my hands.

He groans and looks down.

"Oh my God!"

His arm is covered in blood. There's a big slash across it, and it spurts blood. His car keys drop from his hand. He starts to shake.

I look for something to tie around his arm. There's nothing. I pull at my clothes, but they're the wrong shape.

The grass is wet. The streetlight catches the water, making little lights. I feel around in it, but I'm not even sure what I'm looking for.

I'm kneeling on something hard. I reach down and pull it out. My stomach clenches as I do. "Oh my God!" It's a knife, a big one, like you'd use to cut bone.

"Kelsey."

I look back at Ben as he says my name. His eyes look unfocused. There's so much blood. He's really pale, waxen, like his skin isn't part of him anymore. His lips shiver as he speaks. They're turning blue.

I clamp my hands around his arm, like a tourniquet. It stems the blood a little.

"Stay with me, Ben. Okay? You just stay with me!"

He groans. His eyes flicker and close.

"Wake up!" I scream. "Ben! Wake up!"

He opens his eyes, but they're still unfocused.

"I love you, Ben. You stay awake because I love you!"

His eyes close again.

"I love you! Ben? Ben?" I shake his arm but it makes it bleed more. "Ben? Ben, please!"

I shake my leg, trying to get my phone out of my pocket. It doesn't work. I look around. With all the noise, lights have come on in the neighbour's houses.

"Help!" I scream. "Help!"

A door opens and someone comes outside.

"Help!"

A woman kneels down beside me. "Call an ambulance," she yells over her shoulder. She wraps a scarf around Ben's arm, tying it over my hands. "It's okay. Help's coming," she says to Ben.

Other people come outside. I hear them talking. Others come over to help.

"I love you, Ben," I say again, but it's lost in the noise.

I look up as Pete calls my name. He takes a step back as he sees me. I look down at myself. My clothes and skin are covered with blood. My face too, probably, as I've been leaning my head in my bloody hands.

Pete sits down next to me and wraps an arm around me. I don't push him away, but I groan as he touches me. He squeezes my shoulder. I groan again. The noise seems to well up inside me, making me shake. I keep seeing it, except things change and swirl. I find Mike dead on my lawn. Ben's trapped in a coma. I tell Jacob I love him while trying to stop the blood.

"Have they said anything?"

"No."

I'm surprised Pete even made it to the hospital. I was so incoherent on the phone, the nurse had to take over. She told him to come, while I sat in the chair, trying to breathe. The police talked to me, too, but I can't even remember what I said to them. I could have told them I stabbed him, for all I know.

"God. Who would do this? And why?" He rubs his hand over the back of his head.

I shake my head.

"Fuck." He sighs. "They'd just better catch the bastard."

"I touched the knife," I say to Pete. "I didn't mean to, but–"

"Shhh. It doesn't matter."

I raise my head. The lights hurt my eyes and I have to squint. "I didn't see anyone. I just saw the knife."

"Don't worry about that now."

"We need to call his parents."

Pete nods. "I've done that. They're going to try and get a flight out."

I look up as a doctor comes over to us. "You came in with Ben Graham?"

I nod. Pete shifts his arm from around me.

The doctor turns to him. "And you are?"

Pete holds out his hand. "Pete Morgan. I'm her brother. Ben's flatmate."

I swallow as Pete says his name. "Is he okay?"

The doctor smiles. "He's awake. You can go and see him now. Just one at a time, please, and try to keep it short. He's very tired."

I lean my head down as a rush of relief mixed with nausea sweeps through me. The doctor touches my shoulder as she leaves.

"I thought he was going to die," I say to Pete. I hear him take a breath, a long one.

He stands up. "I'm going to go in. Will you be all right by yourself?"

I nod, but don't look up.

Pete sways on the spot. "Maybe you should wash some of that blood off. You know, before you see him."

I rub my hands together. The blood feels like it's seeped under my skin, becoming a permanent stain. Even if it does wash off, I'll never be able to forget it.

A nurse lets me use the shower in the staff room. The blood runs in a red swirl down the drain. It doesn't look like blood anymore, but like red hair dye washing out. Even so, I keep jerking my feet away from the water as it rushes over them. It's burning my skin.

The same nurse gives me some scrubs to wear. They don't have pockets, so I stuff my cell phone into my bra.

The police take my clothes. Apparently they have to test them. I'm not sure what for. I've already told them it's Ben's blood.

Pete's back in the waiting room when I come out. I tie my hair up with a rubber band I find on the floor, and sit down next to him.

"Aiden's in there at the moment, but you should go in." Pete rubs his eyes. "Ben really wants to see you."

My arms and legs feel funny, like I've got an all-over case of pins and needles. "Does he ...? Is he angry with me?" I say.

Pete frowns. "What? No." He sighs. "You did good, okay? You got him to the hospital. You did everything you could." He shakes his head and closes his eyes. "The nerve damage–"

"Nerve damage?" I look up at Pete.

He doesn't say anything for a bit. Then he looks at me. "His arm. They think there might be permanent nerve damage."

"What does that mean?" My chest hurts. I rub my hand across my collarbone, digging my fingertips into the skin.

"They're not sure yet, but he might not be able to kickbox again."

I close my eyes. All the harm I've caused in the past few weeks feels like it's choking me. It's building up inside me, so there's no room for my lungs.

Pete taps my shoulder. "Anyway, you really should go in."

I take a breath and stand up. Pete stands up, too, and hugs me. It feels weird, like being hugged by a stranger. I want to hug him back, but I can't make myself. Instead, I close my eyes and resist the urge to pull away.

He lets go and steps back. "He doesn't know about his arm. How bad it is, I mean. Don't tell him – it can wait."

Aiden's sitting by Ben's bed. He gets up as soon as I walk in. Ben looks up. My eyes spill over. I cover my mouth with my hand, as if I can squash the emotion back inside, but it doesn't work. My whole body starts to shake.

Ben chuckles. "I don't look that bad, do I?"

I try to smile, but it just makes me cry more.

Ben lowers his voice to speak to Aiden. "I need to talk to Kel. I'll see you later, okay?"

"Yeah, see you later, bud." Aiden taps Ben awkwardly on the leg. He shuffles past me, like he's afraid I'll get snot on him if he comes too close.

I take a couple of breaths in an attempt to stop crying, then look up.

Ben's watching me, his face almost amused. He reaches out with his good arm.

I go over and sit down by his bed. His left arm's all bandaged up now. Even so, when I look at it I shiver, thinking of the blood. I have to focus on his face to see him as he is now. In my head he turns blue again, like he's drowning in the hospital air.

Ben takes my hand in his good one.

I squeeze it and press his fingers to my lips. "I'm so sorry." My tears dribble down my face and onto our hands.

Ben circles my wrist with his hand. He pulls my arm forward until I open my eyes.

"Kel, about today–"

"I'm sorry."

Ben touches his finger to my lips. He shakes his head. "Do you know what I was thinking when ...?"

I look down. I count his breaths. I feel like I have to measure each one or they'll stop. He doesn't say anything until I look back up.

"I was thinking that would be the way you remembered me – me yelling at you."

I shake my head. "It's okay. I–"

Ben jerks my arm, making me stop. He squeezes my forearm, pressing his fingers into my skin. "Don't, Kel. Don't say you deserved it, because you didn't. People treat you like crap, and you just take it. It's not okay."

I turn my face away. Ben takes my chin and forces me to look back.

I drop my gaze so I don't have to look him in the eye. "People don't treat me like crap."

Ben makes a noise in his throat. "You can't even see it. You think it was okay for Mike to hit you. You take all Pete's anger, and you think it's your fault when I yell at you."

"That is not the same thing!" I surprise myself with the

volume of that. I shrink back into the chair and say it again, quieter. "It's not the same thing. Don't you ever compare yourself to Mike. You are nothing like him."

Ben stares at me. His eyes flutter. I realise it's the first time I've even half let on to Ben how I feel about Mike.

I swallow. "I give Pete just as much crap as he deals out to me. It is not the same thing."

Ben meets my eye for a second, then drops his gaze. I swear I can hear the sound of the drops of liquid falling from his IV. Finally he looks back at me. "Did you mean what you said?"

I rub my throat. I have this stupid moment where I think he's still talking about Mike, then I click.

I try to breathe, but it's like trying to fill my lungs with play dough.

Ben runs his finger down my arm. "When I was passing out, you said–"

"I know." I bite the inside of my cheek, chewing a hole in it.

Ben sighs. He looks away, letting his head roll to the side.

"I did ... I mean, I do, but ..." I stop as Ben looks back at me. He frowns as I say the word "but".

I close my eyes and ask the question that's been smothering me. "Did you see ...? Did you see the guy who–" My voice cracks. I stop and bite my lip.

Ben shakes his head. "No. He came up behind me. I couldn't get the car to unlock." His skin pales and a sheen of sweat appears on his lip.

I take a breath. My skin goes cold and clammy.

He looks up at me. "It was so quick. I felt the knife, then I heard him running off, but I didn't see him."

I take Ben's hand and squeeze it, but it does nothing to calm me. He looks so vulnerable. I want to wrap my arms around him, as if I could protect him just with my presence.

"Kel?" His head wobbles back and forth in a shudder. "Before I went outside, it seemed like … like you knew …"

I push the air out of my lungs. It makes my chest hurt, and I have to take a couple of slow breaths. "I … yeah." I shake my head.

"How–?" Ben stops as I press my hand against his cheek.

I draw breath, but I can't make words come out. My eyes start to dribble again. I rub the tears away with my fingertip, leaving a burning feeling under my eyes.

I swallow and force myself to meet Ben's eye. "I …" I look around as my skin crawls. It makes no sense. I know I'm just being paranoid, but even so I lean close to Ben and lower my voice. "I will tell you, just not yet." I gesture to his arm. "When you're better."

"But–" Ben tries to sit up.

I push him back down.

"Kel." His eyes are wide. "Are you …? What if …?"

I get a wobbly feeling inside me as I realise he's worried about me. *You should be angry*, I want to say.

Instead I press my lips against his. I get a feeling, like sparks, around my belly button, as I do. He reaches up and touches my cheek.

I pull back, just enough so our foreheads are touching, and keep my eyes closed. "I love you, Ben," I say, then I move away so I can look him in the eye. "I really do."

He doesn't say anything for a second, he just watches me. I have this horrible moment where I think he's changed his mind, then he blinks.

His eyes are wet, but his lips curl up at the corners. He draws his hand down the side of my face and his fingertips tickle my skin. "I love you too."

21

Chapter Twenty-One

There's a dank smell in the air when we get home. I don't think it's that bad, but Pete's face screws up when he gets out of the car. He starts muttering something about the drains being blocked again, and calling the council. I can't understand him focusing on something like that right now, then I realise it's probably his way of coping.

I'm on my bed, staring at the ceiling, when my cell phone rings. Of course, I get a huge fright. One, because I know who it's going to be and two, because I'd forgotten I shoved my phone into my bra. It buzzes, making my whole chest vibrate.

I fish it out and stare at it.

Mikecell Calling.

The fact that he's still using Mike's phone makes me want to chuck the contents of my stomach. Then I think of everything else he's done, and I feel like I'm going to throw up my intestines as well.

I stuff the phone under my pillow so I don't have to listen to it ringing. It doesn't mask the sound. A second later it stops, and I hear the text message tone. I pull it out again.

ANSWER THE PHONE KELSEY.

It's so stupid. It's not even a threat, and I'm terrified. The phone rings again.

I answer it. "Hello?"

There's a long silence. My skin crawls.

"That wasn't so hard, was it?"

I want to scream, or yell at him, but instead I make a rather desperate gasping noise as I cry. "Why are you doing this?"

"I told you not to tell anyone."

"I didn't tell anyone," I say.

"No, but you would have."

"That's not true!" I squeeze my hands against my lips as they shake.

He doesn't answer straight away. I listen to his breathing. I will it to stop.

"You were about to in the garage," he says finally. "If I hadn't called ..."

It's true. I wanted to tell Ben so much, it was nearly killing me. My mouth feels thick as I try to speak. "You shouldn't have–"

"It was a warning." He sighs. "I could have killed him, but I didn't."

"You killed Jacob!" The words wrench themselves out of me. "And Mike!"

There's a long pause.

"Mike's not dead," he says.

I groan. He might as well be, I want to say. I smooth my fingertips over my forehead. My eyelashes flutter against the heel of my palm.

"Why are you doing this?" I say again. The words sound so

useless. He can't possibly have a reason, at least not a good one.

He drops his voice, so I have to strain to hear him. "I'm trying to … Why won't you …?" I only catch part of what he says.

"What? What did you–?"

He hangs up. I listen to the beeping for a moment, before turning my phone off.

Even after the shower, my skin still has a pinkish tinge from the blood. I couldn't get it out from under my nails, so I'm back to having a red French manicure. Actually, there's not much left to my nails. They're all cracked and ripped down to nubs. I probably bit them, but I don't remember.

I rummage in the bedside cabinet drawer until I find a packet of painkillers. I pop a couple in my mouth, then scull the glass of water from beside my bed. The glass leaves a soggy ring on the cabinet top. I don't care, but it's the kind of thing Pete likes to yell at me about, so I try to rub it in with my fingers. It doesn't work, and I end up with this weird, slimy stuff all over my hand.

I look up as Pete opens the door.

"Hey." He gives me something that almost passes for a smile.

I stare at him. My head feels heavy, like if I try to lift it, it will fall off.

"You want something to eat?"

I make a noise that I hope Pete will interpret as a no. He doesn't say anything, but I don't hear him leave. I open my eyes to see what he's doing.

He stands in the doorway, staring at me. He's so pale, and the circles under his eyes are so dark, it looks like a bad attempt at gothic make-up. He sways on the spot, then leans against the doorframe to steady himself. I hear the mucusy sound of him swallowing.

"You should eat something, Kel."

I let my head flop back and stare at the ceiling. Pete comes and sits on my bed. It groans and squeaks in protest. He rests his hand on my ankle. I'd kick him away, but I don't have the energy.

"Kel ..." He shakes his head.

I look away as I realise he's crying. He sniffs and wipes his face on his sleeve. I think of passing him the tissue box from beside my bed. It's empty, but I think he'd appreciate the gesture. I go to reach for it, but my arm just flops back down next to me.

Pete makes a shuddering, gasping noise and wipes his face again. I look back at him. He stares at me, studying my face. I stare back, but my eyes are unfocused.

Suddenly he stands up. "Get up."

I don't move.

He pulls at the blankets, even though they're not covering me. "Get up, Kel."

I swing my legs over the side of the bed and pull myself upright. Normally I'd argue, but it's easier just to do it. Pete holds my shoulders and stares at me. I close my eyes.

Pete shakes me. "Kel ...? Kel!"

"What?" I squirm away from him.

He grips my chin, forcing me to look him in the eye. He takes a breath. I flinch as he blows it out over me.

"Have you taken something?"

"What?" I shake my head, not understanding, then follow his eye line to the packet of painkillers on the bedside table.

"God, Pete. No!" I rub my forehead. The tablets have done nothing for my headache, and now they've got me in trouble. I can't decide whether I should be angry at Pete, or apologetic. Right now I'm leaning towards angry.

He grabs the packet and empties it out on to the bed. The sheets come out with just the two I took missing. The edge of the foil backing curls up into two bumble-bee-sized wings.

Pete looks at me, then pulls me into a hug. "I thought–"

I shake my head. "I wouldn't do that." Something inside me turns to mush. "I'm sorry," I say, and actually mean it.

Pete sighs and sits back down next to me. "Come downstairs, Kelsey."

I groan. "I need to sleep."

"You can sleep on the couch."

I shake my head.

Pete stands up. "Come downstairs."

I look at him and realise he's not really giving me a choice. It's either go downstairs, or know that I'll be driving him slowly insane with worry.

I stand up and pull my blanket off the bed, ready to bring it downstairs with me. Pete puts the painkillers in his pocket.

I don't sleep on the couch. I knew I wouldn't be able to, but I don't think I'd have slept if I'd stayed in bed, either.

Pete and Aiden drift through the house. Every so often, Pete comes and sits with me. Each time he does, I pretend to be asleep so he'll go away.

He's in the kitchen when the phone rings. I sit up and scream. The phone rings again. I run towards the front door. My feet catch in my blanket and I end up stumbling over it, dragging it along behind me.

"Kel!"

I hear Pete call after me, but I don't stop.

The door's locked. I struggle with it, trying to make it open. There are silver lines around the doorknob, where our keys have scratched the paint. I can feel flakes coming off, under my palms. I tear at the door.

"Shit. Kel, stop!" Pete's right behind me.

I crumple to the floor. I keep shaking the doorknob, as if I'm going to be able to break the lock by force of will.

"Kel, please!" Pete holds his head in his hands. He looks like he's going to cry again. I want to stop, but the logical part of my brain has detached itself.

"Here."

I hear Aiden's voice before I see him.

He steps past Pete and sits down next to me. "Let go of the door, Kelsey."

I shake the knob again, but in a feeble way.

Aiden wraps his hands around my wrists, pulling them away from the door.

"The phone," I say, looking at Aiden. He looks back at me, then his eyes flick towards Pete.

"Answer it," he says.

Pete frowns. "But–"

"Just go answer the phone."

Pete rubs his hand across his mouth then nods. He goes back into the other room.

Aiden stares at his hands. He shifts them, loosening his hold. His palms are rough. They scratch my skin. The clasp on his watch presses into the flesh on my arm. It doesn't hurt, but it's cold.

I let my head flop backwards. It hits the door far harder than I expected. Aiden jerks forward, slipping his hand between my head and the door.

"Sorry." I lift my head up, pulling it away from his hand.

He sits back, wrapping his arms around his knees.

"I'm sorry," I say again. "I need to stop … you know, freaking out." My voice peters out towards the end of that. "Freaking out" doesn't seem quite right, but I'm not sure if there's a word for what I've been doing.

To my surprise Aiden sniggers. "It's fine. I've had lots of practice." He stares at the floor in front of him, smirking.

"Practice?" I shake my head. I squint as I frown.

Aiden looks down at his hand. I watch too as he taps his thumb to each of his fingertips.

"Becky," he says eventually. "She had tantrums, 'freak outs' if you will."

I look away. I can't help feeling he's taking the piss with that last part. Even if he was being genuine, I don't like being compared to his sister having a tantrum.

"That was Ben." Pete comes back into the room with the phone still in his hand. "He's gone and discharged himself." Pete shakes his head as he tries, unsuccessfully, to hide his disapproval. "He said if I don't go pick him up, he'll try walking home." Pete drops his voice and says something else under his breath. *Bloody idiot* would be my guess.

I look up at Pete. He sees on my face what I'm thinking before I have a chance to voice it.

"No." He shakes his head. "You're staying here."

"But–"

"Aiden, can you …" Pete gestures towards me. I love how a small flick of his hand can indicate that I'm a problem to be dealt with.

"Sure." Aiden stands up then reaches down to haul me off

the floor. He draws back his hand as soon as I'm on my feet.

He nods towards the living room. "TV?"

I shrug. I feel my nose wrinkle up as I do. It's weird how this has just become normal. I freak out, Aiden has to babysit me, then we watch TV as if nothing's happened.

I don't actually watch the TV. Aiden sits down and turns it on. I curl up on the couch with my feet underneath me, and watch Pete leave. Then I stare at the closed door, waiting for him to get home with Ben.

It's stupid how people call the nervous feeling in your stomach butterflies. It's more like a whirlpool with sea monsters in it.

Aiden keeps shifting. Every couple of minutes, he throws his arm across the back of the couch, or kicks his leg out, or does an all-over, sitting version of break-dancing. It's like hanging out with a jack-in-the-box.

I flinch away from him as he whacks me in the shoulder.

He looks at me like he'd forgotten I was there, then shakes his head. "Sorry." He tucks his hands under his arms and forces a smile.

"Are you okay?" I ask. It's a stupid question. Obviously he's not.

"Yeah." He stares at the floor in front of us. His hand creeps out, as if of its own will, and starts plucking at the seam on his jeans.

I draw breath to say something, but have to let it out again before I think of what that something is. I watch as Aiden pinches the denim on his pocket into pleats. He stops and smooths it out.

"This isn't helping," he says.

"Huh?"

"This." He points to the TV.

I realise I haven't even noticed what's on. I've managed to tune the whole thing out, even though the volume's up pretty loud.

It's one of those murdery forensic programmes. There's a dead guy lying on a slab in the morgue, while two far-too-beautiful-to-be-real people talk over his head.

I find these shows annoying. The characters are always making excuses to explain the plot to the audience, and I don't believe people working with dead bodies would wear that much make-up.

The dead guy doesn't look dead. He looks asleep, but he's not even that. He's just some struggling actor they paid to lie still for the duration of the scene.

I stand up. "I'm going to ..." I'm not actually sure what I'm going to do, but I find myself gesturing towards the garage, "go practice my punching."

Aiden blinks a couple of times, like he thinks he's misheard me. "What?"

I shrug. "Ben taught me how. You know, to defend myself ... and stuff."

Aiden raises his eyebrows. "Good luck with that." He turns back to the TV and changes the channel.

I want to prove to him that I'm not as feeble as I look. Unfortunately, I think I'll have a hard time convincing him when I don't believe it myself.

I go into the garage, but I don't try punching the bag. I tap it with my toe, making it sway away from me, then go and sit on the bench. The movement of the bag is hypnotic. I look away as I begin to feel sleepy.

The garage smells of sweat – though not unpleasantly,

weirdly enough – and the leather from Ben's gloves. I stretch out my hand. My knuckles are bruised. Not badly, just enough to know I hit the bag pretty hard yesterday.

I squirm as I think of what happened next. The conversation with the caller keeps playing over in my head. *"You were about to in the garage. If I hadn't called …"*

I stop and look down at the floor under the punching bag. There's a grey stain left on the concrete from when this garage was used for cars.

How did he know that? How did he know what I said to Ben?

I get up and move around the room. My hands are shaking. I wind them through my hair but just end up pulling it. It suddenly seems so dark in here. I stare up at the bare bulb, hanging from the ceiling. It feels like it's burning a hole in my retina. I look away, but I'm left with a green splodge in the middle of my vision.

He was watching us. He must have been listening.

I look around the room. There are no windows. There wasn't anyone else in the room. It was just me and Ben.

I run my hand along the wall, as if I'm going to find a secret compartment there. It feels damp. There are little lumps of hard, dried paint beaded on the concrete.

I yank open the cupboard under the bench. It's full of shelves. There's no way anyone could hide in there. Even so, I pull things out as if I'm going to find someone curled up at the back.

He couldn't have been in the room. It was just me and Ben.

Ben …

I stop and look down at the stuff I've taken from cupboard: some of the binding tape Ben wears under his gloves, a mangled paintbrush, and a rusted Stanley knife. I drop them all on the floor and move away. The end blade of the knife detaches as it hits the ground, and shoots off along the floor.

I was about to tell Ben, then the phone rang, but there was no one there … I shake my head again. My throat hurts as I think about it.

I stare at the blade on the floor. It's so brown and porous it doesn't look like it would cut anything. I pick it up and turn it over in my hand, then stop and laugh. Ben was stabbed. The caller *told* me he stabbed him. I never thought I'd be happy about the fact that Ben got knifed, but now it seems like the best thing in the world.

I sit back down on the bench. My head hurts at the memory of finding Ben. The blood, the colour of his skin, the knife … Still something niggles at me.

I run my finger along the rusted blade. My breath catches as it nicks me. I look down at the red oozing from my finger. It's barely bigger than a paper cut, but it's bleeding.

My stomach churns as I realise what's wrong. I never saw anyone else. There was nobody except Ben and the knife. The wound was in his left arm, so he could have …

I groan and rub the sides of my face. Ben wouldn't do that. The Ben I know wouldn't stab himself.

I stare at the punching bag. The Ben I know wouldn't kill two of my friends, either, but the police obviously thought he was capable of that.

I jump at the sound of Pete's voice in the house. Ben's laughing and it sounds weird, hollow almost.

My chest contracts as I start to panic. I lean my head down on my knees and feel myself grow dizzy.

I jerk upright as the door opens. Ben comes in. I try to slow my breathing, but I can't.

He smiles, then frowns as he sees my face.

I slide down off the bench. "Did you …?" I can't look him in the eye, so I stare at his middle instead. His bad arm's in a sling. The muscles in his good arm twitch under his T-shirt sleeve.

I edge my way forward, hoping I can somehow slip past without him noticing.

He moves towards me and strokes my face with the back of his hand.

I pull away from him. "Don't touch me!" It comes out as a hiss. I feel my mouth go hard and ugly.

He draws back, then shakes his head. "I thought–" He half laughs, then reaches out to touch my shoulder.

I hit his sling with my cast. It makes a dull thud as it connects with his skin. He makes a sound, like a groan mixed with a yelp. Then he starts yelling at me.

"What the hell is wrong with you? Why would you do that?" He cradles his arm against his body. He stares at me, frowning.

"I …" I press my hands against my cheeks. "I don't know." I back away. Something touches my arm, and I scream. I bat it away, but it swings towards me, knocking me sideways. I scream again, before I realise it's the punching bag.

Ben steps forward. He closes his hand around the top of my arm. I push him, but he holds tight.

"Let go of me!" I hit out at his face.

He dodges away. "Just calm down." His hand's still around my arm. I claw at his skin with my nails, but it doesn't do anything. They're too broken and ripped to hurt him.

"You killed them! You killed Mike and Jacob!"

"What?" Ben's voice cracks.

I see Pete and Aiden come into the garage. Aiden pulls Ben away from me.

Ben's hand brushes my arm as he goes. "There's something wrong," he says to Aiden. "I think she's–"

"He killed them!"

Pete grabs me. "Stop it, Kel. Just calm down."

I cling to him. "It was him. He killed–"

"I said stop it." He shakes me. "Ben did not kill anyone."

"Listen to me," I say, but it comes out too quiet. I look over at Ben.

He steps towards me. "Kel ..."

I shriek, and Aiden pulls him back.

"What the hell is wrong with you?" Pete shakes me so hard my teeth clack together.

I look up at him, trying to make him understand. "He killed them," I say.

Pete stares at me. A flush creeps up his neck and into his cheeks, then it spews out his mouth. "Have you fucking lost it?" He shakes me again. "Why would you say that?"

I back away from him, but he follows me. "God, you're such a little drama queen. You can't ever let things–"

"Stop it! You need to listen to me!" I push him away.

Pete shakes his head. "You're turning into a mental case, just like Mum."

"Yeah? Well at least I'm not turning into Dad!"

Pete raises his hand, like he's going to hit me.

"Pete, don't!" Aiden darts forward.

I cringe, but the blow doesn't come. I open my eyes. Pete stands there with his hand frozen in the air. Aiden's holding him back.

I stare at him. "Go on. Hit me." I feel my face go hard. "Be like the rest of them."

Pete looks at his hand like he doesn't know how it got there, then lowers it. "I'm sorry. I wouldn't have ..." He closes his eyes and shakes his head. "I can't do this right now." He turns and walks away.

"Pete ..." My voice catches in my throat.

He doesn't look back. Aiden follows after him. I panic as I realise they've left me alone with Ben.

He touches my arm. "Kel, it's not–"

I flinch away from him. "I said don't touch me."

"Kel!"

I ignore him and walk out.

22

Chapter Twenty-Two

I stagger out onto the street. The air outside feels thick. It hurts to breathe it. I need to get away from the house, though.

Mr Humphries' car is still parked across the street. I get a jolt in my stomach as I see it.

My eyes are too wet for me to see where I'm going, and I keep stumbling and tripping over cracks in the pavement. I break into a run.

He hated Mike.

He was jealous of Jacob at the party.

I shake my head. Ben hated Mike because he saw what Mike was doing to me. He was jealous because Jacob …

It doesn't matter. It doesn't make it okay.

My chest hurts so much I have to stop. I sit down on the kerb. Water from the gutter leaks through my shoes. My feet get soaked, and I start to shiver. It's getting dark, and cold. I wrap my arms around my legs and bury my face in my knees. My head's exploding with the sound of my own crying.

"Are you all right, dear?"

I jerk upright at the sound of the woman's voice. She rests her hand on my back. It feels like she's smacked me.

"I can't …" My words get swallowed up. I cover my face.

She sits down next to me. "What's happened? Can I call someone for you?"

My breath makes a wheezing sound. I can't get any air.

"Shh …" The woman pulls me into a hug. "Do you want me to call someone? Your parents, maybe?"

I shake my head and pull away from her.

"Can you tell me what's happened?" She strokes my back.

I swallow. "Ben …" The rest won't come out.

The woman makes a tutting sound. "Bad break up?" She clucks her tongue, agreeing with herself. "I get it. I've been there."

I press my fists into my eyes. I shake my head, but I don't think she notices. She puts her arm around me. I can't stop shivering.

"You need to trust him, honey. If it's meant to be, he'll come back to you."

I nod. I'm not sure if I'm understanding her anymore. My eyes hurt as I crack them open. It's too dark for me to see her face properly. I bet she can't see mine either, or she wouldn't be telling me to "trust him".

She stands up. "Can I give you a lift somewhere?"

I shake my head. "No, I live …" I gesture down the street. I'm not sure which way I'm pointing, but it doesn't seem to matter.

"You'll be okay?"

I nod, then rest my head in my hands.

She pats my shoulder as she walks away.

I watch until she turns the corner and disappears from sight. Once she's gone, I start to wonder if she was ever there at all. It seems like she was just in my head.

I run my hands across my face. My eyes start to close, and I have to wrench them open. If I close them, I think I'll fall asleep and die here on the side of the road.

I pull at the hairs on my arm, tugging each one from the roots. The stinging makes my arm tingle. I keep seeing Ben, lying on the lawn. He stares at me, his face ashen, white against the red of his blood. He moves in slow motion, the car keys falling from his hand.

I wheeze, forcing air into my lungs. His keys were still clenched in his hand. He couldn't have been holding the knife.

It's like something cracks inside my head. I've been so incredibly stupid, I can't even believe myself. Ben was with me in the garage when the caller rang. He didn't make that call.

I hesitate at the corner of Pete's road. While I was lying on the pavement, I tried to think of somewhere else I could go. There isn't anywhere. I walk towards the house.

I catch a whiff of the dank smell Pete was complaining about. I didn't think it was all that bad before, but it's stronger now than it was when we got home. It gets worse as I walk closer to Mr Humphries' car.

It's parked right under the streetlight. I have to force myself to draw level, then I stare into the backseat, ignoring my reflection in the glass. There's nothing there, just some papers and food rubbish, the usual back seat mess.

I walk around to the back. At first I don't understand what I'm seeing. It looks like oil dripping from the boot of the car.

It's pooled underneath, and around the wheel. I step closer.

The pool is red.

My stomach heaves, and I throw up in the gutter. I crouch over and retch until nothing comes up. I get vomit all over myself, but I don't care. I sit down and take out my phone. I dial emergency services and wait for it to connect.

"Fire, ambulance or police?"

I blink. Which service is required for a dead body?

"Hello? Can you hear me?"

I stammer in place of words.

The woman raises her voice. "Can you hear me? Which service do you require?"

"Police," I say finally. "Maybe ambulance too."

There's a click as she connects me. My hands shake as I wait for them to answer.

"What is your emergency?" The man's voice is steady, calming. Even so, I stutter as I answer.

"There's a dead body in the boot of a car across the street from my house. I think it's my teacher, Mr Humphries." Even as I'm saying it, I realise it sounds like I'm confessing to murder.

There's a silence before the man answers. "What is your address?"

"34 Brian Crescent." I take a breath, and it sounds like I'm dying. "Please hurry. You need to get him out of there."

"Can I have your name, please?"

"Kelsey. Kelsey Morgan."

"Why do you think there's a body in the boot?"

"There's blood … and the smell." I shake my head and close my eyes. "Please, can you just come?"

"Stay where you are ma'am. We'll send someone out."

I rub my hand across my face. "I'll wait inside the house; 34 Brian Crescent." I end the call and stand up. In the process, I put my hand in the pool of vomit. I wipe it off on my clothes and keep going.

I stop in the driveway. Ben's car keys are still on the ground where he dropped them. I pick them up. The battery is missing from the unlock remote. I run my hand over it. He couldn't get the car to unlock …

Light glints off the keys as I move my hand. I look up. There's a line of light between the edge of the garage door and the frame. I move towards it. If I squint, I can see into the room. My throat bunches up as I realise anyone could have been standing here, listening.

I don't have my house keys, so I ring the doorbell. My body feels too heavy to keep upright, so I slump against the side of the house as I wait. I scrape my feet on the doormat and a cigarette butt comes loose from the sole of my shoe.

There's a crash, then thumping as someone runs across the floor. I hear Aiden yelling. I back away from the door as it bursts open.

"Oh my God!"

Ben's covered in blood. I start screaming, and I can't stop.

"Shut up! Just shut up!" He grabs hold of me.

I hear someone else running through the house. Ben tries to pull me away but I'm frozen, and he can't drag me with only one good arm.

Aiden appears in the hallway. He's holding a rifle.

I can't do anything except scream.

Aiden grabs me, pulling me away from Ben. Ben's yelling something but I can't understand what. Aiden's arms are wet. My palms come away stained red.

"Let her go, Aiden."

Aiden's between me and Ben. Between me and the door.

"Ben ..." I say. It comes out as a puff of air.

Aiden gestures with the rifle. "Shut the door. Lock it," he says to Ben.

Ben hesitates. Then I see the door closing. I hear the lock click.

Ben raises his hand. "Please ... please just put the gun down, Aiden."

Aiden starts to laugh. "Sure thing." He puts the gun down, propping it up against the wall. He pulls something from his pocket.

"No!" Ben jerks forward, then freezes.

Aiden's arm is around me, a knife against my throat. I scream and try to pull away from him.

His nails dig into my shoulder. "Stop it! Shut up!" His voice echoes in my ear.

"Please ..." I swallow as I feel the blade against my neck. "Please, don't ..."

I stare at Ben. His eyes flick towards the rifle.

Aiden laughs again. "Go ahead. Grab it. See how far a gun with no bullets will get you."

Ben's hand is shaking. He swallows, and I can see his Adam's apple bob. There's blood on his face – three dots, like fingerprints, on his left cheek. I watch him blink, his eyes heavy and slow.

Sweat drips down my temple. I think of it dripping over the blade, mixing with the blood.

Blood ...

"Where's Pete?" I say. My words sound distant. I have to force them out.

I think I hear Aiden laughing. Everything's echoing.

"Aiden ..." Ben shakes his head. He's crying. "Aiden, please don't do this ..." Ben's sling has come loose. His arm dangles, useless at his side, his fingers limp. I stare at his nails. The middle one's black, cracked diagonally in half.

Aiden's pushing me forward. We're moving out of the living room. Ben's saying my name. Then we're in the kitchen, and Ben's telling me not to look.

The floor is covered with blood. There's so much, I can't make sense of it. I step backwards, and the toes of my shoes print red triangles on the lino.

I stare for ages before the shape on the floor turns into something I recognise. Pete's lying on the floor. His stomach is torn open.

"Pete?" I say.

He doesn't move.

"Pete!" I jerk away from Aiden, falling to my knees beside my brother. "Pete, can you hear me?" I lift his head into my hands.

He opens his eyes, but they're not focused. "Kel?"

My face swims in sweat. "Oh my God," I say. "This can't be happening."

Pete groans. His head rolls against my arms.

I look at Aiden. "What did you do to him?" I say. The words feel like they're tearing their way through my skin.

Aiden closes his eyes in a slow blink. "I shot him," he says. He shrugs and looks away. The corner of his mouth spasms, and I hear his jaw click.

"Kelsey–" Ben reaches out to me.

Aiden raises the knife. "Get back or I swear I will slit her throat."

I cringe away from him. Pete's lips are turning blue. I squeeze his face, making him open his eyes. He's shaking, and his eyelids flicker as he looks up at me.

"Kelsey?" His breath makes a huffy sound. Bubbles of spit and blood appear on his lips.

I smooth his forehead. "It's okay, Pete. You're going to be okay."

Aiden shakes his head. "He's not going to be okay. He's going to die."

"Shut up!"

Aiden grabs my arm, yanking me to my feet. Pete's head hits the floor as I drop it. I shriek, hitting and scratching at Aiden with my broken nails.

He snatches my hair, pulling my head back. "Stop it. Just stop it, Becky."

I stare straight into his eyes. They're so dilated I can't see any colour, they're just black. He looks ill. His face is thin and hollow.

"I'm not Becky," I say.

Aiden shifts as I speak. "No. No, you're not." He loosens his hold on my hair then yanks it back again as Ben moves. "I told you to stay where you were. I will kill her if you come any closer."

I feel the blade pressed to my throat again. "Aiden ..." I whisper. My voice cracks on his name.

I hear him breathing. He doesn't answer straight away. He lets go of my hair and takes my arm instead. My skin crawls as he touches me. His palms are clammy. I think he's shaking.

He swallows. "Stand up properly, Kelsey. Can you do that?"

I raise my head. My legs feel frozen. I sway as I try to move. Ben goes to catch me.

"I said I will fucking stab her if you move. Do you want me to kill her? Do you?"

"Don't!" Ben backs up against the wall. His eyes flick between me and Aiden. "Don't hurt her. Just ..." He presses the back of his hand to his forehead.

Aiden nicks my throat with the tip of the blade. I feel a line of blood make its way down my neck to my collarbone.

"Do you want me to kill her?" His voice is quiet.

I squeeze my eyes shut.

"Please," Ben whispers. "I won't move. Just, please ..." His voice cracks. "Please, don't." He keeps repeating "please", over and over.

Pete's groaning. I think I'm groaning too. Aiden's squeezing my arm so hard it's going numb. Suddenly he shifts his hold. I see the knife move.

I scream as I realise he's going to stab Ben. "No!" I dive forward.

Aiden dodges me, and just misses stabbing me instead. He yanks me back.

"Please! Please, don't kill him. Please ..." My voice breaks down into a whisper. "I love him."

Aiden doesn't say anything. He holds me as I struggle against him.

"I'm not going to kill him." He says it really quietly. "Come on, stop it. I'm not going to kill him." Aiden lets go of me for a second, but it's only to lock his arm across my chest. "Ben's just ..." he shakes his head, "going to go sit in time out." He jerks his head at Ben. "Turn around."

Ben stares at me. I swallow. His lips move, but they don't form words. He closes his eyes and turns away.

The carpet in the hall is covered with a layer of dust. I can see it rising into the air with my steps. It's crawling into my lungs and choking me.

Aiden stops outside his room. He nods to Ben. "Go inside."

The photo from Aiden's room is on the floor outside the door. He's torn it in half. Becky smiles up at me. She seems to meet my eye. Aiden's half faces the carpet, the words "happy as always" written across the back.

Ben touches my hand with his fingertips. They make a warm spot on my skin.

He doesn't look at me. "It's going to be okay, Kel," he says. "I promise it's going to be okay."

I lick my lips. I want to say something reassuring to him, but I can't think of anything. Instead, Aiden's voice echoes in my mind: *"How can you possibly promise that?"*

"I said, go inside, Ben." Aiden jerks my shoulder, making me wince.

"Okay!" Ben steps through the doorway, stopping just on the other side.

Aiden nods towards a small package on the bedside table. "That box. Give it to me."

Ben hesitates, then moves across the room, keeping his eyes on Aiden the whole time. He picks up the box and brings it back.

Aiden lets go of me to take it. "The windows are locked," he says to Ben. He goes to shut the door.

Ben blocks it with his hand. His eyes meet mine for a second and then he kisses me, hard, on the lips, and presses his cheek against mine. He drops his voice so only I can hear. "Any chance you get, you run, yeah?"

He steps back before Aiden can react. I don't have time to react either. My lips feel bruised, like he's damaged them by pulling away. I clamp my hand to my cheek, as if I can hold his breath there.

I stare at Ben, but he's looking at Aiden, not me.

"Promise me you won't hurt her, Aiden."

Aiden sniggers. "She'll be fine." He slams the door in Ben's face.

I lean my forehead against the door. "I love you, Ben," I say, but I don't think I say it loud enough for him to hear.

Aiden turns away from me to take a key out of his pocket and lock the door, then he picks up the rifle. He loads it with a bullet from the box Ben gave him. I think of running, like Ben said, but my legs won't move. I just stand there until he's done.

Aiden drops the empty box on the floor. "Let's go see how Pete's doing."

&

I sit back down on the floor next to Pete, cradling his head in my lap. He's shivering. As I look at him, I can't breathe.

"You shot him." I stare at Aiden.

He laughs. "Yeah."

I'm not sure if I meant that to be a question. It came out sounding like I've only just noticed.

Then suddenly I get it.

"You're him," I say. Everything goes out of focus, and I gasp trying to get air. "You're the caller."

Aiden's eyelids flicker as he blinks. He frowns. "I thought that was obvious."

"But ..." I shake my head. "That wasn't you! That wasn't your voice."

Aiden shrugs and smiles. "You can buy apps for everything these days."

I press my hand over my mouth. "No …" A groan wells up inside me as I remember the card: *Tell anyone and I'll kill your brother.*

Pete shifts his head. He looks up at me. "Kelsey?"

I swallow. "I'm here, Pete." I try to sound calm, but it doesn't work. I stroke Pete's head. His skin is so clammy. A sheen of sweat comes off on my hand.

"I didn't mean it." Pete coughs as he says that. His breath makes a rasping sound. "I didn't mean what I said."

"It doesn't matter–"

He shakes his head. "I was trying to come after you. I never would have–"

"It's okay." The words disappear in my throat.

"I love you, Kel." Pete touches my hand, closing it in his. He blinks. I don't think he can see me properly.

"I love you too, Pete." I cry, the tears falling on his face. "And I'm so sorry."

"I'm …" Pete shivers. His words shake. "I'm sorry, too." He closes his eyes.

I hear music from next door. Light from their house reflects against the window, making a star shape. It flickers as someone moves back and forth in front of it. I can't see them. Their house is blocked from view by the garage.

I realise I don't know any of the neighbours' names, not even the woman who helped me when Ben was hurt. I realise I didn't care until now.

I look at Pete. He's not moving.

"Pete? Pete, wake up!" I shake him.

"He's not going to wake up." Aiden sits down opposite me.

He places the rifle across his lap, then leans his head back against the fridge and closes his eyes.

"Shut up! He's not going to die." I rub my hands across my face. I shake Pete again as if that's going to fix him.

Aiden opens his eyes. "Of course he's going to die, Kel." He sniffs. "Anything else you want to say, you should do it now."

I look down at Pete. His chest jerks in shallow rises.

"I love you, Pete," I say.

Aiden laughs. "You already did that bit. Come on, Kelsey. You can do better than that."

"You ... you're a good brother," I say. There's probably something else I should say, something significant. I don't know what it is, though. "I ..." The blood pounds in my ears. I lay my head against his chest. "Please wake up, Pete." I wrap my arms around Pete and bury my head in his shoulder. I feel the sticky, wet of his blood on my skin. He smells sour, like rust and mould. The top button of his shirt presses into my neck.

Aiden goes quiet. He clears his throat. "Aren't you going to ask me why?"

I squeeze my eyes closed. If I could, I'd close my ears too.

"You were so desperate to know on the phone." He sniggers. I hear him move closer.

"I don't care." I shake my head. He can't possibly have a good reason for all this. God, he can barely have a reason at all.

He leans over me. "Come on. You must want to know why."

"You're sick! That's why."

He lets out a breath. I hear him shift back. "Ask me how Becky died."

"What?"

"Ask me how Becky died. Ask me how my mum died, for that matter. But you probably don't even remember I told you about her. You were too self-involved."

I raise my head. I have to force myself to look up at him. "You killed them?" The words come out half formed, like they're dissolving on my tongue.

Aiden gives a short laugh. "No, I didn't kill them. Ask me."

I swallow. "How did Becky and your mum die?"

"My step-dad set the house on fire with them in it. He disconnected all the fire alarms and locked the doors. They died in their sleep."

"Oh my God!"

Aiden looks at me. "It was my fault. I should have got them out of there."

"I'm sorry," I say.

Aiden raises his eyebrows. "Are you really?" He nods towards Pete.

I feel my chin draw back into my chest. The words just came out automatically. I didn't realise how stupid they sounded.

Aiden shakes his head and stands up. "Come on, Pete's dead. There's nothing more you can do."

"No." I bury my face in Pete's shoulder. I think of the hospital and how I didn't want to hug him then. I squeeze him harder.

"You don't have a choice. Get up."

"No."

"For God's sake." Aiden grabs my arm, pulling me to my feet.

Before I have a chance to second guess myself, I pull back my arm and punch him.

"Fuck!" He stumbles backwards, dropping the rifle as he clutches his face.

My hand stings. For a second I don't know what to do. I didn't even know I was going to punch him, let alone hit him hard enough to make a difference. Then my brain clicks in and I run.

"Get back here, you bitch!"

Aiden goes for the rifle, then follows me. I dive for the front door. He grabs me before I can get it unlocked.

"What the hell was that?" He smashes me up against the wall, his hand around my throat. His nose is bleeding. It dribbles, thick and red, over his mouth. He sniffs and wipes his arm across his lip.

"I'm sorry," I say, then scream as he tightens his hold around my throat.

"Kel? Kel!" Ben pounds on the wall. The house vibrates with the noise.

Aiden shakes his head. His face goes hard. "Are you going to behave or do I need to kill you now?"

I swallow, unable to answer.

His lips part, baring his teeth.

There's a knock on the door.

I jump, and Aiden claps his hand over my mouth. His eyes go wide. We both freeze.

Aiden seems speeded up and slowed down at the same time. His breathing's fast, his chest rising in little puffs, but his reactions are dull. He blinks, his eyelids falling, heavy and sick.

"Kelsey Morgan? It's the police."

Aiden stares at me. His hand shifts on the rifle.

The policeman knocks again, but this time a different guy

speaks. "Kelsey Morgan?"

I hold my breath. I'm shaking so much, I swear they must be able to hear my teeth clacking together. The blood pounds in my ears. It pulses against the back of my eyes, making ripples across my vision. I hear the cops shifting their feet.

"Bloody hell. I told you it'd be a hoax."

The other guy laughs. "Come on. We'd better check around the back."

I cry as I realise they're going to leave. Aiden jerks his hand away as my tears dribble on to it.

"Help!" I only get half the word out before Aiden claps his hand over my mouth again. I make muffled shrieking sounds.

"Kel? Don't hurt her, Aiden." Ben pounds on the wall.

The policeman bangs on the door. "Ma'am? Can you open the door?"

I bite down on Aiden's hand. He yelps and lets go.

I dive for the doorknob. "Help! Please. He shot my brother!"

Aiden shoves me hard and I hit the wall. He raises the rifle. I dive sideways, covering my head as he fires straight through the door. The sounds meld in my head. I can't separate it from the banging Ben's making. Someone's yelling, but I can't tell who.

Aiden grabs me, dragging me into the living room. I scramble away from him, but he grips my shoulders, forcing me flat against the ground.

"Let me go!"

His elbow's digging into my chest. I can't breathe properly. Outside a police siren goes off.

"Just calm down!"

"Get off me!" I push him, hitting his face.

"If you stand up, they'll shoot you." Aiden holds my chin, forcing me to look at him. His fingers bite into my cheek. "They'll think you're me, and they'll shoot you through the window."

"Oh my God." My eyes flick to the window, then back to Aiden. There's blood on his face in little freckle-like spots.

His pupils change size as he looks at me. "Stay there."

I nod, too scared not to agree.

He swallows and closes his eyes, then relaxes his hand, dropping it from my jaw to my collarbone. I freeze. My skin feels slimy where he touches it. Red and blue lights flash against the window.

Aiden sits up, leaning against the side of the couch. He's gone pale, green almost. He holds his head in his hands. "When did you ...?" He looks up at me. "Why are they here?"

My throat clicks as I remember. "Mr Humphries," I say. I swallow and close my eyes. "There was blood ... and the smell."

Aiden shakes his head. He sighs and stares at the ceiling. "I wondered how long it would take you to find him."

I cover my face. My chest moves in big, quaking sobs as I cry. I hear one of the policemen yelling, but I can't hear what he's saying.

Aiden shifts. "Stop it."

I shake my head. The sobs don't seem to be a part of me anymore.

"Stop it. Stop crying."

I don't even try to stop. I know I couldn't, even if I wanted to.

"For fuck's sake, stop it!" Aiden yanks my hands away from my face. "Just shut up, okay?"

I stare at him. "Okay. I'll ... Okay." I nod to myself. It's oddly soothing.

Aiden settles back against the couch. He takes the knife out of his pocket and turns it over in his hands. "Who should I stab first?"

"What?"

He tips his head to the side, studying me. "You or Ben. Who should I stab first?"

My mouth shakes, and my eyes start to leak again. I rub under them, but my hand shakes so much, I hit myself in the face.

"Whoever I stab second has a better chance." He stares at me. "The police might make it in time to save them." He shrugs again. "The first person, probably not."

He's still staring at me. I close my eyes and turn my face away.

23

Chapter Twenty-Three

For a while, the air fills with the sound of sirens, then the police talk to us over a megaphone, but I can't make sense of what they're saying. Ben keeps throwing himself at the door. The thumping sound makes me shudder. It's too much like the sound of the rifle.

There's a bloody handprint on the living room door. It's small, probably mine. I press my fingertips to my forearm and think of finger painting. Then I remember it's Pete's blood, and my arm feels like it's burnt.

At one point Aiden makes me get up to close the curtains. He says if he does it, the police will shoot him. I'm terrified as I move over to the window. I'm scared they'll mistake me for Aiden and shoot me. Then I realise it doesn't matter, because Aiden's going to kill me anyway.

After a while Aiden goes to peer out the edge of the curtain. He shakes his head. "This is really messed up."

I stare at the floor. A bead of sweat drips off my forehead and lands in front of me. It holds for a moment, then bursts and sinks into the carpet. I wipe my hand over my face. My skin is warm, but I feel really cold.

Aiden sits down next to me. "I didn't ..." He wipes his mouth with the back of his wrist. "I didn't think it would happen like this."

I'm shivering really badly. My teeth clack together, and I bite the inside of my cheek.

"This was my step-dad's gun. He used to take me hunting, but ..." Aiden gives a half laugh, "I could never bring myself to shoot."

I watch him, but he goes in and out of focus.

"I kept those two bullets hidden, because I always thought one day I'd get up the courage to kill him." He runs his teeth over his lip, scratching at the dead skin. A flake falls and gets stuck to his chin. I stare at that until it makes me want to vomit. I almost ask him who the second bullet was for, but I think the answer is obvious.

"I never meant to hurt anyone else." He lowers his voice. "Mike would have killed you if I hadn't ..." His eyelids flutter. "It doesn't matter now."

"You didn't have to do that." My speech comes out slurred. I lean my head down on my hands.

"Oh yeah? What should I have done?" Aiden's voice echoes. He sniffs, and that sounds louder than anything. "He was still kicking you when you were unconscious. The police don't do anything. You would have been running from Mike for the rest of your life." His voice goes quieter. "This way is better."

Aiden shifts beside me. His knee brushes mine, and I shrink away. I feel a bruise spreading up my leg, infecting me with his ... I don't know what. Evil doesn't seem right. I would have known if I was living in the same house as someone evil.

I wrap my arms so tightly around my chest I think it's going to burst.

He makes a clucking noise with his tongue. "You know you hit me pretty hard."

My hands feel tingly. I'm soaked in sweat. It's dripping down my chest under my clothes. I'm drowning in it, unable to breathe.

"Aren't you talking to me now?"

I fall sideways.

"Shit!" Aiden catches my head. He moves me so I'm lying on my side. "Kelsey? Can you hear me, Kelsey?"

I try to say something, but it just comes out as noise.

Aiden shakes me. "Kel!"

I open my eyes.

He stares down at me. "You're really cold. Here." He takes off his jersey and lays it over me like a blanket.

I let my eyes close again.

"No, don't." Aiden taps my face. "Don't go to sleep." He tilts his head to look at me. "You're in shock. You need to stay awake."

I swallow, trying to get rid of the thick feeling in my mouth. "If I go to sleep, then I can wake up and this can be a dream."

He stares at me, then looks away. "That doesn't work. You don't go to sleep in dreams."

He leans back against the wall and takes a cigarette packet out of his pocket. He slides one out and rolls it against his palm.

I reach to take it away from him, but I miss and bash his leg. He stares at my hand, as if he thinks it will detach from my wrist and attack him.

"You're Ben's friend." I nearly say Pete's friend and have to stop myself. "I like you," I say instead. "I mean ..." My eyes spill over. "I just watched you kill my brother, but ..."

Pete can't be dead. He just can't be.

He stares down at the carpet in front of him. He draws a cross in it with his finger. "You didn't watch me kill Pete," he says. "You watched Pete die. It's different."

I shake my head and groan as bile rises in my throat.

"You weren't supposed to. I didn't think you'd come back." He chews on his lip, then he smiles and twists the cigarette in his fingers. "It doesn't matter now, anyway."

I feel sick as I guess at what he must have been planning. Kill Pete, then Ben, then himself.

I turn my face to the carpet and sob. "Pete likes you. He likes you more than me and ... you're his friend." The words mash together until the sounds pile up inside my head and come out my throat as a wail.

Aiden shoves his hand over my mouth. I scream into it until I run out of air, and he's choking me.

"Stop it! You don't know." He grabs my shoulders and shakes them. "You don't understand!"

My head smacks back against the floor. I see spots and everything closes in.

Aiden's voice explodes in my head.

"Pete was going to hit you. I had to stop him."

"He's your friend!" I scream.

"Pete wasn't my friend. I got fired, and he didn't even notice. He didn't care. No one−"

The phone rings.

Aiden freezes. I taste blood in my mouth. My teeth have gone through my lip. He gets up and backs away. The room swirls as I try to move.

Aiden's whispering to himself. He rocks his body back and forth. He stops and looks at me. "Can you get up?"

"Pete–"

He puts his arm around my waist and pulls me to my feet. I resist but he drags me, pulling me along behind him as he goes back into the kitchen. My breath catches as I see Pete. His skin is turning grey.

Aiden picks up the phone. He holds it to his ear but doesn't say anything. After a second, he holds it out to me. "Talk to them. Tell them you're okay." He forces the phone into my hands. When I don't move he holds it against my ear.

"Hello?" I say.

"Kelsey Morgan?"

"Yes." I look at Aiden. "I'm okay," I say. It's not at all true, but I don't think that matters.

"Who else is in the house with you?"

"Ben." My voice shakes. "And my brother."

Aiden takes the phone out of my hand. "See?" He hangs up.

I stare at him. A feeling like déjà vu crawls over me, making me shiver. I remember the heavy breathing. I remember *Aiden* handing me the phone and hearing the heavy breathing.

"You answered the phone," I say.

Aiden squints like he doesn't understand what I'm talking about.

"You answered the phone," I say again. "You gave it to me and ... you said he asked for me."

Aiden shakes his head. His eyes drift away from mine.

"You were saying all that stuff about Ben, and the phone rang–"

Aiden pulls me back towards the living room.

I stumble over Pete's arm and that makes me angrier. "You were right next to me! How–?"

"It doesn't matter." Aiden drags on my arm.

I hit out at him, trying to make him let go. "It does matter! Who was it?"

Aiden grabs my wrists, but I keep hitting.

"Who? What kind of sick freak–?"

"It was a recording! I called through my computer."

My hands start to shake. Something wells up inside me. "Why?" I'm so angry I can't even shout. "Why would you do this?"

He shakes his head and backs away.

"You said Mike would have killed me, but you were calling before that."

"It doesn't matter."

"It does! You couldn't possibly have known. You weren't trying to protect me, you're just sick." I grab his face, trying to make him look at me.

He pushes me away.

"Was that even true about your mum, or were you just–"

"Of course it was fucking true." Aiden spits the words at me. "Do you think I'd make something like that up?"

"How the hell would I know? I have no idea who you are."

"You sound like her, okay?"

My chest does a jolt like he's hit me.

He screws up his eyes.

I shake my head. "Becky? I sound like Becky?"

He rubs his head. His hands are shaking. He closes his eyes. Finally he looks up at me. "My mum." His voice comes out cracked. "You act like Becky, but you sound like my mum."

I sink back against the wall and cover my face. Aiden sits down next to me, but I don't look at him.

I hear the scratchy sound of him rubbing his hand across

his face.

"I wanted to hear your voice. That was all."

He's so messed up; I just don't even want to know.

I pull my hands back from my face to look at him. "When did you get fired?"

"A week ago." He stares down at his knees. "I stopped turning up. They … they said they had no choice."

"I …" I take a breath. "If you'd told me, I would have cared."

He shakes his head. I can't tell whether he doesn't believe me or if it just doesn't matter anymore.

"Aiden?" My voice cracks. I have to force myself to keep going. "What about Jo?" The words come out as a whisper.

He doesn't answer straight away. At first I think he hasn't heard, then his throat makes a gluggy sound.

"What about Jo?" His voice is really cold. I think he knows exactly what I'm asking.

"She told me you were going to take her to the station. Did you …?" I take a breath as the pain in my chest threatens to burst.

He rolls his tongue around his mouth. "She's just a kid." He sniffs, and for a moment I think that's all the answer he's going to give me. Then he turns and looks at me. "I made sure she got on the bus safely, I even gave her some money for lunch." He shakes his head. "She's just a kid. I wouldn't hurt her." He sighs. "Why do you think I killed them, Kelsey?"

"Because you're sick." My voice makes a hollow sound, like I'm half asleep.

Aiden shakes his head. "I let him kill Becky," he says. He rolls his head, stretching the back of his neck, then he raises his eyes to mine. "Pete could have stopped Mike, but he didn't," he says.

"Pete tried to protect me," I say.

Aiden takes the knife out of his pocket. He runs his finger over the blade, like he's reading Braille off it.

"When he thought Jacob was hurting me." I stare at Aiden, trying to make him understand. "He tried to protect me."

Aiden shrugs. I don't think it matters to him anymore.

"He wasn't, you know?"

Aiden looks up at me.

I chew on the inside of my cheek. "Hurting me. Jacob. I mean, I didn't like him like that, but I don't think he would have … He wasn't hurting me."

Aiden screws up his nose. "It doesn't really matter now, does it?"

His cigarette from before is broken in half on the floor in front of me. I pick it up and mash it between my fingers. In my whole life, I never tried a single cigarette.

I close my eyes and lower my voice. "Stab me first."

Aiden doesn't answer, so I say it again louder. "Stab me first." My throat goes dry. I open my eyes. They spill over, but I don't care. I force myself to look at Aiden. "Let Ben have the better chance. I don't want him to die. He didn't do anything wrong."

Aiden's breaths and blinks seem to be in sync. I watch as he blinks once, twice … He raises the knife.

I cringe away from him, but he raises it to his own throat.

"Maybe I should just kill myself now."

I dig my hands into the carpet. My whole body tenses, waiting.

Aiden lowers the knife and holds it out to me. "Or maybe I should give you the knife, and you can do it."

I stare at him.

He puts it on the floor and pushes it towards me. There's blood on the blade.

"After what I did, you must want to kill me."

"No."

He tilts his head to the side, exposing his neck, and taps his finger against it. "Right here, Kelsey. It'd be quick."

I shake my head and close my eyes. "Please ..."

He laughs. "Fine."

I open my eyes.

Aiden's throat bobs. "I'll have to kill us all, then."

I grab the knife. For a second, Aiden's hand hovers as it was, reaching out, then he raises his palms towards me.

I stand up. Aiden stands too, slowly.

"Kel? Kelsey!"

I hear Ben calling, but I don't answer him. He throws himself at the door. I keep my focus on Aiden.

He looks me in the eye. "Kill me."

Ben hits the door, making me jump. The knife shakes in my hands.

"Kill me, or I'll kill you." Aiden smiles, and then he shrugs like he doesn't care either way.

I glance at the door.

Aiden shakes his head. "You wouldn't make it. You're so beat up, you can barely walk."

"Yeah, and who's fault is that?"

"I didn't beat you up, Kelsey." Aiden steps towards me.

I back away and wipe my face on my shoulder.

"Mike beat you up. I never hurt you."

I squeeze my eyes shut. The floor creaks as Aiden moves towards me. I raise the knife.

He stops. "You know, if things had been different, I think

we would have been friends.”

I shake my head.

“Come on, just do it. Right here.” He taps his neck again. There are drops of dried blood on his palms. They make a join-the-dots pattern across his hands. He closes his eyes and opens them again in a slow blink.

I swallow. “Does Pete remind you of yourself?” I say. I force myself to step towards him. “Do you hate yourself that much?”

His lips curl up into an ugly shape. His fingers clench down into his palms.

There’s a crack. Aiden turns towards the hall.

It takes me a moment to understand the sound, then I get it. Ben’s broken the door.

Aiden’s hands fall to his sides. His whole body seems too heavy for him. His head drops down, too, his chin leaning against his chest.

“You should have done it, Kelsey,” he says.

He lunges towards me, grabbing my head. I bring the knife down stabbing wildly. I hear him shriek as the knife connects with his skin. I keep stabbing. He slams my head against the windowsill. Then everything goes black.

There are colours, sounds, none of it makes any sense. My head hurts. I hear voices, but I don’t know what they’re saying. Finally I just close my eyes again and let it wash over me.

Half of me is cold. The other half is warm, like I'm sitting in a heated bean bag. I'm shivering, and my breath is shaking. I keep my eyes closed. I can't remember why I'm so afraid, but I am, and I don't want to open my eyes to it.

My lips are dry. I run my tongue over them. They shake as I do.

"Kelsey?"

I hear Ben's voice. He shifts, and I realise he's the bean bag.

"Kel? Can you hear me?" He swallows, making a thick, mucusy sound. "Come on, Kel. Open your eyes."

I do, but they don't focus straight away.

Ben touches my face then pulls me into a hug. It's not much of a shift as I'm already sitting in his lap. I want to hug him back, but I don't seem to be in control of my arms. When I look down, I realise what's wrong. My arms are pinned to my sides with a blanket. Ben's sitting on the edge of it, stopping me from freeing myself. I squirm, pulling at the fabric.

"What's wrong?" Ben holds my face, his eyes scanning mine.

I understand what he's saying, but there's a delay in my brain. It's like I've forgotten how to make words.

"Kel?" Ben smooths my hair. His hand is shaking. He's shivering too.

I reach up to touch his face. The blanket stops me. I look down again.

Ben sees me looking, and shifts off the edge of the blanket. I look around as he does.

We're outside, sitting in the back of an ambulance. The doors are open. I watch as police and ambulance officers scurry around Pete's yard. The house is taped off. Neighbours stand at the boundary, peering in.

I look back at Ben. "What happened?" My voice comes out croaky.

"Don't you …?" Ben stops and shakes his head. He runs his hand down the side of my face. It hurts as he touches my temple. "You don't remember?"

I stare out into the yard. It's dark, but the place is lit by flashing red and blue lights. Just like it was when Jacob …

I feel like the ambulance has rolled. I'm tumbling, and I grab hold of the only solid thing I can find. Ben.

"Aiden killed Jacob. He stabbed you and …" I look down at my arms, freed from the blanket. They're covered in blood.

"Pete. Oh my God. Where's Pete?" I stand up.

Ben tries to hold me back, but I pull away from him.

"Pete!" I stare out at the people in the yard. "Pete!" I stumble towards the door of the ambulance.

"Kel, don't–"

It's too far down for me to step from the ambulance to the ground. I throw myself out, jarring my ankles as I hit the ground. "Pete, where are you?"

Ben steps down beside me.

"Where is he?"

Ben pulls me around to face him. "Listen to me–"

I cut him off by turning away.

Then I see it. Two ambulance officers wheel a stretcher out of the house. His head is covered with a sheet.

I remember the blood in the kitchen. The way his skin turned grey. The smell of his sweat.

Ben pulls me against him.

I cover my mouth. I feel dizzy; numb. My head swirls in

and out of focus. "I need to see him," I say to Ben.

Ben shakes his head. "Kel–"

"No." I pull away from him.

He follows me. "Kelsey, don't."

The ambulance officers aren't looking my way. I grab the sheet. I'm about to pull it back when I see Pete. He's in another ambulance, surrounded by several people. They're sticking needles in him, performing CPR.

Ben takes my hand.

"He's alive?"

Ben nods.

The ambulance doors close and it drives off.

"I thought he was dead." I start to cry.

Ben wraps his arms around me. "It's okay. It's going to be okay."

I stare down at the stretcher next to me. *If it's not Pete ...*

I yank the sheet back. Aiden stares up at me. There's gash across his shoulder. His eyes are wide and blank.

My stomach heaves, but there's nothing in it. I dry wretch until I start coughing. Ben holds me.

"Did I kill him?" I say.

Ben doesn't answer.

I pull away, making him look at me. "Did I kill him?" I press my hand against my mouth. "I was holding the knife. I remember stabbing him."

Ben stares at me. His mouth moves, but he doesn't make words. His face goes really pale. He mumbles something to himself, then he shakes his head. "That wound on his neck, it's not what ..." Ben clears his throat. "He fell on the knife," he says, but I hear the waver in his voice.

"You don't know that, do you?" I kneel down in the grass.

The damp creeps through my clothes, wetting my knees. "You don't know." I shake my head. "It was just us in the room. I ... I don't know how many times I stabbed him." I bury my head in my hands.

Ben crouches down beside me. "He fell on the knife," he says again.

"You don't know that!" I rub at the blood on my hands. "If I killed him ..." I swallow, bile rising in my throat.

Ben lets out a breath. "After what he did–"

"It doesn't matter." I turn on Ben. "Don't you get it? I killed someone." I run my hands through my hair. "I killed someone."

Ben stares at the ground. He picks up a blade of grass and rubs it between his fingers. I feel sick as I realise he can't look at me. Finally he raises his head. He doesn't meet my eye, though.

"I should go ..." He doesn't finish that. There are a million excuses he could give, but instead he just says he has to go. He gets up and walks away.

24

Epilogue

I can't see Ben when I get off the bus. It's cold, and I shiver as it starts to rain. I walk towards the station.

Ben's sitting inside. At first I think he hasn't seen me; he doesn't wave or anything, but then he gets up and walks over. I haven't seen him since Dad and Cathy picked me up from the hospital.

"Hey." He forces a smile, but it's more like a mouth shrug. His hands are shoved deep in the pockets of his jacket.

"Your arm's out of the sling. Good." I blush as I hear how stupid that sounds.

Ben smiles a little more at that. He's lost weight. His cheeks look hollow, and there are dark circles under his eyes. I don't know why I'm surprised about that, though. Every time I look in the mirror, I see the same thing on my face.

"Can I ...?" I reach out, stopping just short of hugging him.

He hesitates, then wraps his arms around me. His shoulders are stiff, but he squeezes me really hard. I hear him breathe in, and he presses his cheek against the side of my head.

"I missed you," I say.

336

He nods. "Yeah. I missed you, too."

Even though it's cold, he has to put the air conditioning on in the car. Our breath keeps fogging up the windows, despite the fact that we're not talking. Ben stares straight ahead. Every so often, we catch each other's eye in the rear-view mirror. We both look away when that happens.

I start to get car sick, and I'm sweating, despite the cold.

"Are you okay?"

I look over at Ben. He glances at me, then back at the road.

"Car sick," I say.

He shifts and pats his coat pocket. "Here." He hands me a Mintie.

"Thanks." I unwrap it and pop it in my mouth.

About a minute later, he stops the car. I stare out into the dark, confused, until things grind into place. We're not outside Pete's. Of course we're not. We're outside Ben's new place.

Ben seems to read some of what I'm thinking on my face. "They put the flat on the market. People keep going and looking, but no one's buying."

"I don't blame them."

"Yeah." Ben presses each of his fingertips to his thumb in turn, then stretches his hand out. "We should go inside."

I hang out in the kitchen while Ben makes dinner. He still has boxes of stuff sitting on the counter. He doesn't look at me while he cooks, so I unpack one of the boxes to give myself something to do.

I pull out some knives and forks. "Cutlery drawer?"

"That one." Ben points with his head.

I open it and start to sort the contents of the box.

Ben clears his throat. "You don't have to do that."

I smile. "How long have you been here and you haven't unpacked?"

He shrugs and stares down at the food. "It's just weird, you know?" He looks up at me. "This ... it doesn't feel like home."

I nod. Even though I hated it at Pete's, I know what he means. I don't think anywhere will ever feel like home.

The phone rings, making me jump. I squeeze Ben's arm really hard.

"Kel–"

I shake my head. "It's okay," I manage to say. I force myself to let go of Ben.

He reaches out to touch my shoulder. "What can I ...?"

I wave him away. "Answer the phone."

Ben hovers, then when I force a smile he turns off the fry pan and goes to pick up the phone. "Hello?"

I concentrate on listening to his side of the conversation.

"Yeah, now's not such a good time." He glances at me. I try to look like I'm not eavesdropping.

"She just arrived ... Yeah ... I'll see you Monday." He puts the phone down and stares at me. "Are you all right?" His voice is heavy. I look at his hands. They're shaking. He presses them together.

"The first time the phone rang at Dad's, I ran out of the house. Dad had to chase me down the street." I look up at Ben. "By comparison, I'm fine."

Ben blinks really slowly, like his eyelids are sad too. "Maybe you should–"

"I've been seeing a counsellor." I say that with as much finality as I can muster, then I shake my head and attempt to change the subject. "Who was that?" I gesture to the phone.

Ben sighs. "Jenny." He rubs his face. "She's been calling a bit. Pete won't let her visit." He shrugs. "I don't know what to say to her."

"Pete's ..." I sigh. "It didn't just affect him physically. The rehab staff said the lack of oxygen ... he's not himself."

"I know."

I look up at Ben.

He stares at the floor. "I've been up to see him."

I swallow. "He didn't say." My cheeks grow hot. I pick at the ends of my hair.

Ben shifts. "Yeah, I just came up for a couple of days. I didn't have time to ..."

I nod. *A couple of days and he didn't even let me know he was in town.* I force a laugh. "Pete did keep telling me 'batman' had been to see him. Maybe that was you?"

Ben smiles, but I can tell it's an effort.

"Tell Jenny it will get better," I say.

Ben looks up at me.

"He's making progress every day. He'll be back to himself in ..." I was going to say "no time", but that seems like a lie. He'll be back to himself in a couple of years' time, would be more accurate.

Ben shrugs. "Jenny wants to meet for coffee on Monday. I'll tell her then." He taps his hand against the bench. I try to find something to say.

Ben speaks before I do. "I got you a present."

"Huh?" I look up.

"For your birthday. I know I missed it, but ... I wanted to give it to you in person." He rummages in one of the boxes.

I blush and start talking to cover my embarrassment. "Cathy threw me a party," I say, laughing at the memory.

"Annie insisted on balloons and streamers. Greg wrapped up a rock as a present then made me put it back in the garden so it wouldn't be lonely. Tash came up to stay … I didn't really know what to say to her. Actually, I should call and let her know I'm back."

Ben waits until I've stopped babbling. He hands me a parcel. It's wrapped in purple paper with a blue curly ribbon. I stare at it.

"You're supposed to open it. That's how it works."

I look up at Ben and he smiles.

I twist up my mouth. "I like the paper." I open it carefully, trying to save the wrapping. In the process I manage to drop the actual present on the floor.

Ben picks it up for me.

"Sorry." I blush again.

"It's okay." He gestures for me to turn around. "Here."

I don't know what he's doing at first, then he slips something around my neck.

"Happy eighteenth." He lets my hair fall back around my shoulders.

I look down at the necklace. It's a teardrop-shaped silver pendant. There's a pattern, like a circle of ferns engraved in the centre. It takes me a moment to realise it's a locket. "Oh my God. Thank you."

"It's got a picture of me, you and Pete in it. I thought …"

I turn back to Ben. He stares at the floor then blinks a couple of times.

"Thank you." I give him a hug. This time he hugs me back properly.

Ben serves out the stir-fry, and we sit down at the kitchen counter. He starts to eat, then stops as I push my food around with my fork.

I look up at him. "It's okay. I'll eat." I put a mushroom in my mouth to prove it. I have to force myself to chew. It takes a couple of goes for me to be able to swallow. I hold back a gag. "I'm sorry." I put the fork down and cover my face.

Ben circles my wrist with his hand. "I get it." He drops his fork on the counter. "I haven't been hungry much, either."

I look at the hollows in his cheeks. I reach up and run my finger across his face.

He closes his eyes as I touch him, then pulls away. "Why are you here?"

"What?" I shrink as I hear the rebuff in his voice.

He screws up his eyes and shakes his head. "I mean … you didn't say on the phone. Why have you come back?"

"The police want to talk to me again." I shrug. "They said they could do it over the phone, but …" I force myself to meet Ben's eye. "I wanted to see Mum." I close my hand over Ben's. "And you."

Ben stares at me. He pulls his hand away. "I'll take you to see your mum tomorrow." He picks up his fork and stabs at his food.

My throat bunches up into a lump as he says that. I wait, but he doesn't look back at me.

Ben shows me to my room. It pretty bare. Actually, it's extremely bare. My room at Pete's didn't have much in it except mess, but this room has nothing. I can't even tell where the walls join each other. They all just merge into a beige blur.

"The bathroom's across the hall." Ben shifts like he's trying to decide something. "I'm next door if you need anything." His voice sounds funny when he says that. I can't figure out what it means.

"Anyway." He puts my bag by the bed. "Goodnight." He pats my shoulder then draws his hand away. He hovers for a second. I'm not sure what to say so I just smile.

"Goodnight," he says again. He shuts the door behind him.

I change into my pyjamas, get into bed and stare at the ceiling. In Annie's room at Dad's there was a crack right above my bed. For the first few nights, I was convinced I was going to be crushed in my sleep. After that it didn't bother me so much.

I watch as a spider makes its way across the room. It stops just above my toes and spins a thread, dangling down on it. I draw my feet up and close my eyes. When I open them again, I can't see it. I get out of bed and scan the wall for the spider. Then I get a horrible feeling that it crawled into my mouth and I ate it. The idea makes me sick, and I have to go back down the hall to the kitchen to get some water.

I pour myself a glass to have by the bed, but I don't go back into my room. I hover for a bit, looking around the kitchen then around the living room. Ben hasn't unpacked in there either. His books are still in boxes. I pull a few out. I'm surprised at how many of the same books we have, until I realise they're mine.

It's getting ridiculous. I've got stuff at Dad's, stuff in storage with the rest of Mum's things, and I have no idea what's happened to the crap I left at Mike's. Ben must have had to clear everything out from Pete's. I don't envy him that job.

I head back down the hall to my room but don't go in. My stomach cramps at the thought of lying there, alone in the dark. I think of sleeping on the couch, but it's the same thing. It'd still be dark. I'd still be alone. Instead, I knock on Ben's door.

There's a pause, then he answers. "Yeah?"

"Can I come in?"

I hear him shift, then he calls back. "Yeah, come in."

I open the door, but just stand in the doorway. Ben's lying diagonally across the bed. There's an open library book, lying face down next to him.

"I think I ate a spider," I say. I want to hit myself the moment that comes out of my mouth, but it's too late.

Ben looks like he can't decide whether to laugh or have me committed. He shakes his head. "What?"

"I ..." I stare around his room. He's covered the walls with kickboxing posters. I don't know how he can sleep in a room with so many sweaty, muscly guys staring at him.

"I can't sleep on my own. I had to share a room with Annie, even though they have a spare room. Sometimes Cathy had to come sleep in with us too, because otherwise I had nightmares. And I've started sleepwalking. I'm sorry. I should have told you." It all runs together. I stare at Ben, waiting for him to get angry with me.

He frowns, and it's like there's a delay between what I said and him understanding.

"Do you ..."

I wait, but he doesn't finish that.

"Can I sleep in here?" I say. I shrug as I blush.

There's a pause, where I think maybe I just said that in my head, since I get no reaction from Ben, then he shuffles over in the bed.

"Yeah, come on." He pulls the covers back for me.

Ben lies really still. He folds his arms across his chest and doesn't look at me. It's like he thinks he has to keep himself frozen, so he doesn't accidentally touch me. I want to reach out to him, but it's so obvious he doesn't want me to.

Next to the bed is a poster with a yellow silhouette of two kickboxers fighting, on a black background. I squint at it, which makes it look like a giant bee with a long stinger reaching down to Ben's head. When I relax my eyes, Ben's staring at me.

"It looks like a bee." I point to the picture.

This doesn't seem to clarify anything for Ben, as he just looks more confused. I feel myself blush again.

Ben shrugs his shoulders up into his neck.

I fiddle with the edge of the blanket. "Thanks for letting me stay," I say.

He nods and draws breath, but doesn't say anything.

I rest my head down on the pillow. It smells of apple shampoo.

"Kel?"

"Mmm?" I lift my head up again to look at Ben.

He stares at the ceiling. "What do you remember?"

I close my eyes. I'd kind of hoped we were never going to actually talk about it.

Ben turns to look at me.

"You know Aiden asked me that when I woke up in the hospital? I was scared he was covering for you." I force myself to meet Ben's eye. He looks away as soon as I do. "I thought you'd beat up Mike ... to save me."

Ben's face scrunches up, then he gives something that's

almost a smile. I can't tell if he's pissed off. I decide it doesn't matter – I want to tell him anyway.

"The caller …" I take a breath. "Aiden. He rang the next day and told me he did it. He said he'd kill Pete if I told anyone." I shake my head. The sound of my hair moving against the pillow echoes around the room. "I don't remember anything," I say to Ben. "Nothing new, anyway. He grabbed me, and I started stabbing. After that it's just flashes."

Ben goes still; he looks up at me. "Flashes?"

"You talking to me. The ambulance officers … stuff like that."

"You didn't remember that before?"

I shrug. "It's still all blurry. My counsellor said I probably couldn't process it at the time. The rest might come back, but it might not. She said to plan for it not."

Ben pulls at a thread on the edge of the blanket. It snaps, and his hand jerks back towards his face. "You wouldn't let them near you."

"Huh?"

Ben winds the thread around his finger. "The ambulance officers. You kept screaming when they came close. Then you just shut down completely. I was scared you were going to stay like that."

I let out a breath. I have to stare at the ceiling for a moment, to stop my eyes from spilling over. "I'm so sorry," I say. My throat burns with the tears I'm not letting out. "I'm sorry I thought it was you."

Ben's Adam's apple bobs. "It's okay."

"It's just he knew stuff." I shake my head. "Stuff only you should have known, like what I said to you in the garage …" I stop and close my eyes. "If I'd thought about it, I would have realised he was outside the door." My voice cracks. "But I didn't think about it."

He nods and stares at the ceiling. His eyes flick back and forth, as if he's reading something there.

"I wish ... I wish I had stopped him," I say.

Ben does a really slow blink. "Me too."

I'm not sure whether he means he wishes he had stopped Aiden, or whether he wishes I had. Either way would be my guess.

I take a breath, and tell Ben the other thing that's been playing on my mind. "Mike's woken up."

Ben freezes. I can see on his face that his stomach's dropped, the same way mine did when I heard.

"A month ago. Jo sent me an email."

"Is that why you're here?" Ben's voice is cold. "To see him?"

I shake my head. "No, of course not. Jo asked me to, but I told her no. I don't ever want to see him again."

Ben turns his head to look at me.

I meet his eye without hesitation. "I broke up with Mike that day at the park. I didn't want to be with him."

Mike hadn't been my boyfriend for a long time before that. He'd just been someone who hurt me. Jo didn't deserve any of what happened to her. But neither did I.

I reach out to take Ben's hand. "I'm here to see you," I say.

He pulls away. His shoulder hunches up, making a barrier between us. "It's late. We should ..." He moves his hand to the light switch. His eyes flick towards me, then he turns it off. My eyes dance with spots in the dark.

⌇

I wake later in the night. Ben's talking in his sleep. I can't make out the words. His breathing's all huffy, and his face is covered in beads of sweat. He shakes, turning his head from side to side.

"Ben," I say. "Ben, wake up."

His eyes flutter at the sound of my voice, but he doesn't open them. I shake his shoulder instead. "Ben, wake up."

His eyes shoot open, and he makes a noise like he's trying to suck air through a straw. He shrinks away from me, nearly falling out of the other side of the bed.

"It's okay. It's me." I reach out to him. "It's okay, Ben."

He closes his eyes and crawls in close to me. He wraps his arms around my waist. "I thought ..." His breathing sounds weird, like he's taking three tiny breaths in a row then letting them all out at once.

He buries his head in my shoulder. I stroke his head and the back of his neck.

"It's okay," I say again.

When I wake in the morning, his arms are still wrapped around me. His breathing is steady now. It makes little huffs against my neck. I get this warm spot on my skin that goes cold in between his breaths.

Ben starts to wake. He takes a really long breath, then moves his mouth as if he's chewing something.

I smile. "Hey."

He opens his eyes at the sound of my voice. He blinks a couple of times before he seems to recognise me.

"Kel ..." His shoulders hunch up, and he pulls away. He rubs his face and swings his legs over the side of the bed.

"What's wrong?" I sit up as he stands.

"Nothing." He pulls on a sweatshirt. He turns back towards me, but doesn't quite look at me. "Do you want some breakfast? I'm going to have a shower."

"Ben–"

"Go have something to eat. I'll take you to see your mum after." He doesn't even wait for me to answer. He shuts the bedroom door behind him, leaving me alone.

I eat breakfast by myself. He waits until I'm ready, then appears with his car keys in hand.

He says nothing in the car, he just puts the radio on loud and stares straight ahead. There's not even a chance for me to catch his eye in the rear-view mirror.

Finally, he stops the car outside Mum's rest home.

He puts the handbrake on. "Are you okay to go in by yourself?" He doesn't look at me as he says that. I wonder what he'd do if I said I wanted him to come in with me.

I nod instead.

"Okay then." He draws a spiral on his knee with his fingertip.

I take a breath, realising this may be the only chance I'll have to talk to him properly. "I'm thinking of doing a course. Something I could get a job from."

Ben blinks then nods. He doesn't say anything.

"I don't know, maybe cooking? I always wanted to own a bakery when I was little."

Something that's almost a smile crosses Ben's face.

I laugh. "Yeah, I know, I'd have to start eating again first."

The smile disappears. His eyes flicker.

I keep talking to distract him. "Anyway, I was wondering how you'd feel about me staying. I mean, there're heaps more course options here, and–"

"I don't know. Maybe." Ben looks up at me, then he squints and looks back down. "We'll talk about it."

A pain dribbles down my windpipe. I've spent enough time with Dad to recognise a disguised "no" when I hear one.

"It's fine. I can figure something else out."

"I didn't mean no."

I force myself to look at Ben. "Yeah, you did. But it's okay. I get it." I try to make myself smile, but it's too late. I'm already crying. I rub my eyes to make it stop.

"You get what?" Ben shakes his head. "I didn't say no."

"Do you hate me?" The question pops out before I can stop it. I want to take it back before I have to hear the answer.

"What? Kel–"

"Is it because I thought it was you?" I rub my eyes and hiccup. "I just got so messed up by what the police were saying, and–"

Ben takes my hand. "I don't hate you."

I try to stop my eyes leaking. I really wish I hadn't just wiped my face. Ben's hand must be covered with tears and snot off mine.

I hiccup again. "Why can't you look at me?"

Ben doesn't answer. He doesn't look at me either, which proves my point.

"Is it because I killed Aiden? Is that why you hate me?"

"I don't ..." Ben sighs and rubs his forehead. "You didn't kill him."

I shake my head. "You don't know that."

"Yeah, I do. You know what the police said–"

"Inconclusive ... the wound could have been consistent with him falling." I close my eyes. "It doesn't mean anything. It could still have been me." I sit up and look at Ben. "And if I wasn't me, why can't I remember anything? I know I woke up before the ambulance, but I don't remember anything."

Ben's eyes flick away from mine. "He fell." Ben's voice goes quiet. "You don't ..." He forces himself to look at me. "You don't have anything to feel guilty about."

I'm amazed that he can say that. After everything that's happened, you'd think he'd be the last one to forgive me.

I close my eyes. "He wasn't going to hurt me." I shake my head. "He ... The whole time we were sitting in the lounge I was so scared, but he wasn't going to hurt me. If he was, he wouldn't have ..." I cover my face. "I killed him and he wasn't even going to–"

Ben cuts me off. "You should go in; see your mum."

I stare at him, but he doesn't look at me. His throat bobs as he swallows. I undo my seatbelt.

Ben stops me by touching my arm. "I don't hate you, Kel." He reaches out towards my face, but his hand hovers in the air for a moment. Then he smooths my hair. "I promise."

It seems like such a long time since I've seen Mum. I suppose it's not really that long in time, just in what's happened.

The nurse brings her through to the visitors' room. She smiles when she sees me, then looks puzzled. She seems to be trying to work out where she knows me from.

"I thought my son was coming today," she says. "Have you met him? Pete?"

"Pete won't be coming today," I say.

She shakes her head and tuts. "Hasn't been for such a while. Not like my daughter, she comes to see me every day. She should be along any minute now." Mum glances towards the door.

I find myself looking too, then realise how ridiculous that is. I wonder what I'd do if her "daughter" did walk in. Well, I suppose at least it's nice for her if she thinks I've been visiting that often.

"Are you sure Pete's not coming?" Mum peers at me.

I nod. "I'm sure, Mum."

Mum shows me her knitting. I don't think she knows how to knit – never has, even before she got sick. She seems to have just wound the wool around the needles in knots.

I jump as one of the residents smashes her hand against the door.

"Let me out!"

Mum and I both stare as she throws herself at the door, fighting with the lock.

The noise jolts though me. One of the nurses pulls the woman away, but the sounds continues in my head.

I hear Aiden's voice. "*Kill me.*" I squeeze my eyes shut as a flash of colours goes through my head.

The woman pounds her hand against the wall. In my mind I hear the smash as my head hit the windowsill.

"*Kelsey? Wake up, Kelsey.*"

The colours swim in my head.

My eyes were open. I was lying on the floor. Aiden was leaning over me. He looked out of focus, fuzzy at the edges. He held his hand to his neck, red seeping between his fingers. He said something, but I didn't understand. I think he was smiling. My head hurt.

I closed my eyes.

I heard voices, yelling. I opened my eyes. Aiden and Ben were fighting. It seemed slowed down, like they were dancing.

They stopped suddenly. Aiden backed away from Ben. They both stared at Aiden's stomach; at the knife, its tip hidden underneath Aiden's skin. Aiden looked up, his face panicked. He turned to face me, and his hand crept towards the knife. He was going to pull it out. He was going to stab Ben.

Ben reached out slowly, as if he was going to help. I wanted to call out. I wanted to warn Ben.

Ben shoved Aiden, making him fall.

Aiden let out a breath as he hit the ground. Something between a groan and a sigh. Then he was still.

Ben's breathing was heavy, slow. He closed his eyes, then he looked down at me. His face changed as I met his eye. He looked scared. His mouth moved, but my ears were ringing, and I couldn't understand the words. I closed my eyes and let it all wash over me.

"Oh my God!" I say.

Mum stares at me, like she finds this vaguely amusing.

"Oh my God!" I say again. I rub my face as if I'm going to find flecks of blood on it. "Oh my God!" I whisper this time, leaning my head down into my knees.

Mum pats my back. It feels like she's trying to burp me, rather than comfort me.

I pull away from her. "I … I have to go to the bathroom."

Ben's in the car where I left him. I get in and do up my seatbelt. He glances at me, but I stare straight out the windscreen. I hear him sigh, then he starts up the car.

He doesn't say anything on the way home. I can't tell if that's because he doesn't want to talk to me, or if it's because he thinks I don't want to talk to him. Either way, it's better for the moment. I close my eyes a couple of times, but it makes me car sick. I settle for staring straight ahead and letting my eyes blur a little.

I follow Ben up the path and wait while he unlocks the door. He turns his head towards me a couple of times, but doesn't actually look at me.

I sit down on the couch, inside.

"I'm going to make some lunch," he says. "Do you–"

"Come sit with me for a minute."

Ben hesitates. I watch him out of the corner of my eye. He swings his shoulders, letting his hands dangle, then he sits down next to me.

I take a breath, then take his hand.

His eyes dart back and forth between mine. I watch as the line between his eyes deepens.

I blink a couple of times, trying to think where to start. "Things have been …" My voice gives a little. I force myself to keep going. "The stuff that happened, it happened to you too, and it was hard for me, so you must have found it hard as well, and …"

Ben's eyelids flutter, and he shakes his head. I don't blame him for not following. I barely know what I'm saying.

I sigh. "My appointment with the police is tomorrow." I look up at Ben. "I'm going to tell them I remember what happened."

Ben goes still as I say that.

I force myself to meet his eye. "I'm going to tell them Aiden fell."

Ben lets out a breath. He rubs his eyes. "You can't, Kel. You can't tell them you remember if you don't–"

"Ben." I squeeze his hand, making him look at me. "Listen to what I'm saying. I remember what happened." I stress the word "remember", then pause to make sure he understands.

His face stretches, making his eyes go wide and his lips part.

I lower my voice. "I remember that Aiden fell."

He stares at me and his face slowly crumples. His breath catches.

"Ben, listen to me." I hold his face. "I love you, okay? I love you, and it's going to be all right."

"I thought you were dead," he says. "I thought he'd killed you."

"I know."

"I just wanted to stop him. I didn't mean to kill him."

"It wasn't your fault, Ben."

"I didn't know you'd had the knife." He breaks down. "I didn't know you'd blame yourself. I just … I couldn't believe I'd killed him."

I pull him into a hug and he cries against my shoulder.

"I didn't know how to tell you."

I stroke the back of his neck. "It wasn't your fault."

That night we go to sleep in his bed, but it's different from before. He wraps his arms around me and rests his head on my shoulder. His eyes are closed, and he breathes in that heavy way you do after you've been crying.

"Don't say anything to the police yet." He looks up at me.

"I need to figure out what I'm going to do."

I nod and close my eyes.

"I want you to stay." He leans his head in against my neck. "I wanted to say that before. I want you to stay."

"I'm here," I say.

I take a breath, and let the warmth of him settle against me. I stare up at the ceiling. Right above the bed is a chip in the paint. It looks like a heart.

Also by Helen...

Symbolic Death

A woman finds a Death Curse symbol scratched into the soap scum around her sink. A young boy watches his family fall apart after the death of his father. A butterfly chrysalis hatches, under the watchful eye of a hungry cat, and a teenage grim reaper's job is made harder by the boy who can see her.

Symbolic Death is a collection of sad, poignant, and darkly funny tales about death. If you like unique points of view, heart-breaking moments, and a touch of black humour, then you'll love Helen's short story collection.

Want it for free? You can get it by joining Helen's mailing list at www.helenvfletcher.com.

Coming soon ...

Underwater

Bailey has a lot of secrets, and a lot of scars, both of which she'd like to keep hidden. Unfortunately for her, Pine Hills Resort isn't the kind of place where anyone can keep anything hidden for long.

When Bailey arrives at Pine Hills, she just wants to get through summer quietly, spending as much time in the water as she can.

Then she meets Adam.

Bailey's not looking to make friends, but Adam is not so easy to ignore. Neither is his ex-girlfriend, Clare.

As Bailey grows closer to Adam, she draws Clare's animosity. Will Bailey be able to keep her past a secret, or will Clare discover and reveal the sinister truth about how Bailey really got her scars?

Underwater is the second young adult novel from the author of *Broken Silence*. If you like raw emotions, dark secrets and heart-breaking love triangles, then you'll love Helen's engaging new young adult novel.

Join Helen's mailing list at www.helenvfletcher.com now to be the first to discover Bailey's secret, when *Underwater* hits the shelves.

Enjoyed this book? You can make a big difference.

Reviews are the most powerful tool when it comes to getting attention for my books.

As an indie author, it can be hard to get my books into the hands of readers, but honest reviews of my books help me do just that.

If you've enjoyed this book I would be very grateful if you could spend just a few minutes leaving a review (it can be as short as you like.)

Thank you very much!

About the Author

Helen Vivienne Fletcher wrote her first novel between the ages of thirteen and sixteen. It is, by several accounts, one of the funniest novels ever written. It's just a shame it was supposed to be a psychological thriller.

Helen has worked in many jobs – everything from theatre stage management to phone counselling. She discovered her passion for writing for children and young people while working as a youth support worker, and now helps children find their own passion for storytelling through her business, Brain Bunny Workshops, which runs creative writing holiday programmes and afterschool classes.

Helen is the author of four e-picture books for children. She has won and been shortlisted for several writing competitions, including making the shortlist for the 2008 Joy Cowley Award, and in 2012 she was the recipient of the Wellington Children's Book Association New Pacific Studios residency.

Her poetry and short stories have appeared in online and print publications, and she regularly performs her spoken word pieces in Wellington.

Helen has recently turned her hand to writing for the stage with her first play, *How to Catch a Grim Reaper*, for which she was named outstanding new playwright at the 2015 Wellington Theatre Awards.

Overall, Helen just loves telling stories, and is always excited when people want to hear or read them.

You can find Helen at www.helenvfletcher.com or connect with her on Facebook or Twitter.

Acknowledgements

Thank you to all the friends and family who supported me while writing this book, and who encouraged me to keep going and publish it. Your support has meant so much. Special thanks goes to Hana who loved this story when I first came up with it, and to Mary who encouraged me to start writing it down. Thanks also to Kimberley, Jane and my dad for reading and giving feedback, and to Josh for teaching me about kickboxing.

Thank you to Lesley Marshall for your manuscript assessment, and for the great work you do in fundraising each year, to Sue Copsey for your editing skills, and to the Books Covered team for the beautiful cover design.

Finally a huge thank you goes to everyone from the Evolve Writers Group. I am a terrible secret-keeper, but keeping the ending of this story quiet and seeing your enthusiasm to find out what happens was the best motivation I could have asked for.